The Dark Side

by

John Money

A Black Looks Novel

Published by Regency Rainbow Publishing
Cover by Maria Spada Design at www.mariaspada.com

Introduction

The original first draft of *The Dark Side* was scribbled down by a forty-year-old me between (it says) the 16th November and 29th December in the year 2000 – and it was very much a first draft. The main characters, though, were already 'real' to me, having featured in my first attempt at a novel, *Black Looks*, written some six years before then.

Bill and Franklin have continued to appear in short stories that I have written, and also in my mind, where their disparate characters have been brought together to help me solve day-to-day issues (from missing keys to divorce!).

It's with sincere thanks to my final partner, Sara, that I have finally brought this tale up to proper novel standards, and to all of those lovely people who have encouraged me along the way. The next twelve months or so will see several of my books hit the stands – both new and re-vamped old – and Bill and Franklin will feature heavily in a few of them.

Now, though, it's time to introduce them to a wider audience. The Dark Side is their first story, in terms of publishing, and it will be followed by a much-re-worked prequel later in 2019, and then a third work which is 'in progress' at the moment. I hope you like my odd couple as much as I do – and for everyone's sake, I hope that pleasure is extended to the third member of their small team! Little Dot is *not* to be upset...

As Franklin would say, Stay Cool – and as Bill would say, Cheers!

John Money, 20th December 2018

Chapter 1

Monday 12th November 2018

As he hurried along Cheapside, Franklin Richardson was beginning to think that the old saw about bad things coming in threes was absolutely accurate. He was cold and getting colder, wet and getting wetter, late and, as is the natural order, getting later. November had never been his favourite month and this year was no exception. He hated the dark evenings, the seemingly incessant rain and sleet, the plunging temperatures, and, in particular, taxi drivers who managed to spray pedestrians with filthy water as they passed. His right shoe squelched with every stride he took.

Franklin glanced up at the clock on the tower of St. Mary-le-Bow and cursed under his breath. It was five-forty and he should have picked up the files and computer discs almost an hour earlier. If the office was closed by the time he got there, Dot would not be a happy bunny.

Not that she ever was these days, or so it seemed.

A loud rumble from his mid-section reminded him that he'd had to skip lunch and since he was late already, he decided to make a quick stop at the nearest burger bar for some much-needed sustenance. As far as he could recall, the closest place was a Burger King at the end of Bow Lane and he ducked into the narrow passage. It was, he reasoned, pretty much on his route anyway.

The streets were filling up with office workers heading for their trains or, more likely, the nearest bars and restaurants and as he squeezed past them Franklin felt a pang of envy. Okay, so he had his own office these days, but sometimes the prospect of a steady nine-to-fiver appealed. It appealed even more as someone's umbrella deposited what felt like a pint of cold water down the back of his neck as he ducked past them. Life as a private investigator was not nearly as glamorous as it sounded.

Near the end of the tiny street a crowd of people were standing shoulder-to-shoulder by the entrance to Mansion House tube station, their forms outlined by flashing blue lights and it quickly become clear to Franklin that further progress would either prove painful or impossible. Muttering another mild curse, he turned and was about to make his empty-bellied way back to the main thoroughfare, when a voice from waist level stopped him in his tracks.

"Spare a smidgen of your fortune for an unfortunate like myself?"

Franklin was used to the beggars that over-populated the streets of London these days and would normally have turned a blind eye, continuing on his way. This voice, though, was cultured and sober. It took him a moment before he could make out the figure in the gloom.

The man was sitting on the doorstep of an empty shop, long legs crossed underneath him. As Franklin paused, the man rose to his feet, the movement fluid, almost graceful.

"Actually, it's a little of my fortune that I wish to share with your good self."

Franklin was at a loss, "Sorry?"

"It is the famous Franklin Richardson, is it not?"

Now that the man was upright, Franklin could make out his features. A long mane of dark hair framed a face almost entirely covered with a luxuriant dark beard. Only the eyes, a piercing blue, and a rudder-like nose, gave any indication that the man was white.

"You know me, man?" Franklin asked, puzzled, "I mean I'm not the "famous' anything."

"Yet it would seem I do know you, would it not?" White teeth glittered in the gloom.

Franklin had been used to the occasional stranger recognising him since the Courtney case the previous year with all its attendant publicity, but since he was black, and Bow Lane was dark even in daylight, he couldn't imagine how the man could have identified him so easily.

"Well, yeah," he shrugged, "I'm Franklin Richardson. But how the—"

"Let's just put it down to a fortunate coincidence, shall we?" the man said.

"Just who are you?"

5

"How terribly remiss of me. Peter Charno." The man held out his hand.

Franklin shook it involuntarily, "I still don't get how you recognised me, man."

"As I said, serendipity."

Making a mental note to ask his partner, Bill, exactly what *that* was supposed to mean, Franklin shrugged, "Well, it's me, but I'm in a bit of a rush Mr. Charno. I suggest you call my office if it's business you're interested in."

Charno smiled once more, "Just give me one minute of your time, Mr. Richardson. I'm sure you will find it beneficial. Perhaps this will convince you." He handed Franklin a large brown envelope.

It was unsealed, and Franklin peered warily inside. Then he *reached* inside to confirm by touch what his eyes had told him. They hadn't lied – the envelope was crammed full of banknotes. Large denomination banknotes, at that. "Okay," he said, "Let's say that you've got my interest. What's this all about?"

"An intriguing and… complex problem," Charno said, "It will take me a good deal more than a few minutes to fully describe the situation, but broadly speaking I want you to undertake an investigation on my behalf."

"What sort of investigation? Missing persons? Suspected infidelity?"

Charno paused before answering, a smile playing around his mouth under the thick beard, "I suppose 'missing persons' is the most fitting term, but as I say, the issue is a great deal more complex than it might at first appear."

Everything was conspiring to pique Franklin's curiosity, "Okay, Mr. Charno. I hear where you're coming from and missing persons are my speciality, but I really am in a hurry right now. Why don't we arrange to meet up somewhere tomorrow?" He offered the stranger the envelope.

"Keep it, Mr. Richardson," Charno said, "Call it an advance. A show of faith, if you prefer. I'm positive that you *will* accept this case once you have heard a little more detail, and I'm equally certain that you're the ideal man for the job. However, I'm afraid that I won't be able to meet up with you after tonight. If you really must continue with your errand right now, may I suggest we meet later this evening?"

6

"No can do,' Franklin said, "I gotta get some stuff back to my office or one of my assistants will fry my sorry ass."

"Ah!" Charno nodded, "And how is the delectable Miss Kominski?"

"You know–"

"As I said, Mr. Richardson, I'm certain you're the man for the job. To be that certain, I've had to make a few enquiries of my own."

Franklin shook his head in disbelief, "You're freakin' me out, man."

"That was never my intention, I assure you," Charno went on, "And I apologise if this all seems a little... *strange* at the moment. However, I'm sure things will become clear when you've more information at your disposal."

"I sure as shit hope so," Franklin muttered under his breath.

Charno appeared not to hear, "If you are really positive that you cannot spare me a couple of hours this evening, then I will have to leave you in the capable hands of my own assistant. I will arrange for her to contact you at your office sometime tomorrow if that is suitable?'"

Franklin shrugged, "Fine by me, I guess."

"Splendid! As I say, I'll be... *away* for a while. But I look forward to seeing you on my return Mr. Richardson."

Without waiting for a reply, Charno turned and strode away towards the crowd outside the tube station. Franklin, his jaw hanging open, stared after him.

"Just what the *fuck* was all that about?" he muttered aloud.

Charno was quickly lost from sight and Franklin turned his attention back to the envelope. Another cursory examination of its contents assured him that whatever it was all about, it was looking pretty certain that he'd earn well from it. With another shrug, he thrust the cash into the inside pocket of his drenched overcoat.

*****

Franklin's fortunes seemed to be taking a further turn for the better when he arrived at the office on Ludgate Hill to find the place still open. A security guard at the massive reception desk handed him two small parcels when he'd finally convinced the man that, despite being a twenty-

7

year old black man, he really was *the* Franklin Richardson of the Franklin Richardson Investigative Agency.

He quickly checked the packages' contents and, satisfied that he'd got all he came for, made to head back out into the rain.

"Mr. Richardson?"

Franklin looked back at the security guard, "Yeah?"

"Just thought I'd let you know," the guard said, "If you're gonna be trying to hop on a tube, don't bother."

"Oh?" Franklin asked, when the man seemed unwilling to furnish any further details.

Satisfied that he'd hooked his listener as good gossips everywhere are prone to do, the guard smiled, "All the system's shut down. Seems as if there's been some sort of mass suicide according to Capital News. This city gets weirder every day."

Franklin nodded. After his 'chance' meeting with Charno, 'weird' was exactly the word he'd use to describe the way things were going. "Funny you should say that. Anyway, thanks for the tip, man."

Outside, the rain was coming down harder than ever and Franklin resigned himself to a long, wet walk to Liverpool Street station. Even on a good night black cabs seemed loath to stop for a young black man wearing jeans and a long leather overcoat.

As he squelched his way through the City, he mused on the guard's story. A mass suicide? On the underground? He supposed it at least explained the crowd he'd seen outside Mansion House station, and he knew from his years in the capital that the problem of 'jumpers', as the authorities termed those people who decided to end it all under a tube train, was on the increase. But a mass suicide? Probably just the radio station exaggerating as usual.

After he'd passed similar crowds outside St. Paul's, Moorgate and Liverpool Street tube stations, he began to think again.

Franklin's first stop in the mainline station was the Burger King where three double cheeseburgers finally quelled his incessantly rumbling stomach. He followed these with a swift pint of Guinness in a nearby bar and then headed for his train, a feeling of disquiet buzzing around his head.

8

*****

Back at his office in Walthamstow, he was surprised to find both his partner and his assistant still at their desks. He wasn't *at all* surprised to see that Bill Taylor was sipping from a large whisky tumbler. Bill and his wife Maisie tended to spend most of their time apart – through happy choice, it seemed – Bill working a lot in London and Maisie working equally hard at the couple's home in Norfolk.

"Hi, guys."

"Ah, Franklin, dear boy," Bill looked up from the file he'd been absorbed in, "Surprised to see you back so soon. We've been hearing all sorts of strange tales from the Metropolis – and I don't mean all this moron-fodder, or Brexit as it's more formerly known. No, I mean the transport system ground to a halt and all that."

Dorothy Kominski, Dot Com to friends and foes alike, spun her chair around to face the door, "Yeah. Is it true about these suicides, then?"

Franklin shrugged, "Search me, but there were crowds around most of the tube stations. The mainline services are still running, though. There's nothing on the news sites yet."

"Good," Dot said, "and I do hope them there boxes what you're carrying have got my information in them." It came out as 'An' I do 'ope them there boxes wot you're carryin' 'ave got my information in 'em', but despite the broad East London accent there was something rather mellifluous about Dot's speech patterns.

"Of course they have," Franklin grinned, "When have I ever let you down?"

"If you've got an hour, I can list all the times for you–"

"Children, children!" Bill interrupted, "How many times must I tell you: no squabbling in the office."

William Wilberforce Taylor – Bill to all, except at one time to his late sister – was twenty-nine years Franklin's senior, nearly thirty-one years Dot's, and since taking a more active role in the agency, he'd adopted the role of surrogate father to the pair of them. Much to everyone's surprise, it seemed to work quite well.

9

"Yeah, well," Dot pouted, taking the proffered packages from Franklin.

"Everything okay?" he asked.

"I guess so. I'll make a start on them first thing."

"Good," Franklin went on, "And talking of good, I think we've got ourselves a new case." He extracted the envelope from his overcoat and emptied the contents onto Bill's already cluttered desk.

"Good grief!" Bill's eyebrows rose heavenward.

"Bleedin' 'ell!" Dot added.

Ten minutes later, the banknotes had been counted and stacked into three teetering piles.

"Franklin, dear boy," Bill said, "Would you mind telling me one more time about how you came to be given five thousand pounds in used notes? My logic circuits seemed to have overloaded."

"It was just like I told you. There's me taking a short cut through Bow Lane and this guy Charno stops me and starts into all this weird shit."

"Americanism!" Bill reprimanded him. As well as being a father-figure, he was also trying to break Franklin's habit of trying to live and sound like a native New Yorker. "It is a rather incredible coincidence, though."

Franklin nodded, "You're telling me. There was some fancy word the dude... *guy* used. Began with an 'S', I think."

"Serendipity, by any chance?"

"That's the one, Bill. What's it mean, exactly?"

"Making accidental discoveries or chance meetings that turn out to be extremely fortunate," Bill said.

Dot looked up, "What? Like your car breakin' down and the guy who turns up to fix it turnin' out to be the man of your dreams, sort of thing?"

"A charming example as ever, young Dot," Bill laughed as Franklin rolled his eyes, "And yes, that sort of thing is exactly what it means."

"Let's just hope this Charno guy ain't some sort of weirdo," Franklin said, "I can't wait to hear what this is really all about."

"In the meantime," Bill suggested, "I rather think that a small libation or two at the Swan might be in order. It's been quite a while since we had something to celebrate."

"I'm there," Franklin nodded.

"Count me out," Dot yawned, "I wanna make an early start tomorrow."

"You sure you ain't got some young guy waiting for you?"

"Don't tease her, Franklin."

"I have *not* got a boyfriend, okay?"

"Nah, I guess not. What with the hair—"

"I *like* it like this!" Dot's hair was currently bright green and given her predilection for dyeing it any colour of the rainbow, it was probably intentionally so.

"Children!" Bill interjected, "It is at times like this when I truly realise why I never had any offspring of my own. Now, let's away to our celebration. We'll see you in the morning, Dot."

"Yeah, okay then." She offered Bill a smile, Franklin a scowl, "Have one for me, will you?"

"But of course," Bill said, "I may even make it two."

Franklin laughed, "Now wouldn't that be a surprise?"

*****

The Swan was now – and still – called the Mucky Duck but Bill, being a traditionalist, refused to entertain the idea: "One more nail in our proud heritage" had become the precursor to one of his regular soapbox-style rants on modern trends.

That Monday night it was almost deserted when he and Franklin arrived.

"Mandy, my dear, what have you done to everyone? Has your bounteous beauty finally overcome them?"

"Evening, Bill," the barmaid laughed, "Evening, Franklin. Your usuals?"

They agreed readily and were soon served with – and savouring – a very large whisky and a pint of Guinness, respectively.

As was usual Bill was unwilling to talk about work, but Franklin's nagging sense of unease wouldn't dissipate, even under the non-stop barrage of Bill's anecdotes. A further three pints of Guinness seemed to have little effect on his disquietude and at ten o'clock Franklin decided to call it an evening. Bill, engrossed in a conversation with Mandy concerning the relative merits of malt whiskies barely noticed the young man's departure.

The rain had finally let up for a while and a full moon was almost visible behind a light covering of black cotton-wool clouds. This, however, only served to reduce the temperature still further and Franklin pulled his long leather overcoat tightly around him as he trudged wearily towards his flat.

It was situated at the end of a narrow road which ran from the town centre towards the maze of reservoirs that serviced most of north-east London. Franklin had chosen it specifically for its relatively peaceful location, but on nights like this the ten-minute walk seemed a high price to pay for a little peace and quiet. Not for the first time, he began to wonder whether his Caribbean blood wasn't suited to the English climate.

As he walked, his mind kept returning to the mysterious Peter Charno. The strange man was certainly the main reason for his unease. Or rather, it was the circumstances of their meeting. What were the odds on a chance encounter like that? Especially since Franklin had been taking a last-minute detour from his chosen path. Just what had his rumbling stomach got him into this time?

He was just approaching the front gate of his apartment block when his musings were cut short by a voice in the darkness ahead of him, and for the second time that evening he stopped dead in his tracks.

"Franklin Richardson?"

Franklin fully expected Peter Charno to step out of the shadows by the side of the building, and he breathed a sigh of relief when a uniformed policeman stepped forward instead. "That's me," he managed, a familiar feeling of non-specific guilt creeping over him as it always did in the presence of the constabulary, "How can I help you officer?"

"Is this where you live, Mr. Richardson?"

Franklin nodded, "Why, has there been a break-in or something?" He was half hoping that was the case. A burglary was bound to have tidied the place a bit.

"Not as such," the constable smiled, "But we did receive a call from your neighbour an hour ago complaining about a disturbance on the premises."

"Old Mrs. Jenkins again," Franklin sighed, "But you've got the wrong man. I've been in the Mucky Duck since eight. You can check there if you like."

"That won't be necessary, Mr. Richardson. We're fully aware that you weren't at home when the, er, incident occurred."

"Well, would you mind telling me exactly what's going on, only I'm cold and wet and–"

"Of course," the policeman interrupted him, "Mr. Richardson, are you the owner of a white mustang?"

"What? And what are you grinning at, come to that?"

"It's a perfectly straightforward question Mr. Richardson."

Franklin gave another deep sigh, "No officer, I do not own a white Ford. If you check the records you'll see that I don't even have a driving licence, let alone a flash sports car."

"I wasn't…" the policeman appeared to smother a laugh, "I wasn't talking about a car, Mr. Richardson. I meant a mustang as in Hi-Ho, Silver."

"What!?"

"A horse, Mr. Richardson."

"Of course I don't own a fucking horse! Where would I keep a fucking horse for chrissakes?"

"Language, Mr. Richardson. Given the circumstances, it's a perfectly reasonable question."

Franklin felt as if steam was beginning to pour off him, "Reasonable? What's reasonable about asking someone who lives in the middle of London whether they own a bloody great horse?"

The policeman coughed, now obviously struggling to keep his features under control, "I rather imagine it's reasonable when we're called to a property because of a disturbance and find a, what was it?, '*a bloody great horse*' in someone's flat, don't you?"

Franklin's eyes shot up to his second-floor windows. For the first time, he noticed a light on in his front room, "You're not telling me that someone's put a horse in my flat are you?" A creeping sense of dread was overcoming him.

"Well, sir, that would be the assumption if you didn't put it there yourself."

"Me? What sort of idiot do you think I am? I mean… what…" He trailed off, speechless, his eyes staring in horror at his windows.

"In that case, sir, have you any idea who might have put it there? Or who it might belong to?"

Franklin's gaze returned to the policeman and if looks really could kill, there was a fair chance that Franklin would have been arrested on the spot. "This isn't some sort of wind-up, is it?" He didn't really believe it – not after the weirdness the day had already served up – but clinging to straws was one of his strengths.

"Absolutely not, Mr. Richardson. It's made rather a mess of your flat, I must say."

Franklin chose not to mention that he didn't think that it would have made much difference, "What are you lot going to do about it?"

The policeman's smile slipped away, "*We lot*, Mr. Richardson, now that you deny any knowledge of the animal, will have to remove it from the premises."

"You mean you haven't tried to do that already? You've left a bloody great horse in a tiny apartment for however long it's been there?"

"Technically speaking, there's no actual law against keeping animals in flats as long as they're well cared for."

"As long as… I'm dreaming this, aren't I?"

"No, sir. Now, if you're positive that it's not–"

"Positive!? Positive!? What the fuck do you think I am? I'm a fucking private investigator, not a black Lone Fucking Ranger!"

"Now, now, sir. There's no need–"

Franklin held up one finger, "Right now, *officer*, I reckon that there is every need for me to feel pissed-off," his voice came out in a monotone, "I've had a shitty day, I'm cold and wet and tired. Now I come home to find out that some nutter's put a horse in my flat, and all I get from our wonderful boys in blue is a load of sarcastic crap."

"Talking of crap, sir," The smile was back, "At least you've got a nice fresh supply for the garden." The officer took a hasty step backwards when Franklin's pointing finger became a pointing fist, "Sorry, sir. Just trying to lighten the mood a little. I'll just call through to the station and get them to send a vet along, okay?"

"Any more cracks like that and you'd better ask them to send along some paramedics."

"Now, now, sir–"

"Don't start that again!" Franklin took a deep shuddery breath and tried to relax, "Okay," he sighed, "Here's the keys to the flat. When you've managed to get the bloody thing out of there, just lock the place up and drop these into the Mucky Duck. I think I need another drink or five. I'll sleep over at Bill's tonight."

The policeman took the proffered keys, "Well, if you say so, sir. But we'll need to ask you a few questions down at the station–"

"Tomorrow," Franklin said, "Just give me your name or the incident number and I'll see Sergeant Blake in the morning, okay?"

"Well, I suppose it can wait. Just mention the horse, sir. I'm fairly positive that there won't be many other incidents like this tonight."

Franklin didn't trust himself to respond. Without a word, he spun on his heel and began to trudge back to the pub.

*****

"How big was it?"

"Bill, I've absolutely no idea," Franklin drained half of his Guinness before continuing, "But I reckon it's a reasonable bet that 'too big' is enough of a description."

"This is all most peculiar, dear boy."

"What a fucking day!"

"Language–"

"Don't you start!"

"Of course, we all understand that you're upset."

"Only natural," Mandy stifled a giggle.

"Very trying," Gerry Cooper, one of the regulars, added.

Franklin glared at the assembled company. "Why me?"

"Enough with the black looks, dear boy," Bill said, his shoulders shaking.

"Did the copper really say 'Hi-Ho Silver'?" Mandy asked.

Franklin drained the rest of his pint while the others gave in to their laughter. "Why me?" he muttered again to no-one in particular.

His keys had still not been delivered to the pub before it closed, and he dreaded to think of what sort of state his flat would be in by then. There again, it couldn't possibly be much worse than Bill Taylor's London house.

They were both a little drunk when they reached there, and it took Bill three attempts before he finally managed to insert the key in his front door.

"Come in, come in. *Mia casa*... well... my house is your house and all that. You know where everything is, don't you, dear boy."

"Course I do, Bill," Franklin nodded, "I did stay here for three months, after all."

"Ah! True," Bill said, "In which case you'll know where the whisky is kept. Guests' privilege to pour the night-caps, you know?"

"You want more?"

"The night is young, dear boy. Don't tell me your get-up-and-go has got-up-and-gone?"

"I don't think I had any to start with," Franklin said, opening the glass-fronted cupboard which contained several bottles of Scotland's finest. "Doesn't your Maisie disapprove of your 'London retreat' and your London habits?"

"On the contrary, dear boy. I rather get the impression that my sojourns to be by your side are something of a blessing as far as my wife is concerned. They afford her a little peace of mind to know that I am cerebrally busy, not to mention a little peace in more general terms!"

Several night-caps later, Bill left Franklin snoring on the sofa and staggered off to his bedroom.

Chapter 2

Tuesday 13th November 2018

Bright sunlight speared into Franklin's brain when he awoke the next morning to the smell of frying bacon. Grimacing against the pain, he pulled himself into a sitting position and shielded his eyes from the glare. He was still groaning softly when Bill appeared from the kitchen bearing a large tray.

"Morning, dear boy! Your breakfast awaits." Bill set the tray down on the coffee table in front of the sofa.

"Bill," Franklin sighed, "How on earth do you manage to drink so much?"

"It takes considerable will-power, I can assure you." He thrust a glass of cool water into Franklin's left hand and four Paracetamol into his right.

This routine had been practised on many of the mornings when Franklin had been staying with Bill and it was an almost automatic reflex as he popped the tablets into his mouth and washed them down with the water.

"Good lad," Bill nodded, "Still two sugars in your coffee?"

"Yeah, thanks. What's the time?"

"Eight-thirty, and isn't it about time you bought a watch?"

Franklin's refusal to ever wear a wristwatch was a source of constant mystery to Bill since Franklin refused to disclose exactly why, using his mobile instead. "Not that again, Bill," he said around a mouthful of bacon sandwich.

"As you wish, dear boy."

Franklin looked up as he munched on his breakfast, "Bill? How come you never get hangovers?"

"Good fortune, I imagine. Now, eat up and drink up, and yours will have gone before long."

Franklin knew this to be true and followed Bill's instructions despite complaints from both his stomach and head. When he'd finished, he went through to Bill's cluttered bathroom and plodded through his morning ablutions, dressing in a spare set of clothes that he always left at Bill's for emergencies. By the time he returned to the living room, he was already feeling halfway back to being human.

"What's the plan for today?" he asked Bill, who was reading *The Times* diary column.

"I'm due to meet with that nice Miss Thomson at twelve, and Dot's got all of that data to implode."

"That's 'input' or 'upload'," Franklin grinned. Bill wasn't allowed near the computer anymore after a series of Taylor-esque disasters.

"Whatever, dear boy," Bill said, rising to his feet, "And yourself?"

"I've gotta pop down the nick and get this horse business sorted out and then I guess I'd better get into the office and wait for this Charno guy's assistant to call."

"Dot will be pleased."

"And what's that supposed to mean?"

Bill patted Franklin's shoulder, "I rather think that our little lady is enamoured of you, dear boy."

"Enamoured?"

"To use the modern, vulgar parlance, *fancies* you."

Franklin snorted, "Sure! She's never got a good word for me. Besides, she's a bit too young for all that."

"She's sweet nineteen," Bill said, "And a charming little thing, to boot."

"Funny definition of sweet. Although booting her might help."

"Now, now, dear boy. You'd be lost without her."

"True," Franklin nodded, "But I never mix business with pleasure."

"That theory doesn't seem to hold water if you consider that business with Melanie Forbes."

Beneath his dark skin, Franklin felt a blush rising, "She wouldn't take no for an answer. I really didn't have any choice."

"Franklin," Bill said, "You're six foot two and weigh fourteen stone. Little Melanie, as I recall, was a foot shorter and five and a half stone lighter. I'm therefore fairly positive that you could have repelled her advances should you have chosen to do so."

"Yeah, well. It just didn't seem polite."

"Really very attractive, as well, wasn't she, dear boy?"

"Cute as they come," Franklin nodded.

"In fact," Bill went on, "She could almost be mistaken for Dot's twin sister..."

"I guess she could- Oh, no! You're not catching me out like that."

"I rather, dear boy, think I already have."

*****

Franklin decided to call into the office before facing the gruesome prospect of Sergeant Blake. By the time he got there, Dot was already at her desk, her fingers clattering over the computer's keyboard. She glanced up as Franklin threw his overcoat onto Bill's chair.

"Hi, boss. I hear you had an unexpected house guest last night?"

"Hi, Dot. How on earth did you get to know about that?"

"Sergeant Blake called about ten minutes ago and told me to remind you that you're supposed to be seeing him this morning. He weren't having me on then?"

Franklin shuddered. Charno had been bad enough, the horse was a step too far into the Twilight Zone. "It must be something to do with the full moon, but this is turning into the week from hell."

Dot shrugged, "Does seem pretty odd, don't it? I mean, an 'orse?"

"A norse?" Franklin permitted himself a smile.

"Very funny. Need a coffee?"

"Desperately. Then I'd better get down to the nick. Did Blake say he was expecting me there at any particular time?"

"Something about the sooner the better," she replied over her shoulder as she filled the kettle, "Seriously though, any idea who might've put it in your flat?"

"I don't even know anyone that's seen a horse, let alone got one at their disposal," Franklin said, "It's not even as if we've had any serious cases for the last few weeks."

"True," Dot nodded, "Although there was that Forbes business."

"Oh, for chrissakes," Franklin groaned, "Don't I deserve a little bit of peace over that one?"

Dot's response was inaudible, but the tone of her voice suggested that he might be better off not being able to hear it anyway.

"Anyway," Franklin said, *"Changing the subject*, is there anything in the news feeds about those suicides last night?"

Dot passed him her tablet, open to the online *Times*, "Bottom of that page. Sounds bleedin' weird to me."

"Since when do you read the *Times*?"

She groaned, "It's part of Bill's latest single-handed crusade to 'raise the literacy levels' in the office. Bleedin' cheek is what I call it. He won't even let me load the *Sun* on here anymore. Reckons it's racist, sexist, and populist, and he's doing it for our own good."

Franklin grinned at her, "You know, he might actually have a point. You were always moaning on about the exploitation of women."

"Only because you insisted on leaving it open on the page three-type of story and going on about how I'd never have to worry about appearing on there." Dot straightened the front of her blouse, a movement which served to emphasise her small bust.

"I *prefer* my women on the small side."

"Yeah, sure."

"Really!"

Dot paused for a moment and then nodded, "I s'pose that Melanie Forbes wasn't exactly in the Pamela Anderson category."

Franklin rolled his eyes and settled himself into his chair, quickly scanning the *Times* report. "This is bloody weird," he said.

"Yeah. Creeped me out, it did."

"Seventeen people at sixteen different tube stations all committing suicide within three minutes of each other. No notes, no obvious links between them. But it can't be a coincidence, can it?"

"You'd get bleedin' good odds on it at the bookies."

"You're not wrong, little lady."

"Less of the little, please."

Franklin rose and crossed to Dot's chair, "Sorry." He patted the top of her bright green head.

"Sod off."

"Charming."

"Yeah, well. Why don't you do something useful like go and see old man Blake? Perhaps they'll have found out who put the 'orse in your flat by now."

"Our wonderful police?" Franklin said, "I doubt it. But I guess I'd better get it out of the way. I want to be here when this Charno guy's assistant calls." He drained his coffee mug in three long swallows and grabbed his overcoat, "See you later, little lady." He managed to get through the office door a fraction of a second before a plastic coffee mug clattered against its frame.

*****

To his surprise, Franklin was shown through to Sergeant Blake's desk less than twenty minutes after he presented himself at the police station's front desk.

"Hiya, George."

"Morning, young Franklin. Quite the regular down here these days, aren't you?"

"Not by choice, I promise you."

Blake laughed loudly. He and Franklin's history went back to the days of the young black man's teenage years when he'd been something of a local legend, always in one sort of minor trouble or another. "I must say," the policeman said, "This is probably one of the oddest of your little incidents."

"You're telling me, man. I take it you *have* got the bloody thing out of my flat?"

"Eventually," Blake nodded, "Although apparently there's quite a mess up there now. Actually, if you want to get rid of any of the... manure, I'd always take it off your hands. Fantastic stuff for the roses is horse shit."

"My hands aren't going anywhere near it, but you're more than welcome to help yourself."

"I might just do that," Blake said, "But in the meantime, here's your keys."

"Any ideas about who put it in there?"

"I was just about to ask you the same question. I know that in your line of work you can't help but upset people occasionally, so is there anyone you've upset more than usual recently?"

Franklin shook his head, "We've been pretty quiet for the last few weeks. Just routine stuff."

"What about old man Forbes? I hear he wasn't exactly voting you man of the month a few weeks ago?"

"Who... I mean, how is it everyone seems to know about my personal business? Often, before I do!"

"It's a small town, Franklin."

"It's part of a city with close on eight million people living in it. At least seven and a half million of which have access to my personal life."

"Pardon the term, but you are a rather colourful character."

"Thank you, George," Franklin had to smile, "But anyway, as far as Forbes goes, that was all amicably settled."

Blake nodded, "I know, and besides, he's out of the country at the minute. Thought he'd take little Melanie out of harm's way for a few weeks."

"Then why mention him?"

"Sorry, couldn't resist. Seriously though, *have* you upset anyone recently."

"*Seriously*, no."

"Any interesting cases you're working on at the minute?"

"Nope. Two routine surveillances and a security job. I've just picked up a missing person case, but that wasn't until last night in any case."

"Well, I'm afraid it's all a bit of a mystery, then. We've not received any reports of missing nags and neither have the other local stations, so not even a clue there. It's a bit odd really, because the vet reckons it's a pretty valuable animal."

"Is it really a white mustang?"

"I don't know about mustang, but it's definitely white. Why do you ask?"

Franklin thought back to the constable that had approached him the night before and made a mental note to muddy the waters for the young man in the near future. "Just curious," he said, "What's gonna happen with it?"

"Well, currently it's at the vet's country practice up in Essex somewhere, and I suppose technically, it's lost property. If no-one claims it in the next six months, I guess it's yours."

"What the hell do I want with a bloody great horse?"

"Franklin, when it comes to you, I shudder to think."

*****

Back at the office, the case of the mystery mustang unresolved, Franklin asked Dot to order him a pizza and then settled into his chair to catch up on a stack of paperwork that was coming close to being a life-size representation of the Leaning Tower of Pisa. Dot had been unusually gracious with his request, and it had left him wondering whether – despite every appearance to the contrary – Bill might not be right about her. He was wondering what colour her hair really was when the telephone beside him began to ring.

Before he could answer it, Dot, as efficient as ever, lifted her receiver. A short conversation later, she hit the 'hold' button and turned to face Franklin, "Sounds like the call you were waiting for. Some posh bird called Alexandra Featherington, calling on behalf of Peter Charno."

"That's our boy," Franklin nodded, "Put her through, would you?"

"Sure you don't just want me to say we don't need the work?"

"Sarcasm doesn't suit you." He paused, then added, "You're far too small."

Dot span back around in her chair and pressed another button on the telephone, "I've managed to get Mr. Richardson out of the pub for you, Miss Featherington. He's just about sober enough to hold a conversation."

Before Franklin could say a word, Dot diverted the call to his phone and he grabbed the receiver, "Sorry about that, Miss Featherington, but my assistant, *Dorothy*, does like her little jokes. Now, how may I help you?"

The woman gave a soft chuckle, "It sounds as if you have a very nice atmosphere to work in, Mr. Richardson."

The look he was receiving from Dot had more of a suggestion of broadswords than daggers, "Absolutely, Miss Featherington."

"Please, call me Alexandra."

"And I'm Franklin."

"Well, Franklin…" She paused as if relishing the taste of his name on her tongue, "I'm calling on the request of Peter Charno who, I believe, made contact with you yesterday evening."

"He most certainly did," Franklin said. Either Alexandra Featherington's soft, educated tones, or a sudden memory of the mysterious Charno, sent a shiver along his spine. "What exactly does he want my agency to undertake?"

"It's a rather… *complex* situation, I'm afraid."

"That much I'd already gathered. I was rather hoping your call today might shed a little light on matters."

The young woman gave another quiet, throaty chuckle, "You have a reputation for efficiency, Franklin. I'm beginning to see why."

He just managed to stop himself from saying 'I do?'. "Thank you. Perhaps you'd like to make a start?"

"Actually, I think it would be more suitable if we were to meet on a face-to-face basis, Franklin. It will take some considerable time for me to explain everything in the sort of detail I'm sure you will require."

"Fine," Franklin said. Who was he to refuse a meeting with what sounded like a very attractive young woman? "Name the place and the time."

"There is – now, at least – an element of urgency involved, so perhaps we could meet as early as tomorrow? I know you're a very busy man, but I assure you that this will prove an… interesting challenge for you."

This time, Franklin only just managed to stop himself from saying 'I am?'. "Tomorrow would be fine. Where and when?"

"Splendid," Alexandra Featherington purred, "Shall we say midday at the City Vault? Do you know it?"

"The pub just off Cheapside, down some steps?"

"That's correct."

"In that case, yes I do. And twelve will be fine. If you've got any documentation that might be relevant to the investigation, photos and so on, it'd be a good idea to bring it along."

"Actually," she said, "I believe that a discussion will be needed first. Should you need any further material, then I live close by. We could return there and pick up anything you consider that you might need."

"Great," Franklin said, "How will I recognise you... Alexandra?"

"This may sound a touch arrogant, Franklin, but I think you'll find that when I walk into the room, every male head – and maybe a few of the female ones – will turn my way. Simply follow their eyes. Besides which, I know exactly what *you* look like. I look forward, very much, to our meeting. *Ciao*, Franklin." She broke the connection.

"Well?" Dot asked as soon as he'd hung up.

"Weirder and weirder. I'm meeting her tomorrow."

"I got that much. But did she say anything about the case itself?" Dot's natural curiosity had evidently overcome her earlier temper.

"Not a word, now I come to think of it."

"Are you sure you're in the right profession?"

"I'll find out everything I need to know tomorrow! She did say it was pretty urgent."

"She certainly sounded as if she wanted *something* urgently."

"What *is* getting into you these days? You always seem to be bitchin' about–"

"I'm *not* a bitch! Don't you ever call me that!"

Franklin's eyebrow's shot skyward. Dot was often... temperamental, but this reaction was totally out of character, "Look, I didn't mean that you're a bitch, I was just saying..."

"Like you're always *just* saying something. But what about me, eh? Can't *I* have opinions?"

"Dot?" Franklin rose from his chair and started towards her.

She shot to her feet and grabbed for her coat, "Forget it, okay? It's just little stupid little Dot being stupid little Dot as per usual. Just forget I said anything."

Before he could stop her, Dot had marched out of the office, slamming the door behind her.

25

Franklin was left in the middle of the office, his jaw hanging slack. "What the fuck was *that* all about?" he muttered, "I'm getting the distinct impression that everyone around here is cracking up."

By the time Bill returned from his meeting with Jennifer Thomson an hour later, Dot had still not returned.

"Are you sure you're not exaggerating her reaction?" Bill asked when Franklin had related the details of Dot's outburst.

"If anything, I'm understating them. Honest, Bill, she really flipped out there."

"And you're positive it's not just another of your playground squabbles?"

"We do not have playground squabbles. It's just light-hearted banter."

"There's no need to get defensive, dear boy, but if this is a serious contretemps, I rather think it would be better if you made yourself scarce before she returns. Let me have a little chat with her, I know she'll listen to me. Besides, I can imagine that you might have a few things to sort out back at your pied-a-terre. There's an ironmonger's just round the corner, I'd arm myself with a large shovel if I was you."

"Thanks for reminding me. But perhaps you're right."

"When am I ever not?"

"I won't bother answering that. Actually, though, I think I'll grab a beer first. Dutch courage and all that. You fancy a swift one?"

Bill held up his hands, "I think that I should remain here, dear boy."

"Now this really *is* getting weird," Franklin said, "Dot exploding, Bill refusing a drink—"

"Not nice, Franklin."

"Yeah, well, it's just, you know?"

"Very eloquent. But, yes, I *do* know."

Franklin gave Bill a wry smile, "Look, when – if – Dot comes back, could you tell her… well, you know? Like, if I said anything to, you know… upset her—"

"I'll tell her that you send your heartfelt apologies, that you are, at this very minute, on bended knee praying for salvation, that you are but a callow youth who knows not how to express his true emotions without a masquerade of—"

"Just say I said 'sorry', okay?"

"Oh, very well then. Now, off you go."

"Thanks, man... Bill."

"Do have one for me, dear boy."

*****

The Mucky Duck was almost deserted when Franklin arrived, the lunchtime drinkers back at their desks, market stalls and workbenches. Of the pub's normal crowd of regulars only Richie Davis was present, single-handedly propping up the bar with one elbow and staring morosely into his beer glass. He was, as usual, wearing a large grey overcoat and an oversized Stetson.

"Hiya, Richie," Franklin greeted him.

The gloomy figure looked up, "Why, Franklin! What brings you to the house of fun?"

"I'm on a search for Dutch courage."

"Oh, of course!" Richie nodded, "Not surprising after that business with the horse."

Franklin's jaw dropped open, "Not you as well?"

"How do you mean?"

"Why is it, that everyone seems to know about that bloody horse, and yet no-one seems to know where it came from?"

"Quite the mystery," Richie grinned, "Allow me to purchase some *Irish* courage for you."

"Good idea."

When he had finally taken a long draw from his Guinness Franklin finally found an opportunity to divert attention from his own plight. "I take it the hat-shop isn't exactly crowded today?" he asked Richie.

Richie's latest venture – the latest in a very long line of unsuccessful commercial concerns – was not proving to be the financial bonanza that he had both hoped for, and firmly predicted. "I haven't had a single customer since Saturday," he said, "And given that he was only there is search of car parts, I'm beginning to think that maybe 'Top Gear' wasn't the ideal name for the enterprise."

"Well I thought it was a good name."

Richie sighed long and loud, "You'd have thought that people would be buying hats in droves given the miserable bloody weather we've been having lately. Come to that, with all your outdoor work, wouldn't a hat prove beneficial to your good self?"

"No chance, man. It's a well-known fact that people recognise people by their hats more than by their faces. So if I'm trailing someone or on surveillance, the last thing I'd need is a hat."

"So, no-one has ever spotted a six-foot two black man wearing a long leather overcoat trotting around after them?"

"No chance," Franklin laughed, "That's why they call me 'The Shadow'."

"They do? I thought it was the 'Lone Ranger'?"

"Not funny, Richie."

Two pints later, Franklin felt sufficiently emboldened to take on the dreaded journey to his flat and he left Richie at the bar with a promise that he would give full consideration to the purchase of a piece of headgear for social occasions. Once outside, he almost regretted not taking Richie up on his offer of a special discount. The rain had started up again, a steady drizzle that quickly found the gaps in Franklin's leather armour. By the time he reached the gate to his apartment building, he was almost as wet as if he'd been taking a shower.

The front door of the building opened before he could even locate the correct key.

"Ah, young man! I feel that I should have a word with you."

"Hello, Mrs. Jenkins," Franklin sighed. The old woman occupied the first floor flat and was a constant source of annoyance to Franklin. She must have been watching the street to have got to the door before he could open it.

"You do realise what a disturbance you caused last night, don't you?"

"To be accurate, Mrs. Jenkins, *I* did not cause a disturbance. Someone else put the bloody animal in my flat."

"Be that as it may. But there is a rule in the lease that strictly prohibits tenants from keeping pets on the premises."

"Pets!? You don't seriously believe that I'd get a horse for a pet do you?"

"Well," the old woman said, "Things are no doubt very different where you come from."

"Islington? Not so's you notice."

"You know very well what I mean. It's in your blood, is all I'm saying."

Franklin shook his head. Mrs. Jenkins was one of a very rare breed – an accidental racist. "Well, Mrs. Jenkins," he said, "I'm sorry for any inconvenience caused, but I assure you that I am the innocent party here, and both myself and the police are doing everything possible to find out who the real culprit is."

This seemed to mollify her a little, "I'll let it go this time, but I'm afraid I'll have to contact the landlord if anything like this happens again." She stepped aside, allowing Franklin access to the building.

A thought struck him as he passed her. "Surely you must have heard something when the bloody great animal was being led up the stairs?"

"Oh, you know me, young man. Always keep myself to myself. Not one to pry or interfere."

"Oh, very true," Franklin sighed.

He trudged up the stairs with a mounting sense of dread and paused for a full thirty seconds outside his front door before reluctantly sliding the key into the lock. He had fallen in love with the flat the second he'd seen it six months previously. Situated on one of the very few quiet roads in the area and with its rear aspect looking out over the reservoirs, it had seemed like a little oasis in the metropolitan desert. True, he hadn't kept the place as tidy as he might have done, the blame for this being put firmly at the door of his unsociable work hours, but he now dreaded to think what state the place would be in after temporary occupancy by a bloody great horse.

The door swung back to reveal a scene of utter carnage. Newspapers, books and soiled takeaway cartons, liberally intermixed with dirty washing, formed a three-centimetre-deep carpet across the floor of his front room.

"Not much change there, then," he muttered to himself.

Further investigation revealed that the horse had been almost inconceivably well behaved during its spell as house guest. Other than three large and smelly mounds in the bedroom, and a couple of dozen hoof-prints imbedded in the parquet flooring of the kitchen-cum-dining room, the place was pretty much as he'd left it the previous morning.

Relieved, Franklin set to work bagging up the manure for later collection by Sergeant Blake. This noisome task completed, he decided that he might as well clear up a little more of the flat's normal detritus and set about the living room like a man on a mission. It was six o'clock before he'd finished, and he was sitting, exhausted, on his sofa, marvelling that he'd actually got a rather nice carpet in the living room, when the doorbell rang.

Sergeant Blake appeared at his door a couple of minutes later.

"Evening, Franklin. Just come to collect the manure."

Franklin pointed to a bulging plastic bag in the hallway, "All in there."

"Thanks, lad. I thought you said I'd have to shovel it up myself?"

"Since it was in the bloody bedroom, I decided that it might be an idea to get it out of there in case you changed your mind."

"Probably wise," the policeman grinned, "But thanks anyway."

"Any news about the bloody animal?"

"Neigh, lad. Sorry, couldn't resist. I take it you haven't heard anything?"

"Why me?" Franklin muttered, "No, George, I haven't."

"Oh, well. Better get on home, Mary's expecting me early for a change. Do you want anything for this?" He pointed at the bags.

"Just getting it out of my sight is payment enough," Franklin said, "But if you've got your car with you, could you drop me off at the Mucky Duck, only I could murder a pint or three?"

Chapter 3

Wednesday 14th November 2018

Franklin woke the following morning with another massive hangover and spent the next twenty minutes in the shower trying to steam it out of his system. Water, Paracetamol, coffee and a bacon sandwich finally helped to bring him back to his normal, pain-free self, and he left the flat at ten-thirty. He had decided to go straight into the City for his meeting with Alexandra Featherington rather than risk a confrontation with Dot in the office, and he arrived at Liverpool Street station with nearly an hour to spare.

The interminable rain was still tumbling from a steel-grey sky, and he spent the spare time browsing through bookshops. He had only recently taken to reading as a hobby – mainly thanks to Bill's efforts – and like anyone new to a pastime, he felt a vicarious thrill whenever he could indulge himself for a while. He arrived at the City Vault five minutes early, toting a large carrier bag full of paperbacks. His new Kindle was great when he was travelling around, but for the new bookworm the sensations that holding and actual, bendable, sweet-smelling physical book were a true delight.

Franklin had never been keen on pubs like the Vault – a hangover from the Yuppie days of the 80's and 90's as far as he was concerned, although Bill had insisted that it was one of the oldest and most traditional of City alehouses. The place was, to Franklin's mind, low, dark and dingy, and this, coupled with the limited alcoholic fare on offer – real ale, port or champagne – rendered it unto the category of places to be avoided.

Of course, places to avoid took on another, altogether more attractive facet, if you were meeting a potential goldmine on the premises.

To the left of the main door an area had been set aside for those City workers who believed that lunchtimes could also incorporate solid substances, but since he had no idea of who he was meeting or what her habits at this hour might be, Franklin took up station at the bar where he could keep one casual eye on the door. She had said that she would be instantly recognisable – or at least, that he would have no trouble spotting her entrance, and that she knew what *he* looked like – so he guessed that she was not already present within the bar's gloomy confines.

By ten past twelve, he was beginning to wonder whether he might not have been mistaken. Workers from the myriad local offices were beginning to fill the subterranean bar-cum-eatery, and the view to the narrow doorway was becoming blurred by the number of bodies passing through it. Franklin was just about to move to a table closer to the entrance when the Australian barman called out his name.

"That's me," he waved an arm at the harassed-looking young man.

"Mr. Richardson, a message. A Miss Featherington says that she has been unavoidably delayed but will be here by one, okay?"

"Thanks," Franklin nodded.

"She also said that she'd be starving by then and could she meet you at a table in the restaurant section? Want me to fix it?"

"Why not? I guess I could always use a decent meal." Along with the traditional beverages, the Vault's solid-fare menu stretched only as far as good old-fashioned English meals, and Franklin couldn't remember the last time he'd eaten an honest-to-goodness steak and kidney pudding.

The bar had been filling rapidly during Franklin's wait, and the restaurant section was already heaving with hungry office workers. The young Australian spoke briefly to a waiter before showing Franklin to a small table tucked into the corner of the gloomy, low-ceilinged room.

"Sorry, mate, but this is all we've got left for now."

"No problem, man."

The barman left him, and Franklin chose the seat giving the best view of the entrance. Alexandra Featherington would need to sit directly to his left such was the intimate nature of the table's situation, and he found himself hoping that she would turn out to be as attractive as she had sounded on the telephone. With forty minutes to kill, he decided to start in on one of his purchases. By the time a waiter tapped coughed politely by his ear, he had become thoroughly engrossed and had even stopped glancing at the door every few minutes. When he saw the figure standing next to the waiter, he rather wished he'd been more vigilant.

Alexandra Featherington had ensured him that heads would turn when she entered the pub, and he could see at once that she hadn't been joking or bragging. She was quite simply the most beautiful woman he had ever laid eyes on. Tall and presumably slender underneath the long, dark overcoat she wore, her blonde, silver-streaked hair framed a face that was almost too perfect in its construction. When the beautiful apparition saw Franklin's jaw drop open, she offered him a smile which revealed an even row of perfect white teeth. Her green eyes were locked on him, glittering in the flickering candlelight.

"Franklin," she said quietly, "How wonderful to meet you."

He shot to his feet, the paperback forgotten in an instant, "Al... Alexandra Featherington?"

"None other."

The waiter offered to take her overcoat, and with her eyes still firmly fixed on Franklin, she slowly unbuttoned the front of the garment, shrugging it from her shoulders into the waiter's hands. Franklin had followed the progress of her long, manicured fingers and as the coat fell away, he almost swallowed his tongue.

Underneath it, Alexandra Featherington was wearing a tailored jacket which reached her upper thighs, a short, matching skirt completed the ensemble. And that was the cause of Franklin's inadvertent attempt at auto-cannibalism. Beneath Alexandra Featherington's two-buttoned jacket with the plunging neckline was nothing but Alexandra Featherington. The gentle inside slopes of her breasts were plainly visible to Franklin's eager gaze. With considerable effort, he dragged his point of focus back to her face, finding her smiling, knowingly, at him.

The waiter, standing behind her, the coat draped over his arm and oblivious to the spectacular view that Franklin had, pulled back her chair. In one fluid and graceful movement, the young woman slid into the proffered seat. As she did so, the jacket gaped open to fully reveal her left breast to Franklin, its nipple dark and rigid.

Much as Franklin now was.

Trying desperately to gather his shattered wits, he sat himself back down and fumbled two menus from the hovering waiter. "It's very nice to see you... *meet* you, I mean," he stammered.

Alexandra waited until the waiter had moved off before replying. "I do so hope my... dress doesn't offend your sensibilities, but it's what I'm accustomed to wearing." She rested her elbows on the table, the jacket gaping a little as she did so.

Franklin had to swallow hard before replying. He was beginning to feel that her naked breast had developed a gravity all of its own – he couldn't seem to tear his eyes away from it. "No, that's... They're... Er, that's fine. Great in fact!"

"Marvellous. Shall we order, then, before we get started?"

"Get started? Oh, right! The case."

"Only I know you must be very busy, and I've already delayed you."

"Oh! That's quite alright," Franklin smiled stupidly, "I've got all the time in the world."

The young woman quickly scanned the menu. "I know I shouldn't really, but I simply can't resist their steak and kidney puddings here. Very traditional, but terribly bad for the figure."

"You've got a wonderful br... figure!" Franklin stammered, "Er, I think I'll join you. In the pudding, that is."

"They use only the finest ingredients, of course."

Franklin nodded, "The very breast... best!" He groaned and rolled his eyes, "Look, Miss Featherington–"

"Alexandra."

"Look, *Alexandra*, I'm sorry, but it's not exactly an everyday occurrence for me to be sitting down for a meal with a beautiful woman in a rather... under-dressed state. It seems to be distracting me a bit."

"That's quite alright, Franklin," Alexandra laughed softly, "And thank you for the compliment. If it eases your discomfort at all, most red-blooded men react that way, and I can assure you, that they soon become used to my... unconventional ways. It should really be me apologising to you, but as I said, I'm accustomed to dressing this way. I fear there's a little latent exhibitionist in my make-up."

Franklin just managed to stop himself from querying the 'latent', "It's not a problem, honest. Just… a bit of a surprise, is all. A nice surprise," he added.

"Thank you, once again."

"So, the, er, case?"

Alexandra sat back in her chair, the movement pulling closed the front of her jacket. Franklin couldn't decide whether this was a good thing or a bad thing.

"Where would you like me to start?" she asked, "Only this is a very complex situation."

"So Mr. Charno said. Perhaps you'd like to start with the missing people and then move on to their backgrounds? How many people are we talking about for a start?"

"Thirteen."

"That's a lot of people."

"When Charno set out to find you on Monday, there were thirty."

"But you've already located the other seventeen? Don't you think the rest might just show up?"

"Located, Franklin," she said, "Is hardly the word I would use. The seventeen are dead. The newspapers insist on saying it was suicide."

The penny dropped, "You mean the seventeen jumpers on Monday night?"

"Indeed."

"Why did you say that the papers 'insist' on saying it was suicide?" Franklin asked, small warning bells beginning to ring in his head.

"Because that is all they can conceive of. Charno and I, among many others, know differently."

"Have you contacted the police with your theories then?"

Alexandra leant forward once more, her voice becoming urgent, "That is out of the question. For a start, there are people involved here that would not take kindly to such a move, and in any case, we have no substantive proof. This is exactly the reason why you are needed. We simply *have* to find the other thirteen and put a stop to all this nonsense."

"Are you saying that these thirteen are in danger, then?"

"In all probability," she shrugged, "To be honest, they may already have been... terminated. But we simply have to find out, and if they're alive, then it's imperative that they are located and recovered."

Franklin let out a low whistle, "This all sounds pretty weird to me. Why on earth would you want my agency to get involved in something like this? Why not go to one of the big agencies?"

"It's precisely because you are not well known that you were chosen. In addition, Charno has had your organisation thoroughly checked, and is sure that none of you are already involved in this... situation. We will pay four times your normal rates."

"And if I don't want to take this case on?"

"Then we go to the next agency on our list."

"Okay," Franklin nodded, "Let me get this absolutely straight. You want my agency to try to trace thirteen missing people, who may or may not, already be dead. If they aren't already dead, you believe their lives to be at risk. You're willing to pay four times the going rate. Alexandra, this all sounds pretty dangerous to me. In fact, it's already sounding as if it's out of our league."

"You and your team have proved to be very resourceful in the past," Alexandra said, "And you have the added bonus of being unknown to them. That, together with your very different appearances and characteristics, was what attracted you to Charno."

"Which 'them' do you mean? If it's the missing persons, then it sounds very much as if they might want to stay missing."

"I wasn't referring to the missing persons. But before I tell you who 'them' are, I'll need to have your agreement concerning the undertaking of this investigation."

"And before you get that, I'll need to know a lot more about it," he countered, "Just how much are you willing to tell me?"

Before Alexandra could answer, the waiter arrived with two plates, piled high with steaming pudding. As soon as he left, she took a forkful, blew gently across the surface, and eased it between her lips. "This is good," she nodded contentedly.

Franklin was far from content, but he had to agree that the steak and kidney was one of the best he'd ever tasted. "Delicious." They postponed the discussion of the case until they had finished. By the time they were sipping post-prandial ports, Franklin was even beginning to relax.

"So, where were we?"

He glanced across at Alexandra, his eyes briefly stopping to take in the tantalising curve of naked flesh beneath her jacket, "You were going to tell me how much information I get before I should decide whether to take on the case."

"Of course," she smiled, "Well, basically I can give you full details about the missing persons, and a general outline of the entire situation. Would that be sufficient, do you think?"

She leaned forward once more, and as Franklin's eyes dropped involuntarily to her bared breast, he began to think that her mode of dress was designed to deliberately distract him from matters at hand. With an effort, he turned his attention back to the conversation, "It might be enough. Start with the outline."

Alexandra thought for a few moments before beginning, "This is the part that you might find a little difficult to... come to terms with, to believe, even. But I can assure you that, no matter how bizarre it sounds, every word is the truth."

"This week I'm getting used to weird," Franklin said.

"As I'm sure you know, there are a number of societies and organisations which control their own interests within the City – the Livery companies and so forth – and there is also an extensive underground... world."

"I know about the Livery companies, and I've heard plenty of stories about the London underworld."

"I'm not actually referring to the gangs of petty criminals," Alexandra said, "I'm talking about the physical world beneath the streets."

"The tube system, you mean?"

"That's just a small part of it, Franklin. As well as the train tunnels, there are hundreds of miles of sewers, pipes for gas, electric, cables of all description. Even this new Crossrail system is nothing more than a minor diversion for us, no matter the billions spent on its construction. Then there are the subterranean road tunnels and pedestrian walkways. The Royal Mail even has its own, independent underground railway system.

Hundreds of cellars and deep basements are also connected by pipes and walkways."

Franklin raised an eyebrow, "Really?"

"Really," Alexandra nodded, "In fact, you're sitting in part of one of the largest, right now."

"This place?"

"The Vault is connected to the City Pipe to the West, and to the old Debtors' prison to the East. Although you can no longer traverse its entire length – at least, members of the general public can't – the tunnel stretches all the way to Bishopsgate. Next time you're up that way, pop down to the cellar bar in the Duke of Norwich. You'll see what I mean."

"Fascinating stuff," Franklin shrugged, "But are you trying to tell me that your thirteen missing people have got themselves lost down there somewhere?"

"Bear with me a moment or two longer, Franklin," Alexandra went on, "Wherever there is property, regardless of its look and location, there are people eager to own it. Many of the subterranean tunnels are regarded as property by... elements within the City. Since before the last war, these elements have been acquiring the underground resources for their own, in some cases, nefarious activities."

"Surely most of them are already owned by companies – gas, electric, London Underground for starters."

"That, Franklin, rather depends on your view of the word 'ownership'. Besides, a very large proportion of the tunnels down there are disused and can be legally purchased should an individual so desire. Do you know how many abandoned tube stations there are?"

"I've heard of one or two–"

"There are forty, Franklin. Four-zero. This very room where you're now sitting is owned by someone, as are the cellars of most of the buildings for miles around. I told you at the start that you might find this all hard to believe, but I promise you – virtually every part of London's underside is now in the hands and control of two groups of people. Access is carefully controlled and there are strict boundaries established."

"You're kidding?"

"Not in the slightest, Franklin. Furthermore, one of these groups is... not to be trusted. They have grave plans."

"And you are part of the other group?"

"Very good. I can see why Charno was so impressed."

"Even if what you're telling me is true – and my jury's gonna be out a long time on that one – how do I know I can trust you?"

"You don't," she said, "But I'm hoping that you will come to do so. In addition I have a great deal of documentation at my disposal – it should at least convince you of some truth in my words. Unfortunately, I am not able to go into greater detail until you undertake the case."

Franklin shrugged, "So, okay, let's say all this is kosher, that you show me all this paperwork. What's to stop me from spilling the beans to the papers or the police or someone?"

"Franklin, those involved in this underground... struggle are powerful people. Very powerful. Should you try to name names or spread the information around, things would not go well for you."

Alexandra's voice had dropped an octave, and Franklin was suddenly sure that this was no idle threat. "I take your point," he said, "So, to recap: There's two groups having some sort of property war–"

"It's not just property – it's also *control.*"

"Okay, fine. Anyway, I'm supposed to view one of these groups as the baddies, and since you belong to the other somehow, then by definition, you're one of the good guys, right?"

"That's certainly how we view ourselves."

"On Monday, thirty of your good guys disappear, only seventeen of them subsequently reappear, splattered under tube trains. The other thirteen are missing, presumed either dead or in danger?"

"Quite so."

"Presumably, also, the seventeen dead were murdered by the 'other' group?"

"It seems likely under the circumstances," Alexandra agreed.

"And if any of the other thirteen are still alive then they're likely to be underground somewhere?"

"Once again, you have reached the same conclusion as us."

"And you want me to find them for you? If these groups you're talking about are so powerful, why can't you find them yourselves?"

Alexandra shook her head, "We're known to the other... group. And besides, we believe our own group to be at considerable risk already. Our numbers have dwindled over the last two decades – we really can't afford further losses if it can be prevented."

"Why," Franklin said, "Do I get the impression that this is a particularly dangerous case for me to take on?"

"It's not nearly as dangerous for you," Alexandra said, "You're unknown to them, and if you're found wandering about in a tunnel, they'll hardly think twice about it. People get lost under there every day. Tens of people, in fact. I really do hope you'll take this on."

"Just who are these missing people?"

"Twelve men and one woman. All young and fit, and all of them with years of experience of life underground. That's why we are hanging on to the hope that they're still alive, maybe trapped somewhere, who knows?"

"Is that all I get to know about them?"

"Their names are... unimportant right now. It's fair to say that they are mostly high-ranking executives with major corporations. You're very unlikely to have heard of any of them."

"Young and high-ranking?"

"Quite so," Alexandra said, "There are benefits in being part of a group such as ours."

"I doubt whether the seventeen on Monday would necessarily agree with that."

"That is why we simply *must* get the others back. We need to find out what exactly happened – work out a way to prevent it happening again. And even if they are... dead, then at least we will have tried to give them assistance. I say again, I really hope you'll help us."

Franklin took a long, deep breath, "Where do you and Charno fit into the picture?"

"How old do you think Charno is?"

Momentarily wrong-footed, Franklin shrugged, "It was hard to see clearly in the dark, but about forty, I guess."

"He's seventy-three," Alexandra smiled, "He's a very powerful man. The leader of our group. I'm his assistant, right-hand woman or lieutenant, whichever you prefer."

"Don't tell me you're really forty-something?"

She laughed, "No. I'm twenty-five, just four years older than you. However, by working this closely with Charno I hope to age as gracefully as he."

"I can't say I blame you. When I met him, he said that he was going away for a few days or something. That doesn't sound like the action of a good leader at a time of crisis."

"He *had* to get away, Franklin. Until we know exactly what's going on, he's at too great a risk in the capital. If anything happened to Charno, that would be the end of us, believe me."

"And yet you, his faithful lieutenant, stay here?"

"I have a degree of... additional protection, shall we say. And besides, someone needs to be here to organise the attempted location of the others. Franklin, *please* say you'll take this on?"

Although he hated to admit it, he was becoming intrigued. And of course, there was the money to consider – things really hadn't been very busy in recent months. If it was no more dangerous than Alexandra Featherington had described, then why not? "One last question. What about payment if we fail to turn up anything?"

Alexandra seemed to relax, perhaps sensing that he'd reached a positive decision, "You'll be paid at the rate I mentioned regardless of your success or lack of it. In addition, we can offer you a substantial bonus should you be able to resolve matters to our satisfaction."

"I must be an idiot," he muttered under his breath. Then, "Well, I guess you've got your man, Alexandra."

She gave a sigh of relief and then sat forward, grasping his left hand in both of hers, "Thank you," she said, "I'm truly delighted that you've seen fit to help us."

Franklin was equally delighted to have seen the contents of her jacket once more. He swallowed hard and turned his attention back to the investigation, "Okay. So when can I get to see all these documents you have?"

"Tomorrow morning," she replied promptly, "I'll need to visit each of the others on our team this afternoon and this evening, to tell them that someone has been hired, and to make sure they are in complete agreement. The less contact you have with them the less chance there is of you being linked to the group. I'll also collect the documentation that you'll be needing. I know that this is a somewhat urgent situation, but I'm afraid that it will take at least until the morning to put everything together."

"I guess I'll be needing to re-organise things myself, so it suits me."

"Marvellous," she said, and then pulled a key from her pocket, "This is the key to my apartment. The address is on the tag. Do you know where it is?"

Franklin took it from her, "Close by the Barbican, isn't it?"

"Exactly. It's the second-level basement flat."

"Now why didn't I guess?"

"I might not be there when you arrive, or I might be asleep or something, so let yourself in. You'll find all the documentation on the table in the living room."

"Okay. How early is too early for you?"

"I probably won't get finished until six or seven, so any time after that."

"Just one thing," he said, pocketing the key, "Is it really sensible for me to be seen with you or at your apartment?"

"As I said, Franklin, I have additional levels of protection available to me. It shouldn't cause a problem."

"I seriously pray that you're right on that score."

"I'm really terribly grateful, Franklin. This means a lot to me."

"Well, I guess I'd better go and break the news to my crew," he said, "Let's hope I can meet your expectations. I'd better get the bill."

"No need, it's on me. Since you've agreed to take the case it surely counts as one of your expenses, does it not?"

"I guess so."

Alexandra pushed back her chair and rose with the same fluid grace with which she seemed to do everything. Franklin, anxious not to miss a last glance of heaven, rose with her.

"I'll, er, see you tomorrow morning then?"

She leaned back down to the table and picked up the bill, "I'm sure you'll be seeing a lot more of me in the coming days."

There wasn't, Franklin considered, anything that he dared say in reply to that. Instead, flustered, he waved to a passing waiter, miming putting on a coat.

He waited with his new client while she paid the bill and then accompanied her out into the interminable drizzle.

"Don't you just hate this sort of weather?"

"Underground, Franklin," Alexandra said with a smile, "Rain is not a major problem."

They parted company outside the Guildhall, and Franklin whistled happily all the way back to Liverpool Street.

*****

He was still whistling by the time he reached his office at four o'clock, but by now it had become a far more reflective sound. On the journey back he had replayed the conversation he'd shared with Alexandra – as well as taking a few moments to be sure that he remembered exactly what she looked like – and he was beginning to wonder exactly what he had got himself, Bill and Dot into. Okay, so she had assured him that they wouldn't be in very much danger, and since philandering husbands, full of righteous retribution when caught out, were a staple part of The Franklin Richardson Agency's diet, he reckoned that they were used to the occasional spot of violence. On the other hand, she'd told him that contact with members of her weird group would be unwise, which would presumably make asking questions about the missing ones a rather tiresome process, since it would have to be carried out under a cover of some sort.

On the plus side was the much-needed money – and, of course, there was Alexandra Featherington herself. All in all, he reckoned that he'd made a sound call on this case. Well, probably.

It wasn't until he opened the office door that he remembered Dot's uncharacteristic spat the previous afternoon, and he breathed a sigh of relief when he saw her chair unoccupied.

"Good afternoon, dear boy," Bill greeted him.

"Afternoon, yourself," Franklin grinned, "Where's our little firebrand? She has been in today, hasn't she?"

"Indeed so. She's left early to get some photocopying sorted out, or some such. She'll be back tomorrow."

"You manage to have that word with her?"

"Absolutely," Bill said, "She specifically asked me to apologise to your good self on her behalf."

"She said that?"

"Actually, I think her exact words were something in the order of 'Tell the bleedin' great get I was bang out of order', but I'm almost positive that it counts as an apology."

"That sounds more like our Dot," Franklin said, "Perhaps it's just down to the wrong time of the month."

"Damn!" Bill muttered.

"What?"

"That means I owe the young lady five pounds. She said you'd come out with something stereotypically chauvinistic, and I bet against it. You can be so disappointing at times, dear boy."

"Sorry, man," Franklin laughed, "But at least I've got some good news for us."

"Ah! Your meeting with the enigmatic assistant went well then?"

"I don't know about enigmatic, man, but she sure as shit had great tits."

"Franklin, please!" Bill shuddered, "Sometimes I think that poor little Dot has every justification in describing you as a male chauvinist pig. Plus there were two Americanisms and an expletive in that one sentence. By rights I should charge you three pounds for such vulgar abuse of our mother tongue."

"Sorry, man... *Bill*, but as it happens, the meeting means I'll easily be able to afford your fine."

"You picked up the case?"

44

"And what a case. This is gonna blow your mind."

Twenty minutes later, Bill sat back in his chair and whistled softly, "Intriguing indeed. In fact I would go so far as to say that it all sounds a little far-fetched to me."

"I really think she's genuine," Franklin said.

"There wouldn't seem to be any point in her fabricating something so esoteric, I grant you," Bill nodded, "And I must admit to having heard rumours about strange goings-on beneath our capital's thoroughfares. Naturally, I put it all down to bored minds dreaming up weird and wonderful fancies. I shall have to revise my opinions if this proves true."

"Well, I should be able to find out more tomorrow morning. I've got an early start on the documentation at her place."

"Would you like me to accompany you on this mission? Only I know what you're like with paperwork."

"Not necessary," Franklin said, "My reading's pretty much up to speed now, and I need the practice anyway."

When Bill had first met Franklin, he'd been horrified to discover how close the young lad was to being officially illiterate. Both his reading and writing levels were no greater than those of a ten-year old, and it had been a wonder to Bill that Franklin had managed to take the course in private investigation, let alone pass the final examinations with flying colours.

"Well, if you're quite sure, dear boy," he said, "But should you change your mind, just give me a call."

"I won't," Franklin said, "Perhaps you could fill Dot in with the details and start rearranging our workload?"

"I'll most certainly pass on the potentially good news, but I rather think it will take me longer to do that than rearrange the schedules – I wrapped up the Thomson case this very afternoon."

"That's great, man! Congratulations. Where'd you find the missing fiancé? Come to that, how?"

"In the very next street to where she lives, and I rather think that the congratulations aren't really necessary. I was in the process of delivering the report to Mrs. Thomas, confirming her husband's dalliance with the young harlot in the corner shop, and I found her front door open. Fearing for her safety, and in no way prying at all, I slipped inside. What should I find, but that Miss Thomson's young beau had also slipped inside. Inside Mrs. Thomas, that is."

"You mean he was...?"

"There was quite a little kerfuffle and embarrassment all round. I for one, didn't know where to look – that Mrs. Thomas is a big woman." Bill had, indeed, turned bright pink.

"What the hell did she say?"

"After she'd finished screaming blue murder at me and, rather amusingly, I thought, accusing me of spying on her, she paid me for the report and threatened to kill her husband on his return. Somehow she managed not to notice the paradoxical nature of the situation."

"What did that Grayson guy have to say about it?"

"Very little. Fortunately, he doesn't know we've been tailing him on behalf of Jennifer Thomson. I went straight round to her flat after I left the somewhat mismatched and red-faced pair to tell her of my discovery. Very impressed, she was."

"She doesn't want any further proof?"

"No, she was more than happy to take my word for things, and as it happens, she'd suspected something of this nature and had been harbouring suspicions about Mrs. Thomas all along."

"Why on earth didn't she mention it, then? It would have saved us a lot of time, and her a lot of money."

"I rather believe the poor little thing was embarrassed that her husband-to-be was possibly dallying with a much older and much larger woman."

"Oh, well, I guess she's happy enough with what we've been able to achieve. Was she too upset with the news, though?"

Bill shook his head, "She was happy at both our efficiency and the news itself. She told me that it gave her the perfect excuse to throw him out of her flat and install her new lover."

"They all seem to be at it like rabbits," Franklin muttered, wondering why his own love-life seemed – Melanie Forbes a few weeks previously notwithstanding – non-existent. "I don't suppose it would be very ethical if we contacted Mr. Thomas with certain suggestions, do you?"

46

"Absolutely not, dear boy. I strictly forbid it!"

"Just a thought. Only I sometimes feel a bit sorry for the supposedly guilty party in some of these cases. Especially in a situation like this."

"We're not here to judge, just find evidence," Bill said, "Isn't that what you always tell me? You quite often get far too involved with the clients for your own wellbeing."

"You're right, I guess." Franklin had earlier been wondering just how far involved he could get with the delectable Miss Featherington.

He declined Bill's offer of a celebratory Guinness on the grounds that he had an early start the next morning and was determined not to make it a hat-trick of hangovers. Bill left him in the office and he opened up his trusty notebook and began to write up a series of notes concerning the new case. If they were to be paid four times the going rate, he might as well be as efficient as possible.

*****

Detective Inspector Graham McCoy was not a happy bunny. As the newly appointed head of the City of London Police's latest brainchild squad, the Criminal Underworld Taskforce, he had been assigned the jumpers case. This was not the cause of his bad mood, although he was fairly certain it soon would be given that no-one seemed to have the faintest idea what had actually happened. Rather, it was the person standing almost at attention in front of his desk.

"What on earth did I do to deserve getting you posted onto my team?" He asked the young man.

"Just your lucky day, I guess," DS Green said, his features neutral, "Only the best for the City's finest squad. They don't call us the CUTs for nothing."

"I'd hardly ascribe the word 'best' to you, Green. And as for calling us the CUTs, I think you'll find that they add a consonant somewhere in the middle. Perhaps now that you're here, it'll seem a little more accurate."

"Charming," DS Green said, "What happened on that last case we worked on together could have happened to anyone."

"Bollocks! We let that Streatham mob get away because one of us wasn't in position. One of us, as it happens, was busy shagging a new recruit in the back of their stake-out van."

"It's not really my fault that they turned up an hour early. Lucy and I thought we'd have plenty of time."

"You and DC Loose-knickers Delaney deserve to be *doing* time as far as I'm concerned."

DS Green took a packet of cigarettes from his bomber jacket and lit one with McCoy's lighter, "Well, that's all in the past. You'll have no more trouble like that from me, guv." Smoking regulations did not apply in McCoy's office as everyone knew, and everyone turned a vision-impaired eye to.

"I know I won't," McCoy said, "This is pretty much an all-male squad, worse luck, for the jumpers' case. Although knowing my fortune, you'll have probably turned queer in the last six months. I'll probably find you buggering some unfortunate plod halfway up the escalator at St. Paul's."

"Not a chance, guv. Too much of a draught there for a start."

"Enough with the wisecracks, Green, and please note that if you tell Cox or anyone high up that I smoke in here you may just get shot by me, understand? In any case. we've got work to do. How much do you already know about this case?"

DS Green took a thoughtful puff on the cigarette, "Well, obviously I read what was in the online news reports and listened to the radio news, but I was also hearing some strange mutterings from the boys over in Westminster. Something about a gang war or something."

"I'm getting the feeling that any day now we'll be wishing that's all it was," McCoy said, "It's been almost forty-eight hours since seventeen, apparently respectable business types decided to top themselves in the finest London tradition. Seventeen apparently unrelated people at sixteen apparently random tube stations and all within two minutes thirty-seven seconds of each other. Given that we can rule out coincidence – and I'm absolutely positive we can – you would have thought that we'd have been able to uncover at least one tiny little clue, wouldn't you? But what have we got? Fuck all, *that's* what we've got. Jack shit."

"Not a single lead?"

"Really, nothing! The only thing we've been able to establish so far is that there are some startling similarities between the jumpers."

"That sounds hopeful," Green said.

McCoy slid a sheet of paper across the desk, "Read this and then tell me whether it's hopeful."

DS Green scanned the sheet, "All unmarried, all living alone, all young, all fit and all financially secure and in good jobs where employers universally describe them as efficient, happy and content. With the exception of the unmarried bit, that rules out virtually every motive for suicide. I'm beginning to see what you mean."

"Perhaps that might explain to you why they decided this morning to bring us in on this case."

"You really reckon seventeen people were topped at the height of rush-hour in the centre of London, then, guv?"

"What do you think?"

"It'd take a hell of an outfit to organise simultaneous murders at sixteen different locations at pretty much the same time."

"I'm not denying that, Green. In fact, that's what's worrying me."

"But surely, someone must have seen something on one of the platforms? I mean to say, if these *jumpers* were all as fit as this report suggests, they ain't gonna be easy to chuck in front of a train."

"The platforms were packed solid, Green. You know what it's like at rush-hour. Add to that, there'd been breakdowns on three of the four lines involved that very afternoon, and you can imagine the sort of crush there would have been down there."

"I suppose so," DS Green said, "I take it there are officers posted down there now?"

"Both to make enquiries and to carry out surveillance. It's got all the feel of a one-off hit, but you never know these days."

"What about the stations' CCTV? Surely that's gotta turn up something?"

"Nice try, but no go. In eleven of the stations the tape had recorded over itself by the time any of the dickheads upstairs had thought to check on them, and at the other five, they were out of order."

"*Very* inconvenient," DS Green said.

"Especially since they were the five quietest stations."

"So other than the similarities between what now looks like the victims, and the highly unlikely simultaneous breakdown of the CCTVs, there's absolutely bugger-all to go on?"

McCoy sighed and plucked a cigarette from DS Green's packet, "That's about the size of it."

"I take it the stations' supervisors have all been questioned?"

"Yesterday. Or rather, all but one. He was knocked off his motorbike on his way home Monday night. He's still too ill to speak to us. Robson's at the hospital waiting for him to come around. The rest all moaned about lack of resources being to blame for the mechanical defects."

"What are the press making of it?"

"They still seem convinced that it was some weird cult thing. It won't take long for them to get restive, though, you know what they're like."

"So where do we start?"

"Green, I've got forty-two men *very* temporarily assigned to this case. By this time tomorrow we'll be back down to four and a half. And guess what? I haven't got a fucking *clue* where to start! Jesus wept, this case is still officially classified as a suicide investigation. I guess we just keep asking the questions. Employers and relations of the deceased, employees of London Underground, the great unwashed commuter hoards. Someone, somewhere, must know something!"

"What do you want me to do?"

"Keep your dick in your jeans, for a start."

"Even when I need to take a piss? That'll—"

"Green! You know perfectly well what I mean. Seriously, though, it's after six, pretty much the only people we can easily contact now are the relatives. DS Singh has been getting some lists put together. Go along and see what she's managed to dig up and then take DC Jackson out for a few fun-filled hours grilling grieving relatives, okay?"

"Got it, guv."

After DS Green had left, McCoy sat back in his chair and stared vacantly at the far wall. "Something," he muttered aloud, "In the country of London, stinks."

Chapter 4

Thursday 15th November 2018

It was still dark when the alarm clock's frantic buzzing woke Franklin the next morning. Unusually, he welcomed its strident tones since he'd been having a nightmare in which a giant breast pursued him along dank, dark tunnels. He couldn't begin to fathom how *that* image got into his subconscious.

Refreshed as much by the lack of a hangover than he was by a decent night's sleep and a long, hot shower, he left the flat at ten to seven and strolled through the early morning drizzle towards the station. He picked up a newspaper on the way and began scanning through it as he waited on the damp, cold platform with a handful of bedraggled early commuters.

News of the 'jumpers' was still occupying the front three and a half pages since the names of the deceased had been released the previous evening. Police had apparently called for any witnesses to the 'suicides' to come forward as a matter of extreme urgency, and suicide pact theories abounded. One tiny, two-column, two-inch filler article caught Franklin's eye. The reporter seemed to find the suicide theory 'untenable' and proposed the theory that what had really occurred was a serious disturbance in the ley-lines that 'everyone' knew ran under the City.

"Moron," Franklin muttered aloud.

The man beside him shuffled a few feet further along the platform.

By some miracle the City-bound train turned up on time and Franklin had time for a coffee at Liverpool Street before heading back out into the rain which had graduated from drizzle to torrential. By the time he'd reached the Golden Lane estate just north of the sprawling Barbican complex, he was once more uncomfortably drenched. He was also uncomfortable with the realisation that he desperately hoped that the luscious Alexandra Featherington would be at home when he let himself in. It was bad enough that she'd plagued his dreams without plaguing his thoughts while he was awake.

He fished the key from his pocket and checked the address. A minute later, he'd located the property, an imposing, ultra-modern looking four-storey building. It didn't come as a surprise. A small gate opened onto a flight of steps leading below ground level and as he opened it, small lamps illuminated the well. He made a careful descent down the rain-slicked steps and took a few deep breaths before inserting the key in the lock of the sub-basement flat.

Although she had told him to let himself into the building, he wondered whether he should really knock first. Shrugging, and telling himself he was just following his client's instructions, he turned the key and let the door swing open.

A moment later he found himself in the most incredible flat he had ever seen. The front door opened directly into a vast living room which stretched more than the width of the building above. The walls and floors alike were covered in rugs and suspiciously real-looking furs. Although the room had only one small window, deep in the stairwell, mirrors on the walls, and steel and glass shelving magnified the light from two standard lamps to an almost uncomfortable brilliance. A long, white, leather sofa dominated the rear of the room and a large, glass-topped table occupied the far-right corner. On it were several neat stacks of papers – presumably the documentation Franklin had come to view. Doors led off to both left and right meaning that the apartment must run underneath the properties on either side.

"Wow!" Franklin whistled. He closed the door behind him and shrugged out of his saturated leather coat, hanging it next to the one Alexandra had been wearing at the Vault the previous day. He hoped that the presence of her coat there, together with the glowing standard lamps, indicated that she was present as well. He stepped forward into the room and called her name quietly, unwilling to disturb her should she be asleep. The flat was as silent as politician's honest promise.

He wondered whether he should check the rooms beyond the two closed doors, but finally, and reluctantly, decided that it might appear too intrusive. Instead, he crossed to the glass table.

On top of the nearest stack of paper was a note with his name at the top. The handwriting was an elegant copperplate, its source immediately obvious. He picked it up and scanned it.

"Franklin,

Here are the papers you will need. Although it is necessary for me to give you full access to them, I must ask that you do not remove any from the premises without my express permission, nor take photographic copies with your mobile telephone. There is, as you will see, some sensitive information within these documents. I am sure you will understand my insistence, and I trust that you will follow my instructions.

I would very much have liked to be awake when you arrived, but the night was long, and I really must sleep. However, I absolutely insist that you wake me before you depart should I have not already 'surfaced' – my bedroom is through the door on your left. We will need to discuss certain matters. The kitchen and master-bathroom are through the opposite door, and I have left the coffee machine on. There is also a drinks cabinet in the kitchen and I insist that you help yourself to anything you desire. After reading these papers, you may very well feel inclined to do so.

Do not be concerned about making a noise: not only are all the walls soundproofed, I think that I can probably sleep through a nuclear explosion!

Thank you so much for coming. I really do look forward to seeing you later,

Alexandra"

"And I really do look forward to seeing you, my dear," Franklin grinned, hoping afterwards that the remark about the soundproofed walls was accurate.

He set the note aside and stared at the heaps of documents before him. It was clearly going to take some time to get through them and he decided to take Alexandra up on her offer of coffee.

Like the living room, the kitchen was ultra-modern and ultra-bright. The appliances were brightly coloured, the work surfaces stainless-steel and the cupboards and drawers glass-fronted. The coffee machine was a *Gaggia* espresso special, and Franklin poured a large, steaming measure into a mug, relishing the smell. He returned to the living room and drew up a surprisingly comfortable moulded chair. The coffee was still too hot to drink so he set it aside to cool and opened the first file. It was marked 'Charno' and seemed an appropriate place to start.

Four hours and all twenty files later, the coffee still sat un-drunk.

Franklin sat back, rubbing his eyes. If what he had read was not the most elaborate hoax he'd ever heard of, then something almost unbelievable had been – and continued – going on right under the capital's feet. Something that if not controlled, could lead to destruction, death and chaos. He shook his head, trying to clear images of secret tunnels, secret doorways, mysterious dark figures, and blood on the walls from his mind.

He rose slowly from the chair and noticed the coffee. He picked up the cold cup with a hand that trembled slightly and made his way back through to the kitchen, setting the cup on the gleaming surface beside the sink. Working on autopilot, he opened the glass-fronted drinks cabinet, extracted a bottle of Glenlivet and poured himself a large measure – 'a Taylor' as it was known back in the real world. It was drained in two swallows.

The bite and fire of the amber liquid seemed to clear his head, and Franklin permitted himself a wry smile. He'd thought that this case was weird yesterday – now he was positive it was. And far weirder by far than anything his imagination could have dreamed up.

The documents were a mixture of personality profiles, charts and maps, and a potted history of the way in which London's subterranean world was being taken over by a handful of powerful people. Those powerful people were being aided and abetted by a veritable army of supporters. Given the purported dark aims and ambitions of the group known as the 'Allenites', Franklin seriously hoped that, if all of this was true, Charno and his own group would somehow be able to prevail. He wouldn't want to be within fifty miles of London if they didn't.

Whether Alexandra Featherington had insisted on it or not, there was no way that Franklin was going to leave there without talking to her. Some serious talking. He almost wished he'd taken Bill up on his offer of accompaniment.

He poured himself another, smaller, shot of whisky and drained the glass, before returning to the living room. He'd been making two sets of notes as he'd scanned the documents, one containing detail relevant to the case, the other a list of questions that he needed to ask the mysterious Alexandra. He put the first set into the inside pocket of his overcoat and then tucked the latter set into the breast pocket of the denim shirt that he was wearing.

Two deep breaths later, he felt that he was ready to face her, and crossed to the still-closed door behind which, she had written, her bedroom was situated. He opened it slowly.

After the brightness in the rest of the apartment, the soft glow in the huge bedroom took some adjustment. Franklin closed his eyes for thirty seconds and then opened them.

He was immediately glad that he'd taken the effort to do so. And also that he *hadn't* brought Bill Taylor along.

Alexandra Featherington, her face almost covered by her blonde, streaked hair, apparently still asleep, was laying on her back in the centre of a vast, circular bed, itself situated in the centre of the room. More importantly – at least as far as Franklin was concerned – was the fact that the sheet that covered her reached up only to her waist. In the soft light, he could clearly make out the perfect forms of her clearly firm breasts, her chest rising and falling in the gentle rhythm of sleep.

'*What to do*?' was the question that immediately flashed into his mind. His libido, under-worked of late, came up with a couple of suggestions at the speed of light. Franklin reluctantly rejected these and tried to imagine what Alexandra's reaction would be if she woke and found him gawping at her naked breasts. She had, after all, *insisted* that he woke her, and she had, in addition, yesterday described herself as a 'latent exhibitionist'. Somehow Franklin still didn't think that she would take kindly to him crossing the room and shaking her awake in that state of undress. Presumably, she had meant that he should knock on her door when he was finished.

Finding the manoeuvre far more difficult than he'd hitherto imagined it would be, he stepped backwards into the living room and reluctantly closed the bedroom door. Taking another couple of deep breaths, he lifted his hand and knocked loudly on the door, "Alexandra? It's Franklin! You said to wake you when I was done."

He put his ear to the door and was relieved that the soundproofing wasn't *too* efficient when he heard her sleep-bleared voice, "Be with you!"

At least, he reasoned, she hadn't *known* he'd come into her room and seen her semi-naked. He returned to the table and took the second set of notes out of his pocket. He was still flattening out the creases when the bedroom door opened and Alexandra Featherington stepped into the room.

*****

Detective Sergeant Tony Green was not a happy bunny. In fact, he was a decidedly pissed-off bunny.

"Guv! There was no choice. I could hardly bang on the doors of justifiably already pissed-off people at turned midnight. What else could I have done?"

"Phoned me for starters," DI McCoy growled, "Why didn't you, come to that?"

"I did. Your dispatcher said you'd left for the night and wasn't to be disturbed."

"And you didn't think to call my mobile?"

"These days I tend to take orders from my superiors."

"Well that at least is a relief. Next time, call me regardless, okay?"

"It'd be a pleasure."

"So, what did you and Jackson manage to turn up?"

DS Green lit a Marlboro before replying, "Something and nothing, I guess you could say."

"Very informative. Give."

"Between us we managed to get to see relatives of twelve of the stiffs. Bloody hard work it was too–"

"Just the facts, as that crap sixties TV cop used to say."

"Before my time, guv. But anyway, the story was pretty much the same. The relatives Sunny Singh had managed to turn up were either parents or aunts and uncles. Not a single brother or sister between them all. It turns out that all twelve we've managed to chase up so far were not only successful, young, fit, unmarried and all that crap, they were also *all* single children. Not a single sibling amongst the lot of them."

"And that's a help?"

"As I said, something and nothing, guv. It don't make any more sense than anything else we've got so far."

McCoy filched another of the Sergeant's cigarettes and lit it. Sitting back in his chair, he run his fingers through his hair, "Shit!"

The young DS had enough experience of his superior to know when silence was a positive virtue. He perched himself on the edge of McCoy's desk and waited.

"Okay," the DI said at length, "There's five more families to interview. From what you say, it almost seems like a waste of time, but I want it done. You might as well finish off what you started, so pick up Jackson and get going. When you've finished with them – assuming you don't get anything useful out of any of them – I want you back here. Next job will be the victims' employers. I want to come with you for those."

"Fair enough, guv. You're still certain it's a case of "victims", then?"

"More than ever. While you're out there with the families, I'll be following up a little bit of information that came my way a few minutes ago. It relates to one of the victim's employers. I want to be sure of my facts before we go to see him."

"Does it sound useful?"

"At the moment, Green, even *you* sound useful. I'll tell you all about it when you get back, but for the minute, let's just say that it sounds about as likely as my mother winning the Miss World contest."

"I thought you were orphaned when you were a kid?"

"Green? I rest my case. I'll see you back here about two, okay?"

The young sergeant shrugged, "I'll do my best."

"Now there," McCoy said, "Would be a pleasant surprise."

*****

"I really thought he would have at least called by now," Bill said.

"You *are* still fretting about the same Franklin that we both know, ain't you?" Dot replied.

"You can be ever-so slightly spiteful at times, dear girl. But, yes, of course I'm a little concerned about him. This is a very strange situation he's walking into."

"Always assuming that it's not just some sort of wind-up. It all sounds bleedin' weird to me. Anyway, it's only two-thirty."

"Franklin does seem convinced that the young lady has told him the truth – or, at least, as much of it that she currently may divulge."

Dot snorted, "Franklin and the term 'young ladies' don't exactly fill me with confidence."

"He does seem to have a penchant for the young, petite, female types, I do admit, but–"

"Yeah, right!" Dot gave another derisive snort, "If it's female, alive and vaguely human he'd go for it. Two out of the three at a push."

"Dot!"

"Yeah, well."

"To quote your good self and in no way wishing to think that I would ever use such parlance, what exactly does 'Yeah, well' mean in this instance?"

"Well, even you're saying that he prefers his women on the small side."

"Dot, my dear, what on earth are you trying to convey?"

"Well, you said it right then and that was the sort of crap he was coming out with yesterday. 'I like my women small'. It's all just crap!"

Bill stared thoughtfully at the young woman, "I think I'm beginning to see what the problem is."

"Sure you are!"

"I really haven't the faintest notion as to what the modern parlance may be, but in good, old-fashioned terms, you've fallen for our dusky, young boss, have you not?"

Dot's head snapped up, "Course I ain't!"

"It's as plain as water without whisky, dear girl."

"You must be nutso." The protest was sullen.

"That may very well be the case, but in this matter I feel sure that I've just hit the nail squarely on the head. What would be the harm in admitting as much to my good self?"

"Because you'd be bound to tell him, that's why. You men always stick together."

"Dot, my dear, you have my word as a gentleman of honour that I would not dream of divulging such information to anyone, let alone the object of your desire. And now that you have my word, why not unburden yourself?"

"Why do you have to always use twenty words when two would do?"

"You're prevaricating, dear girl."

"Yeah, well."

"That little phrase is getting rather tiresome. Come on, Dot. Get it off your chest."

"It's embarrassing."

"The facts or your chest?"

"Don't you bleedin' start!"

"Sorry, dear. Just trying to lighten the mood a little."

"Yeah, w... Anyway, what's there to say? He never takes any notice of me does he? Always going on about how lonely he is. How much he likes small women, and he's never once so much as really looked at me. I'm not that bad, am I?"

"Not in the least little bit, my dear. I must admit that the hair is a little... startling, but you're a thoroughly charming and attractive little creature. And before you say anything, 'little creature' is a term of endearment – a compliment of sorts," Bill paused to see what effect his words were having. As usual, it was difficult to tell with the teenager, "But, your charming appearance aside, I think I could possibly offer an insight into Franklin's apparent lack of interest."

This piqued Dot's interest at last, "Oh? And what might that be?"

"When you first met up with Franklin and me, you were but a fifteen-year-old runaway, were you not?"

"Yeah. But that was four years ago. I'm nineteen now, and he knows it."

"Be that as it may," Bill said, "But often, people don't actually deep-down realise that someone they know is getting older. It is more than possible – likely, in fact – that, although Franklin knows that you are nineteen as a general principle, in the depths of his consciousness he still thinks of you as a fifteen-year-old. And not only that, my dear," Bill lowered his voice, "Both Franklin and I know of your past... *difficulties* with men. I rather think that he may see himself as some sort of guardian to you."

"But I don't want him to be! I..." Dot trailed off.

"So I can see," Bill smiled, "Perhaps I could drop the gentlest of hints in his direction? To be thoroughly honest, I've already mentioned something of the sort."

"You've what!?"

"Dot, dear girl, it has been becoming increasingly apparent of late."

"What did he say, then?"

"I must confess that he was somewhat sceptical, and in fairness to the young man, your attitude to him doesn't lend itself to make him believe what I have said."

"Well, I can't just change overnight, can I? I don't want him to think I'm suddenly coming on to him. What *should* I do?"

Bill laughed, "I'm hardly an expert in matters of the heart, but I do know that modern trends indicate that there is far more equality involved in such things. Why don't you invite him out for a meal or some such? After all, you *are* always reminding ourselves that chauvinism is dead and buried."

"*Me* ask *him* out?"

"Why not?"

To Bill's astonishment, a deep blush spread across Dot's cheeks, "I'm not sure I could."

"I am," Bill insisted, "But in the meantime, while you are plucking up the necessary courage, why not change your appearance a little?"

"You mean you reckon that he really hates my hair like this, then?"

"Not at all, dear girl. It would simply give Franklin an opportunity to ask you why. When he does, you could easily say that you thought he might like it."

"I'm not sure I could say that, either," Dot said, doubt creeping into her voice, "But do you really reckon it could work?"

"I really don't see why not," Bill said, "Surely it's at least worth a try. Just out of curiosity, what is the natural colour of your hair?"

She shrugged, "Black, why?"

"Not very dark brown?"

"Nah. Jet black."

"Do you realise, dear girl, that the combination of raven hair and bright blue eyes is considered by many men to be extraordinarily attractive?"

"Really?"

"Absolutely."

"I thought all the guy's prefer blondes."

"Dot, my dear, I assure you that I, for one, am always enchanted by the combination."

An unusual note of hope had entered Dot's voice, "Well, I guess it might be worth a try... only..."

Bill held up his hand, "Just listen to me for one moment, my dear. I know enough about the psychology of your situation to understand that you colour your hair to take yourself away from the traumas of your past home-life, and that you might feel vulnerable without your camouflage. But consider this. Franklin understands about your past, about the manner in which you suffered, and it is for that reason that he views himself as more your guardian than your friend – although friend he surely is – and if you show him the real Dot, the unadorned lady, then you are showing him in a roundabout way that in some respects you no longer need him to be just a guardian to you. On a subconscious level, he will see the different, grown-up version of the girl that he first knew and has known to this day. I don't want to upset you, my dear, precious girl, but I have to tell you that you really are getting over the past now, and it would be time for you to move on, to become the woman that you are destined to be, even if there were no ulterior motive involved."

Dot stared at Bill for a few seconds before she spoke, "I get what you're saying, and I guess you're right, but I don't think I'll ever get over what that bastard... sorry... no, not sorry... that bastard did to me."

"Not completely, no. But in all sorts of ways you are coping better and growing into a new woman. You have a new life now, one that you are in control of, and every step you take away from that traumatised girl that Franklin and I first knew is a joy for us and a triumph for you. Do you see that, my dear?"

A crooked smile gradually formed, and Dot finally nodded, "Yeah, you're right as usual. And yeah, it is about time I got to be the real me, even if he doesn't notice."

"Somehow, my dear, I think there is less chance of him not noticing than of me being elected the next head of the Temperance Society."

"As usual I haven't got the faintest idea what you're on about, but thanks anyway."

"Your gushing gratitude is entirely unnecessary." Bill checked his watch and frowned, "He really is rather late, you know?"

Dot nodded, "Let's hope he's not in any trouble."

*****

It was several minutes before Alexandra Featherington stepped into the room, and when she did so Franklin's jaw threatened to break the thick glass of the table top.

"Sorry to have kept you waiting, Franklin," she said, "But I simply *had* to treat myself to a long, hot shower."

That she'd had a shower was obvious to Franklin. Alexandra was wearing a short bath-robe made of some sort of flimsy material. Wherever it touched a still-damp part of her body – which seemed to be most of it – the garment appeared transparent. To make matters worse – or better, depending on your viewpoint – it was only loosely tied and covered even less of her upper torso than the jacket she had been wearing the previous day.

"I, er, that is..." He trailed off helplessly.

Alexandra looked down at herself and shrugged, "I like to be as casual as possible at home."

Franklin was in no way certain that 'casual' was the word he would have chosen, "I guess I'm the same," he managed.

"Oh, I do hope not," Alexandra laughed, giving her body another lingering look.

Franklin found himself doing the same, but his head snapped up to her eyes as he caught the possible meaning of what she had just said, "Er..."

"You should have come through to wake me," Her green eyes now latched onto his, "It's a very, very long time since I've had the pleasure... of being woken by a man's gentle hands."

"I, er, didn't want to intrude."

"Franklin, after what you've read this morning, all those intimate details of my life, I don't think you could do anything – very much – to intrude further upon me. With all this dreadful business going on, I need some comfort somewhere in my life." The playful smile in her eyes had faded as she spoke, and now they seemed to glisten in the brilliance of the room's reflected light, "These next few days may very well be the last such chance I'll get."

As she took a couple of steps towards him, Franklin rose slowly from the chair, "I..."

Alexandra reached out one hand and placed it on his suddenly dry lips, "I'm not normally like this," she whispered, "But there's something about you... or perhaps it's just the circumstances. I don't really know, and I don't really care. Come here." She took his left hand and led him into the bedroom.

Franklin's brain felt as if it was about to explode and drain out of his ears. After the horrors that he'd read about in the previous few hours, the appearance of Alexandra Featherington in her diaphanous robe had been like a gift from the gods and manna from heaven all rolled into one. And now this...

The young woman stopped beside her bed, Franklin a pace behind her. Slowly, she turned and faced him. At some point on the short journey she had untied the robe's belt, and the motion of her graceful turn caused it to flare open. She stood silently before him as he took in the smooth contours of her pert breasts, her flat belly, well-muscled thighs.

Moving as if in a dream, Franklin raised one hand to Alexandra's long neck, and then let it slide slowly downwards until it cupped a naked breast, the nipple rigid against his palm. She gave a gentle groan which seemed to break some sort of spell. It also broke the last tiny element of resistance in Franklin and he was as naked as she was in seconds, their bodies locked in the most passionate of embraces. At some point they collapsed onto the giant, circular bed and it seemed to Franklin that he had no control left, that matters were destined. He gave into it, rode the passion, rode Alexandra, their coupling punctuated with groans and sighs, cries of joy and yells of pure ecstasy.

Afterwards they lay entwined, panting, sweating, and staring at each other with matching expressions of gentle amazement.

"That was incredible," Alexandra whispered at length.

Franklin nodded, "Fantastic."

She lowered her eyes, "I know you're going to find this hard to believe, but I really had no intention of... *that* happening."

"No?"

"Really. Yesterday... well, there was one thing I told you that wasn't exactly honest."

"Your story was pretty far-fetched in places."

"No, the story – what's happening down there – that's all true. I meant something about me. I don't really dress like that normally. In fact, I thought I was going to die of embarrassment. If it hadn't been for a few stiff drinks before we met, I don't think I could have gone through with it. You couldn't begin to believe how grateful I was that we'd got that tiny table in the corner."

Franklin sat himself up on one elbow, frowning, "Well, why do it then? Not that I'm complaining, you understand."

"It was Charno's idea – a sort of test, he said. To see how distracted you might become. But when it came to the story, you seemed entirely focused, and that was why I asked you to take the case."

"You do everything Charno tells you to, because this sounds pretty weird?"

"Of course. You've read his file. You know that I owe him my very life and you also know that he's never wrong. If he says that it's a good idea or necessary or whatever, then it's done."

"So it seems to say, but we'll get back to that later. Was all this today his idea?"

"No!" She reached up a hand and held his jaw steady, her gaze locked onto his. When she was sure that she had his full attention, she allowed her eyes to close, "I wasn't lying this morning when I said that there's something different about you. The way I look, I get men coming on to me all the time, but I never... get involved. After we'd parted yesterday, I couldn't help but keep thinking about you and me in the Vault, what I'd worn, how you reacted. Actually, what I'm trying to say, is that I got pretty horny about it, if you really must know. Perhaps there *is* some latent exhibitionism in me somewhere. Then this morning, when I got home, and I found I was still having the same feelings I decided to keep up the act. I wasn't absolutely certain until you came into the bedroom and then went out again without 'waking' me."

"You were awake?"

Alexandra kept her eyes closed, "Yeah, sorry. But when you went back outside I couldn't believe how disappointed I felt. That seemed to make my decision for me somehow, and well, I guess the rest is, as they say, history. I hope you're not too mad with me?"

"Hardly," Franklin said, "For some strange reason, I never seem to get mad with beautiful women who drag me into their beds."

"I bet it happens often."

"I wish," he laughed, "But thanks for telling me. I guess we'd better get back to the business in hand, though."

"Is this what you meant?"

Franklin's eyes widened at her touch, "Well, since we're being honest with each other, it wasn't quite what I meant, but I do believe I've changed my mind. Besides, it's only half-two, I guess there's plenty of time yet."

Chapter 5

Thursday 15th November 2018

"There's no time for it, guv."

"Green, there's no choice in the matter. This is now, *formally*, a murder investigation," McCoy searched in vain for a cigarette, and was finally forced to take the one that DS Green offered him, "And it's no good you standing there and telling me that we haven't got time to divert manpower into investigating the station supervisor's 'accident', because I already know that. Whoever was driving the truck that drove him off the road has got to be found. For fuck's sake Green even you can see that it's the only possible lead we've got!"

"Are you really sure about your source though, guv? I mean, a little coming together between an artic and a bike ain't exactly uncommon round these parts, is it?"

"My source, Green, is a damn sight more reliable than anyone that works here. If he says it was deliberate, then deliberate it was."

DS Green shrugged, "I'll have to take your word for it. But if this informer knows that much, then surely he's got more for us?"

"He hasn't. And he's not the type that can be pushed around in any case. The AI crew have now confirmed that it wasn't the tube station guy's fault, and the one eye-witness we've got so far reckons it looked deliberate. Given the circumstances about the CCTVs it looks pretty clean-cut to me."

"If, as I presume, you're talking about someone offing a potential witness, it seems a bloody risky way to go about it."

"Green, if someone wanted to off seventeen people, staging a mass suicide was hardly lacking in a bit of risk, was it? Besides, what else have we got?"

"Fair enough shout, but–"

"Forget the "buts". There's no choice. I *know* we're short of time, short of manpower – so just get on with it. I'll handle the victims' employers, you'll get round to Snow Hill and find out everything you can about the accident. And I want results – names of witnesses, crime scene report, the works, okay?"

"Whatever you say, guv."

McCoy ground out the Marlboro in his ashtray before looking up at the young sergeant, "Just don't fuck things up."

"Me? Fuck things? Not my style."

"Yeah, right," McCoy muttered as Green left his office. He checked the ground out cigarette to make sure it was extinguished and reached for his coat. Time and manpower might already be short, but his temper was getting shorter.

*****

In order to avoid the temptation of yet further distractions, Franklin and Alexandra showered and dressed before turning their attention to the investigation. While Franklin was hunting around the bedroom for his notes, Alexandra prepared them coffee and sandwiches. A few minutes later, now sated in all senses of the word, Franklin shuffled the few sheets of paper, trying to work out what to ask first.

"Start anywhere," Alexandra prompted.

"Easy for you to say," he sighed, "But I guess what I *should* really ask before anything else is whether these documents are genuine – and in particular, the records of 'proprietorship'."

"They're the genuine article, Franklin," Alexandra's voice was sombre, "No matter how much I wish it weren't so. And as for the records of ownership, they're recognised throughout the world below. As you will have read, there have been disputes – bloody disputes – over the boundaries, but what you were given to read today represents an objective picture of how things now stand."

"But this seems to say that every tunnel, every duct, sewer, covered river – even the bloody tunnels under the Thames – all of them are some

67

part of a stupid game being played out by two men leading groups of fanatics who want to control London from thirty feet below the ground!"

"It's not a game, not some sort of subterranean version of Monopoly," she said, "And you're wrong to say that both of the groups are looking to control London. It's only the Allenites – 'aliens' outside of official documents – who seem hell-bent on that course, who want to use their territorial advantage to wreak havoc on those above ground. I promise you, Franklin, our group – Charno's group – wants to stop it happening. As you've seen for yourself, this all started out as some sort of egotistical competition between Allen and Charno, a way for them to prove who was the master of their territory, but Marcus Allen has taken things too far. If you've read the document that describes the events after seventy-nine, you must surely be able to see that? He's an evil character. Ruthless, manipulative and power-crazed. He'll not be satisfied until all of London is under his 'tender mercies' as he calls them."

Neither whisky nor sex had truly been able to divert Franklin's fevered brain from the nightmare of this case – this situation – that he now found himself embroiled in. It was either a total crock of shit – which a young, immature part of his brain desperately wished for – or it was part of something so vast and so awful, awesome, unbelievable, that he felt completely out of his depth.

"Look," he said, "I understand what you're saying. I think I can even understand what those documents are supposed to be telling me. What I'm finding hard to believe is that this is all going on *literally* under the feet of hundreds of thousands of people and no-one, not even the companies that rightfully own these properties, seem in any way aware of it. Take this," he opened one of the maps and pushed it towards Alexandra, "It's dated June this year, and if I'm reading it right, it shows a new tunnel being constructed between the British Telecom access tunnel here and the..." Franklin quickly checked his notes, "The 'interceptory' sewer here. How the hell could that happen without people noticing?"

"Of *course* people notice," Alexandra said, "But think about it. When was the last time you saw some official van parked by the side of a hole in the road full of workmen and actually went up to them and asked to see some sort of official identification? People don't. The *police* don't if someone has given them prior notification that the work was due to go ahead on a given date. As I told you before, and as you can see from all of these charts and maps, the whole City is a honeycomb of subterranean tunnels and thoroughfares of all sorts. Even the companies who misguidedly believe that they are the real owners of these tunnels and sewers don't really notice the new structures. New tunnels are being dug all the time and they, the companies, accept that there will often be access points in their own structures – there's just not the space down there for it to be otherwise. Do you realise that there's only one map of one type of tunnel system down there? It's for the sewer system north of the Thames. It wasn't completed until the mid-nineties and even that's no longer up to date thanks to the work of the Allenites. Those who look after the sewers might believe that everything's in order down there, but they don't realise that some of the images they get back from their CCTV maintenance equipment are not accurate – that their recording devices have been tampered with. Do you see what I'm saying?"

Franklin closed his eyes and nodded. He could see it only *too* clearly. "Okay. After all I've read, I guess I'd better try to get my head round the fact that this really *is* going on. And if that's the case, then, if I've read these maps right, the Allenites are in control of more than eighty percent of the underground territory. Is that true?"

Alexandra nodded, "Closer to ninety percent since they've taken control of the Circle line and it's getting worse almost by the day."

"You've no idea how difficult it is reading the real tube maps," Franklin said, "I've always pictured the Underground system like the maps they show in the tube stations, but they're not even close to the real layout down there, are they?"

"Not at all. And besides, our charts show the disused tunnels and the 'forgotten' stations. The only one that appears on any other map is the one at Brompton Road, and only then because it's still used by the Territorial Army for exercises."

"Haven't they ever seen anything suspicious? Come to that haven't the cleaners – 'Fluffers' they're called, aren't they?"

"They are. There's more than eighty miles of used tunnel and more than one hundred active stations – they've got enough to worry about with that lot. Besides, most access points to the disused tunnels and stations are closed over – either with false walls or securely locked doors. The lack of government funding for maintenance of the tube system and the distraction caused by all the Thameslink work has been a positive blessing for those of us underground – no-one has any time spare to investigate or inspect the abandoned parts. Even the Transport Police have been no trouble since their numbers have been cut back – there's only about three hundred of them now, and they have all their time taken up with beggars, the homeless and buskers."

"Surely some of the homeless wander into the tunnels at night in search of shelter?"

"They do," Alexandra said, "They're either thrown back out by the Allenite patrols, hit by the automated cleaning trains, or they're too drunk or stoned to notice anything strange. No-one below ground thinks they're a real problem – or at least, no more so than the rats."

Franklin shuddered, "Are they really as big as one of these reports said?"

"Huge," Alexandra said, "And bloody vicious. It's one on-going problem that neither the Allenites or ourselves have been able to cure. That and the asbestos danger."

"The what?"

"Asbestos dust. Until recently, all the tube trains had brakes made up of a compound which included asbestos. As the brakes wear down, they release asbestos dust into the tunnels which is obviously a real hazard for those that spend all of their lives underground. Removing it is the main purpose of the automated, night-time cleaning trains – they're called the 'asbestos trains' because of it."

"It sounds like a barrel of laughs down there," Franklin said, "If the rats don't get you, the Allenites probably will. And if they don't, you can expect a case of asbestosis sometime soon."

"It's not that bad if you know the system," Alexandra countered, "We have, as you can see, our own secret places down there which you can retreat to in times of danger. Hopefully, that's where our missing people are."

"Since they haven't shown up in the past three days, that's not much of a comfort."

"We're holding out hope that they've been unable to make a safe escape and are still holed up. There's plenty of provisions down there."

"But *why* wouldn't they be able to escape?"

"Perhaps the Allenites are waiting for them. Perhaps they think they would somehow be attacked. Remember, they probably know what happened on Monday night to the rest of them. That's why it's imperative that we find them."

"This is beginning to sound a damn sight more dangerous than you led me to believe."

"It's not! At least, not for you. Please don't say that you're changing your mind about taking this on? You can't!"

Franklin didn't know whether the last was a plea or a threat, but it any case, it didn't really matter. He felt that he'd come too far to turn away now. "I'm not changing my mind," he said, "Just trying to work out what the hell me and the gang are going to be able to do. And, let's face it, it does sound pretty creepy if we've got to wander round down there in the dark."

"The tunnels are lit at night."

"So the rats and the Allenites will get a pretty good view of us?"

"Not if you use our secret tunnels."

"The same ones that your missing people can't get out of?"

"I keep telling you," Alexandra protested, "That's maybe because they're scared to."

"Very reassuring," Franklin sighed, "But I guess if they are still alive, it's the obvious place to start searching."

"Is that what you're planning?"

He shrugged, "Since, to judge by their profiles, they all live alone – no close relations and all that – then I doubt whether there's much point in questioning friends and colleagues. Especially since their membership of Charno's group is some sort of enormous secret. We'll have to do the rounds of their homes, of course. Check with neighbours, that sort of thing. But I guess your own people have been keeping these places under observation?"

71

"Naturally," Alexandra said, "There have been plenty of visits from the police, as well."

"That's normal, in the circumstances. I'll be getting Bill to find out who they've got assigned to the case. He always seems to be able to get the information out of them."

"Does he have inside contacts?"

"Some, but mostly he just makes a complete nuisance of himself until they tell him what he wants to know. He's got a mind like some sort of ancient encyclopaedia and keeps on quoting archaic laws and by-laws at them. Works every time."

"Charno's report on him suggested that he was a little... eccentric."

"Then Charno's investigators didn't do a great job. Bill is *very* eccentric. One or two last questions: Is the file on Charno genuine?"

"Absolutely. Why do you ask?"

"For a start, it reads more like a sci-fi story than a personality profile. It almost makes him out to have some sort of... supernatural, magical power – all that stuff about hypnotism, levitation, phenomenal strength. Either supernatural or a fairground magician."

"He's neither of those. But you've met him yourself – he has a certain... aura about him. You can sense his power."

"He's certainly not your run-of-the-mill seventy-three-year-old," Franklin conceded, "Which is why I still find it a bit odd that he's scarpered."

"I explained all that yesterday," Alexandra said.

"Yeah, I know. Too dangerous to risk him and all that. But I guess that brings me to my final question."

"Which is?"

"You, Alexandra. There was no profile of you *specifically* amongst these papers."

"I didn't think it would be necessary," she shrugged, "I'm here and mentioned in many of the other profiles. You can ask me anything you want to. Besides, there's very little information on file about me. I only joined Charno's group two years ago."

"Oh? And yet you're his 'right-hand woman'? That's quick work."

Another shrug, "You've seen his own file. He has great vision. He told me that straight after rescuing me, he knew I was the element that his group had been missing, that I was destined to be at his side when the final conflict started. That I would someday take over his mantle. I didn't believe it myself, at first, but once you've been around Charno for a while, you come to trust everything that he says."

"Another 'last thing', then. What exactly were you 'rescued' from? Where you a prisoner of the Allenites, or something like that?"

"A prisoner of them?" Alexandra gave a short laugh, "Franklin, I'm Marcus Allen's bastard daughter. Two years ago I occupied the same position for him that I now do for Charno."

*****

Bill had taken to pacing the floor between his and Dot's desks. "I'm getting very distressed," he said, "This is most unlike the boy."

"It's only five," Dot said, "Anyway, he can take care of himself."

"That is as may be, dear girl. But this is a very strange affair. I have a terrible sense of foreboding."

"Bill, you always do. Even when we're tailing some old wrinkly who's been cheating on his wife. You worry too much, you do."

"You may be right."

"Why don't you pop along to the Mucky Duck? Have a quick whisky. Take your mind off things. I'll call you the second I hear anything."

"I really shouldn't..."

"Bill! If nothing else, I might be able to concentrate on getting these accounts done."

"Oh, right. Sorry, dear girl. If it will assist you in your endeavours, I suppose I could manage a small libation. What with skipping lunch and all."

"I did offer to bring you back something from the Pizza Hut."

"They don't serve whisky there to the best of my knowledge."

"Bill," Dot sighed, "You're..."

"Incorrigible?"

"That's the word. Now, go on. Scoot!"

"And you'll–"

"Call as soon as he rings here or gets back. Now, *please*, sod-off!"

"Right you are, dear girl. Anything you say."

Bill could hear Dot's sigh of relief through the office door as he hurried down the stairs.

*****

Franklin stared hard at Alexandra, "Is that what you mean by having 'special protection' or whatever you called it?"

"Partly. Allen would never let any direct harm come to me if it could be avoided. Unfortunately, my… defection, as he calls it, seems to have intensified his desire for complete control down there. Or if not that, then it has certainly accelerated the process."

"In effect, it's you that's bringing this all to a head?"

"Unwittingly, but, yes. It certainly seems that way. I don't have a choice though, Franklin. Not after getting to know what Allen's true plans are. It wasn't until Charno brought me out of there that I could really understand just how… evil Allen is. There's no choice for me anymore."

"Yeah, I guess not," Franklin sighed.

"When do you plan to start?"

Franklin looked up at the glass and chrome wall-clock, "It's four-thirty now. I'll need to get back and talk to Bill and Dot and discuss things with them, work out some sort of strategy. Judging by your files, and how the territory currently stands, I guess two of us, Dot and me, should start with a visit to each of your group's 'safe houses' in the Underground system. That will leave Bill free to annoy the police and see what he can dig up – no pun intended – above ground."

"You think the little girl is up to it?"

"Dot?" Franklin bridled, "She may be small, but she's probably more capable than me, you and Bill put together. She's–"

"Franklin, I'm sorry," Alexandra interrupted him with a placatory gesture, "I'm sure you know your staff far better than I ever could. I was wrong to suggest otherwise."

"Yeah, well," Franklin muttered, subconsciously echoing Dot, "As I was saying, it's Thursday afternoon now, by the time we've discussed our plans, it'll be too late to start anything today. I guess we'll make an early start tomorrow morning. It's been three days already, I can't see another few hours making much difference. Besides, for some weird reason, it looks like the tunnels will be quieter during the day."

"That's true," Alexandra said, "I would appreciate it if you could call me tomorrow evening with an update on progress. And, of course, on subsequent evenings should that prove necessary." She handed him a business card. "The direct line is probably best."

"I could always pop round here, if you'd prefer?"

"No!" Her reply was sharper than either of them had expected, "That is, please don't. What happened earlier... as wonderful as it was, must be viewed as a one-off. I fear that your presence here in future might prove... too much of a temptation."

"But... surely–"

"No, Franklin. And I'd very much like you to keep... what happened to yourself. I... I swore myself to Charno. Earlier was... wrong of me."

"This is the same Charno that sent you to meet me in the middle of a busy restaurant with your tits hanging out, right?"

"Don't be like that! I told you, explained to you: Charno does everything for a specific purpose."

Franklin shook his head, "And you, of course, will do anything he says."

"Yes! Look, I gave you my reasons for coming on to you. Plain old-fashioned horniness. The simple, exquisite desire to be fucked by a cute, young man, okay? I shouldn't have, but there you go. I wasn't kidding when I said there was something different about you – I haven't felt like that about any guy since I met Charno, so I just reckon it would be better if we stayed at arm's length. In fact, it'd be best if you left as soon as possible, assuming you've finished with the questions?"

"I guess I have," he nodded, "I'd like to take some of the charts with me, if that's okay?"

"Other than the territorial map and the profiles themselves, feel free." Alexandra handed him a small canvas pouch, "Inside here are the keys that you will need to activate the locks at the tunnel entrances, the instructions for their use are handwritten on the backs of the relevant charts." She stood and crossed her arms as he sorted through the documents, "Look, I'm sorry, Franklin, and don't think that I didn't enjoy... what happened. It just mustn't happen again, and even standing this close to you is a temptation."

Franklin looked up at her, "And that's supposed to make me want to leave?"

She stared back at him, "I want there to be complete trust between us. I'm not sure I can trust *myself* around you. It's better this way."

"I guess so. Besides, you're my client. I'm here to carry out your instructions."

"You're mad at me, aren't you?"

Franklin sighed, "Not mad as such. Disappointed maybe."

"Because I'm fickle? Because I've led you on?"

"No," he grinned slowly, "Because I ain't gonna get to see those cute tits of yours again."

Alexandra snorted laughter, "You're a great guy, you know?"

"Sure I'm not great enough for one last wrestle in the bedroom?"

"Don't even think about it."

"Can't blame a guy for trying."

"I guess not. Got everything you need?"

He held up a stack of documents, "This should be enough. And if I'm that much of a temptation, I'd better get going."

"Sorry again."

"It's okay," Franklin tried to keep the hangdog expression at bay, "And thanks for... for earlier."

"Thank *you*."

He resisted the urge to embrace her as he walked past and retrieved his jacket from beside the door. He placed the charts in the voluminous inside pocket and shrugged on the heavy garment.

"Franklin?"

He turned to face her, his hand on the door handle, "Yes?"

"I really am sorry, you know?"

"You said."

"I've been unfair."

"I would have rated you better than fair a few hours ago."

Her right hand was fiddling with the top button of her silk blouse, twisting it back and forth, "You're a remarkable man, especially given your youth."

"You're pretty damn cute yourself."

The button popped open and her hand slid lower, "I can't quite believe the affect you have on me."

Franklin remained silent.

The second and third buttons were undone. Then the fourth. Trembling hands drew the blouse from her black jeans, the front falling open.

*****

"I must be the most stupid guy on this fucking planet," Franklin told the taxi driver three minutes later, "Some gorgeous chick wants to jump my black bod and I walk out the door so she knows she can trust me! What a fucking dickhead!"

"Sounds about right," the driver nodded, "Liverpool Street was it?"

"Or the nearest nut-house."

"The station, then. Bloody awful weather, innit?"

"Not where I'm going tomorrow."

"Somewhere nice and warm, then?"

"Yeah," Franklin sighed, "A constant temperature of twenty-one degrees and absolutely no bloody rain."

*****

By the time he got back to Walthamstow, Franklin was in desperate need of a drink. He collected a surprisingly friendly Dot from the office and they met up with Bill in the Mucky Duck. The first evening rush which comprised the happily-marrieds just popping in for one on the way home, was over, and the second wave, the happily-singles out for the evening, was yet to start.

"Nice and quiet," Bill commented.

"Which is good," Franklin told him, "Because this is going to require a fair bit of concentration. Not to mention a fair bit of believing." Before starting, he took three long swallows of Guinness.

"Get on with it, then," Dot said.

"Where to start?" Another swallow and a deep breath, "Perhaps I'd better start with what these two bunches of nutters call 'proprietorship'."

An hour later he looked up at them, "Well?"

"Actually, a little queasy after your revelation, dear boy. I think I'll head bar-wards and replenish our glasses."

"And this is all genuine, then?"

"Sorry, Dot, but yeah, I guess so."

"And you want me to do an impression of a mole and go crawling about in rat-infested tunnels that don't officially even exist?"

"You got it."

"You must be bleedin' stupid."

"That was never in question," Franklin grinned, "But it can't be as bad as it sounds."

"I bet it bleedin' can."

"You are up for it, right?"

Dot gazed levelly at him, "Course."

"Good girl."

"Don't start that crap again, or you'll be down there on your tod, mate."

"Sorry."

"You'd better be."

Bill returned with the drinks, "Everything okay, dear girl?"

"Yeah, fine," she shot him a warning glance, "But I reckon I'd better drink up and get off home. Loads to do *and* an early start tomorrow, thanks to mole-boy here."

"I'll not be much after you," Franklin yawned, "That was a bloody long, tiring, exhausting day."

"It's amazing how reading and talking can take so much out of one, is it not?" Bill said.

"That, too," Franklin grinned to himself.

Fortunately for him, Dot failed to notice.

*****

McCoy stared at DS Green's face, "Four bloody hours, and this is all you've come up with?"

"Things are getting stranger by the hour, guv. You wouldn't believe what I had to do just to get hold of that much."

They were standing at the bar of the Duke of York, much needed beers in hand, and similar expressions of frustration on their faces. The young sergeant drained the rest of his beer before continuing.

"First the bloody file was missing, and the details didn't seem to have been entered into the system. Then, when they finally did manage to dig it up, half of it had disappeared – no witness statement, no SOCO report. I tell you, guv, it all looked pretty fishy to me."

"You reckon someone had deliberately tried to muddy the waters?"

"I'd bet on it," Green said, "I was at Snow Hill nick for more than two hours. By the time someone had contacted the officers who attended the accident – who, by the way and strangely enough, have been seconded to the Kent Traffic Police and are now working out of Maidstone – I was beginning to think I'd never get any information. Fortunately, one of them still had his notes and he gave me the name and address of our sole witness to the accident. One David Evans."

"Not so fortunate when you subsequently find out that he's buggered off on an unexpected, unscheduled, three-week holiday to Tenerife, though, is it?"

"That's hardly my fault, guv."

McCoy sighed and waved for two more pints, "I guess not. But you're right about one thing – this has all the hallmarks of a cover up. I mean to say, this witness of ours is a state registered nurse. It's hardly normal behaviour for nurses to suddenly pack a bag and piss off for a little fun in the sun. I wouldn't have thought he could have afforded it for a start."

"I don't suppose we've got anyone out there at the moment?"

"I doubt it, but it's worth checking. And while you're at, Green, I want you to try to check and make sure he's actually gone there in the first

79

place. It's a long shot, but you might find a local travel agent or someone that sold him the tickets. If you can, you should be able to find out where he's staying, and we can check that he's turned up."

"I could always fly over there myself and check out all the hotels on the island. This weather is really beginning to piss me off."

"Yeah, right!" McCoy snorted, "There's more chance of that happening than me winning the lottery this weekend. And I haven't even got a ticket."

"Somehow, I just knew you'd say something like that, guv. I'll just finish this and get back out there, okay?"

"Do it," McCoy said, "And check in with me every hour from now on. Use my mobile number."

"What will you be doing?"

"Going around the last of the victims' employers, although judging by the responses so far, I might as well be pissing in the wind. It's been the same story everywhere I've been – and by the same, I mean they all sound as if they're reading from a bloody script. Not a bad word from any of them. If I hear the expression 'It came as a complete surprise to me' one more time, I think I'm going to strangle someone."

"Well, I know one thing, Guv. I'm absolutely positive that those guys didn't jump of their own accord, and I'm positive that there's some sort of conspiracy behind whatever happened."

"You and me both, Green. You and me both."

*****

Franklin left the Mucky Duck half an hour after Dot. Too tired to even think straight, he stopped off at the local KFC and ordered half of its contents before splashing the rest of the way back to his flat with the warm bag in one hand and a plastic file full of very strange maps in the other.

He stopped outside his apartment building and checked to make sure there were no lights blazing in his windows. He shuddered to think what he might find up there. Letting himself into the relative warmth, he made a mental note to ask Alexandra if white horses had any sort of significance to either of the groups when he next spoke to her.

The flat proved horse-free and everything appeared to be where it should be. Satisfied, he settled himself on the sofa and opened the bag containing his supper. On the way upstairs, he'd collected his mail from the desk in the hallway, but right now, food was a far more important consideration than the latest tawdry offers from mail order companies. Flicking on the television, he listened to the news while munching his way through the steaming mound of fried chicken.

After three days, the mysterious case of the 'jumpers' had been relegated to the fourth slot, but there was still sufficient interest to devote more than three minutes to the item. Three minutes seemed to be a collection of clichés centred around 'The police are baffled'. Even the intrepid reporter was baffled. Franklin couldn't blame him.

Belly full and the contents of the bag now reduced to something resembling a major explosion in a cemetery, Franklin sat back, dragging the mound of mail with him. As was his customary habit, he separated the envelopes into three piles: obvious junk mail, bills and other official letters, and lastly, personal mail. To his surprise there were two of the latter. He set these aside to be opened last.

The junk mail was immediately consigned to the same fate as the remnants of his meal, making the bulging paper sack heavier than when he'd arrived with it. The second pile contained just one bill which was good news. It also contained a begging letter, although to be fair, since it was from the landlord, it could also be termed a bill.

He turned his attention to the last two envelopes. After checking the post-marks, he opened the blue one first. It could only be from one person – Kathy Blake, the local Sergeant's sister who had retired to Southampton three years previously. Kathy Blake had been the welfare officer with the somewhat onerous responsibility of looking after the young Franklin Richardson' interests during his many years at orphanages and foster homes. Even this many years on, and despite the fact that she had left the social services a long time before, she still seemed to feel it was her duty. Since she had moved to the South coast, she had taken to writing to him once a month, and this letter was November's effort. Franklin always adored her for it.

He read the missive with a smile firmly fixed on his face. As usual it was a mixture of news of her progress 'down South' and firm reminders about his own behaviour. There was also the normal exhortation for him to 'come visit' as soon as he had some spare time. He'd postponed the promise visit three times so far and guessed that he really should make the effort soon. In the meantime, he made a note in his precious notebook to phone her in the next day or two.

Finally, he turned his attention to the last envelope, a plain, white affair with his name and address written neatly on the front. The post-mark was local, and given that the address was hand-written, he firmly believed that it wouldn't prove to be a bill. The envelope was of the old-fashioned type, sealed by licking the gummed edges of a triangular flap, and he used the blade of his penknife to slit it open. It contained a single sheet of high-quality paper which he extracted, unfolded and read. Then he read it again.

'*Franklin Richardson,*

I am given to understand that you are about to undertake an investigation of an unusual nature. My advice to you is really very simple. Don't.

A friend - would that you knew it.'

"Well, it's certainly straight to the point," he said aloud. Something about its brevity was disconcerting. *But there again*, he thought, *what hadn't been disconcerting this week*? He folded the note and slipped it inside the plastic file to show to Dot in the morning. Right then, what he needed more than anything else was a few hours decent sleep. Weirdness seemed to be especially tiring.

Chapter 6

Friday 16th November 2018

Another unaccustomed early start saw Franklin stepping out into the pre-dawn Friday morning ready to curse the rain. To his great surprise there was none in sight. Looking up, the sky, though still dark, proved cloudless. A slight glow on the Eastern horizon even hinted at the amazing possibility of sunlight in an hour or so. After the discomforting note, the on-going weirdness, confusion over Alexandra, and a general feeling of unease about the coming few days, the thought of a bit of sunlight was more than welcome.

Then he realised where he'd be spending most of his day. Underground. "Bloody typical," he sighed, setting off towards the office where he'd arranged to meet Dot.

A light was burning in their first-floor window and he let himself inside, eager for a coffee before they started out. As he climbed the stairs, he began to make out the clattering of the computer keyboard, and he smiled to himself. Efficient as ever, our little Dot.

"Hiya!" he called as he opened the door, "I hope that's coffee I can sm..." He stopped and stared as the figure sitting in front of the PC slowly turned to face him. At first he thought that it was a stranger. A stranger with Dot's slight build. "Dot?"

"Who were you expecting? Joan of bleedin' Arc?"

Gone was the spiky mass of brilliant green hair, replaced instead by black waves that fell to her shoulders. Gone, too, was the regulation baggy sweatshirt, and in its place a loose, silky, white blouse. Were it not for the bright blue eyes and the black jeans Franklin thought that he really *wouldn't* have recognised her.

"Well, what are you bleedin' staring at?" The words were harsh but delivered with a clearly discernible nervous undertone.

"Er, well, you, I suppose."

"You don't like it, do you?"

"Like it? I *love* it! It's… I mean *you*, look terrific."

Dot's familiar pout appeared, "You're just saying that."

"Yes I was. And I meant it. Don't tell me that's your natural colour and you've been hiding it all this time?"

"As it happens, it is. You're not winding me up here, are you?"

"No. Really."

"Really?"

"Yes!" Franklin rolled his eyes, "You look great. But why change it now after so long?"

Dot felt a blush begin to rise and quickly crossed the room to the kettle. Her already sky-high opinion of Bill had just risen another notch. She took a deep breath, her back firmly turned towards Franklin, "I, er, thought you might like it. You know? As a change, like?"

"It's wonderful," Franklin said, "Really suits you. So does the blouse."

"I'll have to put a sweatshirt on over it when we get started."

"Shame, but I guess you're right."

Her hands were trembling a little as she poured Franklin's coffee, and she prayed that he wouldn't notice when she carried his mug over to him. *A change of subject might help*, she thought, "What time are we actually gonna start out?" She began to stir the coffee.

"We'd better wait until the rush-hour's over, because one of the access points – the one that seems most likely according to Alexandra – is close by an existing station. So I reckon we'll leave here about eight-thirty." He bent down and opened the bottom drawer of his desk, rummaging through it for a supply of spare torch batteries.

Dot took this opportunity to cross the room with his coffee, nearly spilling it at the last moment. "Coffee's up."

"Thanks. I'm sure I put the bloody things in here somewhere."

Dot leant over the corner of the desk, "Want me to look? You're bleedin' hopeless when it comes to finding things round here."

"Good idea." He straightened and then moved his chair back to give Dot some room.

She knelt down and began to systematically remove the clutter from the drawer, "It's no wonder you can never find anything."

Franklin took a sip of scalding coffee and sat in his chair. He leaned forward and peered down. He had intended to peer down into the drawer in case he could catch sight of the missing batteries. Instead, he found himself peering down the front of Dot's loose blouse as she reached into the drawer. Her small, pert breasts were clearly, wonderfully, visible to his gaze. "I don't believe this!" he snorted.

Dot ignored him and continued the search, "It's only a few batteries, and besides, we could always pick up some more on our way."

Franklin suddenly realised that he was in a very awkward situation. Dot had apparently gone to great lengths to change her appearance, and he no longer had any doubt that Bill had been right about her sudden interest in 'the boss'. She was also – for her, at least – in a much better mood. Somehow, pointing out that every time she bent over – like *that* – she would be displaying her perfectly-formed breasts to the eager gaze of anyone more than a few centimetres taller than her. Which was most people. There again, if he didn't make some sort of comment and she found out about it later from someone else, then she would *know* that he'd have had the view he was having now. She'd kill him. Somehow, he was going to have to alert her without mentioning that if her tits had been a bit bigger, it wouldn't have been a problem.

He took a deep breath, "Er, Dot?"

"Are you sure you put them in here?"

"Dot! Forget about them. We'll get some later like you said." He swallowed hard as she looked up at him, grateful that his gaze was locked onto her face.

"Fair enough. I'll just shove this back in." She grabbed a heap of desk detritus and heaved it back into the drawer.

"Er, actually, it'd probably be a good idea if I did that… only…"

She looked up again, "Only what?"

"I, er, that is…"

"What?"

Franklin flicked his gaze quickly downwards and then back to her face, "The, er, blouse? It's a little bit on the loose side."

Dot slowly let her own eyes travel down. As she finally made out what the hell Franklin was trying to tell her, she let out a squeal, shooting to her feet, one hand pressing the blouse close to her chest, "You sod!" she yelled, "You've been sitting there staring at my tits, haven't you? Why didn't you tell me you was getting an eyeful?" Her cheeks were scarlet.

"That's what I was trying to do!"

"Took your bleedin' time about it!"

"Look, I'm sorry, okay? It's a pretty awkward situation, though, yeah?"

Dot's shoulders sagged, and she turned away, "Yeah, you're right. And I guess it's my fault. I just wanted to look… good for you. And as per usual, Dot screws things up again, eh?"

Franklin couldn't be sure, but he thought Dot's shoulders were quivering slightly, "It's okay, Dot," he said softly, "I really appreciate what you did. The hair and everything, I mean," he added quickly, "If it's any help, I won't mention it to anyone."

"So you're not going to add it to your collection of 'stupid little Dot' stories, then? About how she tarted herself up and ended up acting like a tart?"

Franklin rose quickly as he heard the tears in her voice, "You haven't acted like a tart, and I've never thought of you as 'stupid little Dot'. For a start you've got more brains than Bill and me put together," he approached her cautiously. Her middle name should have been 'volatile'. "I didn't realise how you felt about me is all. And I thought I was just teasing, having fun when I call you a little lady and all that…" He rested his hands on her shoulders, kept them there as she first flinched and then finally seemed to relax. He continued when she remained silent, "I guess I just always think of you as the underage runaway. Unapproachable, out of bounds. Bill said something last night after you left us. I guess I finally realise what he was on about. You're an adult, is what he said. Small, maybe, but I weren't joking when I said I prefer my women on the small side."

Dot shook her head, once, black hair flapping across the backs of Franklin's hands. '*You're just saying that*!' seemed to be the meaning behind the gesture.

"I mean it, Dot," Franklin said, "What do you want me to say? You look gorgeous. You've always looked gorgeous, I guess. It's just that 'stupid' Franklin hasn't noticed – hasn't bothered to notice. Dot?"

In one super-fast movement, she spun round and hugged him tightly, her strength always a surprise, "Sorry," she said, her voice muffled against his chest, "I'm so sorry."

"Hey! There's no need," he returned her hug, tried to lighten the mood, "And it's not just your face and build that are gorgeous – those are the cutest little tits I've ever seen." Shocked, and despite Alexandra Featherington, he found himself actually meaning it.

Dot snapped out of the embrace and took a step back. Several emotions seemed to be vying for control of her features and for a few moments Franklin thought that anger was going to prevail. He watched as she swallowed hard, her long, dark lashes working overtime.

"Would you... like to go out for a meal somewhere?" she almost wailed, before spinning round and flying out of the room.

It took him ten minutes of patient urging before he finally coaxed her out of the small bathroom that served their office.

"I feel so stupid!" Dot said when they were both sitting on Franklin's desk, sipping tepid coffee.

He put his mug down and reached out for her free hand, "Never think that. Think it about me, by all means, but never about yourself."

"Yeah, well... And you really mean it about the meal and stuff?"

Franklin leaned across and gently kissed the tip of her nose, "You bet."

Dot's blue eyes grew larger than ever, "You really *do* mean it, don't you?"

Franklin rolled his eyes, "Come here!"

After a moment's hesitation, Dot set down her own mug and scooted sideways until their thighs were touching. She closed her eyes as Franklin's arm slid across her shoulders and kept them closed as his lips met hers. They remained closed as the kiss became more passionate, tongues probing, teeth occasionally touching.

They snapped open as his other hand brushed across the front of her blouse and her rigid right nipple beneath the silky surface.

"No!" she snapped, breaking free of him.

There was a moment of shocked silence and then her eyes closed once more. A burst of laughter, as unexpected as a tax rebate, burst out of her. "Sorry!" she gasped, "But I mean? How bleedin' silly can I get? Half an hour ago I was flashing them at you and now I get all silly-little-teenager about the slightest of touches!" Her face fell serious, "I mean... I don't want you to think I'm a tease or anything..."

"I don't," Franklin said, his face solemn, "Blame me. I was pushing a little too far, a little too fast."

"No," Dot's hair sprayed around her, "I..." A blush rose again to her cheeks, "I don't really mind. I don't mind at all! It's just... I guess it's just the past and... I don't want you to think I'm coming on to you. Which I guess is bleedin' stupid, really."

"No it isn't," Franklin said.

"I mean, what with accidentally flashing my tiny tits at you and everything..."

He pulled her back to his side, "They're gorgeous little tits. Very hard to resist, as it happens."

He'd rested his hand on her upper arm, his eyes locked onto hers. Permission was clearly being sought.

Dot stared back at him. She realised that he wouldn't make any move on her if she didn't want it. No other man had ever shown her that sort of respect. Suddenly, she adored him for it. Adored him anyway. Back in her tiny flat, in the middle of her more torrid dreams, she had wondered what it would be like right now. More than anything, she wanted to know. She craned her neck a little, offering him her lips. Offer accepted, she moved her arm back and used it to manoeuvre his hand until he understood the message and gently cupped her breast in his massive hand. It felt heavenly.

Ten minutes later, they disentangled themselves, both of them panting a little and wide-eyed. Dot's delicate blouse was a little creased. Franklin's jeans were feeling extremely tight.

"I, er, guess we'd better get our minds back on the work?" Dot managed.

"Shame but true," he nodded.

"I'd better go through and change."

"Change here if you like. After all, I have seen it all before."

"Pig!"

"Happy pig. I'll keep my eyes closed, if you like?"

"Yeah, right!"

"Promise. I want you to be able to trust me."

Dot looked at him long and hard, "Alright then. But I'll be watching you. One peek and you'll be a castrated pig. Got that?"

"Got it." Franklin closed his eyes, "Just tell me when you're decent."

Dot went to her desk and picked up the sweatshirt she'd brought in with her. With trembling fingers she quickly unbuttoned the blouse, her eyes fixed on Franklin's firmly closed eyelids. She hesitated for a moment before shrugging out of the garment, a delirious and unexpected thrill coursing through her. Still his eyes were closed. As quickly as she could, she pulled the sweatshirt over her head, covering her nakedness.

"I guess you can open them now."

He did so, smiling at her, "See? I'm completely trustworthy."

"Pig!"

"Now what?"

"If my little tits are as tempting as you've been telling me, you would have had a quick peek."

"Well," he grinned, rising from the desk, "I bet I could soon get that sweatshirt off you."

Dot squealed and, giggling, dashed out of the door as he moved towards her.

*****

After they had agreed a verbal Armistice over their nascent relationship while work was required, Dot unlocked the bathroom door and followed Franklin back into the office. They were just donning their coats when Bill arrived.

To the surprise of all three of them, Dot rushed over, threw her arms around him and hugged him tightly. "You're a genius!"

"I like to believe so, dear girl, and I really must say, you look wonderful," Bill said when he had been released. He looked from Dot to Franklin and then back again, "I surmise from your matching silly grins, that there has been a development on the romance front?"

"Yeah, sort of," Dot nodded.

89

"*Very* sort of," Franklin added.

Bill heaved a huge sigh, "Well, thank goodness for that. If I'm fortunate, I imagine that the bickering level should be significantly reduced."

"I wouldn't go that bleedin' far," Dot grinned.

"It wouldn't seem natural," Franklin agreed.

Bill groaned, "Changing the subject, I take it that you two lovebirds are about to head off into the bowels of the earth?"

"Given where we're going, man, I'd rather you didn't mention bowels."

"Forgive me, dear boy. Point taken. What time do you expect to be checking in with me?"

"I can't guarantee it, but somewhere around two seems likely."

"Very well, then. But please do try to make it close to then – you know how I fret so."

"Our very own mother hen."

"If you will, Dot, my dear. But someone has to look after you youngsters."

"We'll be fine," Franklin said, "But we'd better get going. The sooner we get our explorations over with, the happier I'll be."

"Too true," Dot nodded.

"Take care, you two."

Franklin nodded and made for the door, "Good luck with the police," he called back over his shoulder.

Dot started after him, but then paused and turned, "Thanks, Bill."

"It is an absolute pleasure, I assure you. I hope things work out well for you. For both of you."

She wrinkled her nose, "Me too. See you later." She dashed out after Franklin.

"I certainly hope so," Bill said to himself.

*****

DI McCoy was startled awake when the phone on his desk began to ring. Cursing and groaning as his cramped muscles protested, he sat as upright as his stiff back would allow and picked up the receiver.

"McCoy."

"Morning, guv."

"Green?"

"Yep. Did I wake you?"

"Sort of," McCoy yawned, "It was late when I got back here. Couldn't be bothered to head home. You know how it is."

"Too bloody right, I do. I only got four hours myself."

"What time is it, Green? Come to that what *day* is it?"

"Seven-thirty – a.m. that is – and Friday. You asked me to call you at eight or earlier if we'd got any news."

McCoy immediately snapped fully awake, "Which means you've got some news. Give."

"I'm not sure it takes us much further, but here goes. Travel agent fourteen on the list, one of those late-night, bucket shop affairs. A young girl was working in there and said she'd been on duty Tuesday night as well. Says she always prefers working the late shift and then going straight out clubbing. Maria Walker, her name. A real stunner—"

"Get on with it, Green."

"Sorry, guv. Anyway, she says she remembered our guy coming in on Tuesday night, not long before they were due to close, which would put it around eleven. Maria reckons she's got a great memory for faces, and she certainly seemed positive when she saw the photo."

"Was he alone?"

"I was just coming to that!" There was a hint of reproach in the sergeant's voice, "It was the next thing I asked her. As it happens, she tells me he wasn't. There was another guy with him – a tall, athletic-looking sort. Our man was acting a bit sheepishly, Maria said. She reckoned that maybe the tall guy was our man's boyfriend or something."

"Perhaps he was."

"Not according to his colleagues at the hospital. Apparently our Mr. Evans is a real ladies' man. What had made the girl in the travel agency fairly convinced about this stranger was that Evans booked two return flights."

"This is starting to sound like good news, Green. It's about time we had a lucky break."

"Luck? It was hard work that did it, guv." More reproach, "Unfortunately, it's not all good news. The tall man's ticket was booked under the name John Smith, they paid cash, and they didn't book a hotel room."

"Sounds fishy," McCoy said, "I take it we've got people phoning to check out all the hotels over there?"

"I've had three at it most of the night. Last time I checked, they'd got through about a quarter of the places listed, without luck, of course. Julio Fernandez has just turned up, so I've collared him since he speaks the lingo."

"Good thinking, but I don't reckon we'll find them. This smacks of being a cover story."

"I know what you mean, guv. I'd bet my last dollar that Evans is either still in this country, or he's been offed. I had to get the hotels checked though, just in case. Besides if I hadn't, you would have had my balls for breakfast."

"You're learning fast, Green. Anyway, even if Evans *has* jetted off with this Smith guy, they'd avoid the big hotels. If Smith really wants Evans out of circulation for a while, he'd insist on some tiny place which probably hasn't even got a bloody telephone signal. Still, like you said, it's gotta be worth a try. What happening about this 'John Smith'?"

"I called through to Central from the travel agent's and got the artist to come out. I reckoned it'd be quicker than getting Maria all the way over to the other side of town and using the computer to generate a 'fit. We scanned the artist's impression into the system just after two, but the first search hasn't turned up anything. Sunny Singh has just set a second search running with fewer criteria to match." The new, upgraded computer system could now search a central database of tens of thousands of criminals' photographs in a matter of an hour or so, and it was now even possible to set which features were to be matched. Green had watched as DS Singh had limited the search to eyes, nose and mouth. The results were due through in a few minutes.

"Did Sunny reckon the artist's impression was good enough?"

"You know her, guv. She reckons they're better than the ones the computer can generate, but I've asked Maria to come in this morning, anyway. If nothing else, getting her to create a computer-generated impression will at least give us an idea of just how good her memory for faces really is."

"Not a bad idea, Green. We're getting absolutely nowhere with the victims' relatives and employers. We've had no credible witnesses come forward about Monday night, and now it's starting to look like the one eye-witness to the bloody accident has been removed from the equation. This Smith character looks like our best chance of making any progress. Come to that, our *only* bloody chance."

"There's one thing puzzling me about him, though, guv."

"Which is?"

"Well, it's a bit like the accident in the first place. You know? Using a bloody great lorry to get rid of a witness that might – just might – have seen something at one of the stations. That seemed a bit over the top to me. And now the one witness to *that* accident has disappeared, but not before being seen with a stranger. It's not as if they needed to go into a travel agent's – the tickets could have been booked using a credit card. Oh, and by the way, before you ask, Evans has one Access card and one Visa and they're both being monitored but neither have been used since last Saturday."

"I'll grant you that it does sound a bit sloppy, but there again, if villains didn't make mistakes occasionally, we'd never nab anyone. Besides, maybe this Smith character was just trying to make it *look* like a last-minute thing, an unexpected romantic break. If nothing else, it at least corroborates the evidence we've got so far. You never know, it might all be genuine."

"If you want to bet on that, then you'll be using your own money, guv. Anyway, I've asked all the City division to circulate the picture among their narks and grasses, and I'll have our guys do the same. Me included."

"Good idea, again, Green. There's hope for you yet. Before you head out, though, I want you and Sunny Singh to knock out a press release featuring Mr. John Smith. The usual stuff: we want to identify this man in connection with, and so on. You know the drill. I want to see it on every online newsfeed you can manage and in *The Standard* by lunchtime, okay?"

"Consider it done, guv. Anything else?"

"You'd better send me up a handful of the impressions. I've got a few people of my own that might know something. And if there's any spare, I could murder a coffee."

"You got it. I'll check in with you about ten."

"Do that," McCoy said, "And, er, Green?"

"Yes, guv?"

"Good work." He broke the connection and rubbed at tired eyes.

*****

"Bleedin' typical, ain't it?" Dot, sitting opposite Franklin, stared out of the window of the train.

Franklin looked across at his companion and smiled, "What is?"

"The first decent day's weather for weeks and we… er, we will have to be indoors all day." Although the commuter train wasn't crowded, in their line of work, discretion was always called for in public places.

"I was thinking just the same thing on my way into the office. Still, thanks to the train being on time, we'll be able to have a stroll to the first site."

"Thank heavens for small mercies, I guess."

"Thank heavens for all small things," Franklin stared pointedly at Dot's chest.

She slapped his knee, "I thought we'd agreed that there'd be none of that at work?"

"True, but as far as I'm concerned, work doesn't start until we get to the first site."

94

"That's cheating," Dot giggled, a sound which seemed to take her more by surprise than it did Franklin. She clapped a hand over the offending mouth.

"I'm the boss, I make the rules," he told her.

"Ah! But don't I qualify for a bit more say so? You know, now I'm sleeping with the b–" Her eyes widened in horror as she realised what she'd almost said, and a blush bloomed quickly on her cheeks. She used both hands this time to close her mouth, before groaning and letting them fall into her lap. "What's happening to me? I've lost control of me own bleedin' mouth! I didn't mean that I was, you know, actually, you know?"

"But you'd like to," Franklin grinned, "I reckon that was a good example of one of those Freudian slips that Bill's always going on about."

"No!" When Franklin gave her a downcast look, she gabbled on, "I don't mean that I don't want... I mean, you know, you're..." Crimson-cheeked, she looked around desperately, praying that none of the other passengers were witnessing her embarrassment. Satisfied that they weren't she turned back to face the grinning Franklin, "You're doing this deliberately, aren't you?" she hissed.

"Who, me? By the way, you look really cute when you blush."

She slapped his knee once more, "Stop it! It's been a bleedin' weird morning so far as it is. I think I'm a bit off-balance."

"For some of us it's been a pretty weird *week*, but I rather liked this morning's weirdness, so I guess I shouldn't tease. Sorry."

Dot stared hard at him before realising that he meant it. Strangely, it only deepened her blush. "Yeah, well. I guess this is gonna take some getting used to."

"I'm looking forward to it."

She looked down at her hands, still cradled in her lap, "Me too."

Before her embarrassment became critical, the train rattled into the cavernous Liverpool Street station, and she hurried for the door.

After passing through the ticket barrier, Franklin put a hand on Dot's shoulder and guided her to a quiet corner of the concourse.

"What's up?"

"Dot, I just wanted to check with you before we go on. *I'm* not looking forward to this, let alone you. So, if you want to give it a miss, I'll understand."

"No way! I'm not having you make clucking noises every time I walk into the room."

"I'm being serious, here," Franklin said, "I wouldn't call *anyone* a chicken for opting out of this little venture. And besides, we don't know just how dangerous this can turn out. I'd never forgive myself if anything happened to you."

"Nor me if it was the other way round. And it'll be a bleedin' sight safer with two of us. Watching each other's backs and all that stuff."

"Well, if you're really sure–"

Dot reached up and pulled his head down to her level. "Enough. You're not getting rid of me that quick!" She gave him a quick kiss and let him go. "So, where did you say we were starting?"

"Right where this whole business started back on Monday. Mansion House tube. There should be one of these 'safe houses' close by north platform."

Dot shuddered, "I think I'm going to make the most of our gentle stroll there."

Franklin took her hand, "You ain't the only one, little lady."

"It's weird, you know?"

"What is?"

"For the very first time, I didn't mind you calling me that."

"Things are looking up."

"Well I sure will be from now on."

"Come on then, little lady, let's get to it."

They left the station hand-in-hand.

*****

The desk sergeant was beginning to wish he'd taken early retirement when it had been offered to him. "I'm sorry, Mr. Taylor. The investigation to which you are referring has nothing to do with us, and, for the tenth time, no, I don't even know which force is handling it. And before you ask

96

again, I am positive that none of the senior detectives here know either. I suggest you contact New Scotland Yard. There's an area with a good signal or even a payphone just outside."

Bill fumbled through the small notebook he was carrying, "Actually, sergeant, I think you'll find that if you check sub-section 28, clause 4 of the Metropolitan–"

"Oh, no! We're not getting into all that rubbish again."

"I'd hardly term the very Act of Parliament that gives the Metropolitan Police the right and duty to–"

"Alright! I surrender. Just tell me what your bloody research has turned up *this* time."

"Would you like that verbatim or–"

"*Mr.* Taylor!" The sergeant, a veteran of earlier encounters with the ever-persistent Bill, knew better than to let him start quoting entire paragraphs from the obscure law books that he seemed to know from cover to cover, "I go off duty in four hours. There isn't time. So, what, in a nutshell, is my supposed duty in this case?"

"There's no supposed about it–" A glance at the thunderous expression on the police officer's face brought him swiftly to the point, "Well, it basically comes down to the fact that *you* must find out the information for me. In any crime where death has occurred in suspicious circumstances, any member of the public who may have an interest in the case is entitled to approach the most senior officer in charge. In order to do this, he quite patently needs to know the identity of said officer. This is the bit where you come in–"

"Okay, okay! I get the drift. That was a bloody big nutshell by the way. Take a seat by the door and I'll see what I can come up with. Satisfied?"

"It's certainly a start. But if you could expedite matters, only time is of the essence."

"Believe me, sir, the sooner I can get back to my actual work, the better." He picked up his telephone and dialled a number.

Smiling to himself, Bill headed for the chair.

Ten minutes later, he lifted his head from his newspaper and saw the sergeant beckoning him over to the desk.

"Any joy?"

"I've got two names for you and a seriously sore eardrum, if that's what you mean?"

Bill took out his notebook and pen, "Good man. Fire away."

"Okay," the sergeant sighed, "The investigation is under the ultimate command of Detective Chief Superintendent Cox of the City of London Police. However, the physical process and co-ordination of the investigation is being handled by Detective Inspector McCoy. He's head of yet another new taskforce, the CUT."

"Ah! I know him of old. And were would he be based these days?"

"McCoy? The last I heard, it was a disused office block on Queen Victoria Street, but it could be anywhere by now."

"How very extraordinary," Bill said.

It was the sergeant's turn for a bit of griping, and after the past twenty minutes, he needed it, "It's the bloody government, isn't it? Set up all these wonderful-sounding new taskforces for this that and the other, draft in the staff, equip them all. Then forget to find them some bloody offices to work out of! Sometimes I feel sorry for the poor sods – having to move about every few weeks. If you ask me–"

"Yes, well, thank you for your time sergeant, but I really must be going. I'll pay a visit to the City of London CID in Old Jewry, they're bound to know where this McCoy chap hangs out." Bill gave the officer one of his brightest smiles, snapped close his notebook and marched out into the early morning sunlight.

"They won't know what hit them," the sergeant muttered.

*****

DI McCoy and DS Green arrived back at their latest temporary offices at the same time. Both had been summoned by a somewhat excited Sunny Singh. This in itself was an unusual occurrence – in the tradition of such things, DS Singh had earned her sobriquet precisely because she had never been seen to smile and was totally unflappable.

"Let's hope this really is good news, Green," McCoy said.

"It'd be about bloody time."

They marched straight through to Sunny's room – known, wherever she was stationed, to one and all as the workshop – and found the young Asian in her customary position, hunched over one of the room's many computer terminals. Seated in the room's furthest corner was Maria Walker, the witness from the travel agency. They both looked up as the two men bustled into the room.

"What have you got for us, Sunny?" McCoy, as ever, wasted no time in small talk.

"Nice to see you again, Maria," Green smiled at her.

"Something very strange, Inspector," Sunny said, "But probably very useful."

"Okay, let's have it. We're getting nowhere out in the field."

DS Singh composed her features and took a few moments get her thoughts in order. To some it appeared that she was dithering, but in fact, as McCoy knew very well, she was simply ensuring that she would give a concise and accurate report. Sunny was nothing if not meticulous with detail. When she was ready she began, "Miss Walker," she nodded her in her direction, "arrived one and a half hours ago and we proceeded to generate a computer-fit of the suspect known as John Smith. When that was completed – in a remarkably short time, I must add – it proved to be a very close likeness to the artist's impression that was created last night."

"From which we can deduce," McCoy said, "that Miss... Walker's observational skills are very good."

"Thank you," she said through a yawn.

"Would you like to go and get a coffee, Miss?"

"Actually, Inspector," Sunny intervened, "I am believing that you will want to be asking the young lady some questions very shortly. It would be better if she stayed."

McCoy shrugged, "Whatever. So, we're now pretty certain that we've got a good likeness of this Smith character."

"That is very true," Sunny said, "I had already carried out the second matching run on the first likeness, and with fewer criteria selected we had more than one hundred hits – one hundred and twenty-five, to be precise. Since the process takes less than thirty minutes, I decided to run the match again, but this time using the computer-generated likeness. Twenty minutes ago, I received the results."

"How many matches?"

"One hundred and twenty-eight, Inspector. One hundred and twenty-two of them appeared in both sets."

McCoy's eyebrow's shot towards the ceiling, "Now that *is* incredible."

Sunny nodded, seemingly unperturbed, "As I said before, the likenesses were extremely close."

"Presumably none of them are known as, or use the alias, John Smith?" Green asked.

"There is no such evidence within the system, but that brings me to the... unusual part. I asked Miss Walker to study each of the matches on the monitor and asked her to pick out any that she thought might be the man she saw on Tuesday night. There were no names attached to the images at this point, of course, and I was using just the eyes, nose and mouth features. In each case, Miss Walker selected two men, and in each case, she selected the *same* two men. Or rather, the same two images."

McCoy smiled, "That's about as positive an identification as we could hope for." He paused, "What do you mean by 'the same two *images*'?"

Sunny glanced at Maria Walker before continuing, "This is the first part of this most unusual thing, Inspector. Although there are two images in each of the matching sets, they belong to the same man. In other words, Miss Walker picked out *one man* from each set. The same man in each case."

"But... How could there be more than one image? It's supposed to be a universal database."

"One main reason which leads us to the second part of the thing that is so unusual," Sunny said, "You see, there were many, many data sources used to build the universal database, and there would naturally be duplicates at first. There have been many pieces of software run in an effort to eliminate these, but it is always difficult to determine precisely what constitutes a duplicate."

"Surely, name, date of birth, sex, those sorts of things?"

"Most surely, Inspector. In fact, where possible they have used DNA samples and so forth. However, it was decided that if a person's

100

appearance had changed dramatically between two different sources, then both records should be retained."

"Okay," McCoy said, "That makes some sort of sense, since witnesses tend to see the same things in different ways, and particularly when it comes to their fellow man. This way you give them two chances to recognise the suspect."

"Also," Green added, "If we turn up any photographic evidence from an old case, there's more chance of nailing the perp. if we've got an old image of him in the system."

"You are both, of course, most correct," Sunny said.

"Hang on!" McCoy held up a finger, "This is what's so strange isn't it? If this guy's appearance had changed so much, how come both images turned up in the same run?"

"I'm afraid it is even stranger than that, Inspector," Sunny picked up two sheets of paper from his cluttered desk and handed them to McCoy, "These are the images that were selected by Miss Walker. As I have already mentioned, I showed her only the parts of the images used for the match: eyes, nose and mouth. Remember, using the full image overnight, we had no matches whatsoever."

McCoy stared at the faces. With only the central features clearly visible, they took on an almost ghostly appearance. Regardless of that, they were, beyond doubt, the same man. "I can't see much in the way of dramatic differences here. Perhaps the odd wrinkle or two."

Sunny, for once almost vibrating with excitement, handed him two more sheets. It was immediately clear that they were of the same man, and as far as McCoy was concerned, it was also clear that he'd not had an easy life in recent years. The younger version had the look of an aristocrat about him – high, wide forehead, unmarked by a single line, smooth cheeks below high cheekbones, a square jaw. His hair was jet black, short and with a deep widow's peak, his flat ears almost delicate. The older version looked beaten. The eyes still held their slightly haughty glare and the nose was still as straight as before. The mouth was still formed into a tight-lipped smile. But there, the similarities ended. The hair was longer, unstyled and shot through with a lot of grey. A deep scar ran from his right temple and down his cheek, ending in an ugly 'J' just above his jawline. The lower lobe of his left ear was missing altogether, and another scar ran horizontally across his jaw, a centimetre or so under his lower lip.

"Well," McCoy whistled, "I can certainly see why both of these were kept in the system. At first glance you'd never know they were the same guy. You are certain that they *are* the same guy, though."

Sunny nodded, "DNA does not lie, Inspector. Both sets of records match perfectly. Only the face has changed."

McCoy stared hard at the young Asian, "We haven't got to the weirdest bit, yet, have we?"

"Indeed not, Inspector."

Before Sunny could continue, McCoy shook his head, "Oh, no! You're not going to say what I think you're going to, are you? Only I seem to recall Green, here, telling me our suspect was about thirty according to the obviously observant Miss Walker. Which puts this guy out of the picture. He's got to be fifty now, if he's a day!"

"No, Inspector," Maria Walker said. She rose from her chair and crossed to where he was standing. Taking the image of the younger man out of his hands, she pointed to it, "I'm one hundred percent positive that this was the man I saw on Tuesday night."

"Then this," McCoy said, waving the older image in front of him, "*Can't* be the same guy. There must be some sort of system error."

"Naturally," Sunny said, "That is exactly what I thought. But I checked myself, and I have had others checking who were involved with this man in the past. DNA does not, as I said, lie. Everything about the two sets of records tallies. Except, of course, for the appearance."

"Then it's this one's son," McCoy insisted, "Surely they could have matching DNA?"

"They could not," Sunny said, "No. However, strange it may seem, this is the same man. His name is Benjamin Bannen, and he's known as 'King' or 'King B'. The most recent picture was taken just two years ago. He had been charged with the attempted abduction of a senior official in Whitehall. The case never came to trial. The earlier one was taken seven years ago after what was described as a gang-fight at Queen's Park tube station. He was charged with several counts of ABH. To add to the strangeness, he escaped from Brixton while on remand, and took his cellmate with him."

"Why would that be strange?"

"His cellmate was an up and coming barrister – hardly natural bedfellows."

"I think I remember that," Green said, "The barrister had been refused bail but had claimed that without being freed, he would have no chance of constructing his defence. He was on the run for about three months, then gave himself up. When his case come to court, he was acquitted in two days."

"Okay," McCoy said, "This is all very fascinating, but I still can't believe that these two are one and the same guy."

"Perhaps the barrister paid for him to have reconstructive surgery or something?" Green suggested.

"Not even bloody barristers earn enough for that much plastic. And besides, it's not just the details of his appearance. There's something… older about him in this supposedly earlier one."

"I agree with the Inspector," Maria said, "I was positive that the man I saw – this man – was around thirty. He even moved like a young man."

McCoy shook his head once more, "Well, how old are… *is* he, then?"

"Fifty-seven," Sunny replied, "He was fifty-five last time he was arrested and that is confirmed in his statement at the time."

"Okay!" McCoy held his hands up in surrender, "I'm not willing to say that I actually believe all this but given the weird shit that's been happening this week, I suppose I shouldn't be too surprised if it turns out he's discovered the fountain of bloody youth or something. But if Miss Walker, here, is confident that she's identified our man, then the least we can do is find him."

Maria Walker nodded her agreement, "I'm positive. Sorry if all this has been confusing for you."

"It's hardly your fault," McCoy gave her a wry smile, "When we catch up with this guy, we'll need to ask you to come in and formally identify him in a line-up."

"I… won't have to actually face him, will I?"

103

"No, love," McCoy said, "Not that we would permit any harm to come to you if you did have to at some point. You think he might be the violent type?"

"Maybe, but that's not it. There's something… *weird* about him. He never said a word to me and the few times he did open his mouth to say anything, it was in a whisper that I couldn't catch. And then there was the way he breathed."

"The way he *breathed*?"

Maria nodded, "While the nurse was filling in the booking form I watched the other guy. He was standing close by the desk, side-on to me. He was only wearing jeans and a T-shirt, even though it bitter out. It wasn't until he eventually took a breath that I realised. I watched for the next couple of minutes and he could only have taken three or four breaths. I don't know why, but it was beginning to creep me out."

Green shrugged, "Maybe he's one of those fitness freaks."

"Maybe. I just know for sure I wouldn't want to be alone with him."

McCoy clapped his hands together, "Enough with all this weirdness. Thanks for your time, Miss Walker, you've been most helpful. Sunny, let's have all we've got on this guy. Bannen, you say his name is?"

Sunny handed him two thick files, "There should be some more at the front desk by now. If you like I'll pick up anything that's arrived and escort Miss Walker out at the same time?"

"Actually–" DS Green begun.

"Good idea!" McCoy interrupted, "Green and I have some serious reading to do, don't we?"

"Well–"

"That's the spirit. Have a file."

Chapter 7

Friday 16th November 2018

Reluctance was evident in every step that Franklin and Dot took across the City. The sun was blazing in a cloudless sky – too late in the year to do anything more than take the chill off the skin, but bright enough to warm the soul. The worst of the rush-hour had passed, half a million souls now cramped in the offices, bars, shops and banks of the Square Mile. Couriers buzzed around, more than ever, it seemed, on bicycles, late-starters and dawdlers bustled along, many of them frantically checking their wristwatches and muttering under their breath.

Just a few days before, Franklin had felt a tiny pang of envy as he'd been trudging through the rain-sodden streets. This morning, hand in hand with Dot and the sun burning brightly, he suddenly felt extremely fortunate.

They paused in Finsbury Circus and watched a cursing gardener filling in holes on the normally pristine surface of the bowling green at its centre.

"Vandals," Dot tutted.

Franklin shook his head, "Rabbits. There's been a family of them living around here for years now."

"Yeah, right!"

After a brief and none too friendly conversation with the gardener, they toured the gardens in search of what Dot referred to as 'the rogue bunny'.

"Maybe next time," Franklin said as they left, disappointed, but content in the unspoken acknowledgement of a few more minutes diversion.

He led them on a slightly circuitous route, partly because he didn't really want their walk to end, but mostly because he wanted to approach the start of the physical side of the investigation from exactly the same direction that the whole thing had started from. They passed along the back of the Guildhall and then along Gresham Street, turning left at its end towards St. Paul's. They crossed to the South side of Cheapside and walked towards St. Mary-le-Bow, their footsteps slowing further still as their destination approached.

"Did you know," Franklin said, "that a lot of people believe that it's the sound of the bells from there that you have to be born within earshot of to be called a proper Cockney? Given that there's only a couple of thousand actually live here and no maternity unit in earshot, if that were true then there wouldn't be any Cockneys anymore."

Dot nodded, "Bill's always going on about stuff like that. I was born in Bethnal Green, so I'm a proper one. What about you?" For the third time that morning Dot clamped a hand over her mouth, "Oh, shit! Sorry Franklin, I completely forgot. What a dumb thing to say!"

"Don't fret," he smiled reassuringly at her, "It don't bother me. I could tell people I really am a genuine Cockney, and they'd never be able to disprove it."

Franklin had been found abandoned outside a police station in Islington when he was just a few days old. A note, pinned to the blankets he'd been wrapped in, simply said that his name was Franklin and that although his mother loved him, she simply couldn't give him the care and attention he deserved. It was unsigned. He still had the note, yellowed and battered, barely legible. Every year, on or just after his birthday – an assumed date, since no-one knew the real one – he took the note from an old wallet that he kept in his bedroom, and he read it. He knew the words by heart, of course, but it was different reading them while touching the paper that they'd been written on. Sometimes he'd read them just a couple of times. Sometimes over and over. He always did this alone. He hated people to see him cry.

A WPC, returning to the station at the end of her shift, had heard his cries and discovered the tiny, black baby tucked into the meagre shelter afforded by the building's front steps. After a short stay in hospital where he was declared to be perfectly fit and healthy, he had spent the next sixteen years in a succession of orphanages and foster homes. His mother had never been traced and had never come forward.

"I really am sorry," Dot apologised again.

"There's really no need," Franklin insisted.

"Doesn't it... ever bother you at all?"

"I'd be lying if I said I never thought about it, but it truly doesn't most of the time. I suppose the only thing that I do occasionally regret is my surname."

"There's nothing wrong with Richardson. Who chose it for you, anyway?"

"It was the name of the policewoman who found me. Apparently it's some sort of tradition when kids like me are found abandoned. I sometimes think I'd like it to have been a bit more... I dunno, *exotic*, I suppose the word is."

"You could always change it – loads of people do."

Franklin shook his head vehemently, "I never will. I mean, if that policewoman *hadn't* found me when she did, well, I probably wouldn't be here today. I guess I feel as if I owe it to her somehow. It'd be different if she was my real mother... It's hard to explain."

Dot snorted, "Sometimes I feel like changing mine just *because* of my mother. Stupid cow."

"I like your name. Dorothy Kominski – it sounds sort of glamorous. And when it's shortened to Dot Com, it sounds really modern and hi-tech."

"Yeah, right. Just remember: never call me Dorothy. I hate it. It's her name as well, you know? Only she would never let anyone shorten it to Dot. I remember when I was about ten and one of my 'uncles' called her Dot three times in an hour. She slapped him so hard he lost a tooth."

"Now I know where you get your violent streak from."

"I do not have a violent streak! Say so again and I'll thump you."

They were still laughing together as they made their way down Bow Lane, but it subsided as they approached the tube station entrance. Franklin stopped beside the empty shop.

"This is where Charno was sitting on Monday night."

"Seems too weird to be a coincidence."

"You're telling me! "

"He must have been following you."

"That makes some sort of sense, but if he was, then how come he managed to get past me without my noticing? I came down here on the spur of the moment."

"Perhaps he ran down the other side of the church? There's a little passageway behind it that connects up."

"I wasn't exactly taking my time, and this guy's seventy-odd. He'd have to be some sort of geriatric Usain Bolt to get past me in such a short distance."

"You did say he looked a lot younger than that."

Franklin shrugged, "It's been a bloody weird week, that's for sure."

"Talking about weird, any news about the horse yet?"

"Don't ever mention the bloody horse! If you do, I'm gonna start calling you Dorothy."

"Remember what my mother did to that uncle of mine!"

"It don't worry me," he grinned, "You'll never reach."

"Who said anything about going for your face? There's much easier targets lower down. And they're softer."

"Ouch!" Franklin grimaced, "You wouldn't, would you?"

"Don't call me Dorothy, and you'll never have to find out."

"I think we might have ourselves a deal."

"Good boy."

Franklin pulled Dot tightly to him. "I hate to say this, but I think we're subconsciously putting off the task in hand."

"Where does the 'subconsciously' bit come into it?"

"You sure you're up for it?"

She nodded, "Like I said, we'll watch each other's backs. I ain't going through all that baring-my-soul bit and then letting something happen to you straight after."

"Not to mention that baring-your-cute-little-tits bit."

"I did not bare them! That was a complete accident, and you bleedin' well know it."

"A happy accident. If you hadn't, who knows what might have happened?"

"Yeah, well. Just promise me you won't tell anyone."

"You've already got my word. Of course, should any little lady mention horses while I'm about it might just slip my mind…"

"Okay! Looks like we've got ourselves another deal."

"Fair's fair. Now that's settled, I guess we'd better get moving."

Dot sighed, squeezing him tightly. "Yeah, guess so."

They kissed and then broke the embrace. Silently, hand in hand, they walked to the tube station's entrance. After a moment's hesitation, they walked inside and began to make their way down into London's other City. The dark side.

*****

Alexandra Featherington sat back in her chair, staring at the computer monitor in front of her. She had turned off the room's lighting and the glow of the screen was the only illumination is the basement apartment. Currently, it was displaying a grid-work of what seemed to be randomly connected lines. At some of the intersecting points were small rectangular shapes and in the sector she was currently monitoring, all of these tiny oblongs were solid white. She consulted the photocopied operating instructions for the software and nodded to herself before moving the mouse cursor to an icon resembling a satellite dish. One of the rectangles changed from white to green, and she smiled to herself.

Alexandra picked up a pen and started to sketch out the grid of lines on a sheet of paper. She glanced up at the screen to double-check before adding copies of the rectangles to her diagram. Next to the one representing the green box, she carefully wrote "Mansion House – sub-level 1 access".

*****

DI McCoy threw the file on his desk and grabbed his coat. "I think, Green, that it's time we paid a visit to some of Benjamin Bannen's known accomplices."

"I'm right with you there, guv. Not that we've got much to go on."

"With this bloody case, does that really surprise you?"

They marched out of the office and made their way down the stairs. It was six floors, but the lifts had been playing up again. Since theirs was essentially an undercover squad, there was no formal front desk, but as they walked into the reception area they saw DC Robson in animated conversation with a member of the public.

"What's going on?" McCoy demanded.

Robson looked up and tried to signal something with his eyes, flicking them rapidly from the Inspector to the front doors. Before McCoy could fathom what this strange behaviour was all about, the man at the desk turned round.

"Ah! The very man!"

"Oh, shit!" McCoy groaned, "Just what I need!"

"You know him, guv?" DS Green asked.

"Oh, yes. Mr. William Wilberforce Taylor and I are very well acquainted. I wish we weren't, but there you go. He foolishly invested some of his money in a private investigation firm, and now works as chief busybody for it."

"Inspector McCoy! How wonderful to meet up with you again, dear boy!"

"Mr. Taylor. What the hell are *you* doing here?"

"Mutual interest, dear boy, mutual interest," Bill offered his hand, which was refused, "Very well. I gather that you are the leading light when it comes to the investigation concerning the rather bizarre subterranean events of Monday evening?"

"Does he always talk like that?"

"I'm afraid so, Green," McCoy sighed. He turned back to Bill, "I don't know how you found out as that is classified information, and I'm not going to bother denying it, since you seem to have an uncanny ability to worm information out of people. But we are very busy, as you can imagine, and I haven't time for you and your amateur detective agency. So, if you'll excuse us?"

"I did say this was mutual interest, Inspector. And may I just correct you on one point, there – the agency for whom I work are in no way amateurs. We are a professional organisation with the appropriate accreditation to verify the fact. At all times we strive to provide the very best of service to our many and varied clients—"

"Enough with the advertising spiel. Get to the point. When you say mutual interest, I take it you're referring to the investigation concerning the suicides?"

"Suicides?"

McCoy and Green exchanged a quizzical, slightly worried glance, "The seventeen people who committed suicide on Monday evening. That's what you referred to when you first spoke to me."

"I referred," Bill said, "to the bizarre events, not suicides." He had surmised that this approach would at least pique the Inspector's interest. He was proved right.

"You know something about what went on?"

"My agency has, shall we say, become *a little* involved."

"Why do I get the impression I'm going to really, really regret this," McCoy sighed, "Okay, Taylor. I'll give you five minutes of my time, but let's get this straight, right from the start. I don't want any of your clever-clever beating around the bush and I will not – repeat not – be divulging any information concerning the investigation. You are being permitted this time solely to provide us with any information you have, *and* you will not withhold anything from us. Do you hear what I'm saying?"

"You're coming through crystal clear, Inspector. Like a skylark on a still spring morning, a violin solo in an empty Albert Hall, a—"

"Taylor!"

"I was just trying to assure you that I fully comprehended your—"

"Next time, a simple "yes" would do."

Green nudged his superior, "You sure five minutes is gonna be enough?"

McCoy nodded, "You heard my DS, Taylor. A perfectly valid question. Since you are definitely only getting five minutes, you do well to remember to keep things brief."

"Message understood," Bill said.

"Guv? You want me to go on ahead?"

"No, Green. *Mr.* Taylor might be a right royal pain in the arse, but him and the other two at his agency do seem to be able to dig up the

111

occasional worthwhile bit of information. You'd better sit in." He turned back to Bill, "Okay, follow me. There's an interview room on the second floor."

DS Green and Bill followed McCoy out of the reception area and up the stairs.

"I remember now," Green said as they reached the first landing. He looked over his shoulder at Bill, "Your lot were involved with that Courtney case last year, weren't you?"

"Quite so, dear boy. Although I rather think that the term should be 'solved' the Courtney case. Just the three of us. How many men did you have on that case, Inspector? Sorry, I didn't catch that. Twenty-five, did you say?"

"Shut up, Taylor," McCoy said, opening the interview room door, "For your information, Green, there were fifteen men assigned to the case for two days shortly before Tristram Courtney was apprehended. And he would have been apprehended at least a week earlier if he hadn't received a tip-off that we were about to collar him. If I could have proved it, Taylor and his merry men would be doing time right now for aiding and abetting the suspect's escape."

"Inspector!" Bill said, "How could you possibly suspect our good selves?"

"Easily and with a clear conscience, Taylor. The fact that your cronies at that bloody awful pub of yours provided all three of you with alibis is all that kept me from investigating further."

"A gross slander, Inspector." Bill turned to face Green, "Back at the agency, we put it down to his professional jealousy. Loss of face and all that."

"Can it, Taylor," McCoy sighed, "And take a seat."

DS Green moved around and sat beside his superior. Bill settled himself comfortably and pulled out a box of cigars from inside his voluminous coat, "Do you mind?"

McCoy slid an ashtray across the table and lit cigarettes for himself and Green, "You'll need this," he told the sergeant, "It helps kill the stench of those awful bloody things Taylor smokes."

"They are the finest quality Cuban," Bill said, clipping the end off of the cigar, "but I must say I do so admire a man who flouts the law on cigarette smoking indoors so reasonably." He lit it and inhaled deeply, holding down the smoke for a full ten seconds. He let it drift lazily out of his mouth along with a contented sigh. "My one vice," he said to Green.

"Bollocks, and enough of the plainly artificial compliments," McCoy said, "Okay. Are we sitting comfortably? Good. Then you have five minutes of my time, starting now." Before Bill could speak, McCoy pressed on. "Question one. You said downstairs that your agency was, and I quote, 'a little involved'. Does this mean that your involvement is on a professional basis?"

"In what precise way do you mean, Inspector?"

"Four minutes fifty seconds."

"Oh, very well," Bill said, "The agency has been asked to undertake a *professional* investigation."

"Just what we need. Okay, question two. Who's employing you?"

"Client privilege, Inspector. I couldn't possibly divulge that information at this juncture."

"In that case, Taylor, this meeting is terminated."

"I still have more than four minutes, Inspector!"

"Not if you don't tell me who has dragged you into this mess."

"A mess, is it?"

"See what I mean, Green. You've got to watch every bloody word that comes out of your mouth when he's around." He turned back to Bill, "Now, are you going to tell me or not?"

"Would it be okay if I gave you my word as a gentleman that we will inform you of anything that we uncover during the course of our investigations just as soon as whatever it might be comes to light?"

"Since that's your duty under the laws of this country, that doesn't strike me as a reasonable offer, Taylor. I want the name."

"Perhaps another alternative that might be more appropriate is that we exchange what little we already know about the general background to the case?"

"There will be no exchanges. However, since you've now admitted that you've got some information, I have a perfectly valid reason to lock you up until you tell me what it is. Alternatively, you could provide the information of your own free will. Your call, Taylor."

Bill nodded. He had played this game with Detective Inspector McCoy on a couple of previous occasions. It was time to play the intrigue card. "What if I told you, Inspector, the *reason* that our agency has become involved?"

"I'm assuming that a relative of one of the victims–" He stopped himself, but too late.

"So you've got that far by yourselves?"

McCoy gave Bill a level stare, "What I meant to say was that I am assuming a relative of one of the jumpers does not believe it was suicide and therefore reckons the jumper is, in fact a victim."

"A plausible reason for your slip of the tongue. However, it is largely irrelevant. That is not why our agency has been employed."

"So, why don't you stop beating about the bush and fucking well tell me?"

"Language, Inspector."

"Taylor!"

"Very well, Inspector. I rather think that this is going to raise your eyebrows."

"They'll have gone grey and dropped off by the time you get round to it."

Bill smiled, "Our agency, Inspector, has been employed to trace a missing person."

McCoy shrugged, "What's that got to do with anything?"

"Our client, Inspector, believes that the missing person was also meant to become a victim on Monday night. That the person somehow avoided the fate that befell the other seventeen, and is now holed up somewhere, in fear for their life."

McCoy and Green exchanged a suddenly interested look.

"Why would your mysterious client believe that?"

"The person in question has some sort of bizarre conspiracy theory concerning the... *underworld*, shall we say. The missing person has a very similar profile to the other seventeen."

McCoy sat thoughtfully for a few seconds, "Okay, Taylor. The name of your missing person."

When Bill, Franklin and Dot had discussed this the previous evening, they had decided that it might prove worthwhile to divulge a little information of this sort. The police were likely, in time, to learn of at least one or two of the other thirteen disappearances – they did not fit the normal missing persons profile – and that there was absolutely no chance of them discovering the subterranean connection. Besides which, as Franklin had reasoned, if one of these thirteen *did* turn up above ground as a result of a police investigation, then it would make their own job that much easier.

"The person in question is one Thomas Gerald Parkington. He is twenty-eight years old, works for a merchant bank and has risen quickly to the rank of director. He is both single and a single child. He lives alone. As I said, his profile matches those of the other victims. I have the details in this envelope." He patted his breast pocket.

McCoy turned to his sergeant, "Get Singh onto that right away. The envelope, please, Taylor."

Bill extracted it and handed it to Green.

When the sergeant had left, McCoy lit another cigarette and stared at Bill, "Is that kosher?"

"You have my word, Inspector."

"You won't give me the name of your client?"

"It's irrelevant. If it's a relative of Thomas Parkington, then you'll be speaking to them soon enough. The same applies if it's one of his colleagues."

"Is it either one of those?"

"Honestly, Inspector, and with all my heart, I don't know. Whether you believe it or not, he approached young Franklin in the street and handed him sufficient cash to carry out a thorough investigation. And that is all."

"And just where are you looking?"

Bill shrugged, "The normal places. But it's very difficult with so few people around who know of this man's private life. You know how it is."

"Don't I bloody just. But if you know about the profiles of the seventeen so-called jumpers, and how similar they are to this guy, you've already been doing a hell of a lot of work."

"We're nothing if not thorough. And, no, I cannot divulge my sources. Before you ask, though, I can assure you that it's no-one within your squad that has assisted us."

"Sure?"

"Absolutely positive, Inspector."

"You do realise that this Parkington's disappearance could be construed as extremely suspicious."

Bill nodded, "That he might even have been at least partially responsible for the murders on Monday night. We do know that his body was not found on any of the lines. You have my word, Inspector, that should we locate the man, we shall inform you immediately. Whatever you might believe about Tristram Courtney, he was harmless in the physical sense. If there is any possibility that Parkington is not, then we will make it a priority to keep you informed."

McCoy rose and locked the door, "I'll be extremely disappointed if you don't. Perhaps there's something else that you could assist me with."

This was the part Bill had been waiting for. "We are extraordinarily busy at the moment with this investigation, but of course, if what you require assistance with in any way overlaps our efforts, we will naturally be more than happy to take it under our wing."

McCoy nodded. The rules of the game were being observed. "We are currently looking for one man that may have been a witness to the… events on Monday."

"Not Parkington, obviously."

"No, not if your description was accurate." He reached into his pocket and pulled out a sheet of paper bearing Bannen's photograph and a summary of his personal details and past record. McCoy handed it to Bill, "You'll see this guy's picture online today and in today's *Standard* as well as tomorrow's dailies. The usual 'wanted in connection' stuff, but no mention of Monday. As far as we're concerned, he's pretty much our only lead on what happened down in the tube stations. The only other thing I can – or will – tell you, is that we believe this man to be dangerous."

"I understand, Inspector," Bill said, "And rest assured, that there will be no stories appearing in the press from 'inside sources' linking him to Monday night's goings-on."

"There'd better not be."

"Thank you, Inspector." Bill rose and offered McCoy his hand. This time it was shaken.

McCoy unlocked the door and watched as Bill headed down the stairs. He waited for a few seconds and then turned to the desk, picking up the telephone. "Robson. I want tails put on three people. One William Taylor who will be leaving the building in a few seconds, a Franklin Richardson and a Dorothy... Kominski, I think it is. You'll get the address of their agency in the directory under the second guy's name, okay?"

*****

The northern, eastbound, platform at Mansion House stretched into the distance. Monitors were mounted on the walls at one end of the platform so that drivers could check back along the side of the train as passengers were getting on or off. Further along, past the electronic displays listing the next trains, there were CCTV cameras and a large mirror. Opposite, a small office had views across the rails. To all intents and purposes, every millimetre of the platform seemed to be visible. Currently Franklin and Dot were the only people present.

They walked slowly towards the western end, Franklin explaining what they were about to do. Dot was clutching his hand tightly, her palm slippery and hot.

"Just beyond the end of this platform the main tube tunnels divide for a short distance. According to the file there should be what looks like an access tunnel a few metres down the right-hand branch. It's used by London Underground for storage of cleaning equipment and all that sort of shit. At the end of that tunnel is a large steel door which is permanently locked. Or at least that's what the staff believe. It was installed when the station was refurbished about twenty years back – the contractors responsible were working as much for Charno as LU – and behind it there's a new tunnel which leads down to one of their groups' safe

117

houses. If these missing guys are going to hole up somewhere *real* safe, then that's as likely place as any."

Dot nodded, "Okay, I'm with you so far, but just how do we get there without being seen? There's cameras and stuff all over the place – not to mention bleedin' trains."

A Circle Line tube rattled into the station and she and Franklin stood back as a dozen passengers alighted. They waited until the last of them had left the platform and then resumed their slow stroll.

"Apparently – and I hope to Christ the notes I've got are right – there's one blind spot on the platform. Again, contractors Charno has some sort of control over made sure that the cameras and other monitoring gear can't see that one spot. As for the trains, there's three come through here in every ten-minute period throughout the day. What we need to do is wait until there's a four-minute gap between them, then, just as one is leaving, we simply step down the side of the platform and into the tunnel. We have to wait until the driver's cab is out of sight, though, because those screens at the other end let the driver see what's going on back here. And we'll have to make sure no passengers see us, of course."

"Didn't I just hear you say 'simply step off the platform'?"

Franklin gave her a reassuring grin, "There's a set of steps at the very end."

"But what if a train comes and we're standing there in the middle of the tunnel?"

"That's why we wait for a four-minute gap. That should give us plenty of time to find the access tunnel. If one *does* come, there's recesses all along the walls. Squeeze into one of them, face the wall. We're both wearing black, so the driver shouldn't notice us."

"Of course, in your case you could face outward."

"There are advantages to being black," Franklin laughed, "As long as I don't open my eyes, I guess I could face the tracks. Not sure that I'd want to, though."

"Nor me. Let's hope it don't come to that, anyway."

"One other thing," Franklin said, "Don't step on *any* of the rails. For a start, one of them's live, and the others might well be greased."

"No fears on that score. I'm gonna be hugging wall all the way down there. Er, one thing, though?"

"What's that?"

"Do your wonderful notes say anything about rats?"

"Well... there was some mention of them."

"I didn't like the way you said that. What *exactly* did they say?"

"There's... a few of them about. Er, quite big ones, I think it said. Scared of rats are you?"

"I wasn't till I read those bleedin' books by James Herbert. One of them was set down here, you know?"

"Yeah, I know, but don't worry. There's not supposed to be any in this area." Franklin crossed his fingers and prayed that the first sound they heard down the tunnel wasn't a squeak.

They reached the end of the platform which had narrowed to the point where they were forced to walk single file. Dot peered over the edge.

"Well, the notes were right about the steps, anyway."

Franklin looked up at the indicator board and sighed, "I don't know whether that's a good omen or not, but there's supposed to be a four-minute gap between the next two trains."

They stared at each other and finally smiled.

"Some bleedin' first date."

"You gotta admit it's different."

The rails beside them began to thrum and there was a tiny dip in the temperature. They moved a few metres back along the platform and stood against the cold wall. Accompanied by a surge of air, the tube train thundered into the station, its brakes squealing. When it came to rest the doors slid open and a handful of passengers alighted. Evidently seasoned tube travellers, they all emerged at the furthest end of the platform nearest the exit and the last of them had disappeared before the train even moved off.

As the first carriage disappeared from view, Franklin took Dot's hand and before either of them could back out, they walked quickly to the steps and climbed down onto the banked cinders of the tunnel floor.

Ten paces on and it was like stepping into instant night. Prepared for this, Franklin lit the powerful flashlight he was carrying, its albeit shaky beam illuminating the darkness. Dot followed immediately behind him, one hand firmly grasping the back of his jacket.

They both started as a train roared into the station behind them, the sight of it lost because of the division of the tunnels, the sound of it somehow amplified in the dark confines that they walked through. Neither of them fancied meeting one in the same tunnel they were in, and their pace increased.

The westbound train had just departed when Franklin stopped abruptly.

"What's up?"

"It's the access tunnel," Franklin said over his shoulder, "It really is here."

"I should bleedin' hope so. I'm gonna feel a lot safer down there."

"Come on. Let's get this over with."

They turned into the tunnel which was about half the diameter of the tube tunnel proper. Its ceiling was only just high enough for Franklin to walk upright, and the walls, cluttered with shelves of cleaning and maintenance materials seemed to press in on each side. Faint stirrings of claustrophobia fluttered in his stomach, and he was glad that they'd stopped en route to replenish the supply of torch batteries.

The tunnel was longer than Franklin had expected, and he heaved a huge sigh of relief when the torch beam finally picked out a metallic surface stretching across the width of the passageway.

"There's the door."

"About bleedin' time."

"Not wrong, little lady."

"'Ere, I just had a thought."

"Congratulations."

"Very funny. Actually, I was gonna ask you how we get inside? I take it you do know?"

"I know what it says in the notes, anyway," Franklin said, "The door looks like one structure, but it's really two doors. One for getting in and one for getting out. Both of them are secured with a real hi-tech combination lock. The combinations are changed every two weeks."

"Well let's hope you've got the right one."

"Only one way to find out," Franklin said as they reached the door.

The tunnel's shelving had ended a few metres further back and they now stood side by side in front of the massive steel entryway. A sign which appeared to be etched into its surface warned that the tunnel was blocked at this point and that it was impassable and hazardous beyond. Franklin could well believe the latter. Another sign suggested to the idle tourist that access beyond this point was impossible and any attempt would, in any case, constitute a crime of the highest magnitude.

On the very left-hand edge of the steel surface was a complex affair comprising what looked like a rudimentary handle and a cylinder.

"I don't see any numbers or stuff," Dot said.

Franklin took a small, circular piece of metal from a canvas pouch and placed it on the top of the strange cylinder. When he pressed down, there was a dull, metallic click and a smaller cylinder slid smoothly out of the larger one. It consisted of four steel wheels, each bearing the digits zero to nine.

"Hey presto," Franklin grinned. He carefully pocketed the key he'd used to release the combination cylinder. "There should be a similar arrangement on the inside which will let us out again if we come back this way." He handed a second key to Dot, "You'd better hang on to this in case we lose the other one."

"Very clever-clever. What's the combination, then?"

"Forty-seven, forty-seven." He reached up and aligned the wheels accordingly, then turned the handle upwards.

"It didn't open!" Dot said, worried.

"No sweat, little lady. That's just another part of the security system. Watch this."

He waited for ten seconds at which point there was a subtle click inside the lock mechanism. It was more felt through the handle than audible. He turned the handle back to its original position, spun the combination locked and then realigned it once more. Taking a deep breath, he twisted the handle upwards once more.

The movement was accompanied by a much louder click and then a whoosh of air. The left-hand half of the door swung smoothly outwards on invisible hinges.

"It actually worked!"

"Bleedin' good job. I guess it's onwards and downwards from here, then?"

"Guess so."

Franklin stepped across the threshold and turned his flashlight to the wall. A bank of switches was situated at waist height and he brushed his palm across them to the accompaniment of a series of clicks. Old fluorescent lights flickered into life along the chamber's ceiling and a gentle humming began to emanate from a large steel box suspended from the far wall. To their right, a computer monitor fizzed softly as it began to glow. After the dank mustiness of the ancient tunnels outside, it was like stepping into an operating theatre.

"Bleedin' hell!" Dot stared around her as she moved into the room.

Behind her Franklin pulled the door closed and twisted the interior handle. A series of clicks and whirrings indicated that the mechanism outside had been re-set. With a shrug, he turned and looked about him.

The chamber was about twelve foot to a side, the walls and ceiling a smoothly plastered sterile white. The only furnishings were a long table along the far wall and a typist's chair which faced the computer screen. At the back of the room was a simple wooden door, much as you would find in any house in any town.

Dot had sat herself in front of the monitor, "Any idea what this is supposed to be?"

Franklin crossed the room and stood behind her, "There wasn't much about it in the notes, but it's supposed to be some sort of security monitoring system."

"Looks a bit like a map," Dot said. She moved the mouse around and then pointed at the screen, "Look, there's loads of lines and little boxes. Most of the boxes are white, but there's a green one here."

"Green sounds okay. Perhaps it's us?"

Dot shrugged, "Who knows. Maybe if I had a bit of time I could figure out what it really does?"

"I'm sure you could. Unfortunately, we haven't got a bit of time. The place we need to check out is through there somewhere." He pointed at the door.

"Spoilsport."

"That's me. Let's go."

He opened the wooden door to reveal a narrow passageway which descended at a gentle angle. Dim lights were suspended from the ceiling at regular intervals.

"At least it's lit," Dot said, "After you, though."

Franklin led them through the doorway and began the descent. After the sterile chamber behind them the mustiness and grime were oppressive. According to the notes, the tunnel was supposed to be about sixty metres long. Franklin hoped and prayed that it wasn't much longer than that.

"What exactly is supposed to be down here, then?"

Franklin was grateful for Dot's question. He was suppressing the urge to start sprinting. "The notes refer to it as a 'safe house' – a sort of refuge if any of Charno's group need to hole up for a while. It's actually one of the old tube stations that was used as secondary access to a deep bomb shelter at Chancery Lane during the last war."

"I heard about that," Dot said, "Loads of stations were used as bomb shelters, weren't they?"

"About eighty of them and there were eight more deep shelters built but only a few of them were opened to the public. Loads of tube stations were abandoned after the war and haven't been used since."

"I reckon that was a smart idea, turning them into shelters, like makes a change for the powers that be to do somethin' sensible."

"It wasn't the powers that be," Franklin said, "London Transport didn't like it and said it wasn't legal if the people didn't mean to travel anywhere. So what people did was buy the cheapest tickets available and then camped out down there anyway. They even turned one into a children-only shelter. The Aldgate extension, I think it was."

"Cool idea."

"Not always. Sometimes bombs found their way down there, then it was carnage. More than a hundred were killed like that at Bank station, twenty at Marble Arch. The worst was at Balham where the river burst in. Six hundred people drowned there that night."

"Oh, yuck! I wish I hadn't brought it up."

Franklin tried to be as reassuring as he could – not easy under the circumstances, "It was normally pretty much okay. Did you know that more than a hundred thousand people were down here most nights when the Blitz was at its worst?"

"Where'd you get all this gen?"

"Where do you think? Bill, of course. You know what he's like about the history of London. He told me that there was a whole subterranean society back then. You know? Theatre productions, libraries, canteens. Some stations even produced their own newsletters. There was one really famous one called Mickey's shelter. He was three-foot tall hunchback and he became so famous that the US presidential candidate – Wilkie, I think it was – visited him there on a UK tour. Marks and Sparks donated a whole working canteen to the place."

"I don't think I could have lived underground like that."

"Given what was going on above ground, it might not have been so bad. And from what I read the other day, there's plenty of people living down here right now."

"Rather them than me."

"There's the next door!"

Dot peered under Franklin's arm, "Doesn't look very impressive."

The small steel door was beginning to rust at the edges and the "No Admittance" sign was hanging by one corner from a bent fixing.

"Well," Franklin said, "Let's see what a 'safe house' actually looks like, shall we?"

"Can't bleedin' wait."

He turned the handle and pulled the door open.

Lights automatically began to flicker on along the length of what had clearly once been a tube station. At first sight the place appeared to be neglected and decaying, but as the level of illumination increased, it became clear that this was not the case. Although many of the tiles were chipped and broken, the walls gleamed. The concrete floor of the platform was dust and dirt free, the blocked off section of tunnel was free of litter.

They were standing at one end of a long, straight platform. At the far end they could make out the reinforced glass windows of an office of some sort. The only differences between this deserted, abandoned station and any of the hundred others still in use, was that it was cleaner, and that the advertising hoardings weren't covered in graffiti.

"Bleedin' hell," Dot whispered.

"About half way there, anyway," Franklin said, "Welcome to St. Bartholomew's. Let's check out the offices. If anyone's down here, that's where they'll be." He took a few steps down the platform before he realised that Dot wasn't by his side. He turned back to see her standing just inside the open doorway, "What's up?"

She shook her head, "I... dunno. I gotta funny feeling, that's all. Like... something bad has happened. You know what I mean?"

All Franklin could feel was the vestiges of his mild claustrophobia, "It'll be fine," he told her, "And the sooner we get finished here, the sooner we can think about getting back above ground." He walked back and put his hands on her shoulders, "Okay?"

Dot nodded, but without certainty, "I guess."

Franklin pulled the door closed behind her and, noticing three large iron bolts, decided that it might be wise to slide them home. "Never can be too careful," he said.

He set a brisk pace along the platform in an effort to dispel the growing sense of unease that even he was beginning to experience. By the time they got to the office block they were moving at a near-trot. Without a second's hesitation, he grasped the handle of the ancient wooden door and tugged it open.

The room beyond had the appearance of a barrack room. Small beds lined the walls to left and right, interspersed with writing tables and wooden chairs. An open door at the far end gave a view of a modern-looking kitchen and another to their left looked in on what appeared to be a hi-tech office. There was no sign of life.

A thorough search of the rooms confirmed it and they wandered back out to the platform.

"It looks as though someone was here a few days ago," Franklin said.

"Well, they sure ain't today. What next?"

"We gotta choice. We could either go back the way we come and get some fresh air, or we can use the exit from the other end of this station and head East. There's another tunnel and another station in that direction. In fact, it'll be a damn sight easier going that way 'cos we won't have to use the active tunnels."

"I guess it's probably safer that way, then," Dot said, "Let's do it."

Franklin led them through the old exit barrier into a narrow tunnel of more recent construction than the station behind them. Five metres into it was another rusting steel door. It was standing open and they stepped quickly through into the darkened passageway beyond. As Franklin began to close the door behind him, suspended ceiling lights began to flicker on, and he returned the flashlight to his pocket with a sigh of relief.

"This isn't so bad, after all, is it?" he asked Dot.

She shrugged, a worried expression on her face, "I guess not."

*****

Alexandra Featherington had breathed a huge sigh of relief when the small rectangle on the computer grid which represented the Mansion House entrance changed from white to green. Franklin's search was finally under way. She left the desk, went through to the kitchen and poured herself a coffee. She offered up a little prayer that Franklin was going to follow her suggested search pattern and check out each of Charno's safe houses first. Maybe the young man would even manage to find some of Charno's missing acolytes...

Sipping at the scalding brew, she made her way back to the desk and picked up her hand-drawn diagram. She checked the monitor again and was pleased to see that a line representing one of the subterranean access tunnels was now solid green. As she watched, the rectangle at the end of the tunnel icon also changed to a pleasing shade of emerald. If Franklin really was following her suggested course then this must be St. Bartholomew's, one of the forty abandoned stations dotted around the system – and more importantly, one of the four that were still under

Charno's control. After adding the name to her diagram, she smiled to herself and picked up a dog-eared paperback. *Journey to the Centre of the Earth* was one of her all-time favourites and she was soon engrossed. So much so that it was another half hour before she realised that there had been a further change to the computer map.

She stared at the screen, her expression neutral. The Mansion House icon was glowing brilliant scarlet. Someone had entered Charno's tunnel system shortly after Franklin Richardson.

*****

"It's the same damn story everywhere I go," McCoy said, "'*No, Inspector, I haven't seen him since he was nicked last time round*'. It's doing my bloody head in."

"Same here, guv," DS Green took a long swallow from his pint, "No sightings, no addresses, no capers, no nothing. It's like he disappeared."

"Except he was seen in Willesden last Tuesday."

"Except for then, yes."

"If it weren't for that Walker bird being so positive that it was Bannen – and picking him out the way she did – I'd say that we were barking up the wrong tree."

"There's one other thing that points to Bannen, though."

"Which is, Green?"

"His previous."

"How do you mean."

"He was last nicked for abduction, wasn't he? And that's what we think's happened to our witness, the absent Mr. Evans."

"That or he topped him."

"Bannen doesn't seem too bothered about a bit of violence – look at the first time we had him. Eleven counts of ABH and that was just one incident."

"Right now," McCoy said, "I'm willing to clutch at any straws, so I guess I'll give you the benefit of the doubt..." He trailed off into silence.

"What, guv?"

"Something about Bannen's previous has just struck me as rather odd. Make that 'bloody weird'."

"Not with you, guv."

"He was nicked seven years back for those attacks at Queen's Park, wasn't he?"

"Yeah. It's all in the file."

"And he was refused bail and put on remand in Brixton, right?"

"That's where he did a runner from, right," Green nodded, "Scarpered with that lawyer or barrister or whatever he was."

"And two years ago, he's nicked again. This time for the attempted abduction of some Whitehall bigwig."

"That's right, guv. From what I remember, some civil servant in the Department of the Environment. There was some sort of deal done out of court..." It was DS Green's turn to trail off, "Now I see what you mean, guv."

"Right! Why wasn't Bannen banged up again for the ABH charges and escape? Two years ago, the bloody Met had him in their cells for the best part of a month before they just let him walk out Scot free. They must have known about his previous!"

"I reckon this is beginning to stink," Green nodded.

"I'm beginning to wonder if this Bannen character isn't part of something bigger. Something much bigger."

"Come to think of it, guv, didn't that Taylor guy say that his client thought that all this business on Monday was part of some bloody great conspiracy?"

McCoy looked at Green, "He did, although he didn't seem to believe it himself. Not that that's anything to go by. But I'm beginning to get a very nasty feeling about this. Drink up, Green, I think we need to pop along to the Yard and have a word or two, don't you?"

"Looks that way, guv." The sergeant drained his glass and set it on the bar counter. "Guv?"

"What?"

"We're all agreed that there must have been some sort of link between all the victims, right?"

"I can't believe that there isn't."

"And there seems to be some sort of cover-up going on. Maybe some sort of conspiracy or something?"

"It's looking that way. What's your point?"

"I've just had a thought."

"You won't be doing any more thinking for a while if you *don't* get to the point. You're almost as bad as William bloody Taylor."

"Just getting it straight in my head, guv. The point *is*, that there might be one link between these victims that we've overlooked."

"Green!"

"Bear with me. So far we've checked out there backgrounds, their jobs, relatives, home lives, all that sort of crap."

"It's standard procedure."

"But what about the one possible link after they're dead?"

Light dawned on McCoy's face, "Fuck me! Of course!"

"They were all wealthy professionals," Green nodded enthusiastically, "And what do all good little wealthy professionals do?"

"They make wills," McCoy grinned, "And this particular bunch haven't got a close relative between them! Green, you might just be a bloody genius. Come on, let's get moving. We'll call in at the office on the way over to the Yard. I'll get Sunny and some of the others onto this straight away. Let's just hope and pray there's some common ground in those wills."

Chapter 8

Friday 16th November 2018

Bill enjoyed what he referred to as the cloak-and-dagger side of the business. There was something about the assuming of a completely fictional identity that reminded him of his days at Cambridge.

After leaving McCoy at Queen Victoria Street, he had taken a tube train to Tottenham Court Road and from there he had walked to the British Museum, a favourite haunt whenever he was in the area. The daunting peace of the Reading Room was, as far as he was concerned, perfectly conducive to serious thinking.

The notes concerning Benjamin Bannen were brief and succinct, and Bill committed these to memory within a few minutes. It seemed clear to him that Bannen was somehow tied up with the disappearances and, like McCoy's sergeant a few minutes earlier, the nature of his release following the attempted abduction, struck Bill as very strange.

He checked his watch and sighed. Franklin and Dot weren't due to check in with him for another couple hours at least, and he needed something to take his mind of their potentially dangerous situation. Since there was precious little in the way of leads to chase up, he decided that a trip to the Ministry of the Environment represented his best chance of making any progress. If he was fortunate, the senior figure that had been Bannen's abduction target might still be employed there. The MoE were about to be introduced to Bill's favourite alter-ego, Brigadier William Forbes-Rice.

He left the hallowed building, crossed Great Russell Street and marched into the Museum Tavern, where the considered application of three large whiskies enabled him to make the transition into the former military intelligence officer. Once Bill was satisfied that he was 'in character', he checked that he was carrying the false identification that

Dave The Engraver had provided him with and made his way out in search of a taxi.

Behind him DC Bradford swallowed the last of his drink and followed him outside.

*****

"How long do you think it'll take us to get there?" Dot asked as they started out along the corridor.

Franklin shrugged, "If the map's accurate, then I guess it'll be about ten minutes. The station itself is pretty much straight under the Bank of England, somewhere beneath their own underground railway system."

"They've got one as well?"

"It's beginning to seem like everyone has."

"But if there's so many abandoned London Underground ones, why didn't they use those tunnels instead of building their own?"

"Beats me. Security, I guess. Apparently, the Bank uses their system to transport cash and bullion and stuff."

"Makes sense."

"There's one thing that doesn't quite make sense, though," Franklin said, thoughtfully, "All these abandoned stations..."

"What about them?"

"Well, when I was talking to Bill about them, he said that the government have been trying to sell them off for years. Really cheaply, as well, and yet with only a couple of exceptions, no-one seems to want them."

"You'd think someone would," Dot said, "But it ain't really that strange, surely?"

"It's not the fact that there's been no takers that's bothering me. No, it's just that it doesn't really gel with what I read in Charno's files. Come to that, it doesn't match up to what Alexandra Featherington told me, either. She seemed to be saying that these places couldn't just be bought, and that there was some sort of underworld rule about ownership. If these mysterious groups are so wealthy, why wouldn't they just buy the property through normal channels? And why would Alexandra tell me that it wasn't possible?"

"Did she actually say that?"

Franklin was glad that Dot was behind him and couldn't see his face, "That's the way I remember it, but what with all those files and everything, I guess I could have been a bit distracted."

"There must be some way we could find out whether they really have been bought by someone. Although I don't see that it gets us anywhere."

"We'll get Bill onto it when we check in with him," Franklin said, "And as for it not getting us anywhere, I for one would be happier if I knew a bit more about what is *really* going on down here – at the minute we've only got Alexandra's word for it. Okay, so the place back there was just as she'd described but that doesn't mean to say that everything she said was kosher."

"I get your point, and I guess it can't do any harm to get as much info as possible... What's up?"

Franklin had stopped walking, and he made space so that Dot could stand alongside him. "There's no mention of this on the map."

The tunnel had come to a junction with three others. The one leading away to their left was clearly a more recent addition to the system, its walls and ceiling smooth and free of the damp stains that had accompanied their progress so far. The central branch was almost identical but the branch to the right was slightly narrower than the tunnel they were currently standing in, and appeared to be a little older, more worn and well-used.

"Which one do we take, then?"

Franklin pulled the map from his pocket and unfolded it. "There really isn't any mention of a junction," he said, "According to this, the tunnel should just curve gently south-eastwards about halfway along."

"That's be to the right then?"

"Yeah. And it'd be about here, I guess."

"Well, the one we're in seems to go straight on – dead straight, I mean – and the one on the left is totally wrong."

Franklin nodded and refolded the map, "So our best guess must be this older one on the right. What do you reckon?"

"It's gotta go somewhere, anyway."

Franklin shrugged before leading them into the narrower tunnel, "And at least it's heading in the safest direction."

"How do you mean?"

"Well, according to the files, the only part of the system that Charno still controls – in other words, the safest part of the system as far as we're concerned – is the south-east sector. The Allenites started out somewhere over in the north-west, and they've been making steady inroads into Charno's territory, but they haven't got this far. Well, not yet, anyway. So that's why I'm quite happy to be moving deeper onto Charno's turf."

"You're not alone, there," Dot said, "But... I dunno, the longer we're down here the worse I'm starting to feel."

"How do you mean?"

"I... can't explain it exactly, like, but..."

"Is it a bit like claustrophobia?" Franklin asked the question lightly, but the earlier sensation of being confined, crushed almost, was gradually creeping back over him.

"Nah, not like that at all," Dot said, "It's like I'm here and I'm talking and trying to take a real interest, but underneath it all, I'm beginning not to care anymore. Like it's all pointless, you know?"

"Being somewhere weird like this is bound to have some strange effects on you."

"Yeah, I guess so. It's just... strange. I was so happy just before we came down here, and now..."

"Suddenly realise who you've got yourself lumbered with?"

Dot shook her head vehemently, before realising what a pointless gesture it was, "No, it's not that. I guess you're right – it's just being down here. It's all so... drab and dreary."

"Don't worry," Franklin said, "We'll soon be at the next station. After that we'll go topside and have some lunch. We'll have earned it."

Behind him Dot didn't reply directly. "Did you just hear something?"

Franklin stopped walking and tilted his head to one side, "No, it's a quiet as... wait! You're right."

From a long way behind them came three metallic booming noises. There was a few seconds pause before they were repeated. Franklin and Dot stared at each other.

"I think," Franklin said, "that we've got company."

Dot clutched at his arm, "Tell me you closed those bolts back on the station door?"

"All three," Franklin nodded, "But it must mean someone's come in from the Mansion House entrance. There's no other way into this part of the system until that junction we just passed, and that noise is coming from a bloody sight further back than that."

"Perhaps it's some of Charno's people?"

"Alexandra said that it was probably too dangerous for any of them to come down here at the moment if they aren't already holed up somewhere close by. Chances are, it's some of the Allenites. Perhaps Monday's little exercise has finally allowed them to take control of this sector. We'd better get moving. It's one thing explaining to people that you accidentally got lost in the main tube system, but it's a bit bloody different when you're in somewhere with all the protection this place has got."

"I'm right with you there."

They broke into a trot.

The trot became a mad dash as a thunderous crash of metal indicated that the rusted steel door had finally surrendered to whoever had been battering at it.

*****

Detective Chief Superintendent Jacobs was, if anything, more irascible than DI McCoy. DS Green was just happy that he wasn't standing between the two men as they exchanged laser beam stares.

"McCoy, what happens here has nothing whatsoever to do with you. Or any of the other City boys, for that matter."

"With respect, sir, the events concerning Bannen's release are extremely relevant to our current investigation." It had taken them an hour to find out who the superior officer had been at the time of

Bannen's last arrest, and a further forty minutes before they managed to get to see him. He wasn't about to give up now. "Under the latest Home Office regulations concerning–"

"Don't start spouting that crap at me. I've neither the time nor the patience."

Despite Jacob's words, McCoy could see that the man knew that he would have to assist him. It was just a matter of allowing him time to let off steam, "Nevertheless, sir. It is imperative that–"

"Just who do you think you are to come storming in here demanding my co-operation? All over some bloody stupid bunch of suicides?"

"I'm the senior detective on a multiple *murder* case, sir."

"What do you mean 'murders'?"

"We're almost one hundred percent positive that the so-called jumpers were, in fact murdered. We're also pretty much certain that Benjamin Bannen was involved. Now, I could have gone through official channels, but to be frank, sir, we're running out of time here and if we're to stand any chance of finding out just what happened last Monday we need some answers and need them quick."

"You're seriously trying to tell me that seventeen people were simultaneously murdered?"

McCoy nodded, "And without your assistance, the job of finding out who's behind this is considerably more difficult."

"Who the fuck could organise a hit like that?"

"As I just said, sir, that's precisely what we're trying to find out."

Jacobs stared hard at the Inspector for a few seconds and then slumped into his chair, "Very well, McCoy. Sit down and start talking."

McCoy did as instructed, "Would you like my sergeant to fetch Bannen's file?"

Jacobs snorted, "I don't need a bloody file to tell you anything about Bannen, McCoy. Believe me, it's etched into my memory."

"Something weird happened, didn't it?"

"Something *fucking* weird. Let's see. It was just over two years ago as I recall. A car was stopped outside the Ministry of the Environment building – an official looking Jag. One of the Westminster plods notices it and goes over to ask the driver to shift it or show some official accreditation. The driver – not Bannen – gets out and starts to go through his pockets, only instead of some papers, he pulls out a machine pistol and fires three rounds through the plod's right knee. Next he strips him of his walkie-talkie, drags him round to the back of the motor and dumps him in the boot. All of this is in broad daylight on one of the busiest streets in London. Not a single fucking witness comes forward, of course."

McCoy and Green exchanged a knowing glance.

"As far as we're aware," Jacobs continued, "Bannen comes out of the building about five minutes later, accompanied most unwillingly by Sir Desmond Fairfax. This guy is one of the real bigwigs in the Civil Service – a mandarin's mandarin, probably more powerful than the fucking Prime Minister. Not that *that* would be difficult. Anyway, Fairfax is dumped into the Jag and they start to drive off. Only what the driver hasn't realised is that one of the rounds he put through the plod's leg has ricocheted off of something and lodged itself in the motor's front tyre. Halfway round Parliament Square the tyre goes flat. The driver – we've never traced him, before you ask – tries to keep on driving, but as luck would have it, the car's noticed by a couple of Special Branch guys and they try to get the driver to pull over. When he ignores them, they drive him off the road.

"In the confusion that follows, the driver scarpers and the Branch guys collar Bannen. With Fairfax and the unfortunate plod, we've got an open and shut case. Bannen isn't saying anything – no reasons behind it all, no names, no nothing – but that isn't much of a concern. We've got him bang to rights, to use a very tired cliché, and not only that, there's the unfinished business over the Queen's Park incident and his subsequent prison jump."

"So what happened?"

"Nothing, McCoy. We had him locked up nice and safe right in this very building for the next twenty-four hours. He wasn't going anywhere, and we were busy getting his paperwork sorted out. Then the message comes through: Let Bannen go."

"Who from?"

"Only the fucking Home Secretary himself."

McCoy's jaw had dropped open, "Why the fuck would he have done that?"

136

Jacobs snorted, "Apart from the fact that the man's a certifiable lunatic in my opinion, who the fuck know? When I tried to press for some information, I was told in very, very certain terms that it was none of my business. The official line was that the incident was a 'considerable embarrassment' to the government and that it would be better all-round if it were swept under the carpet, and security arrangements tightened at each of the Ministry buildings."

"Which is a crock, of course."

"Completely," Jacobs said, "I tried a few contacts, made a few private enquiries to certain people, but whenever I mentioned Bannen's name mouths slammed shut. I've tried on and off ever since – the same result every time. To make matters worse, Bannen has disappeared into thin air. So, what's *your* interest, McCoy?"

"We have an extraordinarily reliable witness who places Bannen in a Willesden travel agency on Tuesday night. He was accompanying a potential witness in the jumpers' case. Said witness has since disappeared."

"You reckon Bannen is the magician?"

"I'd bet my pension on it, sir."

"What do want from me?"

"Anything that you've got that's not in the official files. From what you say, you've been doing a bit of digging. You must have some names – known associates and so on. All the ones we've contacted swear they haven't seen Bannen since the abduction caper."

Jacobs nodded, "There's two men you might like to pay a call on. A word of warning, though. These are real heavies, and they're real quiet. My guess is that they've worked with Bannen recently – certainly since the Fairfax business – but we've got nothing on them. Until a few weeks ago they were under surveillance, but they seemed to know it and laid low."

"You reckon someone tipped them off?"

"It certainly looks that way," Jacobs said.

"This is sounding messier by the minute. I'm beginning to think that William Taylor's conspiracy theory might not be too wide of the mark."

"You don't mean the same William Taylor that works with that black guy's detective agency?"

McCoy nodded, "You know him, sir?"

"Oh, yes! Well, if he's tangled up in your case, I wish you the very best of luck. You'll need it."

*****

The passageway seemed to go on for ever and the sudden appearance of the small steel door at its end brought a massive surge of relief to Franklin and Dot's faces. They slithered to a halt in front of it and tried to quieten their panting, straining to hear any signs of pursuit.

"All quiet so far," Franklin whispered.

"Yeah, I think so. Let's get this open quick."

Franklin turned to the small combination lock and checked the numbers on the map. "If we're at the right place, then it should be forty-nine, ninety-four." His fingers trembled as he spun the wheels, and they both breathed a huge sigh of relief when the lock sprang open.

The door opened smoothly, and they stepped into the darkness beyond. Franklin handed Dot his flashlight, "Look around for some light switches while I get this shut."

"Will do."

He took the lock from the outside and pulled the door closed. Like the one at St. Bartholomew's, three large iron bolts secured the door from the inside. He slid these home and put the lock through the internal handle for good measure.

"Found them!" Dot hissed from somewhere behind him.

Franklin turned as a series of clicks issued from the wall to his left. Lights began to flicker on starting at the furthest end of what turned out to be the platform, gradually illuminating its entire length. Like St. Bartholomew's a section of tunnel was blocked off to their right. There didn't appear to be any offices or other rooms.

"According to the map," Franklin said, scanning the document, "There's an exit to street level on the other side of this place. A maintenance shaft rises into the main drain that services Cornhill, we just lift a manhole and pop out."

Dot's face was sullen as she turned to face him, "Lovely."

"Hey, we're nearly there! We'll soon be outside enjoying a bit of well-earned sunshine."

"It's..." Dot paused and took a few deep breaths, trying to compose herself, "It's not going to be a second too soon."

Franklin put his arm around her shoulders and began to lead her briskly along the platform. She walked stiffly, almost seeming to cringe from his touch. "I'm not that bad, am I?"

"No... it's just... that feeling again. It seems even stronger here. Everything just seems so... useless!"

Franklin gave her a worried glance, "Let's get a move on, then."

At the furthest end of the platform a small archway led off to the left. They had just turned the corner when there was a thunderous crash from the end of the platform. Franklin and Dot froze on the spot and stared, panicked, at each other.

"Shit, they're fast!" Franklin breathed, "Come on! We've gotta get outta here!"

Dot was breathing rapidly, almost gasping down each tortured lungful, "You... go," she managed.

"What!?"

"Maybe I should... just stay and see who it is," Dot panted.

"Are you crazy! Have you forgotten that seventeen people – maybe more – died down here a few days ago?" Not waiting for an answer, Franklin grabbed Dot by the arm and began to drag her towards a small exit door. Another thunderous crash rang out from the platform behind them. "That door's not gonna stand up to that sort of battering for long," Franklin said, trying desperately to manoeuvre Dot towards the exit. She had seemed unwilling to move at first, but now went almost limp in his grasp. "Jesus! Dot? What's wrong?"

She stared up at him, all expression draining from her face, "Dunno... just..." Her eyes closed.

"Dot! Dot!"

There was no response and her body sagged bonelessly against his side.

"Oh Christ, man!" Franklin patted her cheeks, one of the gentle slaps delivered much harder than intended as another crash reverberated along the station. "Shit, shit, shit!" He took a few deep breaths, trying desperately not to panic, clutching tightly to Dot's inert form. "You'd better be as light as you look, little lady," he muttered. He reached down with his left arm, hooking it behind her thighs. Another deep breath and he stood up straight, Dot in his arms. "I can do this," he panted and walked quickly to the door.

As gently as he could, he set Dot on the cold concrete and pushed at the door. After a moment's panic when it wouldn't budge, he pulled instead, and it swung open, rusted hinges protesting loudly.

There was total inky darkness on the other side of it and even the lighting from the station didn't seem to be able to penetrate the gloom. He fished the flashlight out of his pocket, switched it on and cast the beam into the chamber beyond.

It revealed a circular vertical shaft no more than six feet in diameter. On the far side a metal ladder rose about ten feet from the floor, ending in what looked from Franklin's angle like a wooden trapdoor. He played the beam over the inside of the steel door and breathed a huge sigh of relief when he spotted two large bolts, one at the foot of the door, the other near the top.

His pulse rate was already racing, but he thought his heart might burst as the next crash from the platform was accompanied by the squealing of metal. One more hit and he and Dot would no longer be alone.

He knelt beside her and tried to rouse her once more, his hands trembling, but there was no response. Sweat had started to poor down his forehead and as he reached his arms underneath her, one hand encumbered by the flashlight, three drops ran into his left eye. He blinked rapidly in an effort to clear it and then heaved himself to his feet.

Another, final, crash echoed along the platform. A split second later came the unmistakable sound of a steel door hitting a concrete wall. Without waiting to regain his balance, Franklin stumbled forward, his right foot catching the door-well. The flashlight slithered out of his sweaty palm, bouncing behind him, in the direction of rushing footsteps. He knew straight away that he had no chance to retrieve it and plunged into the darkness beyond the exit.

He half-dropped, half-laid Dot on the floor and grabbed the door, hauling it closed just as he caught a glimpse of a tall figure turning into the arched exit from the platform. The door clanged shut and Franklin flailed around in search of the bolts, small keening noise escaping his panicked throat. He had no sooner slid the first home before a tremendous thud issued from the other side of the exit.

Once the second had been located and secured he felt a little safer. This door, unlike the others, opened inwards and was therefore much harder to break through. It also seemed much thicker than the others, and although he could hear voices on the other side, he couldn't make out the words that were being exchanged.

Franklin knelt carefully and felt his way around until he located Dot's inert form. Trying not to let the panic get the better of him, his heart pounding thunderously in his ears, he first checked to make sure she was still breathing. Laying his hand on her chest he could feel the gentle rise and fall of normal respiration and breathed a sigh of relief. Next he started to go through the pockets of her jacket before grunting in satisfaction and pulling a small torch from one of them.

He clicked it on and quickly scanned the access shaft, praying that there would be some other way out.

"Shit!" The iron ladder was his only option. And that was only if the trapdoor at the top wasn't locked. *There again*, he thought, *it looked pretty flimsy*. Even if it was locked, he might be able to break through it. Then, of course, all he had to worry about was the dead weight of the unconscious Dot

There was a muffled thud from the door behind him and he shot to his feet, determined to keep his rising sense of panic under control. "Think, you stupid black bastard!' His breathing was ragged and his mind racing. He gave a nod and then stepped to the foot of the ladder. Wedging the torch into his breast pocket, he ascended the steps as quickly as he could and reached up to the trapdoor. A quick scan of the wooden square showed that there were no bolts or locks – at least, on this side of it. Also, there was no sign of hinges. A couple of deep breaths, and he gave a firm push. No movement. He repeated the exercise on the opposite side of the door with the same result. Panic rising in him one more, he moved on to the third side.

At first he thought he must have imagined it, but another, firmer shove lifted the hatch a fraction. Franklin pushed again, much harder this time, and it lifted a centimetre or so before dropping back into place. It might well have been wood on Franklin's side, but unless it was several feet thick, the top side must be covered in metal or concrete.

There was another series of muffled thuds from the door below and Franklin redoubled his efforts, moving up another rung to increase his purchase. He placed his shoulder against the hatch, his ear collecting half a dozen splinters as he did so, and with a desperate cry, surged upwards.

The trap moved slowly at first and then just as he was beginning to think that he wasn't going to succeed, it gained momentum, finally snapping sideways with a tremendous crash.

Gasping for breath, he wedged himself in the hatchway and pulled Dot's torch from his pocket. Casting its narrow beam around, he could make out that he was in some sort of chamber which appeared to branch of a large circular tunnel a few feet in front of him. The ceiling was no more than four feet from his head, its walls running with damp. A dark, musty odour assailed his nostrils, and this coupled with the panic started to make him feel nauseous. He gagged a couple of times, before swallowing hard.

Resuming his scan, he saw a number of crates and a couple of ladders stacked against the wall to his right. "Some sort of storeroom, then," he muttered, an idea forming in his head.

More muffled thuds from below made him wince, and he quickly dropped back down the ladder, praying that Dot had started to come round. A quick check with the torch and then by hand soon made it clear that she was still out for the count.

"You could've picked a better time, you know?" he said.

He desperately patted her cheeks once more, muttering a mixture of prayers and curses under his breath. No response, not so much as the flicker of an eyelid. So hard was he concentrating on bringing her round, that at first he didn't notice the rhythmic pounding that had set up behind him. When it finally permeated his conscience, he stood quickly, eyes wide, and crossed to the door. Pressing his hands to its cold surface he soon realised what was happening on the other side. Clearly, unable to batter their way through, their pursuers had changed tactics and were somehow trying to remove the door's hinges. Franklin had no idea how long that could take, but at least it served to make up his mind about his next move. He turned and looked down at Dot, then slowly up to the hatchway.

"You'd better pray I don't drop you little lady."

With a sigh, he knelt and slid his hands under her body.

*****

"I'm sorry, Brigadier," the receptionist said, "but I'm afraid there's no mention of an appointment for you with Sir Desmond. Are you absolutely certain that's who you are here to see? Only you didn't seem to be too sure yourself when you arrived."

"Oh, I'm absolutely certain," Bill – alias Brigadier William Forbes-Rice – said, "It was arranged ages ago, my dear. It's a standard security procedure, you see? Naturally, I cannot divulge the exact nature of my business here as I'm sure you understand. However, I must emphasise once again that this is an extremely important and urgent affair."

"Well…"

"Why don't you phone through to Sir Desmond? I'm sure he'll be able to make time for me once he knows who I am."

"I guess it can't hurt any," the receptionist shrugged. The military gent had been at her desk for ten minutes now, and she was already late for her lunchtime rendezvous with the dishy Trevor from Accounts. She picked up her telephone and punched in Sir Desmond's number.

Bill stood back contentedly. He felt that he really was getting rather good at this sort of thing.

Three times the secretary confirmed that the Brigadier was with Military Intelligence before replacing the receiver, a scowl on her face. She looked up at Bill and changed the scowl to a fixed smile, "Sir Desmond wished me to tell you that he is a very busy man, that this is most irregular and that you'd better be... I think the term he used was 'bloody quick about it'. He'll see you in his office on the tenth floor in five minutes."

"Splendid!" Bill said, "You have been most kind and helpful, dear lady. Once last thing?"

The secretary suppressed a groan, "Which is?"

"The number of Sir Desmond's office?"

"Brigadier, there *is* only one office on the tenth floor."

"Important man, our Sir Desmond."

"That's one way of describing him," she muttered, "Well, if that's all, I'm late for a lunch appointment..."

"I shan't detain you for another moment. Run along to your young man."

The receptionist stared at Bill in shock, "How did you know...?"

"They don't call us Military Intelligence for nothing, dear lady. Cheerio." In point of fact, Bill had noticed a slight blush form on the young woman's cheeks when she'd mentioned her lunch date. He was nothing if not observant.

She watched his retreating back and prayed fervently that the Military Intelligence guys were as discreet as they were good at finding out about relationships. If her Norman ever got to hear about Trevor, there'd be hell to pay.

It was half past twelve when Bill alighted from the lift to find himself in one of the plushest offices he'd ever seen. A rich, deep-red carpet stretched away from his feet in all directions, the walls were papered in red and gold flock and hung with suspiciously genuine looking oils and watercolours. The one that seemed to have pride of place was of rolling glens with what looked like Balmoral Castle in the background. Matching leather sofas were placed either side of a low table in the centre of the room.

All of this faded into insignificance, though, when the visitor set eyes on the massive desk on the far side of the room. At least twenty feet long and ten deep, its brilliantly polished surface mirrored the two large windows that framed the room's only occupant.

Seated in a leather wing-back chair was Sir Desmond Fairfax, his leonine mane of grey hair framing a handsome face full of sharp lines. He was currently barking order into his telephone and waved Bill towards one of the sofas.

Five minutes later, he cradled the receiver and strode around the end of his desk, his hand already outstretched. Bill stood and shook it.

"Sir Desmond, I'm Brigadier William Forbes-Rice. So very good to make your acquaintance, and so very kind of you to spare me a few minutes of your undoubtedly valuable time."

To Bill's surprise, Sir Desmond gave him a welcoming smile, "Always pleased to see that you boys are looking after our interests. Drink? I have a fine selection of single malts that I can thoroughly recommend."

"That would be most acceptable."

Sir Desmond strode over to a vast cocktail cabinet, "Any preferences?"

"Nothing too peaty, maybe an Islay if you have one?"

"An excellent choice, Brigadier." He returned with two brimming tumblers one of which he set onto the low table in front of Bill. He took a long sip of his own and raised his glass at Bill, "Cheers."

Bill copied him and then set the glass back on the table, "Most pleasant, Sir Desmond. Now, we'd better get down to business. As I've already said, I'm aware that you're a very busy man."

Sir Desmond gave a snort, "Would that it were so, Brigadier. Things are dreadfully quiet at this time of year, you see, and I'm a great believer in delegation."

"I rather got the impression from your receptionist–"

"Ah! The redoubtable Susan. Better than a couple of Rottweilers, that one. I was surprised when you managed to get past her."

"She seemed most charming."

Sir Desmond raised an eyebrow, "I do so hope that your judgement in matters of a security nature are a little more accurate." His blue eyes twinkled with amusement.

Bill laughed, "Fortunately I'm more involved with information gathering, these days."

"I got the impression from Susan that this was a security issue?"

"I would probably describe it as being more in the realms of after-sales service," Bill said.

"From that I would surmise that you wish to discuss the Bannen affair?"

"Very perspicacious, Sir Desmond. As part of our normal routine when it comes to such matters, we revisit those involved after a couple of years have elapsed. The memory is a very strange beast – sometimes things come to light thanks to – rather than despite – the passage of time."

"I rather think, Brigadier, that every ounce of my knowledge of the affair was drained from me at the time. However, feel free to ask me what you will. If nothing else it means that I've had to cancel my lunch with the Minister. Crashing bore that he is."

Bill took another sip of whisky before he began. He set the glass back on the table and pulled Bannen's information sheet from his pocket, "You are absolutely certain that this is the man that attempted to abduct you?"

Sir Desmond grimaced, "That's the bugger all right. Marched right in here, bold as brass, pulled a gun on me. Not the most pleasant of experiences, although I'm sure you already know that in your line of work."

"Unfortunately so," Bill said, "Did he speak to you at all? Give any indication as to his motive?"

"Not as such."

"As such?"

"As far as I can recall – you can check this with the records at the time – what he actually said was 'You're coming with me. There's someone who would like a little word'. That was the general gist of it, anyhow."

"No names?"

"It wasn't until a few hours after his arrest that I learned of Bannen's name."

Bill nodded thoughtfully, "Do you have any idea who might have wanted that 'little word' with you?"

"I've spent the last two years racking my brains over that," Sir Desmond said, "And I've only ever come up blank. As far as I can see, the only plausible explanation is that I upset some businessman or some such

– maybe made a planning decision that frustrated them. All the same it does seem a rather extreme way of trying to get to talk to me."

"Had you made any controversial decisions around that time?"

"Nothing out of the ordinary. I think you'll find that there's always someone who believes decisions like that are controversial, but I can't even recall of a case that was particularly hotly disputed. On top of that, Brigadier, there are not that many people out there that even know of the involvement of the Civil Service in such matters. Less still who would know of my involvement."

"I must say that it came as something of a surprise to me," Bill said. He was getting the impression that he might have stumbled onto a link. "I don't suppose it would be possible for you to locate the files concerning planning cases in the few months prior to the abduction."

"Nothing could be simpler." Sir Desmond set his glass beside Bill's and crossed to a bookshelf beside his desk. He pressed a switch on the wall and the shelving slid almost silently aside, revealing a small, utilitarian office beyond. "Come on through, Brigadier."

Bill rose and followed Sir Desmond into the small room. "The papers you want are in this cabinet here. Everything is filed in date order, so you should find what you want pretty quickly. As I recall, there were only four or five cases in the six months prior to the Bannen thing."

Fifteen minutes later Bill had a list of the four companies who had failed in planning applications considered by Sir Desmond. Along with the company names, he had also listed the directors of the companies involved.

"Did the police check these out at the time?" He asked when they were sitting back on the sofa.

"You'll have to ask them yourselves, I'm afraid. Immediately after the incident I was taken into hospital for observation. By the time I was allowed out, Bannen had been released and nobody was saying a word about what had happened."

"That must have been terribly distressing for you, dear boy. I do hope I haven't added to your discomfort today?"

"Not at all, Brigadier. Is there anything else I can help you with?"

"No, I think that's everything. Obviously, should anything further materialise from my investigation, I would be grateful if I might possibly be able to contact you once more?"

Sir Desmond handed Bill a card, "My hotline is the one at the bottom," he said, "You can normally get me on that one any time between ten and three. Feel free to call if you need any more information. One thing I would like to ask, though?"

"Fire away."

"If you ever *do* find out what was going on back then, would you be so kind as to let me know?"

"Rest assured," Bill said, "Now I'd better get on my way. Things to do, and all that. Thank you once more for your time, Sir Desmond."

"My pleasure." He escorted Bill to the lift, "Good luck, Brigadier."

*****

McCoy and Green made their way straight back to the office after leaving New Scotland Yard, both of them wrapped in a thoughtful silence. Green finally broke it as they approached the building, "Do you really think there's some sort of cover-up going on here, guv?"

"No doubts, Green. I mean, look at all this guff about Fairfax."

"Covering up one failed abduction is a bit different to covering up seventeen murders, though."

"Maybe eighteen if Taylor's missing person turns up toes up. But it wasn't just a failed abduction back then – Bannen's previous was also swept under the carpet. What bothers me most is government involvement. As soon as the Home Office start sniffing around you might as well drop the case there and then."

"There's been no sign of them getting involved in this one."

"It's only a matter of time, Green. Cox was telling me this morning that our beloved Home Secretary is already suggesting that he'd be happy to hear of some positive progress in this case. But, no, what's bothering me most is that no-one seems to know anything, anywhere, anyhow. Given the number of people we've spoken to so far, that just not normal."

Their car pulled up outside the office.

148

"You wait here, Green. I'm just going to pop in and see if Sunny's got anywhere chasing up those wills."

"Fair enough, guv."

Green was already half asleep by the time McCoy came back ten minutes later.

"Anything so far?" he yawned.

"Only two. You know what it's like – lawyers and valuable information, blood and stones."

"Tell me about it. Any similarities between the first two."

"Only in so far as both wills named two beneficiaries who turn out to be 'charitable institutions'. Not the same ones, unfortunately."

"Bit of a coincidence, though, guv?"

McCoy shrugged, "Hardly. Remember, none of these victims had much in the way of close family. I've got Sunny checking out these charities just in case there are any links between them. Let's just hope he can get hold of details of some of the other wills."

"Rather him than me. Where to now, guv?"

"I rather think it might be useful to have a word with Sir Desmond Fairfax. Jacobs never has been the brightest copper – there might be something him and his team overlooked in their investigation back then."

"You want me to come with you, or should I get back to a bit of door knocking?"

"For one thing, Green, I reckon we've pretty much run out of doors to knock on, and for another, if I've got to put up with half an hour in the company of one of these Whitehall bigwigs, I want to spread the pain around a bit. You're staying with me."

The one-mile trip from the City to Westminster took the customary twenty minutes and McCoy was quietly fuming by the time they arrived outside the Ministry building. His mood worsened appreciably when he spotted DC Bradford standing outside it.

"Bradford? What the fuck are you doing loitering around here?"

"Er, I'm supposed to be tailing that Taylor guy."

"Supposed to be?"

"Well, you see, sir. I followed him to the British Museum and then to the pub opposite. He was in there for about half an hour and then left and hailed a cab. I got close enough to hear that he wanted to come here and then spent ten minutes trying to get a cab myself."

"Why didn't you radio through and have someone pick up the tail at this end."

"My, er, that is…"

"Out with it, Bradford!"

"My phone's battery seems to have gone flat."

"God give me strength!" McCoy screwed his eyes tightly shut, "Okay," he went on, "What happened then?"

"Well, I thought that even ten minutes wasn't too long for me to be able to pick up his trail if he was going to be in there talking to someone. Anyway, I got over here as fast as I could, but I think Taylor must have changed his mind on the way."

"And what would make you think that, Bradford?"

"Well, because nobody of that name has been in there today. Someone who vaguely fitted his description had been in there, but it turns out this guy was some Brigadier with Military Intelligence."

"And it didn't occur to your pea-fucking-sized brain that maybe our friend Mr. William bloody Taylor wouldn't use his own name? That Taylor might not, quite fucking reasonably, think that a senior Civil Servant wouldn't see a mere civilian?"

"I did think that… A bit later. That's why I came back here."

"Came back?"

"I…"

"Yes, Bradford?"

The detective constable seemed to shrink under McCoy's glare, "I had a beer in the pub earlier and, well, it was getting a bit uncomfortable. I had to, er, relieve myself, sir."

"Right now, Bradford, I wish I had to. Because I'd do it all over you. How long ago was all this?"

Bradford checked his watch, "About thirty minutes, sir."

"Shit! You are a brain-dead little dick, Bradford. If we weren't so short of manpower I'd have you back in uniform before you could blink."

"Sorry, sir. But it's the first time I've ever had to tail someone, and I was a bit nervous."

Behind the three police detectives, Bill Taylor who had been eavesdropping, sidled round the corner of the building before scurrying away towards St. James's Park.

*****

Accompanied by the persistent hammering at the exit door's hinges, Franklin's first attempt at hauling Dot's limp form up the steel ladder had ended when she had nearly slithered out from under his arm. Gasping for breath, fighting the urge to panic, he returned to the floor of the shaft and tried desperately to figure out how he could get her through the trapdoor ten feet above him.

Finally, after what seemed an eternity but was in reality only a minute, an idea struck him. He slipped the leather belt from the loops of his black jeans and took a handkerchief from his pocket. As gently, but firmly, as he could, he removed her jacket and lifted Dot's arms over her head. Finally, using the handkerchief as a cushion, he bound her wrists together with the belt.

Panting heavily, he lifted her to her feet and then took her weight by the belt binding her wrist. In the dim light from her torch, Franklin could see the edges of the wide belt digging deeply into the flesh of her wrist, but at least the binding hadn't slipped. He set her carefully back on the floor to give himself time to get his breath back before the next attempt.

A screech of tortured metal indicated that one of the door's hinges was being torn free, galvanising Franklin into action. He slipped off his jacket, picked up Dot's and dashed up the ladder, hurling them into the chamber above. Not bothering with the rungs, he slid back down to the floor and quickly rolled Dot onto her side, her arms still stretched out above her head.

The rhythmic hammering at the door had resumed, the second hinge now under assault.

Franklin said a silent prayer and stretched out on the floor, his back to Dot's front. Awkwardly, he reached behind his head and grasped one of her arms. Frantic now, it took him three feverish attempts before he finally managed to pull her arms over his head, one each side. Grabbing

151

tightly onto her thigh which was resting against his butt, he took a deep breath and rolled onto his front. Dot, secured as she was, flopped onto his back.

As slowly as he dared, desperate not to let her slide off him, Franklin struggled to get his hands and knees underneath him. As the sweat poured into his eyes, he finally steadied himself on all fours, and gently guided her body lower down his back until her bound wrists were resting under his chin. It wasn't exactly a piggy-back ride, but at least there was no chance of her slipping away from him.

He took four deep breaths and, using the second rung of the ladder for support, forced himself to his feet. Dot's full weight was suddenly suspended from Franklin's throat, and for a couple of seconds, he thought that his windpipe was about to be crushed. With another gigantic effort he managed to lift her slightly until he could put his chin under her hands. By tilting his head back slightly, her weight was now suspended on his lower jaw, his neck taking much of the strain.

He wasn't at all sure that he could bear it for more than a minute at most and grabbed hold of the rungs once more. Breathing deeply, he raised his right foot onto the bottom rung and hauled hard until his left could join it. Dot's body swayed against his back, threatening to spin him round – to topple them both off onto the floor below. If that happened and he landed on top of her slight form, he was pretty certain that the impact would kill her. And that was just from this height.

He took a few more deep breaths and then went through the same routine again, taking them up to the second rung. As he recovered there, he looked up, the torch beam illuminating the five remaining rungs. "I'll never make it,' he gasped.

The hammering from the door seemed to be increasing in frequency and its echoes spurred Franklin on once more.

By the time he'd reached the fifth rung, his head now just centimetres from the empty hatchway above, muscles in every part of his body were quivering. His neck was the worst, a constant tremor running from his skull to his coccyx, and he felt sure that it was about to snap.

Slowly, he raised his right foot once more. Their height now made it necessary for him to find a purchase for his hands inside the room above, and he gingerly lifted his right hand through the hatchway. The sides of the trap itself appeared to be about five centimetres deep – which at least explained its tremendous weight – and they were also very rough – concrete by the feel of it. He took as firm a grip as he could manage and then lifted his left hand, using the slightly damp-feeling floor as a brace.

He held his breath and lifted his left foot. As he did so, Dot began to swing slowly sideways. Franklin could feel his right foot begin to rotate, and in desperation he hooked his left foot around the side of the ladder. As Dot at first swung out wider, he began to think that his head would simply tear off. After what seemed like an eternity her swing slowed and reversed, bringing her back in line with his own body.

Satisfied that she was in the best position, he gingerly edged his left foot around the edge of the ladder and on to the safety of the sixth rung. Muttering under his rasping breath, he prepared himself for the last push.

Without warning, Dot's weight plunged downwards a few centimetres as her wrists slipped down Franklin's sweat soaked jaw. The impact on his neck was excruciating, and for a second he felt his hands begin to slide off their meagre purchase in the chamber. Pain was also flaring along his chin where the buckle of the belt had torn through the skin.

With a desperate roar he raised his right foot, every muscle straining. Without pausing for thought, he braced his hands and surged upwards.

There was another moment of pure panic as some part of Dot scraped heavily against the edge of the hatchway, threatening to halt his momentum, before he hurled his body out into the chamber.

Pain was flaring all over his body and it was all he could do to extricate himself from Dot's accidental death-grip. Fearing that if he lay down, he'd never have the energy to get up again, he forced himself to his knees. Somehow, he had to close the trap – the door below couldn't possibly hold out much longer.

A bright splinter of pain shot through his right shoulder as he pulled the torch from his pocket causing him to gasp aloud. When it had subsided, he gently moved Dot's still inert form away from the trap and turned his attention to the trapdoor itself.

It was at least five centimetres thick, concrete except for a thin veneer of wood that was visible from underneath when it was closed. He cast his hands along its edges, seeking a handle or a handhold of some sort. There was nothing other than the recessed hinges along one side. Clearly, when it was shut, it would be almost impossible to see from above. No matter how hard he tried he couldn't get a purchase on the solid block.

He shone the torch around the small chamber. Apart from the crates and ladders he had seen earlier, there was a rack of tools at the tunnel's furthest end. Surely, he reasoned there'd be some sort of implement among them that he could use?

Franklin rose to his feet in a crouch and stepped shakily across to the tool-rack. After a few moments' indecision, he selected two straight bladed screwdrivers and a long crowbar.

"Perfect," he muttered, still gasping for breath.

He had just knelt down at the hatchway when there was another screeching of metal. Heart thundering in his chest, Franklin began working the first of the screwdrivers under the edge of the hatch cover. To the background of furious hammering below him, he finally worked the first one home and inserted the second in the tiny gap he'd created. He wormed it along as far apart from the first as he could manage and reached for the crowbar.

The steel door below crashed to the floor, the thunderous boom an almost physical force in the tiny chamber. When the echoes had died away, Franklin could finally make out the voices below.

"Mr. Richardson?" A dark, rich male voice floated up to him, "You'll not get away from us, you know? We view trespass as a very serious offence down here."

Franklin cautiously peered over the edge of the hatch.

Two men were standing just inside the doorway, their faces visible in the light supplied by several torches held by other figures. There was no mistaking the taller man. Marcus Allen smiled up at Franklin.

*****

From St. James's Park, Bill walked past Trafalgar Square and along the Strand, before cutting through Southampton Street and into Covent Garden. It was rapidly approaching two o'clock and he was beginning to

154

fret once more about Franklin and Dot's welfare. The former market was bustling with the normal crowds of tourists, their numbers bolstered by early Christmas shoppers and office workers making an early start to the weekend's festivities. Even Oxford Street on Christmas Eve would seem quiet by comparison, so Bill kept one hand firmly wrapped around his mobile phone, set to both ring and vibrate if anyone called.

The fact that McCoy had apparently set a tail on him was no more than a minor inconvenience, and were circumstances a little less fraught, might even have provided a few hours of light-hearted diversion. Right now, though, he was more concerned with what he had learned in Fairfax's hidden office.

According to Franklin's description of the files that Alexandra Featherington had showed him, there was an ongoing conflict between two factions over the control of property below the capital's streets. A conflict which could result in widespread suffering above ground, and which was tied in closely to the bizarre events that had occurred the previous Monday.

According to McCoy, their prime target was the elusive Benjamin Bannen, who had, just two years previously, been a central figure in the attempted abduction of a senior figure in the Civil Service whose main responsibility was wrapped up in planning applications.

Bill slumped onto a bench outside the Transport Museum and studiously went through the motions of lighting a cigar. When it was finally belching an acrid blue cloud into the unseasonably warm afternoon air he pulled the mobile phone from his pocket and placed it on his lap, his mind alive with the possibilities of this investigation.

If he worked on the assumption that the Featherington woman was at least telling part of the truth and that McCoy had been accurate in targeting Bannen, then there was only one possible factor that provided a possible link. Property.

It made some sort of sense given Franklin's report on Charno's files and the involvement of Bannen. Property – or more precisely, how property was utilised in London – was a major concern for many disparate parties. Parties as diverse as small traders' organisations to the government itself. Again, there was a link.

Bill patted the notes inside his breast pocket and willed Franklin to phone him soon. Right at that moment, he wanted more than anything to be able to get along to the Public Records Office and start digging up information on the four companies who had failed in their attempts to get planning permissions past the eagle eyes of Sir Desmond Fairfax.

And, of course, he wanted to know that the youngsters were safe and sound.

*****

"Marcus Allen, I presume," Franklin tried to sound a lot more cocky than he suddenly felt.

"I thought you might recognise me, given the... *acquaintance* that you have so recently made. And, yes, you are quite correct, I am he."

"You know about—"

"Alexandra? But of course."

"Then you'll know we're not trespassing. Just carrying out a little investigative work."

Allen issued a throaty chuckle, "You know nothing of the rules down here. Putting it simply, what I say goes. More so than ever after the... unfortunate business earlier this week. Now, be a good boy and climb back down. My associates will take care of Miss Kominski."

Franklin felt a strange tingling sensation along his bruised and battered spine. For a split second he almost obeyed the man's suggestion. A soft groan from his left, where Dot lay, seemed to clear his mind in an instant.

"No way, man! There's some weird shit going on down here, and there ain't *any* way I want to get tangled up with you!"

"Oh, really!" Allen gave a disparaging sigh, "I'm not sure what you might have heard, Mr. Richardson, but you are in serious trouble as it is. I strongly suggest that you co-operate with me. Maybe if you proved willing to answer a few small questions, we might be able to sort this matter out to our mutual satisfaction. How does that sound?"

"Dodgy. I'm here on legit business. As far as I know, there's no trespass involved and if you want to take matters further, I'm sure as shit

156

happy to go get some back-up from the law. You got that?" Despite his bravado it felt as if ice water was starting to run through his veins.

"How very bold," Allen said, "But really, young man, just a few questions and you have my word as a true, old-school gentleman that I'll let you off. This once, at least."

"I ain't answering no questions you ask me, man," Franklin said, trying desperately to keep an insistent quaver out of his voice.

"Did I say it would be me asking the questions?" Allen laughed, a mane of long grey hair billowing around his face, "No, young man, things are a little different on our side of the fence. Allow me to introduce you to my assistant, Nadia Melford. I always allow her the privilege of carrying out... investigations of this nature."

The shorter man beside Allen stepped aside and a tall woman who appeared to be draped in a long, black cloak stepped through the empty doorway. At a nod from Allen the torches were trained on the newcomer. Long, dark hair framed an angular face. She smiled at the open hatch.

"Your female Torquemada?" Franklin said.

Before Allen could respond, the young woman took a small step forward, "Not in the least, Mr. Richardson. I am no one's slave or mouthpiece, no mindless fool brainwashed by higher powers," Her eyes flickered towards Allen, "And I am not given to cruelty. I simply ask questions. Reward me with answers, and I reward you with more delight than you could ever imagine." With that, she flung her arms backwards, the robe falling open. Underneath she was naked, her body lithe and slender. "Pleasure is so much more enticing than punishment, don't you think?"

"I..." Franklin found it hard to tear his gaze away from her nakedness, the perfection of her form. His mind whirled, and he felt himself being drawn into the opening of the shaft.

A thought, unbidden and absurd, crashed through his brain. He repeated it aloud, adrenaline-fuelled laughter bubbling in his throat, "What is it about women flashing their tits at me this week?" He shook his head and snorted, "Fuck you!"

Below him, Nadia Melford screeched an imprecation and flung herself out of the shaft. Marcus Allen threw back his head. "Get him!"

In the couple of seconds it took Franklin to get moving he saw the beams of light below spinning crazily as the unseen torch bearers turned to face the steel ladder. In that brief, hectic display, he could see that they were all young females – all sizes, all colours, all creeds – but all dressed in identical robes to the one that Allen's Inquisitor had been wearing.

"Shit, man," he muttered, hefting the crowbar, "Why couldn't they be on my side for a change?"

The rungs of the ladder creaked ominously as the first of the women began to scramble up to the tiny chamber, and Franklin, ignoring the screams of pain from his abused body, shoved the end of the steel crowbar between the two screwdrivers. He raised himself as high as the cramped ceiling would allow and put all of his weight behind his makeshift lever.

The slab of concrete slowly began to rise and with a desperate lunge he grabbed its leading edge, pulling with all the fading might at his disposal. As it reached a vertical position, just at the point where he could let it go – allow gravity to finish the job – a hand grabbed at his ankle.

He squealed, a high-pitched, girlish sound, and kicked out with his other foot. It connected with something soft, and he felt, rather than heard, a sickening crunch reverberate through his leg. His ankle was released.

The concrete slab slammed into place, the diabolical boom of its closing echoing painfully off the walls of the cramped chamber. Close to whimpering, close to tears, Franklin dropped the crowbar and collapsed onto his knees.

He prayed that the adrenaline rush which had kept him going so far wouldn't fail him now and pulled himself towards the largest of the crates that lined one wall of the chamber. The floor was slimy under his hands and knees, the stench of the place threatening to empty his stomach at any second, but he pulled himself onwards until he could reach behind the wooden box.

With a grunt and a smothered cry of pain, he hauled backwards, almost sobbing in relief as the heavy crate moved a few centimetres. Without a thought for any injuries he might already have suffered, he squeezed himself into the narrow space between the crate and the wall and braced himself against the cold, damp surface of the stone.

By flexing his shoulders, he shifted the crate a few more centimetres. Twisting himself around so that his back was to the wall, he brought his legs up in front of his chest and pushed away.

The crate moved with surprising **ease** across the slick floor, and he maintained the pressure until it was immediately above the hatchway. Gasping for breath, he rolled onto his side and then dragged himself across to the second of the crates. He somehow managed to manhandle it alongside the first one, which was beginning to lift slightly as efforts from below were made to force open the hatchway, and with what he truly imagined to be the last of his strength, he heaved it upwards, sliding it onto the top just as his thighs felt as if they were about to explode.

He collapsed onto his butt, staring up at his efforts. The top of the second crate was less than four centimetres from the ceiling of the chamber. Grinning – a rictus of pain and joy – he scrambled back to the far wall and picked up one of the stepladders. With a final grunt, he wedged it between the top of the second crate and the ceiling.

"Get through that, you mothers!" he yelled.

The adrenaline-fuelled turbo-boost of energy that had sustained him so far seemed to drain from his body and he rolled onto his side next to Dot. He allowed himself a couple of minutes recovery time before another soft groan came from her limp form.

"Dot?" Franklin said, "Are you back with me?" There was no reply. He struggled onto his hands and knees and crawled closer to her head. Reaching forward, he gently pulled her hands towards him. The knot in his belt had tightened considerably during their ascent and this, coupled with the trembling of his fingers, made the job of freeing Dot's hands all the more difficult. After a couple of fruitless attempts, Franklin took the torch from his pocket and put the end of it in his mouth so that he could focus the beam directly on the belt.

He winced as he saw the deep gouges on the back of her wrists, her lower arms streaked with blood. At the fourth attempt, he managed to slacken the leather strap sufficiently to free her right hand. The left slipped out on its own, slapping to the floor at her side.

Dot gave another groan and he moved the torch beam up to her face. "Shit," Franklin hissed. He suddenly remembered the moment during his final surge out of the hatch when he felt Dot scrape against the side of the opening. Quite clearly it had been the right-hand side of her head that had come into contact with the rough concrete. A series of raw looking scratches run from her forehead, through her right temple and down her cheek. Blood was oozing steadily from the deepest of these and had turned her ear and much of her neck a dark crimson.

Franklin picked up the tangled belt and pulled out the handkerchief he'd unsuccessfully used as protection. With as much care as he could, he gently wiped the worst of the blood from her ravaged face and took a closer look at the wounds. With the exception of the deepest, the gouges seemed to have already stopped bleeding. Whispering to her all the while, he cleaned as much of the blood off her face as he could, and then moved onto her wrists and hands.   He'd just about finished when Dot gave a small whimper.

"Dot? Little lady?"

"Fr... Franklin?"

He scooted up to her head and leant over her, "Pretty hard to see when it's this dark, but, yeah, it's me."

"What... what happened?"

Relief coursing through him, Franklin laughed, "I thought people only said that in films and books."

Dot tried to sit upright but yelped and then laid back down, "It hurts!"

"Just rest easy for a couple of minutes, okay?" Franklin said, "You remember anything about being down on the station?"

"I... remember feeling... bad. Sort of... depressed, almost," Dot paused for a second, "And I remember we were being chased!" She looked around frantically, "Did they catch us? Are we locked up somewhere?"

Franklin shushed her, holding her down before she could do herself any more injury, "We got out," he said, "There was a shaft at the end of the station with a trapdoor at the top. We're right next to it. But don't worry, no-one's gonna get through there now." He shone the torch beam over the two wedged crates, "It's right underneath that lot."

"Could you help me up?"

160

"Sure you're up to it?"

"It's gotta be better than laying here. This floor's all wet and cold."

Slowly he manoeuvred her into a sitting position and then rolled up the two jackets into a makeshift pillow, wedging them behind her back, "How's that?"

"Better," Dot nodded, then winced, "My head hurts. Guess I knocked it when I passed out." She started to raise a hand to her face, but Franklin stopped her.

"I'm really sorry, Dot, but that's my fault," he shone the torch beam onto her wrists, "That as well. I just couldn't think of any other way of getting you out."

She grimaced at the sight of her wounded hands before a puzzled expression took over, "Come to that, just how *did* you get us out?"

By the time Franklin had finished telling her, Dot's jaw had dropped open, "You're a pretty big guy," she shook her head, "but you must be a bleedin' sight stronger than you look. Why didn't you just leave me down there?"

"Don't be daft. There was no way *that* was gonna happen. Funny you should say that, though, 'cos you said something pretty much like it just before you passed out."

"What?"

"Something like, you thought you'd just stay where you were."

Carefully, Dot nodded her head, "I think I can remember saying something like that. It was really weird. I was feeling as if nothing mattered any more... and it was getting worse the longer we was down there."

"What about now?"

Dot paused before answering, running through a mental checklist, "There's still a bit of it, but it's sorta fading away."

"Now that's something I really am glad to hear."

"Me and all. What about you though?"

Franklin shrugged, "Nothing like that. A bit of claustrophobia, but I guess that's pretty normal."

"And those Allenites didn't get close enough to hurt you at all? Like, when you were closing the hatch?"

161

He grimaced and gingerly touched his jaw, "I managed that on my own."

Before he could react, Dot took the torch out of his hand and shone it up at his face. She let out a long, low whistle, "You silly sod!"

"There's gratitude."

"I can't believe you went through all that just to get me out."

"I told you: there's no way I was gonna leave you with that lot."

"I really owe you, big guy."

Franklin shook his head, "Just protecting each other's backs."

Dot handed him back the torch, "I'll be glad to get out of here, I can tell…" She broke off, a look of alarm spreading over her features.

"What is it?"

"Where are we?"

"Just off one of the interceptory sewers, why?"

"Franklin, if Charno's lot have got all these systems mapped, then so will the Allenites!"

"Probably, yeah. So?"

"*So*, they'll know where we are and more to the bleedin' point they're bound to know how to get here by another route! We've gotta get moving."

"Shit, you're right. Reckon you're up to it?"

Dot rolled onto her side and then onto her hands and knees, "I'll have to be."

Franklin nodded, "Crawl out to the main tunnel then. I'll follow with the jackets."

Muscles already stiffening, he shuffled after Dot holding the torch over his head to light her way. The floor of the chamber was a couple of feet up the wall of the broad, oval-shaped tunnel, and they both slid carefully over the edge. A narrow channel of brackish-looking water was running along the centre of the sewer leaving them a relatively dry – if slimy – path along either side. Coming from every direction was the sound of running or dripping water.

Franklin let out a groan as he finally stood upright, the sound echoing back from the moss lined tiles of the walls.

"You okay?"

He stood massaging his lower back and then his neck, "Just a bit stiff. I'll be fine once we're moving."

"Which way is out?"

"We're about ten metres below street level, so we'll need to walk along here until we come to a point where there'll be a sort of slope leading upwards. Those carry excess rainwater down here when the main drains at street level start to overflow."

"Thank Christ it's dry today!"

"You're telling me. Anyway, we go up one of those slopes into the drain system and then find a manhole. Simply lift it and climb out."

"You don't think it'll look a bit odd?"

"This is London, remember?"

"True. Okay, then. Which direction?"

"If we go to the right, we'll be heading for Cornhill."

"And that's sort of south-east, right?"

"Right. Why?"

"That's the direction the Allenites will expect us to go."

"Good thinking. Left it is."

"Where does that take us?"

"Away from the Allenites is all I know."

"Sounds perfect," Dot nodded, struggling into her jacket, "Let's go!"

Behind them, in the small dark chamber, a tiny electronic sensor lay in pieces alongside a couple of old train tickets, half a pack of chewing gum, a few coins, and other items from Franklin's coat pocket.

*****

"But Marcus, if we send one group back to Mansion House and the other along the parallel interceptory sewer, one of them will find an access shaft and there would still be time to intercept them."

Allen stared at Nadia Melford, visibly biting back an angry retort before sighing, "It's too much of a risk. We don't know exactly what modifications to the system Charno's made down here and unless we follow the blackamoor's route precisely there is a very real chance that we will fall foul of any traps that our enemy has placed in the system to deter unwanted guests." He let out another sigh, "Not to mention the fact that we don't know exactly which routes are covered by CCTV on this side, a risk too far since I would imagine the monitoring would have been stepped up after our efforts on Monday."

Without warning, he spun on his heel and aimed a punch at the nearest wall, tiles shattering under the force of the blow. Breathing heavily, Allen turned back to face Nadia. He reached out and grasped the collar of her cloak, blood running over the back of his hand as his knuckles tightened. With a vicious yank, he tore the cloak away and stared down at her nakedness.

Nadia Melford smiled.

*****

Bill Taylor would not have recognised the version of Sir Desmond Fairfax that now occupied the luxurious MoE office. There again, the sight of McCoy's face had that effect on a lot of people.

"After the way your boys handled things at the time, I see no reason at all why I should be in any way co-operative with you today, do you?"

McCoy took a deep breath before answering, "For your information, Sir Desmond, it was not 'our boys'. The Metropolitan Police are a completely separate entity from us. And as to why you should be co-operative, I'll give you two reasons. Firstly, Benjamin Bannen appears to have been up to his old tricks again, and there's every possibility that he might decide to clear up some unfinished business. Secondly, not an hour ago, you let an impostor into this very room masquerading as some half-senile Military Intelligence officer. Now, I ask you again, what information did you provide the bogus Brigadier with?"

The mention of Bannen seemed to take the wind out of Sir Desmond's sails. He poured himself another whisky and turned to face McCoy. "Bannen is active, again?"

"At the moment, Sir Desmond, he is the prime suspect in a case involving a multiple murder."

Sir Desmond sighed, "Very well, Inspector. Follow me."

When McCoy arrived back down at the reception desk ten minutes later, he was deep in thought. DS Green, who had been forced to wait downstairs crossed the room quickly when he saw the Inspector emerge from the lifts.

"Get anything, guv?"

"I think I just might have done. Let's get back to the office. We've got some cross-checking to do. Oh, and Green? I want Taylor found and fast. I've got a nasty suspicion that he's already one step ahead of us here, and I don't want the bumbling fool to screw up anything."

"Not Bradford, I take it?"

"Not bloody likely. Get Robson onto it."

"Can't, guv."

"What?"

"He's staking out Franklin Richardson' place. There's been no sign of them yet, by the way."

"Who else have we got available?"

"The only other man we've got left is Fernandez and he's just come off a straight sixteen-hour shift. No joy with the hotels, by the way."

"Fucking marvellous!" McCoy snapped. He closed his eyes and sighed, "Oh, well, bloody Bradford it is then. Where is he?"

"In the car, guv."

"Come on then, let's get this over with."

Green followed McCoy out into the early afternoon sunlight, trying to suppress a smile.

McCoy marched over to the car and rapped loudly on the windscreen. Inside, DC Bradford jerked awake, slopping tepid coffee over his lap.

"Out of there, Bradford!"

The young man emerged from the car rubbing furiously at his sodden groin with a grubby handkerchief, "Sir?"

"Another call of nature, Bradford?"

"No, er, coffee, sir."

"Well stop bloody rubbing at it, man! You look like a sodding baboon."

"Sorry, sir." Bradford crumpled up the handkerchief and shoved it back in the pocket of his jeans.

"Right. I want you back on Taylor's trail."

"Sir?"

"What now?" McCoy sighed.

"You mean me, sir?"

"Well I'm not talking to your sodding coffee stained-dick, am I? Although, come to think of it, I might as well be."

"Right, sir."

"Here's what you do, Bradford. First you get yourself a fully functional mobile phone from the office. Second you revisit all the places that Taylor has been today, with one exception. The exception is here, since he wouldn't dare show his face in the Ministry again. Once you have done that, if you haven't found him, you call through to DC Robson and tell him that he should keep an eye out for Taylor as well as the other pair. After that, you go to Walthamstow and find a pub called the Mucky Duck. Take up position at the bar and keep a look-out for Taylor. It's his usual haunt and he's there at some point every night. When he walks in – the very second he walks in – phone me or Green. If Taylor leaves before we get there, you follow him and keep me and Green informed as to where he goes. Got all that?"

"Yes, sir. Definitely, sir."

"Good. And Bradford?"

"Sir?"

"Fuck this up and I really will have you back in uniform. Understand?"

"Yessir!"

"Okay. Now let's move it."

*****

Alexandra Featherington was wearing a puzzled frown as she gazed at the computer monitor, a small cup of now-cold espresso forgotten by her side. She had been staring intently at the flickering lines and boxes for the past hour, monitoring Franklin Richardson's rapid progress through the tunnels. For the past thirty minutes, though, there had been no movement – neither red nor green lights had replaced any of the white ones.

She was confused. If the Allenite party had caught up with Richardson and Kominski at the disused station near the Bank, then they would have taken them straight back out of the system and headed back towards their own territory. The monitors would have indicated as much. The only explanation she could come up with was that there was some sort of stand-off.

She pulled a file towards her and opened it to the page showing the lay-out of the station. There was no way that he would be able to hold out against an entire Allenite squad in the tiny office block there, and the only other structure was the exit shaft. Since the exit hatch was still closed, he must have holed up in there. According to the plan, there was a steel door at platform level.

She shook her head. "Nice try, Franklin," she sighed, "But I think you'll find that it presents less of an obstacle than you might imagine."

*****

Bill checked his watch for the third time in less than two minutes. It was nearly three o'clock and there had still been no call from his young colleagues. His mobile phone was on the table in front of him, and he checked this, too, to make sure it was in perfect working order. He did this by calling the talking clock.

Half an hour earlier, he had moved from the bench outside the Transport Museum and had climbed up to the terrace bar of The Punch and Judy pub at the end of the market building. A copy of the *Times* lay ignored beside his whisky glass.

"This will never do," he muttered.

A passing member of the bar staff paused to check that the posh-looking gent hadn't consumed one too many whiskies and decided to give him the benefit of the doubt.

Bill checked his watch once more and then got to his feet. He drained the last of the whisky and pushed the newspaper to one side, nodding to himself. Since he knew the proposed route that the two youngsters were planning to take, he had a fair idea where they were likely to emerge. He couldn't just sit around waiting for them to call. Besides, if they had experienced any trouble, they might be glad of his presence when they finally came up.

Satisfied that his plan was sound, he marched back down to street level and made for the Strand. If nothing else, a brisk walk would help him take his mind off things for a few minutes. Back on the table, his discarded copy of The Times was picked up by one of the pub's barmen. Along with Bill's mobile phone.

*****

Progress along the slimy floor of the sewer was proving to be much harder than either Franklin or Dot had imagined. In section, the tunnel was egg-shaped, and the gentle slope under their feet caused them to gravitate towards the filthy, odious water trickling along its centre.

"Just pray it doesn't start pissing down, up there," Franklin muttered as his right trainer plunged into the noisome water for the fifth time.

"I'm right with you on that one." Dot, worried about infecting the cuts on her wrists and hands, was trying not to touch the wall, but without its occasional support, she found herself spending a lot of time ankle deep in the centre of the sewer.

"Thank Christ for that," Franklin breathed a sigh of relief.

She peered under his arm and saw the large gap in the wall a few feet ahead of them. They slipped and slithered forward until they could peer up. A square tunnel, four feet to a side, descended into the main sewer at a sharp angle. Small rivulets were cascading down its slimy-looking surface, and a gentle breeze held hints of diesel fumes.

"Looks like our passport out of here," Franklin said.

"Looks a bit bleedin' steep if you ask me."

"Perhaps if we sort of wedge ourselves in there, we can work our way up?"

Dot grunted, "It's a long way to fall back if we slip. I can't even make out the top of it."

Franklin played the torch beam around the shaft's walls, "It's probably only about seven metres, and with the slope it shouldn't be too bad."

"Well," Dot sighed, "Either way, I ain't staying down here a minute longer than I have to. Let's get going."

"You first," Franklin said, "I don't want to do you any more damage if I lose my grip."

"I guess that makes sense. Here goes then."

Dot placed one foot on the bottom of the ramp and by ducking her head to one side, wedged her shoulder against the ceiling of the shaft. "Yuck! This is slimier than it looks." Gingerly, she placed her other foot inside the shaft and then shuffled forward.

"How's it feel?"

"Cold, wet, slimy, and horrible, but I reckon this might work."

Franklin watched anxiously as she inched her way forwards and upwards, "Take your time, little lady."

Dot's reply was muffled.

When she had managed to ascend a few feet, he followed her into the shaft, copying her method. It soon became clear that he was too tall to make the ascent that way. His head and upper body were forced too far forward by the ceiling, cramping his legs and causing him to overbalance. Along with those simple logistics, the position was excruciating for his sore neck. He let himself slide back to the foot of the shaft.

After a few moments thought, he turned his back to the entrance and sat on the damp floor. Using the heels of his trainers, he manoeuvred himself into the shaft at a forty-five-degree angle and then drew his legs up, bracing them on one wall, with his shoulders braced on the one opposite. Tentatively, he shuffled sideways, moving first one foot, then his shoulders, and then the other foot. To his surprise, the method seemed to work pretty well. He certainly *felt* pretty secure, and he just hoped that his legs wouldn't get cramp before he reached the top.

His progress was also faster than Dot's, and by the time he was what he estimated to be halfway up, he was within a metre of her.

"How you doing?" he panted.

"Okay, I guess," Dot was gasping for breath, "Think I can see the top. About a metre. Shit!" Dot skidded back a few centimetres before regaining control, "I'm not sure I can go on much further."

"Stop where you are," Franklin told her.

"What?"

"You'll see."

A minute later he reached her feet. Turning a little squarer in the shaft, he braced his legs against the opposite wall. "Okay. Here's what you do. Rest your feet against my leg, then drop onto your belly. You should be able to reach the top of the shaft and drag yourself out. If you can't then I can push you up."

"You're mad," Dot groaned.

"Trust me. Remember that – you can always trust me."

"You're right. It's me that must be mad."

Slowly she eased one foot against his hip and then the other against his upper thigh. "Here goes!"

There was a distinct slap as she flopped face down onto the floor of the shaft.

"Can you reach the top?"

"Got it," Dot called back, "And there's some sort of rail."

Her feet lifted off Franklin's side and a few moments and much damp scrabbling later, Dot gave a triumphant shout, "Made it!"

Franklin nodded and resumed his own ascent. By the time he reached the top of the shaft and, with Dot's help, had managed to scramble into the drain, his right leg was beginning to seize up.

"Well done, big guy."

"Well done-in, maybe," he panted, "But there's not much farther now."

Dot was shining the torch along the drain tunnel. It was square with damp-stained brick walls and a concrete ceiling. The floor was wet but mercifully it appeared to be only water and contained only scraps of litter and a few bedraggled leaves. The ceiling was only four feet from the floor, meaning that Franklin would have to crawl. Dot took the lead in a semi-crouch.

"What do I look for?"

"Either daylight or some sort of recess in the ceiling," Franklin said.

They had gone less than five metres when Dot gave a cry of joy, "There's one here!"

Franklin joined her and looked up.

170

Tiny shafts of daylight penetrated the gloom through what appeared to be a circular steel manhole cover. Franklin rose awkwardly and reached up, pressing hard on the steel disk. Then he pushed harder still. "Shit!"

"What's wrong?"

"It won't budge."

"It can't be that heavy, surely? And there can't be anyone parked on it, 'cos we can see daylight."

Franklin slumped back to the floor, "Oh, Christ!"

"You're beginning to worry me. What's wrong?"

"Where are we?"

"Somewhere under a road in the City."

"Quite. And one of the anti-terrorist security measures with the Ring of Steel is?"

Dot's face paled in the darkness, "They secure all the manhole covers to stop terrorists planting bombs down them, don't they?"

"They do. Why didn't that Featherington woman remind me? Christ, she as much as *told* me that this was our way out!"

"What are we gonna do?" Dot's voice edged with desperation, "I don't want to go back down there again!"

Franklin rose to his feet once more, unbuttoned the breast pocket of his shirt and pulled out his mobile phone, "Either we get lucky and Bill hasn't lost his mobile for a change, and we can tell him to get help to us fast, or..."

"Or?"

"Have a scout round for anything vaguely heavy that we can use to bang on the manhole and get ready to start screaming for help."

*****

"What's the time, Green?"

"Three thirty, guv. Why do you ask?"

"Because we're getting absolutely bloody nowhere." McCoy sat back in his chair and sighed, "We need more manpower. There's just too much shit to sort through and it's the sort of job that can be done by anyone with half a brain. Much as I hate to do it, I'm going round to Old Jewry and see if they've got any hands they can spare for a few hours."

"Need company, guv? I could do with a break."

"Why not?" McCoy replied, surprising both of them.

They strolled out of the building and chose to walk to their destination on the grounds that covering two hundred metres was quicker by foot than by car. Cutting through Bow Lane, they stopped off in the *Old Watling* for a quick late lunch, and two pints later resumed their journey.

"What beats me, guv," Green said as they crossed Cheapside, "Is that we've now got five wills and four failed planning applications, and they all mention charitable institutions. And yet–"

"And yet, there seems to be no links whatsoever between any of them," McCoy finished for him, "That's why we need the extra hands. There must be something somewhere that ties up. I can feel it, Green, we're getting bloody close to some sort of breakthrough."

DS Green, who was less than convinced about the possibility, opted for the diplomatic response, "And you reckon that the link is something to do with the directors or governors of these charities?"

McCoy nodded, "Too bloody right I do. All we need to do is get a few matching names and we're in business."

"If you say so, guv."

"I do say so, Green. I told you – I can feel it." They turned into the narrow, cobbled street where the City of London Police housed its main CID offices. "Let's just hope the Old Jewry boys have got some time on their hands."

They were just approaching the entrance to the building when Green nudged his superior, "Look up there, guv. Is that who I think it is?"

McCoy stared up the street towards where Green was pointing. He gave a snort, "You know, Green? You may be right." He grabbed the sergeant's arm and pulled him into the narrow alleyway beside the CID building.

Thirty seconds later the figure passed them, and McCoy stepped quickly back into the street, "Mr. Taylor! Fancy seeing you here!"

*****

172

Franklin slipped the phone back into his pocket and held out his hand towards Dot, "Looks like it's banging time. But at least we know Bill's in town somewhere not too far away."

"Silly old sod," Dot said, handing Franklin a short length of scaffold pipe, "I bet no one hears us."

"Nah, someone's bound to. There's half a million people up there. Just get ready to add some screams for help to the racket."

A dull thud sounded from the tunnel to their left, the cause and the distance impossible to determine in their section of the cramped, dark, slimy drain.

"I think," Dot said, swallowing hard, "I'm ready now."

*****

Bill stopped in his tracks and turned on his heel, "Inspector! What a pleasant coincidence!"

"Or should I be addressing you as Brigadier?"

"Ah," Bill smiled, "Well, I'm sure you understand that in my line of work–"

"Committing the criminal offence of impersonating high-ranking members of military personnel is an everyday occurrence."

"Not exactly every day, Inspector. And given the most urgent nature of our current investigation–"

"Shut up, Taylor." McCoy shook his head, "For the very *last* time, I'm going to turn a blind eye to your little fun and games, since you seem to have rattled Sir Desmond bloody Fairfax's cage just enough for him to give us some information that otherwise probably wouldn't have been forthcoming. That, and the fact that we don't have time to deal with you on top of everything else. But hear me, and hear me well, Taylor. If I catch you up to that little trick just one more time, I'll bang you up quicker than you can say William Forbes-Rice, got it?"

"Message understood, Inspector. I don't suppose you've got anywhere with the companies mentioned in those planning applications have you?"

"You don't seriously believe I'd tell you even if we have, do you?"

"So you haven't then?"

McCoy groaned, "See what I mean about him, Green?" He paused and stared at his sergeant, "Green?"

"Can't you hear it, guv?"

"Hear what?"

"Listen."

The three of them stood silently, heads cocked to one side. For a few seconds they could hear nothing but the normal background rumble of the traffic along Cheapside. McCoy was just about to question Green's sanity when the faint noise was heard by all three. A muffled tapping sound followed by what sounded like a hoarse yell.

"What the hell is that?" he demanded.

"Sounds as if it's coming from close by," Green said, turning slowly.

Bill was rooted to the spot, a quizzical expression on his face, "I say," he said after a few seconds, "That sounds like... it couldn't be!"

"Couldn't be what, Taylor?"

"Inspector, hard as this might be for you to conceive of, but I rather think that voice sounds like Dot!"

"What!?"

They waited in silence until the same pattern of noise was repeated. Bill grabbed the Inspector's arm as they heard the muffled cries once more, "It is her! I'm sure of it! She even shouts with a cockney accent!"

"Then where the hell is she?" McCoy span in a circle looking along the street and then up at the surrounding offices. His gyrations stopped when he saw Bill staring at the ground. "What are you looking down there for?"

Bill raised his eyes, "Inspector, my colleagues were undertaking a little... subterranean reconnaissance earlier today. I rather think that they may be somehow trapped under our very feet!"

"Subterranean... Never mind, we'll get to that later. Green! Start checking these manhole covers!"

"Already started, guv," Green called from a few metres up the street. He was bent on one knee over a manhole, listening intently.

Bill strode across to the next steel disk and knelt beside it, "Dot?" he bellowed, "Franklin?" A few seconds later he shot upright and, with

McCoy and Green hurrying after him, he made his way along the narrow street until he reached another manhole. Even from a few metres away, they could all hear the hammering from below.

"Dot! Franklin!" Bill yelled again.

The sounds from below disappeared for a moment before there was a muffled shout of "Bill?"

"The very same, dear boy," he paused and listened to the barely audible response, "I take it from that plethora of expletives, that you are perfectly fit and well. That's Dot with you, is it not? Is she okay?" He waited for the response and then turned to face the two police officers, "It's them and they're trapped there. He says they're okay, but beaten up, whatever that might mean this day and age. And in imminent danger."

McCoy turned to Green, "Get inside the office and get something to break the seals, okay?"

"I'm on to it, guv." He spun away at a trot.

"Taylor? Just what the fuck are they doing down there? Do you realise it's a criminal offence to infiltrate the drainage system? And furthermore–"

"One question at a time, please, Inspector. And do mind your language. All will be revealed when we get them out of there."

McCoy repressed a sudden urge to kick William Taylor's behind as the infuriating man turned his attention back to the manhole cover. "This had better be good."

Ten minutes later a bored-looking member of the City's anti-terrorist team stood up and handed DS Green two steel hooks. "The seals are broken, you'll need these to lift the cover. Give us a call when you're finished here." He wandered away in the direction of the CID offices.

Green stooped over the manhole and hooked the rods through loops on either side of the steel disk. One strenuous heave later, the cover slipped sideways over the cobbles and the entrance to the drainage system was revealed. Also revealed was Dot's pale, blood-streaked face. She lifted her arms through the hole.

"Please!" Tears were springing from her eyes, "Help me out of here."

Trying their best to avoid any further damage to her injured wrists, Green and McCoy lifted her from the drain and set her on the cobbles.

They repeated the exercise with a lot more difficulty for Franklin and then stood back, panting hard.

Bill knelt in front of his two colleagues, his face a mask of pity, "Oh, you poor things! What on earth happened down there?"

"That's what I'd like to know," McCoy grunted.

"Had some company," Franklin said between deep breaths. Even the diesel-laden City air seemed fresh and invigorating after the drains and sewers below.

"Should I call up an ambulance, guv?"

McCoy nodded, reluctantly, "Looks that way." He turned to face Franklin, "Okay, Mr. Richardson, this has gone far enough. I want the name of your client and I want you to tell me who was down there with you."

"Franklin, dear boy–"

"Shut up, Taylor!"

"Bill," Franklin said, "I really think this is getting too hot for us to handle on our own."

"He's right, Bill," Dot added, "It's just too weird."

"Well, Richardson?"

Franklin sat thoughtfully for a few moments. "Inspector...?"

"McCoy. That's DS Green."

"Inspector McCoy," Franklin resumed, "To be absolutely honest, I'm not sure who our client really is. But..." he gave a reluctant sigh, "I was contacted by his assistant, and she was the one who suggested I look for our missing persons, down there."

"Persons?"

"Person, I mean," Franklin shot Bill a glance, "I've been sort of thinking about him as being one of the seventeen jumpers if you get my drift. Anyway, back to this assistant. *She* was the one that suggested we come up this way and *she* was the only other person who knew we were intending to go down there today."

"You think you've been set-up?"

"It feels like that to me. I'll give you her name and address on one condition."

"You'll give it anyway, but just out of curiosity, what is your condition?"

Franklin stared at McCoy, "I want to be able to speak to her as soon as you're finished with her."

"I'm not making any promises, but on the grounds that I seem to owe your colleague, here, a very tiny favour, I'll certainly bear your request in mind. What about whoever was down there with you?"

"You mean *after* us. There was a whole gang of them. Real weirdoes. They were being led by a guy named Marcus Allen. Tall, grey-haired, posh type. The only other one we got a name for was Nadia Medford."

"Nadia *Melford*," Dot corrected him.

"Ring any bells, Green?"

"Allen does, but it's a pretty common name."

McCoy turned back to Franklin, "Okay, now the name and description of this woman who you think might have set you up."

Franklin gave the Inspector the details, only neglecting to tell him that he'd just remembered that he still had the key to her subterranean apartment. While McCoy dispatched Green to the address near the Barbican, Franklin turned to Bill.

"This whole business really is weird, man. And I think it's a damn sight more dangerous than we've been led to believe."

"He's right, Bill," Dot said, "It was... awful down there."

"You poor things. Do I surmise from this latest development that we're withdrawing gracefully from this investigation?"

Franklin shook his head, "No way! We're just gonna be a little more... what's the word?"

"Crazy?" Dot suggested.

"Circumspect?" Bill offered.

"Yeah, that's the one." He lowered his voice, "I've got an idea that I know where we've been conned and I'm pretty sure that I know just how to–"

Before he could explain any further, two paramedics bustled up. Despite Franklin and Dot's protestations they were soon bundled into the back of the ambulance where they were due to be taken to St. Thomas's for more thorough check-ups.

While McCoy was calling through to DS Robson, advising him of their whereabouts and how he was to 'make fucking sure he knew where they went when they were discharged', Franklin took the opportunity to tell Bill about his doubts over the true ownership of the abandoned Underground stations.

"I'll get onto it right away," Bill assured him, "I'm sure my contacts in the Public Records Office and Companies House will oblige me this once. Besides, there's some checking that I need to undertake following my research earlier today."

Despite the fuming of the paramedics, Bill delayed their departure long enough to give them a brief outline of his meeting with Sir Desmond Fairfax. When they had finally been whisked into the early rush-hour traffic, McCoy tapped Bill on the shoulder.

"Don't think for a single second, Taylor, that I'm going to overlook your little masquerade at lunchtime. If that had happened within the boundaries of City Police jurisdiction, you would now be held under the Anti-Terrorist Act."

"Is it my fault that I managed to sweet-talk my way into Sir Desmond's office? Or my fault that, despite the Bannen affair, security is still so very lax?"

McCoy snorted, "At this very moment, those are the only two reasons why I *haven't* bothered to nick you. But you do realise, don't you, that what went on two years ago was looked into at the very highest level? That you're playing with fire over this?"

"Given the state of our present government, Inspector, I rather believe that the application of a little common sense is well overdue. If this Bannen character has surfaced and is involved with Monday night's extraordinary events, then I fervently believe that the application of a bit of the aforementioned common sense might very well represent your best chance of reaching a satisfactory conclusion to your investigation."

"Just leave it to us, Taylor. Ruffling a few feathers in the Civil Service is one thing, but if anything you do jeopardises this investigation I will – and I promise you this – personally make sure you suffer. Got that?"

"Rest assured, Inspector, that in future I will ensure that you are immediately informed of any progress we make. Especially where we seem to be a few steps ahead of you." Before the blustering McCoy could delay him any further, Bill bade him a 'Good Afternoon' and made his way back to Cheapside in search of a cab.

*****

Satisfied that her long vigil had been rewarded with what, from the monitor, appeared to be a successful conclusion, Alexandra Featherington switched off the PC and went through to the apartment's luxurious kitchen to pour herself a celebratory whisky. She added two ice cubes and carried the drink through to the bedroom, sipping thoughtfully.

By her estimation, she would have at least an hour to wait for the phone call – and the praise that she firmly believed she so richly deserved. Patience had never been her long-suit, and she returned to the living room with a large holdall into which she placed all of the files that she had gathered together for the young black man. The next five minutes were spent checking that none of the valuable papers had been dropped behind the Spartan furnishings. Finally, she returned to the bedroom to gather her personal belongings into a second holdall and changed into the suit she had been wearing in the City Vault when she had first met Franklin Richardson.

Leaving the jacket undone, she stood for a few moments in front of the massive mirrored doors of the room's walk-in wardrobe, admiring herself. "Still beautiful after all these years," she crooned in the semi-darkness. She ran her hands over her breasts and was beginning to lose herself in a dark, erotic fantasy when the sudden, unexpected hammering at the front door dragged her back to the present with a jolt.

A moment's panic replaced the sensual, surreal world in her mind before she managed to get a grip on herself. No-one could possibly know that she was here except Franklin Richardson, and he was now a captive. The hammering started up once more, accompanied this time by a muffled voice.

As quietly as she could, Alexandra made her made her way through the living room and pressed her ear to the front door, mindless of the continual blows raining down on it from the other side. Finally she could make out the word 'police', and took a step back, her mind racing.

If it had been Franklin that had betrayed her presence there, it must have been the previous day or early that very morning. That seemed unlikely given that it was now late afternoon. Of course, it was also possible that one of the neighbours had seen her enter the apartment and maybe they had begun to grow suspicious that she was still there. That made a lot more sense.

The hammering came again, and its persistent nature lent itself to the idea that whoever was out there wasn't going to go away in a hurry. And that even if they did, they were likely to return quickly and with a little more force.

Alexandra weighed up half a dozen excuses as to why she should be there, took a deep breath and opened the door.

DS Green had been about to start another barrage on the door when it swung open, and it was only quick reflexes that stopped the side of his hand contacting with thin air. His momentum carried him half a stride forward before he regained his balance and straightened, already holding up his warrant card.

"DS Green, City of London Police, CUT. I'd like…" He trailed off as his eyes focused on the attractive young woman who was warily holding on to the door. He wished with all his heart that the last two words he'd spoken hadn't been 'I'd like'. They didn't do nearly enough justice to the emotion he suddenly felt.

Alexandra looked down at herself. With one hand holding open the door, the expensively tailored jacket gaped open, her breasts fully exposed to the eager officer's gaze. She dropped her arm, partially obscuring his view and increased his sudden discomfort by smiling warmly at him, "Sorry, Sergeant. I was expecting someone else."

Green snapped his gaze up to her eyes, "That's, er, perfectly okay, miss. I, er, that is…" He took a deep breath, "As I was saying, DS Green, City–"

"Please come in. It's a little chilly standing here dressed like this." A shrug of her arms made the jacket glide open again.

Trying to regain his composure, he followed her into the surprisingly bright interior, "I'm, er, looking for an Alexandra Featherington," he told the back of her head, "I was led to believe that she resides at this address."

Alexandra turned and stared at him before settling herself onto the sofa, "I'm very much afraid that you are mistaken, Sergeant Green. This rather quaint apartment is owned by... a businessman."

"And you are?"

She leaned her elbows on her thighs, all the better to distract him with her nakedness, "Shall we just say that I'm an acquaintance of the proprietor? An *occasional* acquaintance."

"And, er, who might that be?"

"Peter Charno. Unfortunately, he's had to leave on an urgent business engagement. I was just about to depart myself." She nodded in the direction of the two holdalls. "It really is most disappointing – I was so *very* much looking forward to a few hours of... entertainment."

"So, you're not Alexandra Featherington?"

She raised an eyebrow and stood gracefully, "Allow me to provide you with a sight of my passport, Sergeant Green. I'm sure that will satisfy your curiosity."

Green watched spellbound, his heart-rate increasing rapidly as she turned and bent over one of the holdalls. Her suit's short skirt rose up the back of her thighs, revealing yet more naked flesh. All too soon, as far as he was concerned, she turned and handed him the document.

"That should reveal everything, Sergeant."

He only just managed to stop himself from saying that it had and took the passport. His eyes flickered over the document's photograph and name before being drawn back to gorgeous apparition before him. "So you're Nadia Melford?"

"In the flesh."

"I, er, noticed." Green cleared his throat and returned the passport to her, "And do you know of an Alexandra Featherington?"

"I'm afraid not. If you're still not convinced of my identity, I believe I have my drivers' licence here somewhere?"

"No!" Green said, louder than he'd intended, "I mean, no. The passport was more than sufficient. Er, do you have a contact number for this Mr. Johno?"

"Peter Charno, Sergeant. And I'm once again afraid not. He was leaving for somewhere in Scotland was all he told me. As I explained, I'm only an... occasional acquaintance."

Green shrugged, "I guess I've got the wrong address."

"You most certainly have. Should you have any doubts, I'm sure we could locate documents here someplace to convince you of the fact." She stretched sideways and pulled a small pile of bills from the edge of the table, passing them into the slightly shaky hands of the police officer.

He quickly scanned the top three: gas, electric and broadband, all addressed to a P. Charno. "That seems to settle it," he passed them back, "I'd better get going."

Alexandra nodded, "As must I. I'm so very sorry that your visit was without success... and also that I couldn't be of more help to you."

"No, er, that is... you've been most... In fact *very*, er, helpful." He stood awkwardly and made for the door. Opening it, he stepped outside and then turned back to face her, "Believe me, miss, it's been a pleasure." He closed the door on her gentle laughter.

Back at street level, he pulled his phone from his pocket and dialled McCoy's number.

"Guv? I reckon I've just been given the run-around by the most gorgeous bit of skirt I've seen in the last ten years. Can you get on to whoever's looking after Franklin Richardson and get descriptions of that Alexandra Featherington and the bird he saw down in the Underground, Nadia Melford?"

"You reckon you've just seen one of them?"

"Melford was the name on the passport I was shown, and believe me this was one bloody weird woman, but she was a physical match for the Featherington woman that Richardson told us about. She also said that the apartment actually belonged to a guy called Peter Charno."

"We can check that out later. Is the woman still there?"

"You got it, guv."

"I'll double-check the descriptions and get back to you. And in the meantime, keep her in sight if she leaves."

"Guv? I promise you, nothing would give me greater pleasure."

Chapter 9

Friday 16th November 2018

McCoy went inside the Old Jewry headquarters and marched up to the reception desk where DS Stan Grayson, an inveterate gambler, was thumbing idly through a copy of *City Index for Dummies*.

He looked up as McCoy approached him and flourished the book, "Fascinating stuff, this is, Inspector. I reckon I could incorporate some of this spread betting into my magical system."

"Still think you're going win a million, Stan?"

"Thanks to this little book, I'm almost positive. What can I do for you?"

"Is DCS Cox in his office?"

"Funny you should ask. He's been holed up in there all day for a change. A constant stream of visitors, he's had, an' all."

"That's not like him. Anyone I'd know, Stan?"

"Doubt it, guv. This morning's lot were from the Home Office, and he's had two parties in this afternoon from Whitehall. The last one only left fifteen minutes back. Want me to buzz upstairs and tell him you're on your way up?"

"No way, Stan," McCoy chuckled, "I don't want to give him any chance to sneak out the back way."

"Right you are, guv."

McCoy took the stairs up to the second floor and strode along to his superior's office. He rapped on the door and opened it without waiting for an invitation. "Super? I need a word." To McCoy's surprise Cox looked pleased to see him.

"The very man! Sit down, Graham."

McCoy slumped gratefully into a chair, "I hear you've had some important visitors."

Cox grunted, "If you think the term applies to concerned members of Her Majesty's Government and a bunch of Whitehall buffoons, then yes.

Personally I prefer the term 'interfering morons'. Which brings me to the reason why I was just about to call you: I need to make a progress report on your investigation. Are you finally getting anywhere?"

"We've got a number of leads, a couple of people we want to get hold of, and we think we may have come across a possible link between the so-called jumpers."

"I already know about the infamous Benjamin Bannen," Cox said, "Who else have you got in the frame?"

"It's hard to know where to start. Do you remember the Courtney case last year?"

"Try as I might, I can't forget it. Don't tell me that interfering Private Agency has got involved in this mess?"

"'Fraid so," McCoy grimaced, "But anyway, it seems that the Richardson guy who runs it was fed some pretty weird information by a woman calling herself Alexandra Featherington. He and his sidekick were down in the sewers or something earlier on and they were allegedly attacked by a gang led by one Marcus Allen. When DS Green went to visit the Featherington woman, she claimed that she was Nadia Melford, who just happened to be the only other member of the underground gang that Richardson got a name for."

"You reckon they're one and the same?"

"We're just checking that out at the moment. Richardson and Kominski are in St. Thomas's for check-ups so I haven't had a chance to formally interview them yet, but I've got DS Singh on her way over there to get full descriptions from Richardson."

"And the mystery woman herself?"

"DS Green is keeping her apartment under observation, waiting for Singh to get a positive ID back to him."

"What about this Marcus Allen character?"

"Singh had been looking into him, but I thought it was more important that we identified this woman first. DC Robson was supposed to be tailing Richardson and Kominski, but he and Bradford were in Walthamstow when all this came up. I've called them both back to the office."

"And Bannen?"

"No sign of him anywhere and not a single tongue flapping as to his whereabouts."

"I gathered from my last party of visitors that you thought it worthwhile ruffling a few Civil Service feathers in your search for leads?"

McCoy shrugged, "It may prove worthwhile. It appears that the original investigation into Bannen's attempted abduction of Fairfax was... not as thorough as it might have been. We're trying to look into the possibility that some sort of property dispute was behind it."

"What on earth would that have to do with Monday's fiasco, Graham?"

"No idea at the minute, Super. Call it a hunch."

"Nothing wrong with a good hunch. You mentioned something about a possible link between the jumpers?"

"Apart from their obvious similarities – all single, successful and so on – we're looking into their wills – see if there's any common ground."

"Seems plausible. Anything so far?"

"We've not had much of a chance to get started. What with trying to keep an eye on the suspects, Richardson and his crew–"

"I get the picture, Graham. You want me to assign you some temporary manpower?"

"Absolutely. Checking into the wills and the property companies doesn't take a bunch of rocket scientists, but it does take a hell of a lot of time even using computers."

"You're pretty positive that it'll yield some results?"

McCoy gave his customary shrug, "Couldn't say until it's done. But on the other hand, it's pretty much the only way forward that I can see."

DCS Cox rose and picked up his phone, "I'll see how many bodies I can round up and get them sent over to your office, okay?"

"Thanks, Super. Tell them to report to Sunny Singh – I'll relieve her at the hospital."

"Will do, Graham. Oh, and Graham?" Cox added as McCoy walked to the door, "Please try to refrain from any more feather-ruffling, would you?"

"I'll try my hardest."

He had just reached street level when he received a call from DS Green.

"What's the news?"

"Sunny just called me, guv, he said that Richardson described Alexandra Featherington as a tall, slender blonde and Nadia Melford as being shorter, heavier and darker. The woman I saw at this address fits Richardson's description of Alexandra Featherington perfectly. Shall I bring her in?"

"As soon as you can. I'm off to the hospital to interview Richardson and Kominski and find out just what the fuck they're involved with and what the fuck they really saw down there. Check in with me once you've got our mystery lady back at the office, okay?"

"Got it, guv."

McCoy rang off and went in search of his driver. He was looking forward to interviewing the young investigators.

*****

DS Green waited until a car arrived from the office, ready to transport himself and the Featherington woman back, before once again approaching the front door of the apartment. It was already growing dark and he was grateful when a spotlight flickered on as he opened the gate.

At the bottom of the stairwell he drew out his warrant card and took a deep breath before hammering on the door.

"Miss Melford? It's DS Green, again. There's something that I forgot to ask you." He pressed his ear to the door but heard nothing. "Nadia Melford! I repeat: this is DS Green of the City of London Police. Open up!"

After five unsuccessful minutes, cursing loudly, he went back up the stairs and crossed to the car. "Open the boot, Jim!"

"Is this what you're after, Sarge?" The driver passed a crowbar to him through the rolled-down window.

"Perfect," Green nodded, "Keep an eye out for nosy neighbours, would you?"

"No problem."

Green hurried back to the front door of the apartment and checked that his sidearm was loaded and ready. He wasn't expecting any trouble of that sort, but he knew from personal and painful experience that it was always better to be prepared for any eventuality. Besides which, the woman was decidedly weird. He spent another minute yelling fruitlessly through the door before returning his warrant card to his pocket and hefting the crowbar.

Five attempts and much violent swearing later, he heard the satisfying sound of splintering wood. He took two paces backwards and then aimed a kick at the lock. The door crashed back into the room beyond and he followed it, crouching as he crossed the threshold. A quick scan of the well-lit room made it clear that there was nobody but him in there. The only other doors were situated opposite each other.

Green moved a chair in front of the one to his right and then crossed the room, continually calling out to the woman who he knew had to be in there somewhere. A thorough search of the bedroom and its en-suite bathroom proved fruitless and as he crossed back through the living room to the final doorway a horrible suspicion was beginning to dawn on him. He moved the chair away from the door and pulled it open. Both the kitchen and bathroom beyond were devoid of life.

He hurried back into the living room and looked around. The two black holdalls that he'd seen earlier were gone. So, however impossibly, was Alexandra Featherington.

"Shit!" He was absolutely positive that no-one had left the apartment since he'd last been in there, he'd not taken his eyes off the entrance for more than the time it took to blink. There was no way a woman with two large holdalls could have slipped out unseen.

The only possible explanation was that there must be another exit, but he'd not seen any such thing during his search. To cap it all, he was in a sub-basement flat which extended below the properties on either side and backed on to an office block. Unless there was some sort of secret tunnel...

Green swore again, Tunnels," he muttered aloud, "And where did Richardson and Kominski emerge from? Where were seventeen people killed?"

188

He ran back into the bedroom and turned up every lamp he could find. The walls were completely smooth, and other than the archway that led through to the en suite bathroom and two small tables either side of the massive circular bed in the centre of the room, there was only the walk-in wardrobe.

He'd opened both of its massive mirrored doors on his first tour of the apartment and now he stepped back inside it. With a sweep of his arm he cleared the rail of suits and shirts, scattering the clothing on the floor behind him, expecting to find a partially hidden doorway.

At first Green saw nothing out of the ordinary. It wasn't until he was just about to step back into the bedroom proper that he noticed the very fine dark line in the otherwise pure-white back wall. He ran his hand along the tiny crack and traced the outline of a small doorway. There was no handle or lock of any type that he could see, just a smooth, blank area.

He dashed back into the living room and returned with the crowbar.

After five minutes of frantic effort, he had managed to do nothing more than scratch the surface of the wall. What he had thought to be plaster was clearly something much harder, and he sat back, panting hard.

The driver, worried about the time DS Green had been inside, had come into the apartment a few minutes earlier, and was sitting on the edge of the bed.

"Looks like we'd better call up some heavy gear," he suggested.

"Yeah. Looks that way. Get onto it, will you? I'd better give McCoy a call and tell him what's happened."

"Rather you than me, Sarge."

Green followed the driver outside and put the call through to McCoy.

Two minutes later, he switched his phone to his other hand and began to massage his bruised ear, "How was I to know, guv? This is getting like something out of a bloody Harry Potter book."

To Green's relief, his superior sighed deeply and lowered his voice, "I guess you're right, Green. Look, make sure Jim has got the heavy access team on the way and then tell him to stay there and keep an eye on the place until they arrive. If anyone tries to get in – or out – of the place, I want them nicked."

"Will do, guv. What do you want me to do?"

"Get back to the office. We've got a few extra bodies coming over and I want to make sure they know what they're supposed to be doing."

Green rang off and went over to the car, "How are you getting on?"

Jim was leaning into the car, the radio mouthpiece dangling from his hand. "They're playing silly buggers as usual. Want to know exactly what sort of door, what it's made of and all that sort of stuff. DS Perryman has just gone off to find one of the engineers."

"Want me to have a word?"

"You might stand a better chance than me, Sarge." He withdrew his tall frame from the car window and handed Green the radio.

While they waited for Perryman to come back to them, Green outlined what McCoy had told him. He was just describing some of the more colourful language that the Inspector had used when the radio crackled into life.

"Jim? I've got the engineer with me, over."

"How you doing, Perry? It's Tony Green, over."

"Tony, you old dog! I hear you've got a bit of a problem, over."

Green explained first to Perryman and then to the engineer exactly what he'd found in the subterranean apartment. "So," he finished, "How long before a team can get here, over?"

"Well…" the engineer sighed.

Green, who's patience was running low, cut in, "Do I need to remind you that this is crucial to a multiple murder investigation? Or maybe you'd prefer my governor to do the reminding? Over!"

"How does one hour sound? Over."

"Fifty-nine minutes too long, but I guess it'll have to do. Over and out." He reached into the car and racked the radio.

"Amazing what a mention of McCoy's name can achieve," Jim observed.

"Amazing what it can do to a bladder," Green said, "Anyway, I'd better get back to the office. You okay to look after the apartment?" He gestured over his shoulder.

"Got nothing better to do. The wife's visiting her sister this weekend."

"I'll leave you to it, then."

DS Green strode away in the direction of the Shakespeare's Head. If he was going to do another twenty-hour shift, he reasoned, he needed something to fill his stomach.

*****

In the hospital, Franklin and Dot were sitting in adjacent cubicles in the vast A&E department, with DS Singh seated outside trying to remain both vigilant and awake. A ten-minute burst of mild swearing from Dot's cubicle had just finished and a relieved looking medic emerged. He turned to the police officer.

"We'll be finished with them in five minutes or so."

The yawning Singh was about to answer when McCoy strode into the room, "Did I just hear that right?"

"And you are?" the young doctor asked.

Singh winced on his behalf.

"DI McCoy, City of London Police. You just said that you'd finished with Richardson and Kominski?"

"Just a few minutes longer, Inspector."

McCoy gave a curt nod and turned to his junior officer, "Singh? If you can stay awake long enough, I want you to get back to the office. We've got some guys coming in to help with the research on the wills and the property companies. In case Green hasn't got back there yet, I want you to make sure they know what they're looking for. How many of the wills have we got copies of?"

"Nine, last I heard, Inspector."

"Not bad at all. Now, assuming none of those are the handiwork of Dave the Engraver, we might be able to make some headway. Okay, when you're sure everyone knows what they're doing, get yourself off home for some kip. You look like you could do with it."

"Thanks, Inspector." Singh rose and, yawning, made for the exit.

McCoy settled into the chair that the young officer had vacated and let out a long yawn himself. He was beginning to forget what his own bed looked like. Ten minutes later, as Dot and Franklin emerged from their cubicles, he was snoring gently.

191

"Reckon we should just sneak past 'im?"

Franklin shook his head, "Nah. He's temper's far too short for a stunt like that. If he wakes up and finds us gone he'd make this morning look like a picnic when he comes after us."

"Good point. What should we do first, though: wake McCoy or phone Bill? I doubt whether 'e's ad enough time to make any progress yet, but you never know."

A passing nurse stopped beside them and wrinkled her nose, "Personally, dears, I think the first thing I'd do in your position was to go home and have a long hot shower."

Dot sniffed at her jacket, "Is it that bad?"

"I'm afraid so. What on earth have you two been up to?"

"That's exactly what I'd like to know," McCoy yawned beside them.

The nurse excused herself and bustled on, leaving the two fragrant youngsters alone with the Inspector.

"Now," he began, "I know you've had a tough time and to be frank, that nurse was dead right about you two smelling like a pair of skunks, but I need to talk to you both as a matter of extreme urgency. So here's the deal. You two volunteer to come back to the office with me, and I don't nick you, okay?"

"On what charges could you do that?" Franklin asked.

"Let's see now. Trespass probably isn't worth the effort, but on the other hand, breaching the City's anti-terrorist defences and jeopardising National Security can result in a life sentence."

"I was just asking," Franklin said, "Of course we'll be happy to come with you, won't we, Dot?"

"Yeah. As long as we don't have to take the tube, mind."

"The car's outside. Come on."

They followed the Inspector out of the hospital and under his direction, climbed into the back of the waiting vehicle. Once all the windows were lowered, they headed for the office. By the time they arrived, the constant stream of cool air during the journey had dissipated the smell a little, although heads still turned when they entered the building.

The reception area was unusually busy, the extra manpower being lectured by Sunny Singh as to their duties. McCoy crossed to the desk where DC Robson was sipping at a mug of coffee.

"What time are you due off duty?"

The constable checked his watch, "It's six o'clock, so two hours ago, guv."

"Good lad," McCoy nodded, "Okay, take off as soon as you like – I'm going to need you fresh for tomorrow. Call me at eight and I'll let you know exactly what you'll be doing."

"Morning or evening?"

"Nice try, but morning. Where's Bradford?"

Robson chuckled, "As soon as we got back here, he asked around until he found out where that Taylor guy had gone and set off after him. I think he's trying to get back into your good books, guv."

McCoy raised an eyebrow, "Green said he'd overheard Taylor say that he was off to the PRO and Companies' House. I do hope that's where Bradford's headed. It might not be a bad idea to keep tabs on Taylor at all times from now on. He may act like a blithering idiot, but he's as sharp as the proverbial eating implement. I'll call through and tell Bradford to stick with him."

Robson drained the last of his coffee, "Well, if that's it, guv?"

"Off you go."

The Inspector checked that DS Singh was happy enough with the extra staff, grunting when he was informed that DS Green had yet to return, and crossed back to where Dot and Franklin were standing. "Follow me."

Rather than risk polluting his own office, he led them into one of the more spacious interview rooms and opened the window. "Coffee, anyone?" he asked, motioning them into chairs.

"Love one," Franklin said.

"I'm gasping."

After ordering up the drinks, McCoy settled himself in his chair and lit a cigarette. "Right," he said, "Normally I'd split you two up and interview you separately along with another officer. Unfortunately, I haven't got the time or the manpower right now, and since this is not exactly a formal little chat, as long as you don't start spouting absolute bollocks, I'll forgo standard procedure."

Franklin shrugged and glanced at Dot, who nodded, "Suits us."

"And by the way," McCoy said, "If I hear the expression 'client privilege' just once during our chat, I'll have you both banged up for the night. Got it?"

"Got it, Inspector."

"Let's get started then," McCoy pulled open a file and picked up a pen, "Alexandra Featherington. You said earlier that she was your client's assistant and that she lived at an address near the Golden Lane Estate. Are both of those little gems true?"

Franklin nodded, "As far as I know, yes. But since this morning, I'm beginning to have a few doubts. Hasn't your sergeant managed to confirm that she lives there yet?"

"I'm doing the interviewing here, Mr. Richardson, but as it happens it won't do any harm to tell you that DS Green did go to the address given and he did see a woman fitting the description you later gave DS Singh. However, she claimed to be someone else entirely and also said that it wasn't her apartment. Any ideas?"

"She did say that she didn't want any police involvement. Perhaps she was just trying to throw you off her scent. Why don't you just ask her?"

McCoy grimaced, "We've experienced a little problem, there. Tell me, Mr. Richardson, where exactly did you meet her, and when?"

"The first time was on Wednesday lunchtime at the City Vault and then yesterday morning at the apartment."

"So you've been inside the building?"

"I was there a few hours," Franklin said, trying not to look uncomfortable.

"What was your impression of the place?"

"Weird, man. It was like some sort of ultra-modern cave."

"How did you get in and out?"

Franklin raised his eyebrows, "Would you believe through the front door?"

"You didn't see, or the Featherington woman didn't mention, any other exits?"

"No, man. But there again, it's not the sort of thing you'd be looking for two storeys under street level, is it?"

"You and Green, both," McCoy muttered, "Okay, did she tell you that it was her apartment?"

Franklin thought for a few moments, "I'm not sure if she said as much directly, but that was the impression I got. I mean, her stuff was all over the place and she knew her way around. I didn't really give it a second thought. What's this 'little problem' you mentioned about her?"

"Mr. Richardson, will you *please* stop trying to interview me. Surely I don't need to remind you how serious this investigation is?"

"Sorry, man, but after what happened to us this morning, you can't blame a guy for being a bit curious." He reached sideways and patted Dot's arm, careful to avoid her heavily bandaged wrists.

"We'll get to that in a moment. For your information, the woman in question appears to have left the apartment by a route other than the front door. A closer examination of the premises has revealed what appears to be a metal door hidden in the bedroom." McCoy paused and studied the expression on Franklin's face, "That doesn't seem to surprise you, Mr. Richardson. Would you mind explaining why?"

"Well," Franklin said, frowning, "As I'm sure Bill told you earlier, our client claims that there's some sort of underground gang war going on. The murders took place on the tube. Alexandra Featherington reckons that the missing person may be hiding below ground somewhere. If there really is some underground exit to the apartment, it wouldn't exactly be going against the pattern, would it?"

McCoy grunted, "Point taken. You really had no knowledge of this hidden doorway?"

"None at all."

"Okay. That brings us to your client. Who is he, and where is he?"

Franklin looked across at Dot.

"You'd better tell him," she said.

He nodded, "Like I told you before, Inspector, I don't know where he is. I only met him the once, and in the street at that. He said that he had to go away for a few days and that his assistant – Alexandra

Featherington, as it turned out – would deal with me directly. He said his name is Peter Charno and–"

"Charno, you say?"

"Yeah, man. What–"

"Hang on, Richardson." McCoy pulled his notebook out of his jacket and riffled through several pages before he found what he was looking for, "Here it is: Green said that the apartment appeared to be in the name of a P. Charno."

Franklin shrugged, "I guess that could fit. Maybe Alexandra Featherington is a little bit more than a personal assistant and she's moved in with him."

"Plausible," McCoy said. He closed the notebook and picked up the phone, "Is Sunny Singh still down there?" He rolled his eyes at the reply, "Well tell her she's a bloody idiot, find out if she's got anywhere chasing up the owner of the apartment Green was at earlier, and find someone to bring us up the bloody coffee I asked for ages ago. Got that?"

He hung up and turned his attention back to Franklin, "Where were we?"

"Charno and Featherington."

"Right. Before you leave, I want you to give a full description of this Charno character to one of my men. Since you tell me you haven't seen him since Monday, then I guess we can set him to one side for now. The Featherington woman is another matter. Care to explain in a little more detail what these 'doubts' are that you're starting to have about her?"

Franklin nodded, "Some of the things she told me yesterday don't seem to make sense, but I guess what really bugs me the most is that it was her that suggested our general route out of the tunnels this morning. I mean, she must have *known* that the manhole covers are all sealed in the City. It feels almost like she *wanted* us trapped down there."

"What else did she tell you yesterday?"

"Shitloads, man. And all pretty weird shit at that."

"Such as?"

Franklin sighed, "That there's these two... gangs, I guess you'd call them. One led by Charno – sorta the good guys – and the other mob led by that character I saw down there earlier."

"Marcus Allen?"

"That's him. Anyway, there's loads of disused tube stations and stuff, and these two gangs are busy buying them up or something. According to her there's some real bad blood between them and..." he paused and glanced at Dot once more, "And that this Allen guy is somehow responsible for the murders on Monday."

"Did she say exactly how he could've pulled off something like that?"

"No. I guess she made him sound like some sort of power-crazed madman, but she didn't go into any details like that."

"If Charno and his gang are so sure, why didn't they contact the police? Did she tell you that?"

Franklin snorted, "Like I said, man, she told me all sorts of weird shit. One of the things she said was that these underground gangs don't believe in... *traditional authority*, I think was how she put it."

"Who does these days?" McCoy muttered, "Okay, I can buy that. What does puzzle me a lot, though, is if these gangs know all about the disused systems down there, why didn't Charno's gang simply carry out their own search for this missing person," he checked his notes, "Parkington."

"More weird stuff," Franklin said, "She reckoned that it was too dangerous for them down there at the moment. Something to do with what happened on Monday. That's why Charno wanted us to carry out the investigation."

"If it's dangerous down there for people that know the systems, surely it would be even more dangerous for people that don't?"

"She said not. That there were always people getting lost down there and that if anyone caught us, as long as we played dumb, nothing would happen to us. After what happened this morning, that's another pretty good reason for me to have my doubts about Alexandra bloody Featherington."

Dot leaned forward, "Yeah, well, she'd better just hope I don't catch up with her."

McCoy nodded, suppressing a smile, "Leave that side of the business to us, Miss Kominski."

"Dot."

197

"Very well, *Dot*. Okay, before we get on to exactly what did happen this morning, can you think of anything else that struck you as unusual – anything potentially relevant to the case?"

Franklin thought for a few seconds before shaking his head, "Nothing comes to mind."

"Has anyone mentioned the name Bannen to you at all?"

"Doesn't ring a bell. Why do you ask?"

"No matter. Your colleague, Taylor, will be able to fill you in on that later."

The interview room door opened, and DS Green stepped inside bearing a tray, a file tucked under his arm. "Sorry about the delay, guv, I was just trying to lever Sunny out of the front door." He set the tray on the table and handed the file to McCoy, "Details about the apartment."

McCoy flicked it open and scanned the contents, "Property title in the name of Peter Charno for the last ten years. About time *something* tied up." He looked up at Green, "Any progress on gaining access to the tunnel?"

The Sergeant shook his head, "Last I heard, the engineers had called up some more specialist equipment. Apparently the door's made of some sort of really tough metal alloy. If they can't get it open with that, they reckon the only other way will be to tunnel round it."

"Just what we need. Okay, Green, you might as well sit in on this. I was just about to ask Mr. Richardson and Miss... *Dot*, to describe exactly what happened to them earlier today."

For the next thirty minutes Franklin explained how they'd followed Alexandra Featherington's instructions and descended into the tunnels. How they'd searched the station at St. Bartholomew's, and how they'd shortly afterwards realised that they were being pursued. Dot added some details, describing how she had begun to feel strange, and then recalling nothing until she'd come round in the dark, dank chamber next to the sewer.

When they had finished, Dot turned to Franklin and gave him an awkward hug.

McCoy had not interrupted their story and now sat forward. "I can see that this has been a very upsetting experience for both of you." Beside him, DS Green raised a surprised eyebrow. "So I'll try to keep this brief," McCoy went on, "You say that this Marcus Allen was with the group that chased you?"

Franklin nodded, "I'd seen photographs of him at Alexandra's... *Charno's* apartment."

"And that he wanted to ask you some questions?"

"That's what he said. But it didn't feel like that to me."

"Are you sure that his intentions weren't just to talk to you? That you didn't succumb to panic, being underground like that?"

"No way, man! If you'd seen what they did to get to us – breaking down steel doors for Christ's sake. And how they were dressed, how they were acting..."

"You make them sound more like some sort of crazed cult than a gang of property dealers."

"That's how it was, man. I ain't never seen such a weird bunch. And it's not just all that stuff. I was getting a really strange feeling coming over me and look at what happened to Dot."

McCoy shrugged, "Perhaps there had been a build-up of gas or something?"

Dot shook her head, "It wasn't like that," she paused and shuddered, "I... I've never felt anything like that in my life. And I never want to, ever again."

"Very well," McCoy slid a sheet of paper across the desk, "Mr. Richardson, I want you to write down the access codes to the tunnel system. As crazy as your story sounds, I've got the feeling that it's all true. I'll have men go down there within the next couple of hours, check the place out." He turned to DS Green, "Get a squad put together and inform London Underground that they'll be entering the system. I want them ready to leave in an hour. Reckon you're up to another two or three hours on duty?"

"I'll do my best."

"Good man. Go downstairs and find someone who can use the software for the compu-fit. I need to get Mr. Richardson to come up with descriptions of Charno and Allen."

When Green had left, McCoy turned back to Franklin and Dot, "This is turning into a very strange business. And not just strange, but seemingly bloody dangerous. While I can't ask you to drop your case, I *can* tell you that you will *not* be undertaking any more subterranean searches. At least seventeen people have already died this week and you are not going to be added to that number. Do I make myself absolutely crystal clear?"

Dot sat forward, "Don't worry. I ain't even going to be using the tube for a few months."

Franklin patted her shoulder, "Any more investigating we do will be strictly street level and above."

McCoy seemed satisfied, "Okay. Go downstairs and find DS Green. As soon as you've got the descriptions done, you're free to leave."

He watched them out of the room and then sat back, rubbing at his eyes. Were they finally getting somewhere? "Buggered if I know!" he muttered aloud.

When DS Green returned, the Inspector was asleep at the desk, his head resting on his arms. He quietly slipped the sheet of paper on which Franklin had listed the combinations out from under McCoy's arm, and pocketed the strange shaped key that the young man had said released a cylinder on the main access door. With a final, envious, look at his superior he left the room and made his way back downstairs.

*****

Bill glanced at his watch and shook his head in surprise. It was eight o'clock, meaning that he'd been pouring through documents in Companies' House for more than three hours. He rose from the desk, stretching to ease the stiffness in his back, and then gathered up his notes.

Once the files had been returned to their proper places, he made his way down to the security desk at the front of the building.

"Evening, Mr. Taylor," the guard greeted him, "Finished for the night?"

"I rather think so, Tom. Thanks once again for letting me stay on."

"Always a pleasure." He reached under his desk and pressed a concealed button, "Front door's open."

With a final expression of gratitude, Bill let himself out into the cool night air, pleasant despite the exhaust fumes, after the stuffy confines of the offices behind him. He fumbled his new mobile phone out of his pocket and stepped into narrow alleyway which served to deaden to traffic noise. Eager to learn of his colleagues' welfare, he dialled Franklin's number.

Ten minutes later, when Bill was finally satisfied that Franklin and Dot were not at death's door, and, though still at the police station, hadn't been arrested, they arranged to meet at the office the following morning to discuss progress. He rang off and stepped back out into the street in search of the taxi that would take him in the general direction of a very large whisky.

Behind him, DC Bradford, worrying whether he was beginning to suffer from exhaustion or even hypothermia, groaned as he saw his quarry's arm rise and a black cab screech to a halt. Throwing caution to the wind, he dashed forward and began waving frantically at every passing taxi.

*****

By the time they finally emerged from the police building, Dot and Franklin, were beginning to feel that their exertions and injuries were catching up with them. As they stood sucking in great lungsful of the cool evening air a wave of exhaustion washed over them, and they turned to face one another.

"What a bleedin' 'orrible day."

"True. I've definitely had better. Still, there has been one compensation."

Dot smiled happily up at him, "Yeah." She reached up and gave him a quick kiss. "Just promise me our next date will be a bit nicer."

"I'll do my best."

"You'd better. Okay, how are we gonna get back to the Stow?"

"Well, the tube's out, and to be honest I don't think I can manage to walk all the way to Liverpool Street."

"A taxi then?"

Franklin looked around and a smile spread across his face, "I think I've just come up with an even more convenient idea. Follow me."

Dot trotted along after him as he turned and made his way back along the street. Ten metres on he angled towards the kerb and approached a Ford Focus that was idling there. He rapped on the windscreen and stepped back as the driver wound down the passenger window.

"Evening, officer. Constable Fernandez, isn't it?"

"That's, er, right, sir. What can I do for you?"

"I seem to recall overhearing Sergeant Green telling you to keep tabs on us. Did I hear right?"

There was a groan from inside the car before Fernandez answered, "Well... that is..."

"Thought so," Franklin said. He winked at Dot, "Only I've been thinking. If we take the train back towards home, you'll have to ditch the car and try to follow on foot. Alternatively you could just head straight for Walthamstow and hope that we go back there. On the other hand, if we got a cab, then you'd have to try to keep up with us in all this traffic."

"Your point, sir?"

"Wouldn't it be easier all round if you just gave us a lift back?"

Dot laughed, "Good idea!"

"I'm not sure–" Fernandez began.

"You know it makes sense," Franklin interrupted.

"This is most irregular." The young officer was nothing if not stoic.

"I know I'd feel a lot safer travelling with a copper," Dot put in.

Fernandez, who had been weighing his options, gave in, "Okay. But don't let anyone see you when we pass the office." There was a loud click as he unlocked the back doors.

"You're brilliant," Dot told Franklin as they climbed into the Ford.

"Young, gifted and black," he agreed.

Once they had hunkered down in the back seat, Fernandez pulled into the traffic. After a minute he told them to sit up.

After another minute he told them to 'open the bloody windows'.

By the time they were approaching Walthamstow, Dot was almost asleep, her head resting on Franklin's arm. He nudged her gently.

"We nearly there?" she yawned.

"Almost. I was thinking, why don't you come back to my place?"

"Fast worker."

Franklin shook his head, "It makes sense. for a start it's closer than your place, and, well, maybe Allen knows where we live. We'd be safer together." He faced forward, "I'm guessing that part of Constable Fernandez's duties is to make sure we're safe, isn't that right?"

The driver nodded, "Sergeant Green seemed to think there might be some small element of danger."

"Well," Dot said, "If you put it like that…"

"That's settled then."

Fernandez glanced over his shoulder, "You sure that's what you're going to do?"

"Definitely," Franklin said.

The constable picked up his radio and informed the station that a second tail wouldn't be needed for Miss Kominski, carefully avoiding any mention as to how he knew.

They had just passed the Mucky Duck when Franklin asked him to pull over for a couple of minutes.

"But you live down there."

"I know, but us two haven't eaten all day, and I ain't up to any cooking after what we've been through. I thought I'd grab some KFC. When we get home, we can shower and then heat it up in the microwave."

"Sounds good to me," Dot said, licking her lips.

Grumbling to himself, Fernandez pulled up outside the red-and-white-fronted building, "No funny business, okay?"

"Man, all I want is shower, food and bed. I'll be back in a couple of minutes. Can I get you anything, Constable? On me, of course, after you've been kind enough to give us a lift."

"I guess a couple of pieces of chicken would at least help mask the stench in here," he nodded.

Ten minutes later Dot and Franklin climbed from the car outside his apartment, a giant family sized bucket of chicken and fries clasped in Franklin's arms. "Thanks again, Constable."

"Just promise me DS Green doesn't get to hear about this?"

"You got it, man. One last thing?"

"Now what?"

"Your mobile number. In case there's any problems?"

Fernandez recited the number.

"Thanks, man. I would have invited you in, but it's pretty cramped up there."

"Don't worry, I'm used to the car. See you in the morning."

"Not too early, you won't," Dot said.

They made their way over to Franklin's building and he let them inside. There was his customary stack of mail on the hall table, but he decided it could wait until the morning.

"Hang on a sec," he said to Dot as she made for the stairs, "I'll go first."

He limped up the stairs and set the KFC beside his door. He'd used all three of the door's locks that morning and it took him nearly a minute before he let the door swing open. The flat was dark and silent. Reaching around the door frame, he flicked on the hallway and living room lights.

"Looks all clear."

"No horses?"

"Very funny. I thought we'd made an agreement about that?"

"Sorry. It just slipped out."

Franklin picked up their supper and walked into the apartment. He made a quick check of the bedroom, bathroom and kitchen and then came back to the living room where Dot was gazing out of the full-length windows at the back of the building.

"I never realised what a lovely view you've got from here."

"Great, ain't it? It's almost like being in the countryside. Especially at night." He set the bucket on the coffee table, lowered the level of the lighting and joined her at the window.

Other than a faint amber glow in the far distance, only the moon, bright and nearly full in a clear sky, illuminated the scene. Three large reservoirs stretched into the distance, their surfaces smooth and glassy. In the centre of the middle one a small island sprouted a dense copse of trees and bushes.

Dot pointed to it, "That looks a bit odd. Sort of out of place."

"Believe it or not," Franklin said, "It's a protected island, the largest Heronry in England."

"Heronry?"

He nodded, "Where herons breed. There's hundreds of them. Sometimes they come right up to the channel at the back of the building to feed. If you're lucky, there might be one or two down there in the morning."

"You having me on?"

"Nope. It's one of the reasons why I like this place so much."

"You like wildlife, then?"

"Except for horses. But talking of wildlife, I think we'd better get ourselves a shower."

"I hope you mean one each?"

"Absolutely."

They turned away from the window and Dot followed Franklin through to the bathroom.

"I'll get you some fresh towels and a couple of shirts and shorts," he said, "They'll be a bit big for you, but I'll bung your stuff in the washing machine and it'll be ready to wear in the morning."

She nodded, "Maybe a T-shirt, as well?"

"Got it, little lady. You get the shower running and I'll get the things."

When he returned a couple of minutes later, the shower was still off, and Dot was standing where he'd left her.

"Problem?"

She looked down at her hands. They were bandaged from above the wrist almost all the way to her knuckles, "I'm supposed to keep these on and dry for the next twenty-four hours."

Franklin stared thoughtfully at them for a few moments, "I've got an idea."

"This doesn't involve you joining me in the shower, does it?"

"Not at all. Unless of course—"

"No!"

"Back in a minute."

He reappeared with a pair or bright yellow rubber gloves and a roll of Clingfilm, "Get the picture?"

"Clever."

"And because the gloves are extra-large, they shouldn't hurt your wrists."

Two minutes later, Dot's bandages were waterproofed, and she shooed Franklin from the room, "I'll give you a call when I've thrown my stuff out of the door," she told him. Noticing that there was no lock on the door, she added, "And no peeking!"

"You can trust me," he called, wandering through to his bedroom for a fresh change of clothes for himself.

When Dot called out that her dirty clothes were outside, he stripped off his own and put on an old robe until he could clean himself up. He took everything through to the kitchen and set the washer-dryer for a full cycle.

Dot re-emerged twenty minutes later, her face pink and slightly shiny above a white T-shirt over which she'd draped one of Franklin's shirts. "Sorry I was so long, but it was a bit awkward."

"You should have called for help."

The pinkness of her face seemed to deepen, and Franklin wondered whether the idea had crossed her mind, "Anyway, the bathroom's free now," she said.

"Let's get those gloves off you first."

"If you insist, I wouldn't say no. They feel horrible."

Five minutes later, he finally stepped under the steaming shower and within seconds he could feel the tension draining out of his battered muscles. It felt like the most luxurious shower he'd ever taken, marred only when shampoo ran into the gash on his chin. Afterwards, he towelled himself off and slipped on a clean T-shirt and shorts. Sighing happily, he tossed damp towels into a hamper and stepped out of the steam-filled room.

"Good wasn't it?" Dot called from the living room.

"The best."

"Why didn't you ever tell me you had a cat? He's really cute!"

Franklin dashed into the living room to find Dot on the sofa with a small ginger and white cat curled, purring, on her lap. "I don't! I've never seen that animal before in my life!"

"What?"

"I'd been thinking about getting one, but I've never got around to it. Where on earth did you find it?"

"It's a him. I think he must have been over in the corner there, on his bed."

Franklin stared frantically to where Dot was pointing. In the furthest corner of the room, at the front of the building, there was a large blue pillow. In front of the cat-bed were two bowls on a small plastic tray and to the side was a scratching post. Several small fluffy toys were scattered underneath the window.

"You really haven't seen him before, have you?"

Franklin, dumbfounded, shook his head, "Really!"

"Well, it's bleedin' odd, then, 'cos there's a litter tray in the kitchen under the worktop, and half a dozen packets of Whiskas in one of the cupboards. I found them when I was searching for some plates for our supper."

"This is weird, man. You saw how my door was locked. Who on earth..." he ran out of words.

"Maybe someone overheard you say you were going to buy a cat and found one for you?"

"Even if someone did, how did they get in here?" He dashed from the room and checked all of the windows. Not one was open.

He returned to the living room where Dot still sat with the young cat. Shaking his head in puzzlement, he checked the tables and front door for any notes that might have been left, and then examined the cat's bed, toys and even the litter tray.

"Beats me," he groaned, staring at the feline.

"I think he's cute," Dot paused and giggled.

"What?"

"Better than a horse, anyway."

Franklin sighed heavily, "I suppose you've got a point."

"What are you gonna call him?"

"Call him? I was thinking of reporting this to the police."

"You can't do that! They'll put the poor little thing in some horrible little cage or something. You gotta keep him!"

Franklin crossed to the sofa and tentatively stroked the little cat. It let out an even louder purr.

"See!" Dot said, "He likes you already."

"I'll think about it," Franklin said, "Tomorrow. Right now, I'm starving."

As if on cue, Dot's stomach let out a low growl, startling the cat, "Guess that tells you all you need to know about me." She took the cat over to its bed and settled it onto the pillow with a couple of its toys.

Franklin, still shaking his head in disbelief, went through to the kitchen and started preparing the chicken and fries.

Despite being reheated, the chicken was still juicy enough to require another application of Clingfilm to Dot's bandages. Twenty minutes later, their stomachs heaving, they fed the few remaining scraps of chicken to the cat and settled back on the sofa with a cold beer each.

"What a day!" Dot yawned.

"Tell me about it. Or rather, don't."

They sipped their beers in a companionable silence for a while before Dot let out another long yawn, "I don't think I can keep my eyes open much longer."

Franklin nodded, "You're not alone. Go on through to the bed. I'll kip here."

"Nah. You have the bed. I'm smaller than you, it'll be easier for me out here."

"I'm not in the mood for arguing. Why don't we both have the bed? It's massive." He'd said it in a half-jokey voice, fully expecting one of Dot's barbed responses.

Instead, she reached over and laid a bandaged hand on his arm, "Don't take this the wrong way, but, okay then."

"Pardon?"

"I said, yes, we can share. Don't go getting any funny ideas, though. I mean, I'm not saying that I want to… you know, *do* anything."

"Well, if you're sure?"

"I am," Dot said, "After all that business earlier, I just feel as if I don't want to be alone, that's all."

"I'll behave," he promised.

Dot was blushing slightly as she rose from the sofa, "Well, er, I'm going through, then."

Franklin set his beer on the table and joined her, "Let's go."

He turned off the lights, despite Dot's protest that the cat might be scared of the dark, and then led her through to the bedroom. "Which side do you want?"

"I'm not fussed," she said, "you have whichever's normal for you."

He moved to the side closest the door, turned out the main light, and made to unbutton his shorts. He stopped abruptly, "I guess I'd better leave these on."

"Please." Dot shrugged out of Franklin's shirt, made sure that the immense T-shirt adequately protected her modesty, and then dived under the duvet.

Franklin climbed into bed a little more gingerly, his muscles once more stiff and sore. "Am I allowed a goodnight kiss?"

"Course," Dot smiled at him.

She moved closer and he reached for her. His hand snapped back as he realised that he'd accidentally brushed his palm across her breast. "Sorry, I didn't–"

"It's okay..." she reached for his hand and pulled it back towards her, settling it the breast that he'd just touched, "I don't... mind. It's nice. Nice to be wanted. As long as it's by you."

Even in the dim light from the bedside lamp, Franklin could make out high colour on Dot's cheek. He caressed her gently through the flimsy material of the T-shirt, marvelling at the tiny perfection of her form. He eased himself closer and kissed her softly.

Slowly, deliciously, their embrace became firmer, their kisses deeper and hungrier.

Panting hard, Dot pulled her head back a little, "I really didn't have this in mind."

"Nor me. Honest."

"I know. I can see. I've wanted you for ages, you know?"

"I do now."

"It's like…" Dot paused, "It's like we've already gone through all that getting to know each other stuff."

"I didn't know how cute you were under all those sweatshirts," Franklin traced the contour of a breast.

"You really mean that?"

He pulled her close, their bellies touching, "If that doesn't convince you, nothing will."

"I'm getting really hot in here," she swallowed hard, "What do you think would happen if I took off this T-shirt? You know? To cool down a bit?"

"I guess I'd have to take off my stuff, and then make sure you don't cool down too much."

"Do you want me to?"

"Right now, more than anything in the world."

"But wouldn't you think I was being… a bit cheap?"

"Never. Not you. Like you said, we've got over all that getting-to-know-you business, and besides I can't ever remember a woman turning me on like you have."

"This may not be a good idea."

"It sounds like a wonderful idea to me."

Dot bit her lip, "I mean, it might not work out. You know, sex."

"There's only one way to find out. Better now than months down the road."

She shook her head, "No, I mean I might… react bad."

"Because of that 'uncle' your mother went with?"

Dot nodded.

"Don't worry. You're with me now because I care for you," he slid his hand under the back of her T-shirt and caressed her back, "And I really want you bad."

She nodded again, and kissed him deeply, "The feeling's mutual." She gave a small groan of pleasure as Franklin's hand moved under her arm and cupped her breast, its smooth, hot flesh perfectly filling his palm.

"I guess that settles it, then. If you're sure?"

"I'm sure."

They stripped off in a frantic blur, before falling hungrily on each, mindless of their injuries. Franklin's hands explored every millimetre of Dot's lithe form, bringing constant groans of pleasure, before she finally managed to grasp him tightly, "I don't just want you now, I need you," she panted at him.

He nodded, breathing heavily, "Let me get a condom."

"No need if you're clean. I am, and I'm on the pill."

"Good," Franklin kissed her deeply, "Because I don't think I can wait."

As he entered her, Dot gave a deep grunt.

"Sorry–"

She shook her head frantically from side to side and pulled him deeper inside her, "That weren't pain, big guy, that was pleasure. I never realised it could feel this good."

Their sweat-slicked bodies writhed and pumped together, in an unspoken, natural rhythm until finally, Franklin could hold back no longer. With a guttural cry and a final thrust, he climaxed deep inside her. As he felt his fluids fill her, her stomach muscles began to tremble, and he pulled his head back to watch her expression as she orgasmed beneath him: first amazement, then wonder, then pure, unadulterated ecstasy.

They lay panting together afterwards, Dot giving an occasional sigh, Franklin idly stroking her breasts and neck.

"I guess we could say that wasn't so bad," he said after a while.

"The best," Dot purred.

"I don't think you'll need to worry any more about problems in that direction."

"I will if I don't get a regular service." She clapped her hand to her mouth, giggling and blushing at the same time.

"Put it this way," Franklin said, "You'd better wear a chastity belt in the office."

"Either that or we'd better send Bill out more often."

"Good compromise," Franklin nodded. He bent and took a nipple into his mouth.

Through a groan, Dot said, "I thought you were tired?"

"Not all of me."

"So I can feel."

It was another half hour before they fell asleep, still coupled, thoroughly sated.

*****

DS Green yawned and tried to concentrate on what the young constable from A Wing was telling him.

"So you see, Sarge, that makes ten thousand possible combinations. It'll take us all night to try every one."

"Not if you find the right one in the first few attempts. And besides, we've *got* all night."

"So you want us to carry on?"

"Isn't that what I just said? And for the tenth time, no, we can't use a drill on the doors. They're flood doors and even the one we're using at Golden Lane wouldn't get through that." Tiredness was getting to him, and he was becoming worried that he was starting to sound like McCoy, "I want the four of you to work in relays for as long as it takes to crack the combination. Since it doesn't look as if we'll be getting anywhere for a while, I'm going to head back to the office. Call me there as soon as there's any news, okay?"

"Okay, guv." The constable's reply was sullen but resigned.

Green walked back to the Mansion House platform and trudged wearily up the stairs and into the night. As he walked the short distance back to the office, he phoned through to the team at the Golden Lane apartment, receiving another report of zero progress.

When he'd reached the steps outside the building he checked his watch and yawned once more. Ten o'clock and time, he decided, for a couple of hours' shut-eye. Carefully side-stepping the crew researching the wills and companies he climbed the stairs to McCoy's office without waking his DI, and settled himself into the room's one comfortable armchair, placing his telephone on the table beside him. Less than a minute later he was asleep.

*****

Bill stared thoughtfully at the stack of notes he'd arrayed on the bar counter, a puzzled frown on his face. His whisky glass sat untouched to one side, drawing worried looks from Gerry Cooper and Mandy, the barmaid.

"What's up with him?" she asked in a stage whisper.

"Ten-thirty on a Friday night and still working," Gerry said, "Something very strange, to say the least." Then to Bill, "Fancy another?"

Bill looked up, "Um? What was that, dear boy?"

"Just wondering whether you fancied another drink."

He stared in surprise at his still full glass and picked it up, "How terribly remiss of me. I rather think that another might go down splendidly." He drained the glass and set it back on the counter.

"So," Gerry said, "An interesting case, is it?"

"Absolutely. Intriguing, as well."

"Need a sounding-board or a friendly ear?"

Bill looked at Gerry for a few moments and then nodded, "Under normal circumstances, I would have to decline your most generous offer on the grounds of client confidentiality, but I'm afraid to say that there is absolutely nothing normal about the investigation we are currently undertaking," he paused to sip at the fresh whisky Mandy placed before him, "In addition, I have the feeling that my research has uncovered something of relevance, but I cannot, for the life of me, work out what it is. A definite case of not being able to see the wood for the trees. Maybe a second head might do the trick, Gerald."

Gerry, surprised and delighted at being honoured in such a fashion, pulled up a barstool and settled himself close to Bill, "So, what's the background?"

"Do you recall the awful, tragic events of last Monday evening?"

"Well, we lost the darts match to the... Oh! You mean the suicides?"

"Quite so, dear boy."

Gerry's eyes were wide open, "You mean that you, Franklin and Dot are investigating what happened?"

"Not exactly. It's a related matter, though. Missing persons."

"Sounds intriguing so far. Do you reckon it really was some sort of weird cult-thing?"

"You've been reading too many tabloids again, Gerald. Between you, me, the police and the bedpost, the very strong suspicion is that the unfortunate seventeen were murdered."

"Murdered!"

"Hush, Gerald! This is not information for public broadcast."

"Sorry, Bill. Go on."

"Very well. In the course of our investigation so far we have uncovered a number of facts concerning various properties and property companies. Indeed, so many facts that I am totally convinced that some sort of vast property war is being raged across and under our fair city as we speak."

"Did you just say 'under'?"

"I most certainly did, Gerald. This very morning, Franklin and Dot undertook a sortie into a disused part of the Underground system–"

"They did what?"

"Gerald!"

"Sorry," he lowered his voice, "They actually went down into the old tunnels?"

"Quite so. Unfortunately they were pursued and only just managed to escape capture."

"From the police?"

"I wish that it were so, Gerald. No, their pursuers were a rather strange and sinister bunch, by the sound of it, and along with other information we have received, I am inclined to believe that they were something to do with the aforementioned property war."

"How are the kids?"

"A few minor bumps and cuts, but happily not too damaged – they should be sleeping off the excitement by now." As it happened, Bill was absolutely right. "Anyway, while they were playing moles and tunnels, I visited a certain gentleman in Whitehall in connection with another possible lead. This gentleman had, two years previously, been the subject of an attempted abduction which was subsequently hushed up at the highest level."

214

"You were right about this being intriguing. It's beginning to sound like something out of a John Le Carré novel."

"Hardly, Gerald," Bill said, "The Whitehall gent turned out to have high-level duties in certain types of planning application, and, sniffing another link to property, I managed to wheedle out of him details of the cases he'd been working on prior to the failed abduction attempt."

"Sherlock Holmes, eat your heart out."

"Thank you, Gerald. Armed with that information, and following a request from Franklin to look into the true ownership of the disused stations, I made my way to Companies House, and spent several hours poring over records. These are the results," he pointed to the stacks of paper beside him.

"And what did you manage to turn up?"

"That is my problem," Bill shook his head, "I'm really not sure – there's just so *much* information that I can't work out what is going on."

"But you're sure there's something a bit strange?"

"Positive."

"Okay, so who really owns the stations?"

"According to one set of papers, it would appear that they are owned or part-owned by a number of small, non-profit making companies. According to another, older, set, they are mostly still owned by Her Majesty's Government."

"That can't be possible, surely?"

"Quite so. It's just possible that the older set have been retained for some sort of historical interest, but I can't check that out until Monday when the senior registrar and the official record keeper return to work."

"Is there anything odd about these companies that are supposed to be the new owners, then?"

"Not at first glance. They all seem to have the correct incorporation papers and judging by the fact that they all seem to have boards of directors as long as your arm, you would have to assume that they are quite legitimate."

"Have they got any directors in common?"

"A very good question, Gerald, and one that I have been researching for the past couple of hours. As I said, there are scores of names to cross-check and the process is not an easy one by any stretch of the imagination. It doesn't help that a number of the companies have charitable status, meaning that their papers also list dozens of patron's names."

"Surely it's not too bad?" Gerry asked, "I mean, there can't be that many disused stations down there, surely?"

"There are forty, Gerald. Judging by the look on your face, I rather think it is time to replenish our glasses." He turned and beckoned Mandy over.

Once she had served them, Bill resumed his narrative, "Leaving the matter of the station ownership to one side for the moment, I next looked up details concerning the four companies that had been involved with planning applications overseen by the gentleman from Whitehall."

"Don't tell me," Gerry said, "They were all perfectly legitimate companies with proper papers and so on."

"That is what I discovered," Bill nodded.

"Do any of them match the ones that are supposed to own the stations?"

"I was rather hoping that would be the case, but unfortunately it is not so. Although, two of them do have charitable status."

"Is that not pretty common these days?"

"I wouldn't have thought so, Gerald, but again, I'll have to wait until Monday to be able to find out for sure."

"What about the directors? Any common ground?"

"See for yourself. There doesn't appear to be a single link. At least there are only four of them to check through." He handed Gerry four photo-copied sheets. "My next job, of course, is to check those four lists against the ones for the ones who seem to own the stations."

Gerry peered at the sheets individually, and then laid them out on the bar counter side by side. He studied them for a few more seconds and then shuffled two of them a couple of centimetres further forward, and the one on the far right a centimetre further back.. Next he pushed them together sideways until the all overlapped.

"What do you see, Gerald?"

"Look for yourself. You're the crossword expert."

216

Bill leant forward and studied the sheets, "What exactly am I supposed to be looking for?"

"Check out the names of the company secretaries."

"Sara Cullmen appears more than once, Lance Maslur... Oh, I see!"

"Anagrams, right?"

Bill drained his whisky and beckoned to Mandy before replying, "Absolutely. And not just any old anagrams. They're anagrams of *another* name and decidedly awful ones at that."

"And?"

"*And*, Gerald, dear boy, it's the name of one of the protagonists in our investigation."

"Well, put me out of my misery, then?"

"Marcus Allen. We have him currently cast in the role of bad-guy, and from what Franklin told me earlier, that is exactly what he is. But really, they are truly dire. One would have thought that this self-confessed master of the underside or whatever he calls himself could have come up with something better than that. I always say you can tell a person from their anagram."

"Ok, Bill, I'll buy it. What does it say about you?"

"I might be termed 'a royal wit mill', which seems appropriate although not as appropriate as Alec Guinness who surely is 'genuine class'. It may seem somewhat un-gentlemanly of me to mention Virginia Bottomley, who translates as 'I'm an evil Tory bigot', but it does rather make my point, don't you think?"

"Very clearly," Gerry said, "But before you start telling me what the significance of me being a 'groped oracle' is, how about you telling me if all this anagram stuff actually helps?"

"I rather think it does, dear boy. We now have a positive link between Marcus Allen and property deals of sorts. If nothing else, it serves to confirm some of the alleged facts that we have about him. Now, of course, what we need is some sort of link to the companies that supposedly own the disused stations. Care to start scanning a few lists in search of cross-matches or more anagrams?"

"Delighted to," Gerry nodded.

An hour later, the pub now officially closed, but with a dozen or more trusted regulars still in attendance, Gerry sat back with a sigh. "You were right about there being hundreds of the buggers," he said, "And talk about how the other half live, just listen to some of these posh names: Tristram Granville-Tompkinson, Justin Chalmondsley, at least there's one sensible one: Thomas Gerald Parkington, then back to the toffs–"

"Gerald! What did you just say?"

"Back to the toffs. Alex–"

"No, before that."

Gerry looked back at the list, "Thomas Gerald Parkington?"

Bill nodded and pulled yet another list from his pocket. He scanned it quickly then passed it to Gerry, "Fourth name down."

"Thomas Gerald Parkington. Who are *these* people?"

"You remember me saying that we are undertaking a missing persons case?"

"Something like that."

"Well these thirteen are the missing persons in question, and you've just spotted one of their names listed as a director of one of our mystery companies!"

"And that's good, is it?"

"While I haven't the faintest idea what this may indicate, any sort of link can only be good news. Let's turn our attention to this list."

Gerry laid it on the counter between them and picked up the list he'd been scanning, "Fair enough. Now, where was I? Ah, yes! Granville-Tompkinson, Chalmondsley, our man Parkington. Next was Alexandra Featherington. I'll start from… Now what?"

Bill took the piece of paper from him and stared down at the name. "Well, well."

"Well, well, what? She's not on your missing persons list, is she?"

"Not at all, dear boy. But she does just happen to be the very self-same person that gave us the list in the first place. Mandy! Drinks, please, dear. I think we might finally be getting somewhere."

Chapter 10

At first DS Green thought that he'd been woken by the sound of a car backfiring. It turned out to be Inspector McCoy.

"Sorry, did I disturb your beauty sleep?"

"Just thought I'd grab a couple of minutes while the going was good," he yawned.

"Don't worry, I don't blame you," McCoy crossed to his desk and opened the bottom drawer. He pulled out a half empty bottle of Glenfiddich and two glasses, "Fancy a livener?"

"Bloody good idea, guv. What time is it?"

"Four-thirty."

Green let out a groan and checked his phone. There had been no incoming calls. "Looks like the lads are having problems getting underground."

McCoy handed him a half-full tumbler and nodded, "I've just done a quick check round. The engineer at Golden Lane reckons another half an hour, the squad at Mansion House say they've got up to four thousand, Fernandez has both Richardson and Kominski safe and sound, and Bradford has just left that pub in Walthamstow and followed Taylor home. I've told him to get some kip and be back there at eight. I doubt whether Taylor will be going anywhere for a while if he's been on the piss for seven hours."

"What about downstairs?"

"Nothing obvious, so far, but a couple of the boys are busy piling all the information into databases or some such. Reckon that it's our only chance to get some cross-checking done because of the sheer weight of names and so on."

"Sunny Singh's our woman to get that going. What time's she in, guv?"

"Knowing our Sunny, any time about now."

Green took a long sip from his whisky tumbler and sighed, "That hits the right spot. Any news on the computer searches for Allen, Charno and Featherington?"

"Three or four directorships listed under the name Alexandra Featherington. Nothing for Charno and Allen. Allen's name turned up as an expert witness in one of the planning application cases, though, which is interesting. The trouble is, we haven't got anywhere trying to locate an address for him. Nor for Featherington, for that matter."

"I wouldn't mind finding her again," Green said.

"Oh? I thought you said she was a right weirdo?"

Green explained how she'd behaved.

"And you didn't jump on her? You really are getting better, Green."

Before he could answer, his phone rang. He answered it and spoke quickly for a minute then rang off. "They've got the apartment's tunnel door open, guv."

"Let's go." McCoy drained the rest of his whisky and grabbed his jacket, "You told them not to touch anything?"

"Earlier, yeah."

"Good. I want to see this first hand."

The drive through the dark, deserted streets of the City was almost eerie, but the absence of traffic was a tremendous relief. They arrived outside the apartment in just three minutes.

A group of men in overalls, with safety visors and breathing masks hanging around their necks, were standing at the top of the steps leading down to the apartment. The tallest of them looked up at the sound of the car doors slamming. "McCoy!" he called.

"That you, Derek?"

"One and the same. Nice job you got us into. What a bastard."

"I hope you're referring to the job and not me?" McCoy gave a short laugh.

"Both as it happens, but Christ, I've got into bank vaults easier than that."

McCoy patted him on the shoulder, "Good work." He turned to Green and motioned with his head, "Ready?"

"You bet."

McCoy led them down the stairwell and into the brightly lit living room. Even through here, there was a fine coating of dust on every surface, and the smell of burnt metal permeated the air.

Green pointed towards the bedroom door, "Through there, guv."

The formally pristine bedroom was a total shambles. The giant circular bed had been shifted to one corner and the entire wardrobe structure had been ripped apart, its mirrored doors shattered. A monstrous drill stood in the middle of the room, two pipes running through the archway into the adjoining bathroom. The floor was at least three centimetres deep in dirty water and more was seeping from the drilling machine as they took in the scene. At the back of the place where the wardrobe had been, a section of the wall, now blackened and charred, stood ajar, three braces holding the hidden door open.

"I don't reckon Mr. Charno's gonna be a happy bunny when he gets back," Green said.

"He'll be a bloody sight less happy when I get my hands on him. Okay, let's see what's through there."

The door was at least fifteen centimetres thick, a dark metallic colour which seemed to absorb light, and it took both of them to force it open wide enough for them to sidle through. McCoy adjusted the braces to make sure that it wouldn't swing shut behind them and then felt around on the wall, finally locating a light switch.

Concealed lamps illuminated a long corridor which appeared to turn left twenty metres down its length.

DS Green was examining the door, "Looks like a bloody great motor opens and closes it," he observed.

"So did a bloody great drill, but I see what you mean. Must be operated by remote control, or something."

"Anyway, we're in now, guv."

"True. Let's find out where this goes, shall we?"

"Can't wait, guv."

"Get your torch ready, these lights might be on a timer, and I for one, don't fancy stumbling around in the dark."

Green nodded and set off in the lead, torch in hand, and heart beating faster than he would have liked. He reached the turn and peered cautiously round the corner. Another, shorter tunnel run on for a few metres then curved away to the right. Taking a deep breath, he stepped around the corner and continued moving cautiously forward. At the start of the curve he paused again and peered as far along the next section of tunnel as he could. At first sight it appeared to come to a dead end, and he moved on once more, praying that the other end wasn't blocked by another security door.

McCoy moved to Green's side, "I don't like the look of that."

"Me neither, guv."

They quickened their pace before McCoy groaned. Green saw the rungs in the wall a fraction of a second after his boss. "Oh, no!"

Green arrived a step in front of McCoy and peered up into a dark shaft. Iron rungs, set into the wall disappeared upwards. He switched on the torch and shone it up the shaft. Twenty feet above them, it ended in a circular steel plate.

"Street level, would be my guess, guv."

"Shit!"

Green handed McCoy the torch and quickly scrambled up the ladder. At the top, he pushed at a steel catch and the manhole swung open, letting in cool night air. He poked his head over the edge and looked around.

"Well?" McCoy called from below.

"Would you believe that I'm in the middle of the Shakespeare's Head's car park?"

*****

Franklin awoke with a start, a tickling sensation from his right foot dispersing dreams of darkness and claustrophobia. Momentarily disorientated, it took him a few seconds before he realised where he was and, more importantly, who was with him. Dot's small form was curled up, completely covered by the duvet, her back brushing against his side.

The tickling sensation came again, and Franklin tried to sit up to locate its source.

Pain coruscated along his spine, the wave running from his hips to his neck. He lay back on his pillow and took a few deep breaths. Gingerly, he rolled onto his side, his shoulders now protesting, and gradually eased himself up onto his elbow. He turned his neck slowly, half expecting a loud click followed by his head dropping off.

The cat, seeing this, stopped rubbing against Franklin's foot and made its way up the bed until it reached chest level. Purring loudly, it curled itself into a tight ball and settled itself under Franklin's arm.

"Cute," Franklin muttered through his pain.

He would have loved to have settled back under the duvet, a warm furry body purring on one side of him, a warm, silky smooth body on the other. Unfortunately, the pressure he felt in his bladder indicated that this would not be the luxuriously comfortable situation that in other circumstances it might prove to be.

With a barely suppressed series of groans, he forced himself to sit upright. He carefully manoeuvred the cat around him, until it was comfortably curled against Dot's back, and then swung his legs slowly over the edge of the bed.

Standing upright proved to be a little more difficult – and considerably more painful – than usual, an exercise that he doubted he could have managed without the help of his bedside table. Despite the increasingly urgent signals from his bladder, he allowed himself a full minute to try to stretch some of the pains from his battered muscles. When he finally felt that his spine wasn't about to crumble into dust, he began to take tentative steps in the direction of the bathroom.

Five minutes later, relieved and increasingly mobile, he put on his tattered old robe and padded through to the kitchen. The clock indicated that it was only eight, the bright sunshine belying the earliness of the hour. As quietly as he could, hoping not to disturb Dot, he filled the coffee maker and set it bubbling, returning to the sink for a glass of water. This he used to wash down four Paracetamol. He had just set the glass on the draining board when he caught a movement out of the corner of his eye.

The cat strutted into the room and made a quiet mewling sound.

"Hungry?"

Another meow seemed to indicate that Franklin was right.

He opened a couple of cupboards before locating the packets of Whiskas that Dot had told him were there and took one down from the shelf. The little ginger tom trotted out of the kitchen towards the living room, Franklin's own progress considerably more measured.

"I don't suppose you could hand me up that bowl?" he asked the expectant-looking feline.

With a series of groans, he lowered himself to his knees and fiddled with the packet. Despite the interference of the cat crawling all over his lap, he finally managed to tear the packet open and emptied its contents into the empty bowl. The cat settled down and began to tuck into its breakfast.

"Not even a thank you," Franklin smiled. He watched the cat for a few moments before his own stomach began to rumble. "Maybe breakfast is a good idea."

On his way back to the kitchen, he checked the bedroom and saw that Dot was still sleeping soundly. What he really wanted to do was slide back into the warmth and comfort of his bed, curl himself around her sleeping form, and simply enjoy the intimate contact. Not wanting to disturb her, though, he blew her an unheeded kiss and went back through to the kitchen.

The fridge was not exactly well-stocked, but it did at least contain fresh eggs, milk and bacon. He decided that an omelette was the order of the day and took the ingredients over to the worktop.

Increasingly over the recent weeks, he found the preparation and cooking of food a relaxing activity, and one that allowed his mind to wander freely in search of answers to any problems he was experiencing. This morning, he tried to keep his thoughts away from the investigation, not wishing to disturb the pleasant calm and delight he was feeling. There would be time enough later for the case when they met up with Bill at the office.

When the omelette was ready, he turned it out onto a plate and took it over to the small breakfast bar beneath the front window. He left it there to cool for a few moments and padded through to the front door, laboriously unlocking it before he could finally pull it open. His newspaper, the overweight Saturday edition of the Times – thanks to Bill's campaign – was folded carefully on the welcome mat outside. Strange woman that she was, Mrs Jenkins always collected the newspaper from downstairs and took it up to his flat, but she would never touch his post, preferring instead to leave it stacked on the table on the downstairs hallway.

Franklin had not bothered to bring yesterday's mail bring upstairs the previous evening and cursed himself under his breath. There was every possibility that whoever had smuggled the cat into the apartment may well have left some sort of clue amongst his post.

He carefully bent and picked up the *Times* and was about to head downstairs when a faint tinkling noise from somewhere in the flat stopped him in his tracks. He closed the door and quickly made his way back inside. Another sound came from the kitchen – a sound suspiciously like cutlery knocking gently onto china – and he grinned to himself. Dot must have woken and discovered the omelette.

"Hope you like it," he said as he entered the kitchen.

Judging by the amount of egg in its whiskers, the cat most certainly did.

"Oi, fleabag! Leave that alone!" He crossed the room and picked up the purring cat, "I just gave you your own breakfast, you're not supposed to eat mine as well."

The cat, hanging limply over his hand began to wash its paws.

Franklin put the newspaper on the counter and turned the cat round so that they were eye to eye. "If you're going to stay here, then we'd better get a few things straight right from the start, okay?" He could have sworn that the cat was smiling at him. "Number one. You do not eat any of my food." Remembering the previous night's KFC, he added, "Unless, of course, I specifically give it to you. Number two. You do not shred the furniture. Number three. You use your litter tray at all times and not the carpets. Do I make myself clear?"

The cat began to purr, and Franklin set it down on the floor. It eyed the edge of the breakfast bar, but after a glance up at Franklin, seemed to think better of it. With a swish of its tail it turned and padded out of the room.

Satisfied that dominance had been established – for a few minutes, at least – Franklin turned his attention to the omelette. Fortunately, the cat had only nibbled at one end of it, and he trimmed this off with a knife. Sighing in self-reproach and fully aware that it was probably a very bad idea, he carried the trimmings through to the living room and dropped them into the cat's bowl along where they formed a rather attractive garnish to the half-eaten Whiskas. The cat, looking, Franklin thought, insufferably smug, dipped its head back into its bowl.

The diversion had served to ensure that the omelette was now cool enough to eat, and he wolfed it down while scanning the headlines, pausing only twice to remove cat's hairs from his plate.

After the omelette and a strong mug of coffee, he began to feel almost human again. He was just rinsing the plate under tepid water when a yawn came from the doorway.

"Mornin', big guy."

Franklin set the plate down and turned to face Dot. His heart felt as if it lurched when he saw her.

She had draped one of his large shirts over her shoulders, the sleeves rolled up to her elbows. It was unbuttoned, one of her pert breasts exposed to his eager gaze, the dark thatch of hair at her groin a stark contrast to her pale skin.

"Wow! And good morning to you. I know how you look, but how do you feel?"

Dot grinned, "Believe it or not, I feel absolutely wonderful!"

She spread her arms wide, and Franklin hastily rearranged the front of his robe, "You sure as hell look it. Whatever happened to the shy little lady?"

"Don't know, don't care," she giggled, crossing the room.

They hugged each other tightly, kissed deeply.

When they broke off, Dot issued a mock sigh of relief, "I ain't 'alf glad last night wasn't a dream."

"It was in one way," Franklin said, "I don't suppose you'd like to pop back to bed for a few minutes would you?"

Dot gave a wry smile, "I'd *love* to, but... well, to be honest I'm feeling decidedly sore this morning."

"Sorry."

"Don't be! It was wonderful! I guess I'm just not used to it yet."

"Let's hope you soon will be."

"I will, I promise."

Franklin laughed, "Okay, so how about some breakfast instead?"

"It's not much of a swap, but thinking about it, I'm starving."

"Would a bacon omelette do you? I've just had one myself. Or rather, most of one." He told her about the cat's breakfast raid.

Giggling, she nodded at the offer, "So you are gonna keep him then?"

Franklin shrugged, "Guess so."

"So he's gonna need a name."

"Not if he keeps nicking my breakfast, but I'll think about it, anyway. In the meantime, I've got an omelette to cook."

"Need some help?"

"Nope," Franklin grinned, handing Dot a mug of coffee, "Go through and relax for a few minutes – I'll call you when it's ready."

"I could get used to this. I'll go and see if there's any 'erons outside."

"Erons... oh, the herons. There might be, I haven't looked, but about this time of the morning's pretty good for them." He glanced up at the clock and then back down to Dot, "By the way, I know there's no neighbours at the back and we're on the third floor, but old Sid, the gardener, normally starts about this time."

"And?"

"Well, if you're standing at the window dressed like that, he's gonna be a very happy old gardener."

Dot looked down at herself and shrugged, "I'm not bothered, are you?"

Franklin raised an eyebrow, "Well... no. I'm too proud of you for that. I just thought I'd warn you."

"Thanks, but there's really no need." Dot looked puzzled for a moment, then grinned, "I guess I just suddenly feel... liberated, I suppose."

"Amen to that." He watched her retreating form trying not to feel at all uneasy.

She returned after a few minutes and set the empty coffee mug in the sink, "No 'erons and no gardeners," she reported.

"Don't worry, they'll probably be back tomorrow." He was busy flipping the bacon over under the grill and didn't see her expression.

"Tomorrow?"

He looked up sharply, "Oh! I mean, if you'd like to stay on for a bit, you know? I mean, only if you want to… which is a dumb thing to say… what I mean–"

"You'd actually like me to stay… on?"

"Well, yeah. I mean… after yesterday and… last night…"

Dot crossed the kitchen and hugged him tightly, "I'd love to," she told his chest, "But are you really sure?"

He turned her face up and smiled at her, kissed her gently on the lips, "I'm positive. Besides," he grinned, "If I'm keeping that cat, I'll need someone to help me look after him."

"That's a deal!"

Franklin kissed her again and then released her, "I'd better get on with your omelette, I don't want your first home-cooked meal to be blacker than me, do I?"

Dot, hugging herself like a happy five-year-old, giggled, "Sure I can't do anything to help?"

"Actually, there is," he said, "When I picked up the paper this morning, I remembered that I hadn't brought up the mail last night. I thought that maybe our cat delivery expert had left some sort of note down there."

"You want me to go down and collect it?"

"If you don't mind."

"Glad to be of service." She made for the door.

"Er, Dot?"

She stopped in the doorway and half-turned, "What?"

He nodded at her flapping shirt, "The hall's at the front of the building and at street level. Anyone passing can see in, and when I checked earlier, our friendly policeman was watching the place."

Dot shrugged, "Like I said, I don't care. I just feel too liberated, too… free!"

She turned, and before Franklin could say a word, headed off to the front door. He stared after her before shaking his head and returning to the bacon. He just hoped that old Mrs. Jenkins didn't pop her head out of her flat – he could just imagine the complaints he'd get about naked women running all over the place. The feeling of unease that he'd experienced a few minutes earlier returned with a little more force.

By the time Dot returned, the omelette was ready, and after a quick check on the cat, he turned it out onto the same plate he'd used himself. "Hope you like it."

"I'm sure I will," she grinned, handing him four envelopes which was the sum total of two days' worth of mail.

"I'll leave you to it," he said.

"The way I feel, I won't be long."

"I won't make any smart comments about your height, I promise."

Dot stuck her tongue out at him, and then turned her attention to her plate.

In the living room, Franklin opened the four bills and stacked them on the coffee table for later consideration. No note about the cat was a disappointment, but it had been a long-shot, anyway. He walked over to the windows and stood gazing out over the reservoirs, letting his mind drift. Below him, Sid arrived, and they exchanged a brief wave before the gardener got himself busy pruning the rose bushes. A couple of minutes later, a clattering from the kitchen indicated that Dot had finished her breakfast.

Franklin was just about to walk through to her when a fluttering out of the corner of his eye caught his attention. He looked down and immediately spotted the heron, knee-deep in the drainage channel, it's long head darting left and right.

"Dot! One of the heron's has turned up."

She shot into the living room, the shirt trailing behind her, "Where is it?"

"Hey! Sid's turned up as well as the heron."

Dot shrugged and marched straight up to the window, "How many more times? I don't care. Now where's this... There it is!"

229

Franklin stared at her, worried. He glanced down into the garden and as he did so, the old gardener looked up. Even from the third storey, Franklin could see Sid's eyes open wide in surprise. A broad smile spread over the old man's face.

"Dot, Sid's seen you."

She turned to face Franklin, a grin on her face, "Lucky Sid, eh? I hope that…" Her voice trailed off slowly and the smile slipped.

Dot took half a step back from the window and then slowly looked down at her nakedness. With a high-pitched squeal, she pulled the shirt around her and span from the window, diving onto the sofa. By the time Franklin reached her, she had her head buried behind a cushion and was crying.

"What was I *doing*?" she wailed, "I'm not like that! I've never been like it!"

Franklin put his arm around her and tried to comfort her, "It didn't seem very like you–"

"It's *nothing* like me! What the hell was I thinking?"

"Perhaps it was just a reaction to yesterday's horrible things? You know, a sort of opposite reaction?"

"What I just did wasn't opposite! It was almost as bad! I'll never be able to look that old man in the eye. I'll never… I can't move in here now, not after that–"

Franklin pulled her tighter against him and began to stroke her hair, muttering soothing noises in her ear. When she had quietened a little, he managed to pull the cushion from her face. Dot wouldn't look at him.

"It's okay, little lady."

"It's not," she sniffed.

"Tell you what I'll do, okay? I'll go downstairs and tell Sid that you're my new flatmate and that I forgot to tell you he'd be down there. That it's all my fault, and that you told me to tell him that you hope he isn't as embarrassed as you are. How does that sound?"

She finally turned to face him, "I don't know… It was just so awful of me!"

"There's nothing awful about you. And especially not that gorgeous little body. Accidents happen, and that's all Sid will think it was when I tell him. It really isn't so bad."

Dot's shoulders slumped, "I guess you're right," she sniffed, "I guess what was really bad was that I felt almost… *made* to do it. Now that it's gone I can sort of feel what It was lIke."

"Nothing like the normal you?"

She nodded, "Yeah, that's it. Almost like I was watching myself from the outside, somehow."

Franklin frowned, "I know this is gonna sound weird, but there again what doesn't this last week?"

Dot stared at him, "What's gonna sound weird?"

"All the women I've met in connection with this case," he said slowly, "have been barely dressed. Those women down in the tunnels yesterday – that Melford woman was wearing nothing under her cloak and let me get a right eyeful, and the others were dressed the same. Alexandra Featherington was even wearing that revealing suit I told you about when she met me in the Vault."

"But–"

"Let me finish. Yesterday, when we were at the second station, just before you passed out, you said that you felt that it wasn't worth carrying on, right?"

"Well, yeah."

"Would you say that you felt almost suicidal?"

"I… don't know. I mean, I've never felt suicidal before, but… yeah, I guess so. And the feeling was getting worse and worse."

"Do you see what I'm getting at?"

Dot shook her head.

"Down there yesterday you got to feeling almost suicidal. On Monday, at least seventeen people 'committed suicide'. Today, like some sort of reaction to what went on underground, you had an overwhelming urge to flaunt yourself – sorry, but I don't know how else to put it – and all of those women seem to have the same urge. Permanently, in their cases."

"Are you saying that you think I only felt like that because of something down there?"

"Maybe some sort of nerve gas and then a reaction to it leaving your system."

"You're right. It does sound weird."

"What hasn't been?"

Dot nodded, "Perhaps you might be on to something. I'd like to think that it wasn't just me cracking up."

"You're not. And I'm here to make sure you don't."

"What did you mean by the seventeen 'committing suicide'? You mean they were definitely murdered, right"

"Well, they did jump in front of trains, but, yeah, I'm absolutely positive they were murdered now, and I think I'm beginning to see how."

"This nerve gas idea?"

"Or something like it. After seeing what you were like down there yesterday, I reckon those people were somehow *made* to jump."

Dot shuddered, "But why were just a few people affected?"

"That's what we've gotta find out."

"I just hope there's no more reactions to it, if it really was some sort of 'orrible gas."

"I doubt it, but I promise I'll keep an eye on you, okay?"

"I'd like that."

"Right now, I'd better pop down and set the record straight with our lucky gardener, then we'd better start getting ready to go into the office."

Dot blushed furiously, "Thanks," she muttered.

By the time he'd returned, Dot had moved into the bathroom and was gingerly removing the sticking plaster from her right temple. Franklin came up behind her and peered at her reflection in the mirror, "Want me to get that?"

Dot, grimacing, nodded at his him, "I just can't seem to get up the nerve to do it quickly. How was the gardener?"

"He thought it was hilarious, but sends his own apologies about enjoying the view," he grinned as she rolled her eyes. He gently lifted one corner of the plaster, "Okay, ready?"

Before Dot could reply, he'd ripped it from her face. Dot squawked as much from surprise as pain. She turned and looked at her reflection.

"There's virtually nothing there!"

Franklin, eyes wide, nodded, "You can barely see where the scratch was."

"Maybe it's true what they say about a little bit of blood making things look worse than they really are."

"How do your hands feel?"

A puzzled frown came over Dot's face, "Now you mention it... they feel fine. Not sore at all."

"Let's have a look." He took a small pair of scissors from the shelf and carefully cut through the bandages on Dot's right hand and wrist. He gently pulled the material back. "I don't really believe it."

They stared down at the hand. Where there had been a deep gouge and numerous other scratches and cuts, there was now perfectly healed flesh showing just a faint suggestion of the earlier wounds. Redundant butterfly clips formed a zigzag pattern on the back of her hand.

The left hand proved just as healthy and they stared at each other, dumbfounded.

"Well, I guess there might have been another side-effect to that gas," Franklin said, "And if that's the case, at least this one is beneficial."

"It may be good, but it ain't 'alf scary." A troubled frown furrowed Dot's brow.

"This bit of it is actually more of a nuisance as far as I'm concerned."

"How's that?"

"Well, I was going to suggest that rather than using the rubber gloves again, I'd volunteer to help you shower."

"You were, were you?"

Franklin nodded, "It would have been much easier that way. The offer still stands, by the way, miracle cures or not."

He'd succeeded in lifting Dot's flagging spirits, "Well," she said, "there's two reasons why I'll have to turn you down. First, it'd be too tempting, and I really am a little too sore just yet. And second..."

"Second?"

"Well, believe it or not, I... I'm feeling a bit... shy."

Franklin laughed, "I'll buy the first one, anyway."

Dot shook her head, blushing, "I'm being serious. I've *always* been pretty shy, and even after... last night, and planning to move in and everything... well, I guess it's gonna take me a bit of time before I feel really comfortable with you... seeing me undressed."

Franklin pulled her into a tight embrace, "I ain't gonna rush you, little lady. You've got a gorgeous little bod, but it's *your* gorgeous little bod."

"Thanks. Really, really, thanks."

He stepped back and grinned down at the front of her shirt, buttoned now, but because of its size, still quite revealing, "I'd better leave you and your bod to it. It's already having quite a strange effect on me."

Dot glanced down and blushed harder, "Yeah, the effect's poking through the front of your robe."

"Consider it a compliment," Franklin said, adjusting the robe again, "I'll, er, go and get your things out of the dryer. They'll be in the bedroom by the time you're done."

An hour later, they finally managed to make their way down to the street to find Constable Fernandez in deep conversation with a local bobby.

"Could be our chance to give him the slip," Franklin whispered.

"Personally, I'd rather have him around for a bit of protection," Dot said.

"Yeah, maybe you're right."

Fernandez looked up as they approached, "Morning. You must have slept well."

"All the better for knowing you were there," Dot said.

The local bobby said his goodbyes and left them alone.

"So," Franklin said, "Anything interesting happen while we were tucked up in bed?" He could feel Dot's blush and made a mental note to apologise to her later.

"There was a couple of people nosing about at about six this morning, but they disappeared as soon as I got out of the car."

"What?" Dot sounded alarmed.

"They looked more like your typical housebreakers to me," Fernandez said, "They seemed to be casing a number of the places down here so I'm sure they're nothing to worry about, miss."

"Dot," she said automatically.

Franklin put an arm around her shoulders, "Like he says, if they were looking at loads of places, it can't be them. They would know *exactly* where I live." He declined to mention that it is almost impossible to see the house numbers in the dark. He turned his attention back to the police officer, "I take it you're supposed to be keeping tabs on us today?"

"At least until I'm relieved," he said.

"In that case, fancy giving us a lift to our office? We're supposed to be meeting Bill there and we're already way late."

Fernandez nodded, "Hop in. You needn't worry about being late though, because last I heard he was still at home."

"Someone watching his place, too, then?"

"Bradford's been there since eight and no-one's emerged. Since your partner didn't get home from the pub until after four this morning, it's a pretty safe bet he's not going to surface for a while."

Dot gave a quiet laugh, "You don't know our Bill."

The Walthamstow streets were crowded with Saturday morning shoppers and their progress was probably slower than if they'd gone on foot. It was one of the reasons that Franklin seldom used his recently purchased second hand Ford Ka, which was currently sitting in Gerry Cooper's garage.

They finally arrived to find a note Sellotaped to the office door.
'Dear Franklin and Dot,

Thought I'd make an early start. Have gone to continue research. Much to tell you when I get back. Probably late afternoon. Bill. BSc., MA.'

"Looks like your partner has the constitution of an ox," Fernandez said, reading the note over Dot's shoulder. "What?" he asked, as he saw the consternation on their faces when they turned towards him.

"This note's not from Bill," Franklin said.

"How do you know?"

Franklin pointed at the sheet of paper, "If it was from him it'd be about ten times as long. Our Bill *loves* words."

"Perhaps he was in a hurry?"

Dot shook her head, "It doesn't matter. We know it's not from Bill because it's printed. He never, *ever* uses the PC."

"Refuses point blank," Franklin added.

"You sure about this?"

"Positive," they said in unison.

"Okay," Fernandez said, "You two wait here. I'm going to call through to Bradford and have him check out Mr. Taylor's place."

He left Franklin and Dot staring worriedly at each other.

*****

Green and McCoy were taking turns in pacing the floor of the latter's office. It was nearly nine o'clock and there had been, in McCoy's terms 'no bloody progress at all'. Sunny Singh had arrived at six o'clock, took one look at the volume of data they had been assembling and gave an immediate estimate of six hours before they could start cross-checking. The last report from the team at Mansion House was that they had reached seven thousand, five hundred and that they were 'bloody knackered'. Green had sent out four men to relieve them.

McCoy was just about to call down for yet more coffee when his phone rang.

"What's the news?"

"We've got the lock open, Inspector. Eight thousand–"

"I don't give a shit about the number, just stay there until we arrive. No-one's to go in there until we do, got that?" He rang off before the officer could reply.

DS Green had already slipped into his jacket and the two men dashed from the office and down the stairs. The street outside was almost deserted in stark contrast to the normal weekday bustle, and they arrived at the entrance to the tube station without having passed a single person.

The Sergeant led the way down onto the platform and they waited impatiently while a train stopped at the station. A seemingly pointless exercise since no-one got on or off. As soon as it had departed, they climbed to the floor of the tunnel and ran along to where the four officers were nursing bleeding fingertips.

"Well done and about bloody time," McCoy greeted them.

"Thanks, guv," one of the four muttered.

McCoy ignored him, "Okay, Green. Let's find out just where Richardson and Kominski went yesterday. I want the rest of you to come with us."

"Can't wait, guv," Green said with a shudder.

McCoy stepped through the open doorway and found a bank of light switches. Brilliant fluorescent light flooded the chamber and the two men stared around. Although the room had been sparsely furnished, every single item had been destroyed. The shattered remains of a computer and monitor littered the floor, glass and broken components crunching under their feet with every step they took.

"Looks like someone was a bit annoyed," Green said.

"If they were frustrated at Richardson and Kominski getting away from them, it's probably understandable. Let's see what's down on these supposedly disused stations."

At St. Bartholomew's, they found the broken remains of the steel access door, and then moved on to the office complex at the end of the platform. Everything was as Franklin Richardson had described it – save for the wrecked furniture. The officers continued on into the tunnel beyond. When they reached the junction where three tunnels joined, McCoy and Green took the right-hand branch, aware that this was the route the investigators had taken the previous day. The others were split into pairs and sent into the remaining two tunnels.

McCoy and Green arrived at the unnamed station to find debris everywhere. Whoever had been after Richardson and Kominski, had clearly not taken kindly to their evasion. The tiles had been ripped from the walls and furniture had been taken from somewhere and systematically smashed to pieces all along the platform.

Green knelt down carefully on the floor and plucked something from the debris, "What do you make of this, guv?"

McCoy peered down at him, "Looks like some sort of cloak or cape."

"There's another one just over there," Green said.

McCoy crossed to where he'd pointed and picked it up, "You're right."

"Didn't Richardson mention that the women in the group were wearing these?"

"And nothing else. There's a couple more over there," he pointed further along the platform.

"Er, guv?"

"What?"

Green was peering intently at the cloak in his hands, "It looks like there's some sort of stain on here. A dark stain."

"Blood?"

"Could be, guv," Green sniffed at the material, "In fact, that's a definite yes."

"Okay. Leave it where it is. In fact, we'd better leave everything where it is. We'll check out the rest of this place and then get Forensics down here."

They made their way along the platform and through the archway that Franklin had described to them. A vast steel door had been forcibly removed from its hinges at the end of the passageway, and they stepped into the gloom of the access shaft with their flashlights already switched on.

The floor was littered with more debris and another couple of cloaks. On the far side, steel rungs led up to a trapdoor. In the twin beams they could see that the surface of the hatchway had been hacked away at with considerable force. There was no longer more than a couple of splintered pieces of wood attached to the underside of the hatch, and in one place the concrete had been hollowed out by almost five centimetres.

"Looks like they were pretty desperate to get at Richardson and the girl, guv."

"Not wrong, Green. How Richardson ever managed to carry a dead weight up there is beyond me. The lad must be a bloody sight stronger than he looks."

"I think if I'd been being chased by the mob he described, I might have managed it myself."

"Well at least they were telling us the truth about this place, but it's taken us fucking forever to follow the trail this way. Perhaps we really should have started out where we found Richardson and Kominski at that manhole. Too late to change our minds now, though so come on, we'd better get back to the others and get the lab boys down here."

The other four were already waiting for them when they reached the junction.

"What's the news?"

The youngest of the two officers that had set off in the central tunnel stepped forward. "This one comes up in the basement of one of the shops on Poultry. There's a separate door to the side of the shop that leads straight out onto the street."

"Same story here, guv," one of the other pair said, "Only it's not a shop, it's a pub. The Pavilion on Watling Street."

"So that tunnel must nearly curve back on itself?"

The officer nodded, "We thought we were going round in circles."

McCoy looked hard at Green, "According to Richardson, that Alexandra Featherington woman told him that the best way out of that station was through the sewers which she must have known were sealed, right?"

"I'm with you, guv."

"And yet, here are two perfectly easy exit points. No seals, nothing."

"They couldn't have got back to here with that mob after them, though."

"That's not the point, Green. The point is that she didn't tell them about these exits in the first place. They already knew someone was after them back at St. Bartholomew's. If they'd known there was an easy way out they would probably have abandoned their search and legged it out when they got here."

Green nodded, "It sure as hell looks like they were set-up."

"I'm positive they were. As soon as we get up top, I want you to get through to Fernandez and tell him that he's not to let Richardson and Kominski out of his sight for a single second. If necessary he's to take them into protective custody. Got that?"

"Got it, guv."

"Okay, let's get out of here. This place is beginning to give me the creeps."

*****

DC Bradford had decided that he was not the sort of creature that could survive on only three hours sleep per night, but his short break had at least given him time to collect his own car and he was now lolling in its front seat dozing gently to the background mumblings of a rock station DJ. Parked as close to the front of William Taylor's house as he was, he was pretty sure that if anyone came out, with his window rolled down, he would be able to hear them.

Rather than the closing of a front door, though, it was his phone that disturbed his increasingly deep slumber. He bolted upright in the driver's seat and fumbled with the buttons on the phone. "Bradford," he yawned at length.

"It's Fernandez. You been keeping a real close eye on Taylor's house?"

"Er, of course. I was back here just after eight and haven't moved since."

"Anyone gone in or come out?"

"Not a soul."

"Okay. I want you to go up to the house and start banging on the door. Don't let up until someone answers. If no-one *has* answered after five minutes, you're to break in."

"What? Without a warrant?"

"This is an emergency, Bradford. Just do it. As soon as you know what the situation is, call me."

"Well, if you're—"

"Just fucking do it, okay?"

The phone went dead in his hands and he stared at it with a look of near-panic on his face. Fernandez had sounded pretty wound up and pretty worried at the same time. Surely if this was such an emergency, it might also be dangerous? Steeling himself, he climbed stiffly from the car and took a few deep breaths.

His walk along the short path seemed to take an age, and his hands were trembling by the time he reached the front door. With as much authority as he could muster, he balled his right hand into a fist and hammered on the door, "Police, open up!"

He repeated the exercise a minute later, increasingly content at the lack of response. Just as he was beginning to think that there was no one at home a muffled curse issued from somewhere inside the house.

"Oh, shit," he muttered aloud.

Footsteps approached the other side of the door and the lock gave a loud click. The door swung slowly open.

Bradford stared aghast at the sight that met him. "You're not William Taylor!"

Gerry Cooper, eyes squeezed into slits, peered blearily at him, "Neither are you."

"Where is he?"

"Who?"

"Taylor, of course! Tell me he's still inside."

"What's the point of that? He's probably not."

"What?"

Gerry held up his hands, "Look, I've just woken up, I've got the hangover from hell, and I can't seem to understand a word you're saying. Can we start again?"

Bradford took a deep breath, "Is William Taylor inside?"

"Don't know."

"What do you mean you don't know?"

"I told you, I just woke up."

"So have you checked his room?"

"Funnily enough, I didn't seem to have the time. I was too busy answering a persistent hammering at the door."

"Well can you check now, then?"

"Could do, but there's not much point."

"Why?"

"He left early this morning. The bugger woke me up to tell me."

"So why did you just say you don't know whether he's inside or not."

"Thinking logically for a second, doesn't it appear possible that he might have returned while I was asleep?"

"Ah, well. Okay. Can you go and check now?"

"Say 'please'."

"Mister... what did you say your name was?"

241

"I didn't. You never asked. All you did was point out that I'm not Bill. Actually, with this hangover that was probably a favour. Thanks."

Bradford's earlier nervousness had by now been replaced with mounting frustration, "Could you please tell me your name, sir?"

"Gerald Cooper. Gerry to my friends."

"Well, Gerry–"

"Mr. Cooper to you."

"*Well*, *Mister* Cooper. Would you please be good enough to see if William Taylor is inside?"

"Certainly, officer." He closed the door in Bradford's face.

By the time Gerry returned, Bradford had formed a worrying possibility. Before Gerry could say anything, he blurted, "What time did Taylor leave?"

"He's not inside. I've checked all the rooms. Now, what was this second request?"

"What time did he bloody leave?!"

"Please! A little quieter if you don't mind. I've a splitting headache."

"*Mister* Cooper, I'm rapidly losing patience with you. Just tell me: what time did Taylor leave the building?"

"Seven-thirty."

"Thank God for that!" Bradford heaved a huge sigh of relief. If it had been after eight he would have been a dead man walking as far as McCoy was concerned.

"Wouldn't you like to know where he was going?" Gerry asked.

"Er, of course. Just coming to that," Bradford said quickly, "And where was it?"

"He didn't say."

"What? Why ask me whether I wanted to know where he was going if you didn't know yourself?"

"I didn't say I didn't know. I just said that Bill didn't say."

"Are you taking the piss?"

"A smidgen, possibly," Gerry conceded.

"Do you want me to nick you?"

"Not in the least."

"Then I want a straight answer. Where do you *know* he's going?"

"When I say 'know'–"

"I'm warning you, Cooper!"

"I strongly *believe* that he would be headed off to Companies House. He has some unfinished research which we were discussing last night."

"Thank you! At last. Companies House makes sense, anyway."

"Anything else, officer? Any messages you'd like me to pass on to Bill should I see him before you?"

"Tell him to contact me through the Queen Victoria Street office if I haven't already spoken to him. Oh, and tell me, have you any idea how he might be travelling?"

"Alone, as usual, I would suspect."

"I *meant* by what means?"

"On foot and then by train, tube, bus or taxi."

"Thank you, that's been... totally useless," he finished lamely as the door closed once more.

He returned to the car and relayed the information to Fernandez. He'd expected that his colleague would be happy with the news, but instead he seemed even more alarmed than before. With the final instruction that 'he, Bradford, was to get himself over to Companies House, pronto, and check to see if Taylor was there', still ringing in his ears, he turned the key in the ignition and pulled into the traffic,

Chapter 11

"I don't like this at all," Dot said, pacing from her desk to Franklin's and then back again.

"I'm sure he's okay."

Dot turned and stared at him, "Let's get real, okay?"

DC Fernandez had locked them in their own office with strict instructions not to admit anyone other than himself into the building and had gone to fetch Gerry Cooper from Bill's house. The young officer had not tried to hide the fact that he thought Bill was almost certainly in trouble of some sort, and after a call to DS Green, his demeanour became even more concerned.

Franklin sighed. "Why would anyone want to cause trouble for Bill?"

"Well, for a start, he's your business partner and someone sure wanted to make trouble for us. I reckon it must be that Allen mob."

"They sure seemed to want to talk to us real bad," Franklin nodded, "Maybe they think they can get to us through Bill?"

"If they knew where he lived, they must know where we live – I mean you – so why not come straight to us?"

"Fernandez sitting outside?"

"You really think that a mob like that would be bothered by one lone copper?"

Franklin shook his head, "No. But what if there were only a couple of them? What if they didn't want to risk too much exposure, or bring to much attention to themselves by travelling mob-handed?"

"Maybe…"

"Remember, Fernandez said that he'd spotted two people nosing around outside *our* place," he permitted himself a smile, "That was around six o'clock."

"But he reckoned they were just casing a few places. Housebreakers, he reckoned they were."

"Yeah, well…" Franklin gave an apologetic cough, "I didn't want to worry you when he said that, but, well, you can't actually see the house numbers very clearly at night. Unless they knew exactly where my place was, they'd have to check out the numbers."

"Oh, Christ!" Dot shuddered.

Franklin crossed to her and draped an arm around her shoulders, "Still want me to carry on getting real about this?"

"For Bill's sake, we'd better."

"Okay, so how about this for a scenario? Two of Allen's stooges are sent to round us up so he can ask his questions, or whatever he really wants. They have my address and walk down the street looking for the number. Fernandez spots them and gets out of his car. They leave before there can be any trouble with the law – they'll know he's the law because they're bound to think that we'll have gone to the police. Besides, who else would be sitting outside in a car at that time of the morning?

"So, having been frustrated at our place, they fall back on their plan B, and hike over to Bill's place. No-one's watching there because the dozy plod that had been on Bill's tail has buggered off for a couple of hours kip thinking that Bill wouldn't be going anywhere after a long session in the Duck. By the time he gets back, Bill has already left."

Dot nodded, "We'll ask Gerry when he gets here."

"Right. So, Bill leaves his place and Allen's two stooges can see that there's no police presence. They follow Bill as he come towards the office and catch up with him as he comes inside. They question him, find out what his plans are and then produce that note before taking him off somewhere."

"They wouldn't have been able to use the computer, though. They don't have the passwords."

Franklin nodded, "But Bill does. In fact, maybe they forced *Bill* to produce the note."

"That's a point," Dot said, "He point-blank refuses to use the PC, but he does just about know *how*. And it'd be just like him to knock out a note that he would somehow let us know that there was something funny going on!"

"Let's have another look at it."

They pored over the sheet of paper for a few seconds and then turned to face each other with triumphant smiles on their faces.

"I never noticed it before!" Dot said.

"Me neither. "Bill, BSc., MA." How often has he told us about his degrees?"

"Every time he starts reminiscing about his misspent youth. And he's always going on about the differences between them and what all the letters mean."

"Right. He hasn't *got* an MA. His Master's is an MSc. Bill *did* type up this note and he was trying to tell us something."

"MA has gotta stand for Marcus Allen, right?"

"I'd bet on it," Franklin said.

"Me too. So I guess we'd better tell Fernandez as soon as he's back?"

"Right on. And here he comes now."

Franklin crossed to the door and opened it to reveal Fernandez and a worried looking Gerry. "Come on in, guys. We think we've just stumbled on a clue."

"What's going on here?" Gerry asked before Fernandez could speak.

"Gerry," Dot said, "We think that Bill might have been kidnapped or something like that."

"Yeah, man," Franklin said, "Do you know what time he left this morning?"

"You, too? Half-seven I think."

Franklin turned to Fernandez, "What time did you say the other copper got back on duty outside Bill's place?"

"Bradford? About eight. Now what's all this fuss about?"

Franklin and Dot exchanged a nod, and Franklin related their theory to the policeman and Gerry.

When Franklin was finished, Fernandez looked thoughtful for a few moments and then turned to Gerry, "Does that business with his degrees sound plausible to you?"

Gerry snorted a worried laugh, "Everyone in a five-mile radius must know about Bill's degrees. It's not that he brags about them or anything, just that he feels it's important that people get the details right about things like that."

"Yeah," Dot agreed, "He reckons that if you've spent years working for something, the least people can do is use the proper letters."

Fernandez nodded, "I'll phone that little gem through to DS Green."

The other three watched anxiously as the policeman related the news to his superior and exchanged worried glances when they heard him say "So, he's not there then?". As soon as he rang off, Franklin demanded to be told the news from Companies House.

"DC Bradford got there about five minutes ago, and the security guards said that no-one has entered the building all morning. It's officially closed, but they're known to allow a select few individuals inside. They've checked the main records office and they're absolutely positive that there's no-one there. In other words Mr. Taylor never got there."

*****

Green turned towards McCoy. "Looks like Taylor has definitely been abducted. It's almost twelve now and he left his place more than four hours ago."

"Jesus fucking Christ! That's all we need! Fernandez was positive that he didn't get a good look at the pair who were snooping around outside the flat?"

"Both tall, but it was too dark to make out their features."

McCoy slumped into his chair and reached for the Glenfiddich bottle. "I don't suppose Singh's got anywhere yet?"

"I checked with her half an hour ago and she reckoned they'd be starting their first runs around twelve. She said—"

There was a knock on the door and DC Robson poked his head around it, "Thought you might like to see this," he brandished a file, "It's probably nothing, but I thought you'd better know."

McCoy took the file and opened it on his desk, Green moving behind him, so he could peer over his shoulder. It contained a standard crime report and was dated the previous Monday. A young woman, Monica Leigh, had been murdered in her penthouse apartment overlooking Tobacco Dock in the heart of Docklands. There was no clear motive and no other crime had been committed at the scene. McCoy turned to the last three pages which were headed 'Witness Statements'.

The first was from a neighbour who had heard 'strange' noises issuing from the apartment above hers. A typically concerned young professional that she was, she kept her door firmly locked until well after things had quietened down. Not wishing to lower the tone of the exclusive building, she had decided against calling in the police and only admitted hearing anything when officers carried out a door-to-door.

The second had both Green and McCoy staring at each other as soon as they'd finished reading it. It was written by the building's supervisor, a retired council officer. Shortly before the time the 'concerned' neighbour had reported hearing her strange noises, he had seen the occupant of the penthouse apartment enter the building with another woman in tow. They seemed to be having a heated debate about something, but, not being the nosy type, he didn't get close enough to make out the words. He also only had a rear view of the pair of them as they made their way to the lifts.

Five minutes later, he made his customary security patrol, starting in the basement and working his way up. He summoned the lift from the fifth floor, the one immediately below the penthouse and when it arrived, the woman that had been with Monica Leigh a few minutes earlier, was inside. He was sure it was the same woman because, even though he'd only seen her from the rear before, she was very unusually dressed and had a very uncommon hair colour.

She was wearing a very short skirt under a well-tailored jacket with a plunging neckline. There was nothing underneath the jacket, and despite it being undone – indeed, to the supervisor, it didn't appear to have buttons – she made no move to cover herself. In his own words, he 'copped a right eyeful of a pair of drop-dead gorgeous knockers'. Her hair, he went on to write, was 'a sort of striped silvery-blonde'. He also reckoned she was about six foot tall.

When they got to the ground floor, she smiled at him and said that she hoped that she had brightened his evening.

"I bet she bloody did," Green muttered.

"This has got to be that Alexandra bloody Featherington, hasn't it?"

Green nodded, "It sounds exactly like her, guv."

McCoy turned to DC Robson, "I want everything we've got on this Monica Leigh. And also, I want everything there is to know about that building and that apartment. If this business really does centre around property, then I reckon that's the best place to start."

"I'm on to it, guv." Robson hurried from the room.

McCoy stared back at the file, "Why weren't we told about this murder before?"

"I suppose because it doesn't seem in any way related to the so-called jumpers, and besides, it's a Met case. We didn't even know about Alexandra Featherington until a couple of days ago."

"Whatever. At least this should get us *somewhere*."

Green reached forward and turned to the Scene of Crime Officer's report. "Murder by strangulation. Signs of a struggle. Forensics came up with pretty much nothing." He stood back and sighed, "Bugger all to link it with the jumpers, but plenty to link it to Alexandra Featherington and therefore to Marcus Allen."

"Which in turn, means there's a link *from* Allen *to* the jumpers."

Green nodded, "It's got to be something to do with these so-called property wars but...I can't for the life of me see where anything fits together."

"I think we soon might, Tony," McCoy said, "I got one of my hunches. Something's going down. And it's going down soon."

Green, an eyebrow still arched at the use of his first name, nodded, "I'm getting the same sort of feeling, guv."

The telephone on McCoy's desk rang, "Give!"

"It's DC Robson, guv. Thought I'd let you know right away. The entire building is owned by one Peter Charno, purchased ten years ago when phase two development started. The penthouse apartment was leased to Monica Leigh shortly afterwards and she's been there ever since."

"Good work," McCoy said, "Any more on her yet?"

"Just getting on to it, guv."

"The quicker, the better." He rang off and related Robson's news to Green.

"Well that settles it then," Green said, "Forget Marcus Allen for a minute. We've got to find Alexandra Featherington. She's murdered someone who this Charno character must have known pretty well – in a property belonging to Charno – and then turns up in another one of his properties, supposedly as his personal assistant or something."

"You're right, Tony," McCoy said, "She's a ringer. If there's just a bit of truth in this property war story, then she's a principal player. I want as many men as we can spare to get after her. And I want more media coverage. Get someone downstairs to arrange a press conference for one o'clock. National newspapers, all internet feeds, locals, TV news teams, the works. "I'll straighten it out with DCS Cox."

"You got it, guv."

When Green had left, McCoy closed the file, a thoughtful look on his face, "I don't know where they've taken you William Taylor, but just for once, I actually feel sorry for you."

*****

The blindfold was finally removed from Bill's face after what had seemed to him like a three-hour journey. After being forced to produce the bogus note, he had been led back down to the street and the placed none too gently in the back of a black nondescript saloon car. The taller of his two captors had climbed into the driver's seat, and Benjamin Bannen, who Bill had instantly recognised, climbed into the back alongside him.

"Gentlemen, would you be so kind as to inform me of what is going on?"

"Shut it!" Bannen had said, producing the blindfold from his pocket.

And that had been it. Neither man had said another word during the car journey, and, after another failed attempt to elicit information from them, had resulted in a hard poke in his ribs, Bill went quiet himself.

To try to take his mind off of his predicament, he attempted to work out where he was being taken. At first the car travelled at a crawl, constantly stopping and starting as they made their way through the busy East London streets. After what Bill gauged to be forty minutes or so, their pace increased, although the traffic noise outside was no less. This, he surmised, indicated that they must have reached one of the Capital's main cross-thoroughfares. The heat of the morning sun, amplified by the car's windows, was falling directly on one side of his face, the left, indicating that they were heading pretty much due South.

Bill tried to think where they might be. The Seven Sisters Road, possibly. Maybe even the Caledonian Road or Commercial Lane.

After a few more minutes, the traffic noise began to subside, and their speed increased still further. The driver made a series of mazy turns, presumably following the one-way systems at the edge of the City, but Bill still managed to hang on to the mental map that he was following. By the time the car stopped, he was fairly certain that they were just south and east of the heart of the Square Mile, somewhere in the vicinity of the Tower of London, possibly. Not too close, though, because he couldn't make out the voices of tourists or street vendors.

They waited silently in the car for a few minutes, before he was unceremoniously bundled onto the pavement and frog-marched a few metres. His captors stopped, and he heard the jangling of keys as a lock was being opened. Another jangle met his ears and a second lock clicked open.

He was led forward through a doorway into a cool corridor – he could sense walls close by on either side of him – and was made to stand still while the door was locked behind them. A rough push on his shoulder indicated that he should start walking once more.

Without the benefit of sight, he found himself becoming increasingly alarmed – an irrational sense of fear pervading his normally calm mind. He began to picture himself walking off the edge of a deep pit, of plunging into a gloomy disused shaft, falling and falling... The first time a spider's web draped itself over his head, he let out a yelp, his heart beginning to race.

The corridor began to descend, the angle steep enough to make balance – especially being blindfolded – a precarious matter. As they progressed, the silence now cloying, the temperature plunged further, and the sweat of his fear began to induce shivering fits.

During this part of the journey, Bill lost all sense of time, and much of his sense of direction. He was fairly sure that they were travelling north-west but could no longer be certain.

Three times, they arrived at locked doors which were silently opened by one the men. After stepping through the third one, he was jerked to a halt by a rough hand. This newest section no longer felt like part of a tunnel or corridor – there was no sense of walls pressing close, and this was confirmed when he was led across an echoing chamber on a diagonal path. There was also hushed voices coming from a distance ahead of him, too far away to be intelligible. He didn't know whether he felt this to be a comfort, or the complete reverse.

He was stopped and spun around one hundred and eighty degrees before a firm hand pushed down on his shoulders. His instant of panic subsided as he realised that there was a chair behind him and he let himself fall onto it.

He raised his hands to the blindfold, but they were pulled away, the strength of the manoeuvre leaving Bill in no doubt that it would be unwise to remove it without permission.

"So, here's the infamous William Wilberforce Taylor!" A cultured voice intoned.

"I prefer Bill, but, yes, it is I."

"I imagine you're wondering why you have been invited here?"

"An interesting turn of phrase, dear boy, but the thought had, I must admit, crossed my mind."

"Do you have any idea where you might be?"

"Under the ground seems to be a perfectly safe wager," Bill said.

"Mr. Taylor! Bill, I should say," the voice sounded amused, "You are a highly educated man with a quite remarkably efficient memory. I believe you know perfectly well that I was referring to your geographical location, not geological one. However, I also believe that such disingenuity is a hallmark of your character, and I shall permit you your little diversions. For now, at least.

"I ask you again, Bill, where do you believe you might be?"

"Somewhere under Whitechapel?"

"Is that what you seriously believe? No, I doubt it. Try again."

"Leadenhall Street?"

"My word! Very impressive. Of course, I'll not be telling you whether you're correct, but I will let you know that you're in the very least, very close."

"Thank you, dear boy."

The voice lost its amused edge, "You have been brought here, Bill, because you and your colleagues have been meddling in affairs that do not concern you. Affairs that are also far beyond your scope and powers."

"Wouldn't it have been easier to simply telephone with your views?"

"Do not mock me, Bill. I have power, Bill, more power than you can possibly imagine. And you are on my territory, now – the Dark Side. I have more control over this City – these Cities – than you can possibly imagine. You would be wise to remember that fact."

"Point taken, dear boy, pray continue."

"I take it you know who I am?"

"The infamous Marcus Allen, I presume?"

"I like that," the voice resumed its lighter tone, "The *Infamous* Marcus Allen. For in just a few weeks, that will most certainly be how I am titled. In a few weeks when even those poor souls above ground will know my name. And fear it."

"This is all getting a little too much James Bond for my tastes," Bill said, "Could we not get on with more immediate and pressing concerns?"

"Not a man who relishes the drama of a situation? You surprise me, Bill."

"I'm not a man who relishes *melodrama*, Mr. Allen."

"Please, it's Marcus. Very well, I shall hasten to the point."

"Consider my gratitude boundless, Marcus."

"Don't press me too hard, Bill. Melodramatic or not, my threats are not groundless. You have been brought here for two specific reasons. Firstly, I want to know everything that you have learned about the wretched Peter Charno and his dim-witted, holier-than-thou followers. I also want to know everything you have learned about what is going on down here."

"There's not actually—"

"Not yet, Bill. Let me finish. That was just the first reason. The second concerns yourself and your colleagues. Your interference has been a distraction that my people do not need at this juncture – particularly at this juncture. Word will be got to them to that effect. In order that they see sense, they will also be informed that you are my... guest."

"You haven't let them know already?"

"After the problems they caused us yesterday, I felt that it would do them good to fret a little – to make them sweat, in the modern parlance."

"I'd like to think that they'd be fretting anyway."

"That may be so, but in addition to my admittedly rather childish gesture, the exact nature of the message I give to them will be entirely dependent on how helpful you are when answering the manifold questions that shall shortly be asked of you."

"I get the picture," Bill said, "Never fear, Marcus, I am sure that you will find me a paragon of helpfulness. Besides, I'm really rather squeamish and have never believed that I could stand up to organised torture."

"Torture, Bill? You have not entered some godforsaken underworld where its denizens have been reduced to savagery. Ours is a very civilised society, much more so than that from which you come. We believe in the pleasure principle. We do not punish bad behaviour with violence – unless, of course, it is the last or only resort – ours is a system based on reward for good behaviour."

"Pavlov had much the same notion with his rats, Marcus."

"I trust you are not, by *deliberately* confusing rats with Pavlov's *dogs*, likening us to those vermin?"

Despite the blindfold, somehow Bill got the impression that their eyes locked for a moment, mutually acknowledging that one verbal thrust had been successfully parried.

"Not in the least. I was merely wondering if your society is based on conditioning. Pavlov's *dogs*, Huxley's *Brave New World*, that sort of thing?"

"Everyone here is free, Bill, so the answer must be a resounding 'no'. This world is brave, I admit, but it is not new. In fact, it is older than even I had once imagined."

254

"Very well, so what comes next?"

"Next, Bill, I shall introduce you to the person who will carry out the questioning. You will find the rewards that she, and her assistants, may bestow upon you, a rather wonderful experience. I feel sure that you will co-operate."

"Whenever you're ready, dear boy."

Hands grasped his shoulders and he was led from the chair deeper into the room. The voices he'd heard earlier were louder now, and he could sense a buzz of excitement underlying the whispered conversations.

As before, he was stopped and turned, hands pressing him into another, more comfortable chair. The footsteps receded and for a moment, he thought that he was to be left alone for a while. Then, at the edge of his hearing he could hear soft footfalls approaching, bare feet on smooth concrete.

Hands reached behind his head and the blindfold dropped free. Although the light in the large room wasn't overly bright, Bill still had to blink his eyes a few times before his vision cleared. Then he blinked them a few more times.

In front of him stood a young woman, a fine silver necklace the only thing on her naked body.

"I'm Nadia Melford," she said, smiling, "I'd like you to answer a few questions."

*****

DC Fernandez was relieved in more than the one sense of the word when DC Bradford appeared at one o'clock to take over from him. Franklin Richardson and Dot Kominski had been driving him around the bend with their constant fretting and non-stop pleas to be allowed to do something. While their concern was perfectly understandable, coming on top of his long shift, it was more than his tired mind could stand.

"Thank God you're here," he greeted his colleague.

DC Bradford looked less than happy himself, "I'd rather be home in bed. I only managed a couple of hours last night. This morning, rather."

"If you hadn't had those couple of hours, you wouldn't be here now, would you?"

"McCoy told me—"

"Yeah, I know," Fernandez sighed, "I was just making an observation. Any more news back at the office?"

Bradford glanced across to where Franklin and Dot were standing, apparently deep in conversation, "DS Green said there was another murder on Monday night that ties in with this case. Reckons it's pretty obvious that the perp was Alexandra Featherington. There's going to be a press conference in about half an hour. McCoy wanted it for one o'clock, but they couldn't organise it in time. You can imagine what sort of mood he's in now."

Fernandez could, to judge by the shudder that ran down his spine. "With a bit of luck I'll be tucked up in bed by then. Okay, you know what to do here?"

Bradford nodded, "Keep those two locked up nice and safe here until Green or McCoy tell me any different. Mr Cooper is free to leave when I go."

"And no-one is to be allowed in here, either."

"Got it. Don't worry, I'm quite looking forward to a quiet couple of hours."

Fernandez grinned, "Don't count on that." He left without answering Bradford's quizzical look.

As soon as the door closed behind Fernandez and Gerry, Franklin and Dot zeroed in on the hapless relief constable.

"Did we just hear you say there's gonna be a press conference?"

"Er, yes, miss."

"Dot."

"Pardon?"

"Call me Dot, okay?"

"If you say so."

"And did you also say that there was another murder on Monday?" Franklin asked.

Bradford looked from one enquiring face to the other, "I'm not sure that—"

"Listen, man. Our colleague is being held out there somewhere. Yesterday we were nearly trapped by some crazed mob. We've been set up and pissed around with for the last week. We're stuck bang in the middle of the weird shit that's going down and we're running out of patience fast. Just answer the question, okay?"

Bradford looked up into the young black man's lowering face, noting how his nostrils were flaring, "Of course. A woman named Monica Leigh was murdered in her apartment," he said quickly, "From eye witness reports, it appears clear that the perp – murderer that is – was Alexandra Featherington. The apartment belongs to Peter Charno."

Franklin and Dot stared at each other.

"Er, is that what you wanted to hear?" Bradford asked.

Dot shook her head, "Not all of it, anyway."

"Dot," Franklin said, "You know what this means, don't you?"

"I guess that this Monica Leigh was Charno's real assistant and for some reason, that Featherington bitch took her place when you were supposed to be contacted by Leigh, right?"

"That's exactly what I'm thinking."

"What worries me is that she *murdered* her," Dot said, "Why go to such an extreme when all we were being employed to do was try to track down some missing people?"

"There's gotta be something more to this case that we don't know."

Dot shuddered, "I thought I was relieved when we got away yesterday. But now…"

Franklin gave her a hug, "Well we did, and we're safe now."

"But Bill–"

"I know," he soothed, "Constable?"

DC Bradford, who had been watching the exchange with a growing sense of disquiet, looked at Franklin, "Yes, Mr. Richardson?"

"There's a kettle in that small room over there. It looks like you could use a cup."

"Pardon?"

"What he means," Dot said, "Is that we want a private word. In other words, get lost for a couple of minutes, will you?"

"I don't think that–"

"We're not going anywhere," Franklin said, "Just give us a bit of privacy for a minute, okay?"

With a shrug, Bradford crossed to the office door, checked that it was locked and pocketed the key. "I'll give you five minutes," he said, "But no messing me about, okay?"

Franklin and Dot both nodded.

When he had entered their little utility room, Franklin closed the door behind him and locked it. "Talk about a dozy plod," he said, over the hammering from within. He pointed to Bill's desk, "He even left his jacket and phone in here."

"So, what's your plan?"

Franklin put his hands on Dot's shoulders. "I've still got the map," he said, "My guess is that they'll be holding Bill in either one of the stations we went into yesterday, or one of the other two that were supposed to be under Charno's control. Allen's arrogant enough to do just that."

"Oh, no!" Dot began.

"Listen to me!" Franklin interrupted, "It was *me* that Allen wanted to talk to yesterday."

"Tell the police. Let them go down there."

"That won't work. You saw how secure those places are. Even if they did manage to get through, I'd bet anything that Allen's mob will just move on. But if it's just one person – if it's me – they'll *let* me in."

"You can't be serious?"

"Deadly ser... I mean, *really* serious."

Dot shook her head, "You *can't*! You heard what that copper just said: Alexandra bleedin' Featherington *murdered* someone!"

"She's already had her chance to do me in, and she didn't."

"But–"

"There's no choice, little lady. Remember Bill."

"Of course I bleedin' remember Bill! No! There's got to be another way!"

"Can you think of anything?"

Dot changed tack, "They're bound to let him go when he tells them what they want. Why don't we just wait a while? A few hours at least?"

"We can't be sure of that. Besides, Bill doesn't really *know* that much."

"What can they possibly want to know anyway? If Featherington is one of theirs, then all we know, all any of us know, is what she told us!"

Franklin shook his head, "It's just come to me. There's one thing they can't know!"

"Well?"

"They don't know what Charno said to me – what he might have told me."

"But he didn't tell you anything much, did he? Just that there were thirteen of his people missing and that he wanted you to find them."

"No he didn't. What he actually said was that there was an... intriguing and complex problem, and when I pressed him to describe what sort of investigation it would be, he said that he supposed 'missing persons' was the most fitting term. He didn't mention numbers, or even say just what he meant when he said 'missing persons'".

"So in other words, *you* don't know any more than Bill either."

"They don't know that."

"If you go down there, they soon bleedin' will. You reckon they'll be happy with that? You reckon they'll even *believe* that you don't know any more?"

"There's only one way to find out. Maybe if I convince them, they'll back off."

Dot shook her head again, "You've heard what's going on! This Allen guy's got some master plan and by the look of it, they're quite happy to murder people to see it through."

"Tell you what. How about we get me a one-hour head start and then have the police follow me down? Allen's mob won't be finished questioning me in just one hour, will they?"

"No! You said yourself that if they see a bunch of people entering the system they'll block the accesses or move on. If you're already down there, they'll know you've set them up. What will happen then?"

"Maybe Bill and I can distract them, keep them entertained."

"All of them? You don't even know how many are down there."

"It's gotta be done. For Bill's sake."

"But you're not even sure where they are! What if they're not where you think?"

"Then I'm not gonna be in any danger, am I?"

"What about the old bill following you? They ain't gonna be happy if you lead them on a wild duck chase!"

"Goose."

"What?!"

"It's a wild *goose* chase."

"That's what I'm trying to tell you," Dot was determined not to be distracted.

"I really *do* think they'll be where I said. Allen really comes across as being that sort of type."

"But–"

"No buts, little lady. This has got to be done. No buts, no choices."

Tears sprang into her eyes, "You can't!"

Franklin pulled her to him and hugged her tightly, "I can. Bill means a lot to me. I can't just do nothing. You know he'd do the same for either of us."

"Then..." she swallowed hard, "I'm going with you."

"No way!" He broke the embrace and stood back a little so that he could stare her in the eyes, "There's something down there that has a bad effect on you. You can't risk it happening again."

"Maybe it was just a one-off–"

"And maybe not. It's too much of a risk. You might even become a liability to us – we don't even know what other side-effects there might be. And besides, I'll need someone up top to help me get the head start I need, and that someone will also need to get the police on my tail."

"What about Gerry? We could call–"

"We're not getting anyone else involved."

"Well how about we just both go now and leave a note for that copper in the utility room. He's bound to get out of there in a while."

The hammering had started up again, and there were muffled shouts coming from the small room.

"That door's pretty solid. There's no guarantee that he'll ever get out."

Dot's shoulders sagged, "I ain't gonna be able to stop you, am I?"

"It wouldn't be right, anyway."

"Yeah well…. Look, if you go getting yourself hurt, I'll never forgive you."

"I won't, I promise. And I keep my promises, remember?"

She nodded sadly, "I remember."

"Besides," he said, "I'm looking forward to going home with you every night. I'm not gonna risk missing out on that, little lady."

Dot flung her arms around his neck and hugged him tightly. "Moron."

"You're not that bad."

It brought a choked laugh from her, and the mood lightened a little, "Okay," she said at length, "You'd better get going before I change my mind. I'll let dopey out of the utility room in half an hour."

Franklin shook his head, "That press conference is due on in a couple of minutes and I wanna see it. And I'm starving. Can't go on rescue missions on an empty stomach."

"There's nothing in the office fridge," Dot said.

"I have a cunning plan, worthy of Baldrick himself," Franklin grinned.

He crossed to the utility room and unlocked the door. A red-faced DC Bradford tumbled into the main office, a look of relief flashing across his face when he saw that both of his captives were still present. It was replaced with a look of indignation, "What did you do that for?"

"We just wanted to make sure that we had our private word, that's all," Franklin said.

"But I told you that you could have five minutes!"

"Check your watch. We needed twenty. Now, what channel is this press conference on?"

"What?"

"The press conference?" Franklin pointed a remote-control unit at the small TV in the corner of the office.

"Oh," Bradford said, "I'm not really sure, but I suppose it's bound to be on Sky News."

Franklin nodded and pressed the appropriate button. The conference was just starting, DCS Cox introducing an unshaven, tired-looking Inspector McCoy to the assembled press corps.

It turned out to be a run-of-the-mill affair, McCoy spending much of the time assuring the press that it was a matter of extreme urgency that the woman named as Alexandra Featherington was located. As soon as the news media realised that she was wanted not only in connection with a single murder, but with the events in the tube stations on the same night, they hurled question after question at the increasingly agitated Inspector.

By the time McCoy had tersely thanked the press for their attendance, departing with DS Green and DCS Cox in tow, Sky News were displaying a 'Breaking News' banner which read: "Mass murder on the tube – not suicides. Police identify suspect".

"Inspector McCoy's going to love that," Bradford said, as Franklin switched off the TV.

"Let's just hope someone knows where the bitch is." Dot said.

"Amen to that," Franklin said. "Look, I don't know about you guys, but I'm starving."

Unseen by Bradford, Dot gave Franklin a pleading look. He shook his head with a sorrowful smile.

She returned the look and took a deep breath, "I'll see if there's anything in the fridge, should I?"

"Nah, I don't fancy anything cold. How about I pop round the corner to the KFC and grab us all a bite?"

"Sorry, Mr. Richardson," Bradford said, "But I can't let you do that. I'm as hungry as the next man... er, and next woman, of course, but orders are orders. I'm not to let either of you out of the building and if McCoy finds out that I did, well, let's just say that I'm not exactly in his good books as it is."

"Well I gotta eat something, man. Tell you what, why don't I phone that cab company that deliver takeaways, get them bring it round to us?"

Bradford shook his head, "I can't allow that either. No-one's to be allowed in the building. It's my–"

"Yeah, I know, your orders. Tell you what then, why don't *you* go? That's not against your orders."

"You think I was born yesterday?"

"Hey, man! You honestly believe we're gonna scarper as soon as you're out of sight? With a murderess on the loose? Man, she knows the address of this place. She could be outside right now, waiting to follow us to a quiet spot where she could top us the same way she topped that Monica Leigh!" Franklin shook his head, "No way, man. We ain't going nowhere."

"Yeah, come on Constable," Dot said, "It's only just round the corner – won't take you more than five minutes. Just make sure you double-lock the front door on the way out."

"Well…"

"It's our treat," Franklin assured him, "We did the same for Constable Fernandez last night."

"You did?"

Franklin nodded, "The least we could do. Hey! And you never know. Perhaps she really is watching this place. Keep an eye out for her and if you see her… well, think how pleased McCoy's gonna be."

Bradford's resistance caved in, "You'll not get up to any funny business while I'm gone?"

"Scouts' honour."

After he had taken their orders and twenty pounds from the petty cash, he lectured them once more and then dashed down the stairs two at a time, determined that he wouldn't be gone more than five minutes. He had also taken the precaution of relieving Franklin of his keys.

"You were never a scout, were you?" Dot asked when the street door had closed.

"I was never even a cub."

"Do you think it'll be busy in the KFC?"

"At two o'clock on a Saturday afternoon when the town's full of shoppers? I hadn't really thought of that. I suppose it could be."

"You're a devious sod, aren't you?"

"I prefer the term cunning strategist."

Dot laughed, despite her fears, "What now?"

"Okay. Let's have your office keys, that combination lock key that we never gave to McCoy and a flashlight. I reckon he'll be at least twenty minutes, maybe more. When he gets back, if it's any earlier than thirty minutes from the time I left, tell him I'm in the loo. Say something about all the excitement upsetting my belly. That should delay him for another few minutes and I should be long gone." He pocketed the keys and flashlight.

"I wish you weren't doing this."

"Me too, I guess. Just think of me as a dusky Arnold Schwarzenegger."

"What!?"

"I'll be both back and black. That's a promise."

Dot hugged him tightly, "Make it soon."

Franklin kissed her and then broke the embrace, "Time's wasting. Wish me luck."

"Yeah, good luck, moron."

"I adore you too."

"Go on, scoot! Before I change my mind and stop you."

He kissed her once more and then trotted down the stairs before he changed his own mind. "I must be mad," he muttered to himself as he stepped into the crowded street.

*****

"I thought you handled that pretty well, guv."

"I hope you're not being sarcastic, Green," McCoy said.

DS Green shook his head, "No, really. Those press boys can be absolute animals."

"Let's just hope something comes of it. I really do get the feeling that everything's coming to a head."

"Like you say, guv: Nothing wrong with a good hunch."

"Who said anything about good? How many men have we got on the phones?"

"Ten plods from Wood Street with experience, five of our own men, and Robson co-ordinating."

McCoy nodded, "Sounds about right."

A turbaned head poked around the doorway, "Inspector?"

"Come in Sunny. I hope you've got some good news for me?"

DS Singh came through the doorway, four large files tucked under her arm, "I am not certain whether news such as this can be termed good or bad, but in any case or either case we have completed our cross-checking."

"Have you been hanging around William Taylor, Sunny?" McCoy said.

"I am not getting your joke, Inspector."

"Never mind. Take a seat and tell us what you've come up with."

Singh settled herself and went through her normal practice of gathering her thoughts into order. "Well, Inspector," she said, "There are some quite interesting matches that have come to light and they fall into two distinct categories. One series concerns a particular group of people and the other concerns the various companies associated with the wills and the planning applications."

"And you're totally sure they're all genuine?"

"Completely."

"Definitely no sign of Dave the Engraver's involvement?"

"Definitely not, Inspector."

"Good. Start with the companies then."

"Very well, Inspector." Singh opened two of the files and turned them to face McCoy, "As you will see from this first list, many of the companies have charitable status. In fact, seventy-eight percent, which is far more than the norm of eighteen percent. If we look at the board memberships when these companies were formed, there are no more than eleven people who appear on more than one company's list of directors. However," she pointed to the second list, "If we look at the directors as they stand this very day, there are more than six hundred matches."

"Are you saying that a group of people having been steadily moving in and taking control of these business?"

"That is exactly what I am saying, Inspector. In fact, most of the changes have been made within the last two years."

"Would the people who made the wills be aware of this fact?"

"Not unless they specifically checked. And of course, if they made the wills more than two years ago and have not kept abreast of these changes, then again, they would be totally unaware."

Green held up his hand, "Guv, do you think it's possible that these six hundred or so, deliberately moved in on companies and institutions that were due to receive large payments should their potential beneficiaries die?"

"It's as good a theory as any."

"There is more, Inspector, which might support such a theory," Sunny opened a third file, "You see from this file that although many of these companies remain, in name, separate entities, closer examination of their share registers show that many of them own substantial portions of the others."

McCoy scanned the list, "It looks like bloody nearly *all* of them are interrelated."

"Ninety-seven percent, Inspector."

Green and McCoy exchanged a nod.

"Okay, Sunny, what about the wills themselves?"

"We have now received details of fourteen. And before you ask, Inspector, Dave the Engraver is definitely not the author of any of them. In each and every case there has been two main beneficiaries alongside much smaller amounts donated to individuals who we can discount as being distant relatives. The main beneficiaries are, without exception, charitable institutions."

"In other words, Green's theory is correct?"

"In all probability, Inspector. I believe that these poor people have been inadvertently exposed to some sort of corrupt manipulation, believing themselves to be endowing charitable concerns, when in fact, these concerns are being systematically taken over by a group of unscrupulous individuals."

Green nodded, "Couldn't have put it better myself."

"Okay," McCoy said, "Let's proceed on that basis for a minute. Assuming we've been able to identify six hundred potential crooks, what do we know about them?"

Sunny Singh opened the last file, "There are two names that we already know of, which are listed at the top."

"Alexandra Featherington and Peter Charno," McCoy read aloud, "That's consistent, anyway."

266

"There is an interesting difference between these two individuals, Inspector. In the case of the lady, she is only listed as having interests in companies that have been subject to the invasion of the six hundred people. In the case of the gentleman, the companies with which he is involved have none of those six hundred names listed."

"But surely if his name appears many times, then he is one of that group of six hundred?"

"No, Inspector. Mr. Charno's name has been associated with these companies or charities since their formation. In many cases, this stretches back to just after the Second World War."

"And Featherington?"

"All within the last two years."

"Okay, so what about the rest?"

"Our preliminary search indicates that the individuals are no longer to be found at the addresses last given, and none appear to have police records."

"Six hundred people moving home in the last two years?"

"In many cases, Inspector, they were never *at* the address listed. To further complicate matters we have carried out searches on records held by the HM Revenue and Customs, Social Security and the Passport Office. None of the names are to be found."

"What!?"

"It is as if these people do not exist, Inspector."

McCoy closed his eyes for a moment, desperately trying to assimilate this information, "So," he said, "The immediate assumption must be that these are mostly false identities created to allay suspicion that one – or at least, a few – individuals are infiltrating these companies and charities, right?"

"Sounds good to me, guv."

"And this in turn, matches up with these crazy stories about some property war, insofar as someone is taking control of any property held by these companies."

"Inspector," Sunny said, "I have undertaken such a check. According to the balance sheets, in eighty-nine percent of cases, the companies' principal holdings comprise property. In seventy-six percent of cases, this is mostly based in London."

"Bloody hell," McCoy said, "This is fantastic work, Sunny."

"And it's just what we needed," Green added.

"Thank you, Inspector."

"Well, if that's everything, we've got some serious thinking to do–"

Sunny held up her hand, "There is one last thing that I noticed when I was collating the duplicate files. Look at a few of those names I have marked with an asterisk and a number."

McCoy and Green both peered at the sheet.

Green looked up, "They're pretty weird I grant you. What's your point?"

For the second time that year, Sunny smiled, "Those I have given the same number to are anagrams of each other."

McCoy looked up sharply, "Bloody well-spotted. What happens if the anagramatical duplicates are removed?"

"My earliest calculation is that the list is reduced to just one hundred and twenty names, Inspector. I will complete this task as soon as I go back downstairs."

"Thanks, Sunny," McCoy nodded, "I'll not forget this."

Singh stammered her own gratitude and backed out of the room as quickly as she could.

McCoy opened his desk drawer and pulled out a fresh bottle of Glenfiddich. "Time for a small celebration, Tony."

"I reckon you're right, guv."

"What do you make of it all?"

"I reckon that no matter how preposterous it sounds, that story Taylor gave us was true. Everything we've come up with so far seems to point the same way."

"I agree. We desperately need to get hold of Alexandra bloody Featherington, Marcus Allen and Peter Charno. The question is, how?"

"As far as Featherington goes," Green said, "I reckon we've done as much as we can for the time being. Who knows about Charno? He could be anywhere. But we're pretty positive that Marcus Allen is close by. Shit, he could even be right under our feet as we speak. Maybe we should send some sort of task-force down in the tunnels?"

"But where would they start? There's more than seven hundred miles of legitimate tube tunnels, without all the abandoned stuff. And look how much trouble we had getting into the tunnels behind Mansion House station. We could pick manholes at random and go down that way, but we wouldn't stand a chance of finding them."

Green nodded, "Needles and haystacks. I reckon the best we could do is try to flush him out somehow. Maybe send a small squad down there and cause some sort of disturbance."

"It might be worth a try," McCoy said, "We've got bugger-all else in the way of options. Get someone to put together a list of the abandoned stations, we'll pick one of them to start with."

DS Green took another sip of his whisky and rose to his feet, stretching his cramped back. He was just about to leave the room when the phone rang.

"Give!"

There was a pause and McCoy's face began to redden. "He's what, Bradford?!"

*****

DC Bradford had been gone thirty-five minutes before he returned, and Dot was beginning to worry that Franklin had too much of a head start. The Constable arrived at the office door, sweating profusely, three large KFC boxes leaking aromatic fat onto his jacket sleeve.

He took one long, worried look around the interior, "Where is he?" Fried chicken scattered across the carpet tiles.

"I don't know," Dot wailed, no acting required.

"You mean he's gone?"

"I… I guess so. I really don't know what he's doing!"

Panicking, Bradford made for the stairs. He got half way down and then clattered back up them, even before Dot could call him back, "How long's he been gone?"

"Fifteen minutes, maybe. You will find him quick won't you?"

"I'd better," Bradford muttered under his breath, "Did he say where he was going?"

Dot nodded emphatically, "He said that he had to go back down there. Our Bill's in trouble and…" she broke off and handed him a sheet of paper.

The constable snatched it out of her hands and stared at it, his mind full of images of McCoy at his worst, "And this is where he's supposed to be headed?"

"It doesn't really say, does it?"

The sheet of paper contained a list of possible destinations, each annotated with Franklin's barely legible script. Bradford seemed on the verge of literally pulling his hair out. "These places… they're… all over the place! Surely he said where he was going?!"

Dot shook her head, "Not in so many words."

"But…" Bradford took a few deep breaths, "You must have some idea?"

She did a mental calculation, and reckoned that if he'd been lucky with transport, Franklin would have reached his destination by then. She took the sheet back and pointed at two of the names listed, "These two. They're the places we were going to check out next after we got past the first two, and knowing him, he wants to make sure that we finish the job."

"Finish the…"

"And he said a little while back that he reckons that's where this Allen guy would take Bill. You've gotta get someone to help him!"

"Are you sure—"

"Just do it! If anything happens to Franklin because—"

"Okay! But you're really positive—"

Dot kicked him square on the shin, "Now!"

Chapter 12

Saturday 17th November 2018

Franklin found a cab with remarkable ease, and after promising the driver a ten-pound tip, managed to persuade him that a fast trip into the City was a splendid way of spending a few minutes on a busy Saturday afternoon. The young Scottish cabby was initially as verbose as if he'd been loosening his tongue for a few hours back in his beloved Glasgow but lapsed into silence at his fare's increasingly nervous state.

"Is you on the run, or summat?" he tried as they barrelled down the Seven Sisters Road.

"Just drive," Franklin muttered, a roll of the eyes enough to silence the driver for the remainder of the journey.

When they arrived in Cornhill, just fifteen minutes later, Franklin paid off the cabby and took the map from inside his jacket. The two remaining stations were clearly marked, but he knew that he could no longer trust the access routes that were detailed on the plan. The closest of the two appeared to be very near the infamous Lloyds building, and he hurried along the road in that direction.

Now that he was back in the City, he no longer felt nearly as confidant that he would be able to locate Bill. Nevertheless, he knew he had to try. His only unresolved problem now was how to get down there. According to the map, he was standing pretty much immediately overhead of a station listed as St. Priaulx, and he looked around at the surface of the street, wondering where to attempt to gain access. All of the manhole covers bore seals and it was soon clear to him that these offered no chance of entry.

Franklin was beginning to despair, cursing himself for a fool, when he noticed the square, concrete structure at the side of an empty office building. Six-foot-tall and five wide, the nondescript block suddenly nagged at his memory. Something about....

He walked over to the structure and stood on tiptoe. A metal grille covered the top surface and from inside he could hear the sounds of large electric fans whirring away. A constant current of warm air flowed up past his face.

"Of course!" he said aloud, a smile beginning to spread over his face.

After checking that there was no-one in sight, he boosted himself on to the top of the structure and knelt to one side of the metal grille. He pulled the flashlight from his jacket and shone it into the depths.

The powerful beam revealed a deep shaft, and in the depths, he could just make out some sort of metal casing. The noise of large fans and the stream of warm, dry air were more apparent here, and he grinned to himself, nodding. This, he reckoned, must be one of the one hundred and twenty air regulation shafts that were used to keep the air in the Underground system relatively clean and at a constant temperature of twenty-one degrees Celsius. If that were the case, then there must be a direct connection to the tunnels below. St. Priaulx was listed as a formerly used station and tunnel which had simply been bypassed some forty years earlier, which in turn meant that he should be able to gain access to it through a concealed entrance, much as he and Dot has escaped from the unnamed station the previous day. By using the air ventilation system, he should be able to find the exact location of the station without recourse to the sewers or the main tunnel system.

With trembling hands, he pulled a set of small screwdrivers from his pocket, checked that he was still unobserved, and then started to unscrew the metal grille. Surprised to find there was no other security devices in place, he quickly removed the grille and eased it to one side. A set of metal rungs led down into the darkness, and after a final check along the street, he swung himself inside the shaft.

The descent was longer than it had looked from the top of the shaft, and after his exertions the previous day, Franklin's muscles were trembling by the time he reached the bottom. The noise of the massive fans was almost deafening in the confines of the small chamber that he found himself in, and he felt the first flutterings of claustrophobia begin to assail him.

Forcing himself to breathe slowly and deeply, he switched on the flashlight and stared around.

At floor level, small square tunnels led off in three directions from the noisy chamber, each of them about three feet square. By shining the flashlight beam into them, he could see that they led slightly downwards and that they appeared to be dry and smooth. Air rushed up each of them, warmer than in the shaft above him, and carrying a faint metallic tang.

He eyed the narrow tunnels with a mounting sense of dread. There was no way for him to know how far they went, or even whether they would remain sufficiently large enough for him to be able to navigate them.

Before his nerve completely deserted him, he dropped onto all fours and awkwardly crawled into the central one.

"This ain't so bad," he told himself, "I can do this."

He moved forward as quickly as he dared, careful not to let himself go too fast as the angle of descent was steeper than it had appeared from the shaft. Not ten metres into the tunnel, sweat began to stream down his face as the humid air rushed part him, and coupled with the constant pressure of the walls at either side and the ceiling overhead, his claustrophobia was threatening to overwhelm him.

Franklin paused for a few seconds, trying to calm his ragged nerves, and then closed his eyes and pressed on, counting slowly under his breath. Every time he reached thirty, he opened them and peered ahead. When he did so after the seventh, increasingly rapid, count, he could see that he was approaching some sort of junction or exit point. He also fancied that he could hear a distant rumbling noise – hopefully the sort of noise made by a tube train passing through a tunnel. Aching muscles complaining, he struggled onwards as quickly as he could.

The end of the tunnel approached, appearing as a solid black square with no defining features beyond, but Franklin could sense space beckoning. With an almost manic grin stretched across his face, he plunged out of the air duct, heedless of what might lie beyond.

An escape from claustrophobia or not, he immediately recognised this to be a very bad manoeuvre. The fall was no more than a couple of feet, but the impact when he landed was enough to knock the breath out of him. After checking that nothing felt broken, he rolled onto his back and lay gasping in the darkness.

By some miracle, the flashlight had survived the impact and its welcoming beam finally drew Franklin onto his knees. He picked it up and shone it around.

He found himself in a large chamber that apparently served a number of purposes. As well as the air duct that he'd entered from, there were several other small tunnels leading into the room, one of which appeared to be blocked off by a metal grille similar to the one at the top of the access shaft. Metal cabinets lined one wall and a panel on the opposite side was covered with switches and electronic gadgetry.

Wincing, Franklin stood slowly and walked across to the first of the tunnels leading out of the chamber. It was seven feet tall and was clearly the main access point to the room he'd tumbled into. He was about to move on to the next one when something just inside the tunnel entrance caught his eye. He turned the beam of the flashlight and shone it at the wall at eye level. Clearly etched into the surface was the word 'Monument' and a small arrow pointing into the depths of the tunnel.

Heart beating faster, he moved onto the next one. This time, the wall had been etched with the word 'Bank'. Holding his breath, he crossed to the third tunnel, the one with the metal grille. A single line was scratched through the name 'St. Priaulx'.

"Yes!" Franklin punched the air with joy, already scrabbling in his pockets for the screwdrivers.

Three minutes later, he was scurrying along the winding tunnel praying fervently that he'd guessed the right location, and even more fervently that he'd be able to gain access to the abandoned station when he reached the end.

After maybe thirty metres, his flashlight picked out what appeared to be a solid wall of bricks directly ahead of him, and he let out a groan. Fearing the worst, he slowed his pace to a walk and stepped forward.

The sudden sound of human voices nearly made him yelp with fright. He stopped and shone the flashlight onto the walls ahead of him, realising as he did so that the tunnel wasn't blocked after all. Instead it appeared to turn sharply to the left.

He began to edge forward, his mind a raging mixture of hope, fear and excitement. He was less than five metres away from the corner when he realised that there was a little light filtering into the tunnel and he switched off his flashlight, not wishing to be discovered too quickly. As he inched his way around the corner, the noise level rose appreciably, and he guessed that there was a large number of people somewhere close by.

The new section of tunnel ran straight forwards for about ten metres, ending in a well-lit room of some sort. Franklin crept forward until he was a few centimetres from the tunnel's exit.

Ahead of him, he could make out the floor of a typical underground tunnel. Typical other than for the fact that the rails were covered in a thick layer of rust. His heart lurched in his chest as three large rats skittered past in front of him. Trying hard to control his ragged breathing, he inched forward and peered around the corner, jerking his head back as soon as he'd taken in his surroundings.

The end of the access tunnel met the abandoned tube tunnel at an oblique angle a metre above floor level and two or three metres from the end of the platform. St. Priaulx appeared to be much larger than two stations they'd visited the previous day, and at the far end of the platform there appeared to be a cluster of offices and rooms, doors standing open. It was from them that the voices were issuing.

Franklin took a deep breath and stepped into the tunnel, quickly crouching down below platform level. Ignoring the annoyed squeaking of a couple of worryingly large rats, he made his way along the station until he reached a position opposite the offices. He was just preparing to take a quick peek over the edge of the platform when a familiar voice rose above the general hubbub.

"Dear lady, for the very last time, I promise you that I am in no position to answer your questions. Now, if you would be so good as to ask your assistant to stop rubbing her breasts around my ear, I'd rather like to talk to Mr. Allen."

In the tunnel, below platform level, Franklin punched the air.

*****

Unlike DC Bradford, Dot was in no way cowed by DI McCoy's rage as they stood in his office.

"Look, it don't matter *how* he got away! You can talk about all of that later. Right now, you've gotta get some men to go down after him. You've *got* to!"

McCoy stared down at her, "Have you quite finished ordering me around, Miss Kominski?"

"But–"

"Enough! Jesus fucking Christ! Of all the brain-dead, dim-witted, fucking *stupid* things to... Didn't I make it perfectly clear to both of you yesterday that I would not tolerate your interference any longer? Do you realise just how much danger Richardson has put himself in?"

"Yesterday was the day before you let our Bill get abducted."

Both Dot and McCoy shot DC Bradford a hard look. "It's not my–"

"Shut up, Bradford," McCoy snapped, "You've no idea how much I'm looking forward to dealing with you when this mess is sorted." He turned back to Dot, "Why didn't Richardson just tell us what he thought had happened, eh? Does he think that a specialist crime unit isn't equipped to deal with a situation like this?"

"Yeah well... you hadn't exactly done anything yet, had you?"

"For your information, Miss 'yeah-well', we were just organising something when that useless bastard cringing over there called to say Richardson had scarpered."

"If a great big gang of you go charging down there, Allen will just move on and we'll never find him again. He's got all sorts of security systems and stuff."

"And he won't move on if Richardson finds him?"

"Course not. It's Franklin he really wants to talk to." She quickly outlined Franklin's theory.

"Richardson may have a point," McCoy conceded, "But it's not exactly much help is it? Now we don't know where either Taylor *or* Richardson is. Even if he does manage to locate Taylor, your idea about Allen moving on if we send a squad down there still applies, doesn't it?"

"We'll have one advantage, though."

"How?"

Dot pulled a small black box from her jacket pocket, "I tagged Franklin's jacket before he left. It's got a really powerful signal, so we should be able to locate him even if he's underground."

"Just how powerful is powerful?"

"On the surface it's got a fifteen-mile radius."

McCoy nodded, "It might be enough. Does he know about it?"

"No. What he don't know about, he can't talk about."

"Well at least you've done one sensible thing." He picked up his phone, "Green? Have the squad ready to leave in two minutes, and make sure we've got every bloody map London Transport gave us, okay?" He rang off and turned back to Dot, "You're coming with me."

"Too bleedin' right I am."

"You, Bradford. Stay here – you've fucked up enough things for one day."

Dot had to trot to keep up with McCoy as he made his way down to the reception area where DS Green was waiting with six officers wearing flak jackets. Each of them were carrying folders, presumably containing maps.

"Ready, Green?"

"All set, guv. Decided where we're going yet?"

"Pretty much. You lot just follow our car, right?"

"Yessir!"

Outside the squad jumped into a waiting van and McCoy, Green and Dot climbed into an unmarked car.

"Where to, guv?"

"Cornhill first, then take it slow and make for Leadenhall."

In the back seat beside him, Dot stared intently at the receiver, willing the bank of tiny bulbs to flicker into life.

*****

Franklin could scarcely believe his ears as Bill's voice came again.

"Isn't it about time that you abandoned your clearly wasted efforts – not to mention all that clearly wasted sexual energy – and allow me to speak to Mr. Allen himself?"

"You've no idea what you're missing." A female voice, rich and deep.

"I have a very clear idea, dear lady. Especially after so many demonstrations by your assistants. However, the fact remains that I've nothing more to tell you."

"Very well. You've had your chance."

Franklin took a quick peep over the edge of the platform. His eyes widened as he took in the scene. Bill was sitting on a comfortable-looking sofa, surrounded on all sides by young women. Naked young women. In front of him, her back turned towards Franklin, was a dark-haired female who Franklin thought was probably Nadia Melford. There was no sign of Marcus Allen – or any men, come to that – but there were figures moving around behind the frosted glass partition that formed the back wall of the room Bill was in.

He had hoped that the women would leave Bill unattended while they fetched Marcus Allen, but the one he took to be Nadia Melford ordered just one of the girls from the room. She returned after a couple of minutes alongside Marcus Allen and another man – Benjamin Bannen.

As they turned into the room, Franklin eased himself onto the surface of the platform, staying low. "Oh, well," he muttered, "Time to make an entrance."

Inside the room, all eyes were focused on Bill, Allen and Bannen standing either side of Nadia Melford.

Allen took a step towards Bill, "I am told, Bill, that you are being uncooperative."

"Not at all, dear boy. I find myself unable to be co-operative, since I'm afraid I do not know the answers to the questions I have been posed."

"Do you recall what I said earlier?"

"Almost verbatim, Marcus. I have a very good memory."

"The you will recall that I told you our society is based on rewards and not punishments?"

Bill nodded, "Adding the codicil that you would entertain violence in the last resort."

"Quite so."

"Hi, guys!" Everyone looked over as Franklin sauntered into the room, "Looks like my kind of party."

Marcus Allen's jaw dropped open, "You!"

"In the flesh. How you doing, partner?"

"Marvellous to see you, dear boy. And I'm being treated very well, thank you."

Franklin stared around at what seemed like acres of naked flesh, "Nice place. Room for one more?"

"Shut up! Both of you." Allen turned to Bannen, "I thought you told me that this place was secure?"

"I said that we'd be finished checking it over by this evening. It's a big station, Marcus."

Allen gestured towards Franklin, "If he can get in, so can others. Get guards posted at every possible access point and get the monitoring system up and running."

Bannen nodded and left the room, pausing long enough to give Franklin a look that suggested violence might play a part in their mutual future.

"So, Mr. Richardson, we meet again." Allen seemed to have regained some of his equilibrium, "I take it that you have come here in search of your colleague?"

"Whatever gave you that idea, man?"

"Don't play smart with me. You have already made one grave mistake by entering my domain, do not add to your troubles."

"Franklin, dear boy, I do believe that Marcus is running a little short of patience. It may be wise to heed his warning."

"Your colleague is quite right, Mr. Richardson. Now, take a seat and behave yourself."

Franklin did as instructed, "You want to ask me something?"

"Indeed I do, Mr. Richardson."

Nadia Melford stepped forward, "Shall I start?"

Marcus Allen put a hand on her shoulder, "Not this time, Nadia. Time is pressing, and I think it would be better if I took over this part of our operation for a while. Do not take this as a rebuke, my dear, I am sure

279

that you would have proved successful with this young man." He allowed his hand to slide down her chest, her eyes rolling with pleasure as he cupped her naked breast. "Go now. All of you."

The naked women trailed out of the room, a few of them gazing longingly at Franklin as they left. He returned their looks with an apologetic smile on his face. "Maybe later," he waved as the last of them closed the door behind her.

"I wouldn't count on that, Mr. Richardson. And just in case you have any ideas about overpowering me and making off, perhaps this will dissuade you from such a reckless course of action." He withdrew a small handgun from his pocket and flicked off the safety catch.

"I'm happy to sit right here. How about you, Bill?"

"Quite so. It's a very comfortable sofa, very–"

"Shut up. You just heard me say that time is running short, so let's get straight to the point, shall we?"

"You're in charge."

"More so than you can possibly imagine, Mr. Richardson. And remember, you're on the Dark Side now."

"I've been on the dark side since the day I was born. It comes of being black."

"You may fancy yourself as a comedian, Mr. Richardson. Try thinking of yourself as a corpse before trying my patience anymore."

"Whatever you say, man."

"Question one. Why did Peter Charno employ you?"

"He said it was something to do with missing persons."

"*Something* to do with?"

Franklin nodded, "I only spoke to him for a couple of minutes. He said his assistant would give me the details later."

"You expect me to believe that?"

"Sure. Why not?"

"Two reasons, Mr. Richardson. Firstly, why would a man such as Charno employ a two-bit little agency when his wealth could utilise the resources of the finest agencies in the world? And secondly, why should he need to employ anyone in the first place?"

"We may be little, but we're good at what we do. How else would I have found you today?"

"I admit, you do seem to have a modicum of talent in your field, but you received substantial assistance from my own people."

"What did you mean by your second point?"

"Do you not realise the power that Charno possesses?"

"I know he's rich."

Allen made a dismissive gesture with his free hand, "I'm not talking about mere worldly worth, Mr. Richardson. I mean, were you not aware that Charno has mental capabilities beyond those of the herd? Not as strong as mine, maybe, but far stronger than any average man."

"You're kidding me, right?"

"Not in the least, Mr. Richardson. Peter Charno can locate people by the power of his mind alone."

Bill and Franklin exchanged a disbelieving look.

"I know it's not an easy concept for people such as yourselves, but it is nonetheless true. Once Charno has been around a person for a few minutes, he can later trace that person by, as he calls it, 'tuning in to their aura'. So you see, I can hardly believe that he would employ you if he wished to locate a missing person. I am aware that you've been using this as a cover story from the very start, but I'm afraid, as you can see, it doesn't pass muster."

"I'm being straight with you, man. Charno stopped me in the street, told me 'missing persons' was the most fitting description of what he wanted us to get involved in, and then said his assistant would contact me the next day."

"The most fitting description?"

"That's what he said."

"If I told you that if you repeated what you've just when I ask the question again, I'll put a bullet through your partner's foot, what would you say?"

"Hey, man! What else *can* I say. It's the truth!"

Allen pointed the gun at Bill.

"Listen, man! Don't do it! I'm not shitting you!"

There was a tense silence for what seemed an eternity before Marcus Allen finally nodded. He turned the gun to one side. "Could it be possible that he wasn't referring to missing people in the general sense of the word?"

"That was the impression I got. It's what I've been trying to tell you."

Allen looked thoughtful. To himself he said, "It was the obvious assumption to make. Charno, fearing for his life, leaves the search for his missing colleagues in the hands of a small, unknown agency..." He looked up sharply, "But what if his colleagues left for safer pastures at the same time as him?"

Franklin shrugged, "We sure as shit haven't found anyone. Or any sign of anyone. All the information I received was courtesy of the Featherington bitch. I take it she works for you? She is your daughter, after all."

Allen barked a laugh, "My daughter? She's Charno's daughter, Mr. Richardson. She came over to the Dark Side just two years ago, unable to resist me any longer. Be very careful what you say about Alexandra, Mr. Richardson, and she means the world to me. She has proved to be a wonderful addition to my little team – all that inside knowledge of Charno's pathetic little band, all that lush beauty."

"I knew it!" Franklin said.

"I say, Marcus, dear boy," Bill said, "Now that you seem to believe that we've been telling you the truth all along, wouldn't it make sense to let us go?"

"I haven't finished with you two by a long chalk," Allen said, "Even if Charno didn't employ you to trace people, there must have been some reason why he called on your services. You're still hiding something."

"We're not, man! Look, as far as I'm concerned we've got ourselves wrapped up in some really weird shit that's way over our heads. All I wanna do is get out of here and forget all about this case. Jesus! Special powers, for chrissakes!"

"I've warned you before about mocking me, Mr. Richardson. Myself and all of my male followers have the power to some greater or lesser extent. Perhaps you might recall what happened to your charming little colleague, yesterday?"

"What are you saying, man?"

"Don't you recall how... depressed she became? Suicidal, even?"

"You mean–"

"I mean, that one of the powers we possess is the ability to induce such feelings into some people. Not all, I'm afraid, some simply experience a tingling sensation and no more."

Franklin's jaw dropped open.

"I see you're starting to believe, Mr. Richardson. A wise move. I trust that you had a rather... intimate night? Only there are some quite wonderful side-effects to encounters with this power. The women down here, as you may have noticed, are given to sexual excess. This is another way in which we may use the power."

"That's sick!"

"It is perfectly natural, Mr. Richardson. It is a liberating experience for them. For all of us. After you had eluded us yesterday, we enjoyed a most wonderful way of venting our frustrations. Although I'm afraid that there was considerable damage to the two stations that you had infiltrated. Such a release does, on occasion, get a little out of hand."

"Look, man, this is getting weirder by the minute–"

A thunderous crashed reverberated along the length of the platform.

"Stay there!" Allen barked. He span on his heel and poked his head out of the room, "What is it?"

An answering yell came from the other end of the platform, "There's someone on the other side of the tunnel block. Sounds like they're trying to break through!"

"Shit! Okay, get Bannen. Assemble everyone here within one minute." He came back into the room. "Who is it, Mr. Richardson?"

"How the hell would I know?"

Allen levelled the gun at his head.

"Okay, man! I told the police where I was headed."

"And they just let you?"

"I had a head start."

"Right. Out of the room. No funny business. You two are coming with us."

McCoy was watching the receiver as closely as Dot, and they both saw the dim glow at the same time. He glanced up to check their location, noting that they were level with the Royal Exchange.

"Take it steady, Jim," he told the driver.

"Got something, guv?"

"Looks that way, Green."

"We have, definitely!" Dot said, "Look! They're getting brighter. He's somewhere ahead of us."

By the time they reached the junction with Leadenhall, all five lights on the receiver were burning brightly and Dot was almost wriggling in her seat with excitement.

"Slow right down," she told the driver, heedless of the black look she received from McCoy, "I think… Stop!"

"Do as she says, Jim." McCoy studied the receiver and could see that one of the lights had begun to dim. They had just passed over the spot where Franklin was currently located. "Let's wait for a minute and see if there's any movement. There's no point in diving down there if he's on the move until we know which way he's headed."

Dot nodded, but reluctantly, "I guess so."

The two of them sat side by side staring intently at the battery of lights, DS Green leaning over the back of the front seat.

After a full minute, McCoy nodded, "Okay. The signal's not changing. Looks like he's stationary and about ten or twenty metres back up the road. Tony, where do you reckon that places him down there?"

The Sergeant pulled open the folder he was carrying and thumbed through a few pages. Finally he found what he was looking for, "Could be the abandoned station at St. Priaulx."

"Closest and easiest access point?"

"Well, the station's built on a disused stretch of the Metropolitan Line. That part of the line used to stretch all the way from Aldgate to Bank, but it was closed after the War because of extensive bomb damage. Most of the tunnel from here to Aldgate was destroyed by the look of it, but there's a complete section running from Bank. There should be an access point there, give me a minute and I'll see what the station map says."

"Please hurry!"

"I'm doing my best, love."

McCoy got out of the car and went back to the van to relay the news. After a few words with the officers inside, the van performed a U-turn and sped back down Cornhill towards Bank station.

"Found anything yet, Tony?" he asked, climbing back into the car.

"Got it, guv! There's two connecting tunnels between Bank and Monument. About halfway along the eastern one is an unused spur that leads into the tunnel we want. According to this they use the first fifty metres for storing carriages. After that it runs all the way to St. Priaulx."

"Right. Jim? Turn us round and get back to Bank station. Tony, I want you to go down with the squad and keep a radio link open with me. Band forty should be powerful enough. We'll be up top and keep an eye on the receiver in case Richardson starts to move off before you've got to him."

"I want to go with them," Dot said.

"Sorry, miss, but there ain't any way I'm going to let another one of you down there," McCoy said, "And it's no good arguing, got that?"

"But–"

"I said, no arguments."

"I'll feel so helpless up here."

In a rare show of sympathy, McCoy patted her shoulder, "I'm sure you do, but you could easily end up being a liability to my men down there. And don't forget what happened to you last time."

Dot hadn't, and shuddered, "Perhaps you're right..."

"I am, and you know it."

The car pulled up outside the station and DS Green hurried over to where the squad were waiting. With a final wave towards the car, he led the men inside.

"Okay, Jim," McCoy said, "Take us back to a spot a few metres closer than where we were stopped. The closer we are to where Richardson is, the easier it'll be to spot if he starts to move."

They had only just arrived back at the spot when the radio crackled into life and DS Green's distorted voice boomed into the car, "Are you receiving me, guv? Over."

McCoy reached over the front seat and turned down the volume, "Loud and clear, Tony. And cut all that 'over' crap, it gets on my tits. Sorry, miss. Where are you now, Tony?"

"I've got hold of a station manager, and he's leading us to access point. He's not exactly happy, because he's had to stop a couple of trains, but he's doing it anyway."

"Tell him the City of London Police are very grateful," McCoy permitted himself a smile, "Let me know what you find when you get there."

"Shouldn't be long now, guv. Our guide reckons the more rats you see, the closer you are to the disused sections. Currently we're knee deep in the bloody things."

"Don't get the idea that you can adopt one as a pet and bring it back to the office."

"Guv? Sod off, will you?"

McCoy turned to Dot, "I don't think my Sergeant is keen on that particular rodent, do you?"

Dot looked up, "It's not funny, Inspector."

"Sorry," he turned back to the radio, "There yet, Tony?"

"Just about..." There was a pause and muffled conversation in the background, "Right. Guv? We're at the start of the disused spur. The station manager's going back to get the trains running again and we're to call him on the way out. There's just one carriage in here at the moment, but apparently there's power in the rails so that they can manoeuvre the rolling stock, so we've got to be careful."

"Quick as you can, Tony."

"We'll maintain radio silence until we're at the station. Don't want to announce our arrival too early."

"Good thinking, Tony. Call me as soon as you can."

McCoy sat back in his seat and turned to face Dot, "Any movement?"

She shook her head, "The lights haven't changed since we got back here."

"Should make our job a bit easier."

"Unless he's not moving 'cos he can't move."

He patted her shoulder again, "Try not to worry, I'm sure—"

The radio crackled into life once more, "Guv?"

"Right here, Tony."

"We've got a problem."

"What's up?"

Beside McCoy, Dot sat forward, her mask a face of concern.

"I'd guess that we were no more than ten metres from the station platform, but someone's bricked up the tunnel, guv. Looks like a pretty professional job and all."

"Reckon you could break through?"

"We've got a couple of sledgehammer-rams with us, so sure. But it's gonna make a hell of a racket. If they really are on the other side, they'll have time enough to scarper, I should think."

"Shit!" McCoy muttered, "Can you think of anything else?"

"Maybe we could use the train carriage back there to crash straight through it?"

"No way, Tony. There's been no movement from Richardson, and if they're right on the other side of the wall, there'd be carnage. I don't think you've got any choices. Just get at it with the sledges as quick as you can. We'll be monitoring the receiver."

The first echoing boom issued from the radio even before Green had turned down the volume.

"They'll get through there sharpish," McCoy tried to comfort the fretful Dot.

"They'd better."

*****

Like a well-drilled military unit, Allen's people were assembled on the platform within the one-minute deadline he'd set, the women now wearing the long black cloaks that Franklin remembered from the previous day.

Marcus Allen himself strode to the head of their uniform ranks, Benjamin Bannen at his side, and Franklin and Bill following behind.

"Okay," Allen said, his voice calm despite the look of fury that contorted his features, "We shall clearly have to abandon St. Priaulx for now. Consider this as nothing more than a temporary nuisance. We are too close to gaining access to the Bank of England's booty to let this little matter divert us from our true goal."

There was a muted cheer and Bill and Franklin exchanged an astonished glance. "So that's the man's little game, is it?" Bill whispered.

Franklin nodded, "Makes sense, I guess. Gotta fund the property war somehow."

A look from Bannen silenced them.

"The plan is as follows," Allen continued, "I want four men to stay with Bannen and myself, the rest of you are to use the ventilation shaft in the back office to access street level through the office block on Leadenhall. Make yourselves as conspicuous as possible, a fairly simple task for the ladies, I would have thought."

There was nervous laughter and one or two of the young women spread their cloaks wide, naked underneath.

"Go now. We shall all meet up again at Westminster later this afternoon. Everyone know what they are to do?"

A ragged chorus greeted this, and four men stepped from the ranks and took up position either side of Bannen and Allen. The remaining Allenites turned and trooped quickly through the office complex.

When the last had disappeared from sight, Allen turned to face Bill and Franklin, the background hammering echoing around them, louder now to Franklin's ears.

"Time is short, gentleman. You will follow me, and you will not try any delaying tactics. It seems that neither of you are susceptible to my powers, but you are both more than vulnerable to a bullet. Any false move will result in the death of one of you. Do I make myself clear?"

"As crystal, dear boy."

"No worries on that score."

"Come, then."

Allen led them to a small room at the end of the platform and walked inside. On the rear wall a stepladder had been placed under a large trapdoor and he climbed it quickly, disappearing into the darkness above. With a shrug to Bill, Franklin followed.

He found himself in a long, low chamber, dim lights in the ceiling providing enough illumination to make the use of flashlights unnecessary. After Bill had made the ascent, Allen motioned for them to follow him and set off towards the entrance to a tunnel at the far end of the chamber.

"This is a construction made by Charno," he said, "Foolishly, he had marked it on the maps left with his assistant."

"The assistant being Monica Leigh?"

"That is correct, Mr. Richardson." Behind them, a solid thud indicated that the trapdoor had been closed, "It interconnects with the last four stations under the stupid man's control, which is rather convenient for us now that we have extended our territory. We are headed for Mansion House station at this very moment."

"Why didn't I guess."

"Indeed, Mr. Richardson."

"Can I ask you something?"

"You *may* ask. I *might* answer."

"Why did you get Alexandra Featherington to go through that whole charade on Thursday? Why not just come to me direct?"

Allen laughed, "I felt that you might prove more co-operative in Alexandra's presence, and if it were at all possible, I wanted to avoid giving up any knowledge of the Dark Side. When you failed to provide her with the information required, we fell back onto plan B."

"To lure me and Dot down here where you would be waiting?"

"That indeed was the original intention. Unfortunately, you proved a little more ingenious and versatile than I had anticipated. For this reason, I reluctantly had to make moves on the surface, hence the presence of yourself and your colleague here today."

"And what happens to us now?"

"You'd really rather not know. For the present, at least, you will take the form of an important piece in a much larger picture. All will become clear within an hour."

289

"Okay, so what's really going on down here? Is this all about some property war or not?"

"I must commend you, Mr. Richardson, on a very convincing act."

"What act?"

"Why, trying to appear perfectly ignorant when you clearly have much more information at your disposal."

"There's no point in starting all that shit again. I really am ignorant."

"Very well, let me indulge you. To answer your principal question, there has indeed been a struggle going on for control of property. With the annexation of these last properties, the struggle has ended. The Dark Side now has complete control of subterranean London and Charno is defeated. I've known the man for close on fifty years, and I'm sure that I've seen the last of him. He'll not return now that there is nowhere safe to run to."

"You mentioned the Bank of England back there."

"So I did. Are you aware that they have their own railway system? Oh, of course you do – Alexandra told you. Did she also tell you what they use it for?"

It was Bill that answered, "They use it to transfer cash and bullion, especially between the Clearing Houses. It's far safer than using street-level vehicles."

"It *was* safer, Bill," Allen said, "The last station in Charno's failed empire lies just feet away from the Bank of England system. It is going to be a simple matter to gain access to their otherwise heavily guarded railway. A simple matter that will result in the biggest robbery of all time."

"Even now that the police know a lot about what's going on down here?"

Allen's temporary silence told the two investigators that the events of the past two days had come as a wholly unexpected and wholly nasty surprise for him, "As with all great plans, there are perforce circumstances in which details must be altered. The intrusion of the constabulary will simply mean a slight change in tactics. I promise you, Mr. Richardson, Bill, that whatever you might think about my plan being thwarted, you are quite wrong. As you will soon discover, a sufficiently well thought out diversionary tactic may bring riches beyond the dreams of avarice."

"Why don't you just make a stand down here while you get on with the robbery? You're all armed, you've got your 'special powers'. And after Monday, it's pretty clear you don't mind killing people."

"That was part of our war, Mr. Richardson. Unfortunate in the extreme, but nonetheless necessary if I was to gain full control of the systems."

"I think I've worked out how you did it." Franklin said.

"Yes?"

"You really have got those special powers, haven't you? You and your men?"

"I prefer the term 'heightened mental capabilities', but I was telling you the truth."

"So, on Monday evening, you and several of your men followed those poor sods down into the tube stations after they left their offices and somehow forced them into a suicidal state. No-one needed to lay a finger on them to make them jump."

"Bravo, Mr. Richardson. I'm beginning to see why Charno went to you when he needed help."

"I wish I did."

They arrived at another chamber and Allen motioned for them to stand still.

"You shouldn't feel too sorry for those victims of war, Mr. Richardson. They – all of Charno's people, in fact – were not worthy of the riches that life under London can offer. They spurned the chance to come underground, to spend all their lives down here, to create new life, clean life, under the rotted streets of our once fair City. Instead they spent their time in cramped offices, treating the Dark Side, the very foundation of London, as a game. They invested in Charno's attempts to keep some level of control down here, blindly, stupidly.

"He only recruited people of a certain type, you know. Don't begin to think of him as some sort of saint as opposed to the sinner that you may perceive me to be. Those he recruited were all young, single, professionals with no close relations. He suggested to them which charities and institutions they should name as beneficiaries in their wills. His way of ensuring that funding would continue into the future, you see.

Like myself, he may have reached his eighth decade, but there are many more years left in us yet."

"He really is seventy-odd?"

"We both are, Mr. Richardson."

"But how's that possible? Neither of you look a day over forty."

"As I've already mentioned. There are treasures down here that are beyond measure. London is an ancient city, and as a settlement is more ancient still. For millennia, it has been fed by underground rivers and wells. Ten years ago, under a property that at the time was in the neutral territory that lay between Charno and I, an incredibly old well was discovered. Its source is a natural spring or aquifer deeper than any other yet discovered, the water, when tested, pure and fresh, but with an unheard-of combination of trace elements. You can see for yourself, the effect that it has on us. It's not exactly the Fountain of Youth, but it's the closest thing anyone has ever discovered."

"That's gotta be bull."

"It is no such thing. There's an interesting side-effect that you may have noticed for yourself. According to one of my men, your ladyfriend, Miss Kominski, suffered a number of cuts and abrasions yesterday."

"How could you know that? She was out of the station by the time you got there."

"I sent men up to street level to search for you, of course. Unfortunately you surfaced at a most awkward place as far as we were concerned. This morning, Mr. Richardson, did you not see for yourself that Miss Kominski's injuries had healed with an amazing speed?"

Franklin stared at Allen. Finally he nodded. "That's true, but we didn't drink anything down here."

"You wouldn't need to," Allen said, "We've no idea quite how or why it works, but when we use our heightened mental capabilities, we seem to somehow transfer the effect of the well's capabilities. Unless the person in question receives regular... doses, the effect wears off after a few days."

"I wish I hadn't seen any of this happening," Franklin sighed, "I'm in grave danger of believing all this crap."

Bannen stepped forward, "Marcus, we should move on now. The shuttle is due in ten minutes."

Allen nodded, "Let us proceed."

He led them to the end of the chamber and knelt down. With a grunt, he lifted a heavy-looking trapdoor. "Welcome to the private railway of the Dark Side." He turned and lowered himself into the shaft below.

*****

Just under five minutes after the police squad had started attacking the tunnel wall, Dot let out a cry of dismay. "He's moving!"

McCoy glanced down at the receiver, "Shit! Tony? How's it going?"

"Slowly, guv, the wall's bloody thick."

"It looks like Richardson is on the move. I'll keep you informed." He patted the driver on the shoulder, "Jim, drive forward slowly. It'll tell us which direction he's headed."

Jim started the engine and let the car crawl forward.

"It's the other way," Dot said, "The signal's fading in this direction."

"Turn it round, Jim."

They had travelled twenty metres before Dot said, "That's it! We've got him again."

With Dot guiding him, the driver moved the car forward at walking pace, first down the length of Cornhill and then across the junction into Queen Victoria Street, past the police offices and slowly on to Mansion House station.

"I think he's stopped again."

The car came to a halt and McCoy looked across at the entrance to the tube station, "Not this bloody place again!"

The radio crackled into life once more, "Guv?"

"I'm here."

"We've got through, but there's no-one here. I've just found a stepladder underneath a trapdoor, and I'd bet that that's the way they went. The trouble is, we can't budge it and it's in too awkward a position to use the sledges on it."

"Don't bother, Tony. We've just followed Richardson's signal to Mansion House, and it looks like he's stopped again. Get the squad out of there and go back down to where we were yesterday. If they've gone down there, there's no way out. I'll be at the entrance waiting for you."

"See you in two, guv."

McCoy turned to Dot, "You *must* stay here, okay. If Richardson starts moving again, get Jim to use the radio to alert Green and then, and only then, come down onto the platform and call for me. Under no circumstances are you to climb into the tunnel proper. Have you got that?"

Dot nodded, "Yeah well, okay. But hurry."

The Inspector clambered out of the car and dashed across the street to the station's entrance. Without a backward glance he disappeared inside.

Dot sat back in her seat, willing Franklin and Bill to be down there. And to be safe and well.

*****

Allen led Franklin and Bill down the deep shaft, their progress taking them deeper than the station itself. Although the shaft itself was dark, there was light filtering from both the top and bottom and it served to keep Franklin's claustrophobia at bay. They arrived in a long, low-ceilinged room that ended in a blank wall at one end, and a tunnel entrance at the other. Down the centre of its length were narrow rails, pinned to the floor.

"Good grief," Bill murmured.

"The latest extension to my own version of the District line," Allen said, "As you will soon see for yourselves, this track runs along the same route as the London Underground version, ten feet above our heads. It currently terminates at Victoria, although today's journey will be a little shorter."

"This is incredible," Franklin said, "It must have cost a fortune!"

Allen laughed, "Several people's fortunes, Mr. Richardson. This last section was built literally under the noses of Charno and his hapless gang.

A fact which serves to much amuse me." A humming noise began to emanate from the tunnel entrance, "Here comes our carriage, right now."

The tunnel entrance began to glow before the small train trundled almost silently into the room. It consisted of three sections, a motor at either end, and a series of low seats in-between. A driver was sitting in the foremost seat.

"It's electric, of course," Allen said, "The main benefits being its quietness and efficiency. We now have seven lines and ten trains, servicing more than forty percent of my little empire. Impressive, isn't it?"

"Looks a bit like a grown-up Hornby set to me."

"Nevertheless, Mr. Richardson, it serves its purpose more than adequately. Please step aboard, our journey will take approximately twelve minutes."

Franklin and Bill lowered themselves into the seats behind the driver. Franklin turned to look at Allen, who had taken the seat behind Bill, "Where are we going?"

"You'll find out in twelve minutes or so, Mr. Richardson, I'd like it to be a surprise."

Franklin shrugged and faced Bill, "Where do you reckon we're going?"

"Given the clear evidence of megalomania," he at first whispered, then louder, "I rather think that our host is taking us to somewhere that he considers his rightful place. The District line passes through Westminster and the station entrance is opposite the Houses of Parliament. The clock tower of Big Ben and all its invasive scaffolding is the first thing you see when you reach street-level."

Allen leant forward, "You are showing nearly as much perspicacity as your colleague, Bill. I really am most impressed."

The train began to roll forward and Franklin turned to face forward, "I'm getting a bad feeling about this. Check that. I'm getting an even worse feeling about it."

*****

The van containing the six squad members and DS Green screeched to a halt outside the station. The Sergeant was the first out, running ahead of the heavily armoured squad. Dot watched them disappear inside and then turned her attention back to the receiver.

Her eyes widened as she saw the five bulbs begin to dim. She blinked once to make sure that it wasn't some trick of the light, then tapped the driver on the shoulder, "Jim! Call Sergeant Green right now. Franklin's on the move again."

Jim nodded and picked up the radio. Static filled the car. "Jim Cooper to DS Green... Come in, Tony..." More static was the only reply. "Something's blocking the signal," he called over his shoulder before trying again.

"Come on!" Dot wailed.

Jim racked the radio, "It's no good. I'd better run down there and get them."

"Hurry, then," Dot cried, staring at the rapidly dimming lights.

The driver bolted from the car and sprinted across the road.

As soon as he was inside the station, Dot climbed over the back seat and sat herself behind the wheel. Given the speed with which the lights were fading, Franklin wasn't just moving – he was moving fast. She set the receiver on the dashboard in front of her, adjusted the seat and turned the ignition key, the engine roaring into powerful life. Praying that her six driving lessons would be enough, she put the car in gear and jerkily pulled away from the kerb.

Fifty metres further down Queen Victoria Street, the lights began to brighten, and she breathed a sigh of relief – at least she was headed in the right direction. She was already approaching Blackfriars Station when the radio crackled into life.

"Kominski!" McCoy's distorted voice roared at her, "What the fuck do you think you're playing at?"

Reluctantly slowing the car to a crawl, Dot reached for the radio and fiddled with the switch on the side until McCoy's outraged voice went dead. Assuming she was now transmitting, she said, "Inspector, can you hear me?" and released the switch.

"Yes, I can bloody hear me! Where are you?"

"Just passing Blackfriars and heading down towards Embankment. Franklin's moving real fast and I wasn't going to risk losing him. You've got to come after me!"

"Come after... Oh, I'm going to come after you all right, you stupid... Look, are you sure you're still on his tail?"

"Yeah, positive! Now come on!"

There was a muttered conversation that Dot couldn't make out then the Inspector came back on the radio, "Kominski, I'm going to kill you when I get hold of you, but in the meantime keep following the signal. There's a switch on top of the dashboard to the right of the wheel. Flip it on and you'll show flashing blue lights on the front and rear of the car – it should make progress easier. Don't go any faster than you have to, and we'll be with you in a couple of minutes. Keep the radio on and give us a running commentary on your position. As soon as you see us, pull up. Got all that?"

"Got it. Just hurry!"

The van roared up behind her less than two minutes later and Dot pulled up at the kerb with a relieved sigh, stalling the engine in the process. She was only half way out of the car when McCoy ran up to it, Jim Cooper and DS Green a few paces behind.

"In the back!" he yelled, his face thunderous.

The four of them scrambled into the car, Jim Cooper uttering a curse as his knee hit the steering wheel because the driver's seat had been moved so far forward, and they were moving again within twenty seconds.

"Okay," McCoy was breathing heavily, "Are we still with him?"

Dot nodded, "He's travelling faster than walking pace, but not much."

McCoy took the receiver from her and passed it to DS Green in the front passenger seat, "Keep an eye on it, Tony. Tell Jim where he's to go." He turned in his seat to face Dot, "By rights, I should tear you limb from limb for pulling a stunt like that. Don't you realise how bloody dangerous that was?"

"Yeah well... I just had to keep track of him. It looked like he was moving really fast."

McCoy shook his head, "So you hijack a police car? My police car, come to that."

"What was I supposed to do? Flag down a bleedin' cab?"

"On the grounds that there was a remote chance that we *might* have lost him – and the fact that we've got more important things to think about just now – I'm going to let you off, Kominski. But that was the very last time you cross me without getting nicked, okay?"

Dot shrugged, "I had to do it." They were slowly passing the Ministry of Defence building.

"I don't suppose you've even got a driving licence, have you?"

"Yes I have!"

"Well that's something, at least."

"I got my provisional two months ago!"

"Your provisional–"

"Guv! They've either stopped or changed direction."

Both Dot and McCoy sat forward, peering over the back of the front seats.

"Okay, Jim," McCoy said, "Do a U-turn and let's see which it is."

A minute later they returned to where they had first stopped, and it had become apparent that Franklin was now stationary. The car pulled up at the kerb, the van idling on the other side of the road. The Inspector looked up and turned to face Dot, "Now what's he up to? Some sort of Guy Fawkes caper is it?"

They were parked next to Westminster tube station, Big Ben towering in front of them.

*****

When the electric train finally stopped, Bill and Franklin were ordered off and made to stand against the wall of the room they had arrived at. Next to Franklin was a digital clock flashing 15:28 in green numbers twelve centimetres tall. Allen produced a tiny video camera from within his jacket and smiled at the two captives.

"Gentlemen," he said, "When I give the signal, I would like you to state your names and your location."

298

"We don't know our location," Franklin pointed out.

"Your colleague was quite correct, Mr. Richardson. You are currently standing just under the streets of Westminster, close by the Parliament Building itself – as will become clear in a few minutes. Now, if you will kindly follow my instructions?"

Franklin shrugged, "We have a choice?"

Bannen took two steps towards them, "Want to find out?"

"I'm cool, man."

"Very well," Allen said, "On three..."

First Franklin, and then Bill, recited what was required while Allen filmed them. He nodded at them when they'd finished and passed the camera to one of the silent men who had accompanied them from St. Priaulx.

"Take this to Dennis in the communications room. Tell him he's to splice it into the PC 'Demand' file and prepare it for transmission by four o'clock."

The man nodded and walked from the room.

"Now, gentlemen, I'm sure that you're wondering what happens next."

"No shit."

"Mr. Richardson, your sarcasm is beginning to tire me. Refrain of your own accord, or I shall be forced to have Benjamin persuade you. Now follow me."

He led them through a second doorway and into a brightly lit corridor. Three metal doors were set into the right-hand wall and he opened the last of them. It revealed a room lined from floor to ceiling with computers and monitors. Sitting at a terminal with her back to them was a figure familiar to Franklin. At the sound of the door opening, she slowly turned her chair to face them.

"Why, Franklin! We meet again!"

Alexandra Featherington's dulcet tones sent a shiver up his spine, "So it seems, bitch."

A fist connected squarely with his ribs and he gasped in shock and pain.

"Mr. Richardson," Marcus Allen said, "You will not be permitted to insult any of my people. Particularly Alexandra. Benjamin will ensure it. Do you understand?"

"Yeah," he rubbed at his bruised ribs, "I understand all right."

Alexandra Featherington rose to her feet, the cloak she was wearing opening sufficiently to reveal her nakedness beneath. "Marcus, my dear, Nadia informs me that we are moving to our back-up plan. May I be permitted to remain with you while it is carried out."

"I'm afraid not, Alexandra. Should anything go awry, it will be your duty to continue in my absence. You know that, don't you?"

She sighed and looked down at her feet, "I suppose you're right. But I'm scared for you – we've had so little time to prepare–"

"We've had *enough* time. Just because we've had to advance our plans, does not mean that we're not fully prepared. There is precious little risk to myself or Benjamin, but I will not expose you to any risk at all, no matter how marginal. You will accompany the others to the Goodge Street base and await further instructions."

"If you insist, Marcus."

"I do. Do not worry, Alexandra, this matter will be resolved in just a few hours and tomorrow… Tomorrow will be the biggest celebration the Dark Side has ever seen."

She looked up and smiled at him, "It's come so fast, hasn't it?"

"Thanks to you, my love."

"Thanks to your vision, Marcus."

"How very sweet," Bill said.

Allen turned to face him, "I trust that was not a sarcastic comment?"

"Not at all, dear boy. I'm a terrible romantic at heart, that's all."

"For the very last time, you have my benefit of the doubt." He turned back to Alexandra, "Go now, my love, I have much to prepare."

She nodded and crossed the room to embrace him. Over his shoulder, she flashed a hungry look at Franklin before breaking away from Allen and wordlessly leaving the room. Allen ordered Bill and Franklin into chairs and then left them under the watchful eye of Bannen.

"Any idea what's going down, Bill?"

"I've been puzzling over that very matter, dear boy, but I'm afraid the only thing I've come up with is the rather preposterous notion that Marcus Allen intends to re-enact the Gunpowder Plot."

"As long as he ends up like Guy Fawkes, I don't care."

Bannen stepped forward, "You will show respect to Marcus Allen."

"Lovely bloke, it's been a real pleasure to meet him."

"Keep it that way."

Bill turned to face Franklin, "What do you reckon all that business with the video camera was about? I haven't a clue about these hi-tech gadgets."

Franklin's eyes suddenly widened, "Of course!"

"Of course what, dear boy?"

"Allen gave the camera to one of his men and told him to take it to someone called Dennis. He was to splice it into a computer file named 'Demand'."

"And your theory is?"

"He's planning to make some sort of ransom demand, with us as the hostages!"

Bill nodded, "That does seem somewhat feasible. Although I can't imagine that we're worth much to anyone – excepting yourself to young Dot."

"You're right. Given that Allen reckoned he was going to pull off the robbery of the century at the Bank of England, whatever he could get for us two would be chickenfeed in comparison. Maybe I was wrong."

"Maybe not," Bill said slowly, "Maybe we're both partly right."

"What's the Gunpowder Plot got to do with using us as hostages?"

Before Bill could answer, the door opened, and Marcus Allen walked into the room, a grim expression on his face. "And so we come to the end game. Follow me."

With Bannen following them, they hurried out into the corridor and trailed after Marcus Allen as he led them along a series of corridors and up a number of staircases. Two minutes later, he stopped by an unmarked door and unlocked it. After the modernity of the rooms and corridors they had already passed through, the chamber behind the door came as a stark contrast. It was clearly very old, the walls rough-hewn, moss-covered and damp. The only sign of more recent building work was a series of steel columns that rose from the floor and through the vaulted ceiling.

"Gentlemen," Allen said, "Welcome to one of the four foundation chambers beneath the clock tower of Big Ben."

"Very impressive," Bill said, "A pity about all this steelwork, though."

Marcus Allen laughed, "A pity indeed, but I'm sure you remember why it's there, Bill?"

Bill nodded, "The tower was beginning to develop a lean some years ago. Something to do with tunnelling work, I believe. The foundations are being reinforced to prevent London having its very own Leaning Tower. Hence all the scaffolding outside."

"Quite correct, Bill. And as you can imagine, it was a terrible inconvenience for myself and my plans. It delayed us for more than a year. Time has now come for me to have my revenge, gentlemen. Time has now come to right a wrong."

Franklin looked at Bill, "I don't see any kegs of gunpowder."

Allen looked up sharply, "What was that, Mr. Richardson?"

Bill nodded for Franklin to explain, "Bill reckons that you're planning some sort of modern-day version of the Gunpowder Plot."

"How very remarkable," Allen's eyebrows rose in surprise, "Your perspicacity is truly astonishing. Had you not caused me so much trouble, I might even consider enlisting you into my service. However, that is not the case and so I am forced to continue with my plan as it stands. For your information, Bill, Mr. Richardson, the Gunpowder Plot was attempted over four hundred years ago. Technology has improved somewhat during the interim." He pointed to the wall next to one of the steel supports. A small black box had been buried in the surface. "That device, and the thirty-nine others of its type, will provide an explosive charge equal to more than fifty times the power of all Fawkes's gunpowder put together. They will be detonated in sequence, providing a series of explosions which will completely destroy the foundations of the tower above us. And before you say something inane like 'surely the builders will notice', there is so much work going on covered by so many different teams, no one will raise an eyebrow to an odd little box or two."

"You can't be serious?"

"I'm deadly serious, Mr. Richardson. If my demands are not met by nine o'clock this evening, Big Ben will be destroyed, as will much of the Palace of Westminster. And this is just the first target."

"What demands?"

"That's none of your business, but since you have temporarily thwarted my plans for the Bank of England, perhaps you can guess for yourselves."

"And what about us? Where do we fit into all this?"

Allen smiled darkly, "You will be in the tower, gentlemen. To the outside world I will portray you as the human side of this situation, a demonstration of my ruthlessness. In fact, I am merely using you to kill two birds with one stone to use a most appropriate cliché. You have become involved in things that do not concern you. You know too much for me to simply let you go."

"That's hardly our fault!"

"Did I say it was, Mr. Richardson? *Fault* is not the problem here. The fact remains that you are too dangerous to us."

"What if they meet your ransom demands?"

"Then you will be killed anyway."

"But what about the police? They know all about your little empire now, don't they? Even if you do somehow get away with this, they'll be after you."

"Mr. Richardson," Allen laughed, "They know about that tiny part of the empire that was once Charno's. You've seen for yourselves our little railway line. We have hundreds more secrets down here and the security that protects my territory is far superior to that used by my former enemy. If we don't want to be found, we won't be."

"This is crazy!"

"However you may perceive it, Mr. Richardson, the one thing you can be sure of, is that it's happening. And it's happening today."

*****

When the transmitter secreted in Franklin's jacket had moved from somewhere near the station, finally coming to rest near the foot of Big Ben, McCoy decided that it was time for action.

The Inspector had called up every available man from the office and had sealed off the end of Victoria, and closed Westminster Bridge and Parliament Square to both traffic and pedestrians. The District and Circle Line services west of Westminster had also been suspended. Detective Chief Superintendent Cox had reluctantly agreed to the measures, on the proviso that if the operation was unsuccessful, McCoy would 'spend a week scrubbing out the stables in Wood Street'.

"I must be mad," McCoy muttered to himself as he surveyed the scene.

Dot had been stationed in his car to continue monitoring the receiver, accompanied this time by both Jim Cooper and DC Robson.

The Inspector, DS Green at his side, strode from the car towards the assembled officers and called for silence.

"Okay, lads, here's the situation. We believe that one Franklin Richardson is being held somewhere below ground by a group of people headed by Marcus Allen, wanted, as you know, in connection with the tube murders last Monday. We have reason to believe that there is every chance that a second captive, William Taylor, is also in their company. As some of you are aware, there are a number of disused tunnels, stations and other such places below ground, and we know that these are utilised by Allen for his nefarious purposes.

"We have detailed plans of the subterranean regions in this immediate vicinity, conveniently updated thanks to the restoration work, and your task is to search every single millimetre of every single tunnel, maintenance store, air duct – you name it. Squad assignments will be given out to you in a couple of minutes, and you are to maintain radio contact at all times during the search. If any of you find anything out of the ordinary, it is to be reported to me immediately. Any questions?"

A middle-aged Sergeant raised her hand, "If we do come across these characters, do we arrest them on sight?"

"Call me first if you can – if there's time, that is – but whatever you do, make sure that anyone found down there is taken into custody.

London Transport have cleared the stations and there are no scheduled maintenance works being carried out by any of the utility companies. In other words, anyone found down there is at the very least guilty of trespass."

A younger Constable waved at McCoy, "We've all been issued with shooters. Does that mean we are entitled to use extreme force if required?"

"You'd better have a bloody good reason to do so, but if push comes to shove, then yes. We fully believe Allen to be dangerous having already seen evidence of extreme violence and given his connection with the tube murders. Obviously you are not to use a 'shoot to kill' policy. Apart from the fact that there are probably two captives with him, we need to be able to talk to this guy.

"Right, if there aren't any more questions, each of the squad leaders is to receive his team's instructions from DS Green and DS Singh."

The assembled company split up into groups of four and were given detailed maps of the search area. One by one, the armed squads descended below the surface – two groups entering via Westminster tube station and the others through various manhole covers and ventilation shafts. The last group, headed by DS Green, and guided by a Government employed surveyor, made their way into the Palace of Westminster, headed for the deeper vaults beneath the clock tower of Big Ben. Sixty uniformed officers were stationed at the hastily erected barriers on the surrounding streets, already struggling to keep back curious civilians and eager press and television crews.

When the last of the squads had disappeared out of sight, McCoy made his way back to the car.

"No movement?"

Dot shook her head, "I keep thinking that I can see some sort of change, but I guess it's just one of them optical illusions."

"Don't worry, love. We'll get him out of there."

"I bleedin' well hope so."

McCoy checked his watch. Four o'clock. The first reports from the squads should start coming through at any time. As if on cue, the radio crackled into life and he reached into the car, "Identify and give!"

"DC Chapman back at the office, Inspector."

"What the hell do you want? I need to keep this line open–"

"Inspector, this is important."

"Make it quick then, Chapman."

"Yessir. First, we just got a report from Special Branch at Whitehall. They were setting up a new system of underground surveillance equipment when they registered the movement of up to forty people below ground. Knowing what case we're investigating, they thought we should know."

"They didn't stop these people?"

"According to the guy I spoke to, they couldn't. Infra-red detected heat sources, but according to their engineer, there shouldn't be any tunnels or anything down there. They're still investigating."

"Tell them from me this is absolutely top priority. Okay, Chapman, thanks–"

"There's something else, Inspector. The Yard have just received a coded telephone call."

"Terrorist?"

"Same codes, but according to the flash we just received, it was some nutter wanting to establish a television broadcast. They'll be calling back in ten minutes with more details."

"What's that got to do with us?"

"The officer who took the call heard a tube train in the background. It's probably nothing, but I thought you should know."

"You're right, Chapman. Well done, lad. Keep on it and get back to me if there's any developments, okay?"

"Yessir."

McCoy cradled the radio and sat himself in the front passenger seat.

"What was that all about?" Dot asked.

"I'm not sure..."

"What if Franklin's was with them, what if–"

McCoy held up his hand, "His signal's still stationary, isn't it? We'll be finding out where he is in the next few minutes–"

"But what if he took off his jacket and left it here? What if–"

"Miss Kominski! Dot. Please calm down."

"There's gotta be something you can do!"

"We're doing it right now."

DS Green's voice crackled from the radio, "Guv, It's Green."

"Give, Tony."

"Something fishy, guv. We're under the Palace, but the surveyor can't get into the vaults by Big Ben. Says the locks have all been changed and that there's some sort of extra security devices on them."

"Ask him if there are any other ways inside. If there are, get in that way. If not, get back to me and I'll send down the engineers."

"Got it, guv. Over and out."

McCoy looked back at Dot, "Sounds like someone wants us to stay out, doesn't it?"

"You reckon that means he's still inside, then?"

"We'll soon find out."

"DC Chapman, Inspector." The Constable's voice made Dot start.

"Give!"

"You've got to stop the search! Right now!"

"What are you blathering about?"

Chapman spoke rapidly but clearly, "The Yard received the second coded call and routed it straight here. It's from a man purporting to be Marcus Allen. He says that his security systems have discovered a large number of people moving around in restricted tunnels and that he's very disappointed that you're attempting to invade his domain."

"Invade his..."

"That's his words exactly, Inspector. If the men don't pull back within the next... three minutes, then William Taylor will be killed."

"Oh, shit!"

"You've gotta get them out!" Dot wailed. DC Robson hushed her into silence.

"How can we be sure this isn't some sort of hoax?" McCoy asked Chapman.

"He said to tell you that you've got a number of garments in your possession which you unlawfully took from one of his newly acquired properties."

"The cloaks we found down in the disused stations," McCoy nodded, "Okay. What else did the bastard say?"

"He'll be calling back very soon."

"Okay, Chapman, stay with it. If or when he calls, route it through to my mobile and have it taped your end."

"Yessir."

DC Robson sat forward, "What are you gonna do, guv?"

McCoy reached for the radio, "It doesn't look like I've got much choice, does it?"

*****

Allen led his captives into what he called his 'communications centre', a large room filled with flashing, bleeping, buzzing pieces of hardware, just as the man seated at a control panel was reaching for a telephone. He stopped and turned quickly at the sound of the door opening.

"Marcus!"

"Dennis, my faithful friend."

"We have visitors!"

"You were informed these two would be–"

"No, Marcus! The tunnels have started to swarm with bodies. I have camera confirmation close by the Westminster entrance, at least a dozen infra-red sensors have been activated in the ventilation system under Parliament Square, and the main sewer under Westminster Bridge has been opened."

Marcus Allen span on his heel and grabbed Franklin by his lapels, "You're bugged, aren't you? That must be how they located us so soon! Too soon!"

"No way, man. I swear."

Allen pushed him roughly towards Bannen who was standing in the open doorway, "Search him." He turned to face Bill, "And him." He slammed his fist against the wall, "Stupid! Why didn't I... Come to that, Benjamin, you're my senior security man. Why didn't *you* think to search them?"

Bannen looked up from where he was patting down Franklin's legs, "I thought—"

"You did no such thing!" Allen raged, "I am very disappointed in you, Benjamin."

"I'm truly sorry, Marcus. But it doesn't really make any difference, does it? I mean, you were going to make the ransom broadcast in a few minutes, anyway."

"But now it's going to look like some amateurish knee-jerk reaction!"

Bannen, who had been continuing his search of Franklin, gave a grunt as he located the transmitter. He pulled it out of Franklin's breast pocket where it had been buried amongst some spare batteries. "Found it, Marcus."

Franklin stared at it in astonishment, "I didn't put that there!"

Allen rounded on him, his fist flashing through a perfect arc, connecting squarely with Franklin's jaw. The young man staggered under the blow, his head ringing. Somehow he managed to stay on his feet."

"Mr. Richardson," Allen said, rubbing the knuckles of his fist, "You may be a consummate actor, but you have now overstepped the mark."

Bill held up his hand, "I know this lad, Marcus. I truly believe that he didn't realise he was carrying a transmitter. I would hazard that it was placed in his pocket by our colleague. She frets terribly over our safety, you know?"

"Then," Allen smiled, "she'll be in for a lot of fretting in the next few hours, won't she? Benjamin, continue searching Mr. Richardson and then check that Bill hasn't anything concealed about his person, either. I think I have a telephone call to make." He took a few deep breaths to compose himself, and then crossed to where the man called Dennis was already preparing a telephone link.

*****

"But we're above ground now, guv." DS Green pointed out.

McCoy paused and then nodded to himself, "It's worth a risk," he said into the radio.

Behind him Dot leapt forward, "You can't! Allen said he wanted everyone to pull back!"

"Keep her quiet, Robson," McCoy snapped. To Green he said, "I'd guess that he's got some sort of motion sensors down there. Maybe even more sophisticated stuff. But I doubt whether he'd risk installing anything above ground. Get inside the clock tower and check around – just you and the surveyor. Even if Allen does have some sort of surveillance inside the place, he'll just think it's a couple of maintenance men or guys from one of the restoration teams. If he challenges us on it, that's what I'll tell him, so make out you're looking for rats or dodgy wiring or something."

"I thought that's what we *were* doing, guv."

"Keep your radio open, Tony, and if you've got anything to tell me, make it look as if you're talking to the engineer."

"Got it, guv."

McCoy racked the radio and turned to where Dot was still squirming in her seat, "It'll be okay, you'll see."

"If anything happens to–"

"Please! I know you're worried, but you need to keep calm. We all do–"

Chapman's voice interrupted McCoy's lecture, "Inspector?"

"Give!"

"Marcus Allen is on the line again."

"Patch him through to my mobile."

McCoy attached the telephone to a speaker and microphone set on the dashboard, and a few seconds later, Marcus Allen's cultured tones filled the car.

"I believe I am speaking to Inspector McCoy?"

"You are. Identify yourself."

"My name is Marcus Allen, Inspector."

"Are you holding captive Franklin Richardson and William Taylor?"

"Straight down to business! A man after my own heart, Inspector. First, though, I would just like to inform you that my intentions are, quite literally, deadly serious. When I make my demands, I am effectively promising you what will happen. Please bear that in mind at all times."

"I hear you. Richardson and Taylor?"

310

"They are indeed enjoying my hospitality."

Dot leaned forward, "Let them go!"

"Ah!" Allen said, "Miss Kominski, I take it. Perhaps young Mr. Richardson was right after all about that transmitter."

Dot gave McCoy a frightened look and he pushed her gently back in her seat, one finger to his lips.

"Are they both unharmed?" McCoy asked.

"Perfectly fit and well. At least, for the time being."

"I want to speak to them."

'But of course, Inspector. There must be trust between us." There was a pause before Allen came back on line, "Mr. Richardson?"

"Hi, guys, I've been told to tell you that we're okay. Presumably, if I don't Benjamin Bannen here—"

There was a scuffling sound before Allen's voice came back, "A tricky customer, is our Mr. Richardson, do you not think?"

Dot was close to tears, "You haven't hurt him?"

It was Bill who replied, "Indeed he hasn't, my dear. We are both still quite well. Marvellous idea of yours, by the way—"

Allen interrupted him, "Enough idle chatter! Inspector, it is time to talk business."

"What do you want?"

"Two very straightforward and simple things, Inspector. Three, if you include my desire for your honesty. I need first, however, to ask you a question."

"Ask it."

"Do you know the whereabouts of one Peter Charno?"

"No, but we'd certainly like to."

"That is an honest answer?"

"Completely honest, Mr. Allen. Together with yourself, Benjamin Bannen and Alexandra Featherington, he is one of the prime suspects into the investigation of the tube station murders that were committed last Monday."

"Very well, I shall accept your word on this matter. Particularly as I know from personal experience just how difficult a man he can be to track

311

down. My first demand is therefore very straightforward. I want to speak to Charno."

"I've just told you, we don't know where he is."

"Then I suggest that you use the media to make contact with him. Perhaps a television appeal and a podcast?"

"You can't seriously expect us to go on television or the 'net and ask one murder suspect to contact another one, can you?"

"I've already stated that I'm deadly serious, Inspector. Should Charno not have spoken to me by half past seven this evening, William Taylor will be killed."

"No!" Dot yelled. DC Robson, pulled her back into her seat.

"You could speak to Charno and kill Taylor anyway. How would we even know if you have spoken to him?"

"That, at least, is very simple. When Charno 'goes away', what he actually means, is that he moves above ground. He'll still be in London somewhere, possibly in the suburbs. At five-thirty I will interrupt the BBC 1 television channel with a broadcast of my own. I strongly suggest that you prepare yourselves to make your own broadcast immediately afterwards urging Charno to place himself in your custody. I repeat, should he not have done so by seven-thirty, I will regrettably be forced to kill Mr. Taylor."

"What do you mean 'a broadcast of your own'?"

"You'll see for yourself at five-thirty. Once again, I thoroughly recommend that you prepare your own broadcast. Maybe you can persuade Charno should I fail."

"What if he's not watching television, for Christ's sake?"

"Peter Charno is a man of habit, Inspector. Mainly pathetic habits such as an addiction to Saturday evening television. He is also a traditionalist and has no time for commercial television or the internet."

"You can't possibly be sure of that!"

"Let's just say that I'm ninety percent positive. Besides, even if the loathsome man himself is not watching, at least one of his pathetic little band of followers is bound to be. They'll know where to contact him."

"This is preposterous!"

"You have little more than an hour to prepare, Inspector, I suggest you drop your preconceived notions of what is or isn't 'preposterous' and concentrate on saving the life of Mr. Taylor. I will speak with you again in due course and will discuss the second demand then." The phone line went dead.

*****

It seemed to take the surveyor an age to locate the keys that would allow them access to Big Ben's clock tower, and DS Green was becoming more and more impatient. The surveyor, a rather pompous little man, finally returned with a set of keys jangling by his side. "Got them at last, Sergeant!"

"About bloody time. By the way, once we're inside, you're to call me Tony, okay?"

"You've already told me that at least five times."

"Better safe than sorry, *James*."

The grumbling surveyor tried a number of different keys before the door finally emitted a series of clicks and he stood back with a triumphant look on his weasel-like features. "There!" he said.

"Right. Remember what I told you. We're maintenance staff–"

"Yes, yes, Sergeant. We're maintenance staff inspecting the clock tower for signs of damage to wiring caused by the restoration work and so on. I'm to call you Tony but we're to remain silent as much as possible."

"Okay, I'll come back for you in a few seconds. I need to check that everything's safe." Into the radio, he said, "Guv? I'm going in!"

The radio remained silent, and Green guessed that McCoy was back in contact with Allen. He shrugged and pushed the heavy door open. The inside of the tower seemed incongruously larger than it appeared from the outside, an effect exaggerated by its low lighting. Steps spiralled up the walls of the tower into the murky gloom above, and the floor was littered with haphazardly arranged machinery and cabinets.

He stepped forward and made a quick tour of the ground floor. Once he was sure that there was no-one present, he returned to the door and stepped back outside. "Guv? It looks empty, and I couldn't see any

313

surveillance gear. Any sign that someone underground picked up my presence?"

There was still no reply from McCoy.

"Oh, well," he said, "Looks like we're on our own for the moment. Follow me inside and start searching the equipment in there. Thoroughly. We're looking for anything suspicious – anything that seems out of place, got that?"

"Yes, Sergeant. Let's get on with it, shall we?"

Green bit back a curse and went back inside the tower. He motioned for the surveyor to start searching the ground floor on the right and then closed the door behind them. They moved around the maze-like array of cabinets and machinery, finally meeting back at the door after five fruitless minutes.

"Nothing out of the ordinary, James?"

"Nothing, *Tony*."

Green nodded, "I guess we'd better start making our way up then. How many–"

A grating sound cut him short, and he cast around for its source. By good fortune, he was facing the base of the stairway, and spotted the small, concealed hatchway starting to swing open. Clamping his hand over the surveyor's mouth, he dragged them behind a tall cabinet, crouched down and peered cautiously across to the stairs.

The first person to emerge was Franklin Richardson, swiftly followed by William Taylor. A voice told them to stand still, and Green switched off his radio for fear of McCoy calling through to him at that very minute. A few seconds later, gun in hand, Benjamin Bannen emerged from the hatchway.

"Okay you two. Into the lift!"

Green weighed the chances of taking Bannen down but decided that there was too much risk to Richardson and Taylor, who he now saw were handcuffed. Once they had taken up position in the lift, Bannen closed the hatchway behind him and joined them. The lift rattled into life and began to ascend the tower.

He waited until it was out of sight, its progress barely audible, and then switched on his radio, the volume as low as he could make it. "Guv!" he hissed.

"Tony?"

"Keep it down, guv, we've got company. Bannen has just taken Taylor and Richardson up in the lift."

"No sign of Allen?"

"Negative."

"Well, he's just made the most outrageous demand. Says he's going to broadcast on BBC One at five-thirty and if Charno doesn't contact him by half-seven, he's going to top Taylor. No matter how daft it sounds, I reckon he's serious. Looks like Bannen's going to be the one doing the dirty work."

"I'll follow him up, guv. Get some men ready outside the door of the tower. No point in making a racket and scaring him off."

"I'll second that, Tony. Take care up there."

"You got that in spades." He turned to the surveyor, whose eyes were wide with fear, "You're to stay right here. Got it?"

"No-one said this was going to be dangerous," he hissed, "That man had a gun!"

"Quiet! Just stay here and you'll not get hurt."

"Wouldn't it be easier if I just left you to it?"

"No. He might hear the door, and I'm not having this operation buggered because of some whining little coward. If you move from this spot until I tell you otherwise, *I'll* be the one shooting you, okay?"

Without waiting for a reply, Green rose from his crouch and crossed quietly to the foot of the stairs. He'd taken the first flight when a noise from above stopped him in his tracks. He stood still, holding his breath for a few seconds, before giving a silent curse. The lift was descending.

He took the stairs three at a time and dashed back to where the surveyor was cowering.

"What's happening–"

"Shut it!"

315

A few seconds later, the lift rattled to a halt and Bannen stepped out. He took a radio from his pocket and pressed the transmit button, "Marcus?"

Allen's voice came faintly to Green's ears, "I'm here, Benjamin."

"Taylor and Richardson are secure in the bell chamber, and I activated the video link. Can you pick them up?"

"Ah, yes! Trussed up like turkeys. This will make a splendid accompaniment to my broadcast. I particularly like the way you've placed them so that the clock face is visible behind them. A nice touch, that. Adds to the drama of the occasion. Did you remember their ear plugs, by any chance? It gets awfully loud up there each hour now that we've re-activated the bells."

"Seems to have slipped my mind, Marcus," Bannen gave a dark chuckle, "Would you like me to go back up there?"

"Oh, I'd rather you didn't. As soon as the authorities realise where our captives are, there's bound to be some sort of attempt at a rescue. Since the only two ways into the tower are by the outer door and our own, modified access points, I think that you should stand guard right where you are. I'll be monitoring Taylor and Richardson on my video pick-up. Should they attempt to extricate themselves, I will let you know."

"Very well, Marcus."

"I shall now go and prepare for my broadcast and will be incommunicado for the next couple of hours. I'll call you when I have any news concerning Charno. Or, of course, at the very latest, seven twenty with instructions concerning William Taylor."

"I'll be right here."

"I know I can count on you, Benjamin."

The radio went silent and Bannen switched it off, returning it to his pocket.

Green tensed as the man took a couple of paces towards them, and then breathed a silent sigh of relief as he watched Bannen move a large packing case into a position near the centre of the room. When the big man had settled himself on the crate, the Sergeant drew his gun and took a few deep breaths.

316

Training the gun on the back of Bannen's head, he rose to his feet and crept silently out of his hiding place.

Bannen had taken a newspaper from his jacket pocket and opened it with a noisy rustling sound that conveniently covered any noise that Green might have made. He stopped just three paces behind Bannen.

"Armed police! Freeze!"

Bannen's shoulders tensed at the shock of Green's voice and the newspaper fluttered from his hands.

"I said freeze!" Green yelled as Bannen's right hand moved towards his pocket, "Both hands above your head. Now!"

Bannen complied, "You'll not live long enough to regret this."

"Now put them on the top of your head. Right now or I'll shoot! Okay, James, get over here now!"

"W-w-what!?"

"Get over here right now!"

The surveyor moved cautiously into the middle of the room, "I really–"

"Take the cuffs from my belt."

"I–"

"Now!"

The surveyor fumbled them from their clip, "You surely don't want me–"

"Go to the right-hand side of my friend here and place one cuff on his right wrist. And don't piss yourself. If he so much as twitches, I'll blow his fucking head off."

With shaking hands, the surveyor did as he'd been instructed, "Now what?"

"Take the hand out to the side and then down behind his back. Right, that's good. Now, Bannen, very, very slowly, put your other hand behind your back. Well done. James, put the other cuff on."

As soon as Bannen was relatively secure, the little surveyor dived away from him.

"There, that wasn't so difficult, was it?"

"Easy for you to say, Sergeant."

"Now, go to the door and ask for two officers to come in. You're free to go after that."

The little man gave an audible sigh of relief and dashed to the door. Ten seconds later, DC Robson entered cautiously, followed by DC Fernandez.

"Come on in lads," Green said, "It looks like Allen's wonderful surveillance systems don't stretch to anywhere above ground. Mr. Bannen here had no idea that he'd got company. Robbo, he's got at least one gun somewhere on his person, and a radio."

Robson strode forward and began to frisk the prisoner. His search revealed two guns, the radio and a lethal-looking sheath knife. Once they'd been taken from him, Bannen was forced to lie face down on the concrete floor.

"This is not over, copper."

"Since we stand between Allen and his captives, I rather think that for them, at least, it's all over."

Bannen grunted a laugh, "If anyone goes near, them, they'll die."

"What are you talking about?"

"If anyone goes near, them, we'll *all* die."

"Are you trying to tell me there's some sort of bomb in here?"

"I've told you all I'm going to, copper."

Green's radio crackled into life and he turned up the volume.

"Green here."

"McCoy. What's happening?"

"We've got Bannen. Taylor and Richardson are up in the bell chamber."

"Good work. Have someone go up and get them."

"I don't think it's going to be that simple, guv."

"Now what?"

"According to what I just overheard, they're trussed up in front of some sort of video camera up there, and it's being monitored by Allen himself. Bannen, here, has just told me that if anyone goes near them, we'll all die. Sounds like he's talking about a bomb, but he's clammed up."

"Reckon he's telling the truth?"

"What with all the weird shit that's been happening, would you bet against there being some sort of device here?"

"I guess not, Tony."

"I reckon our only chance is to try to find the damn thing, guv. It must be here somewhere."

"I'll get the dogs in and a bomb crew. Rather than bring Bannen out straight away, perhaps you could try to... persuade him to be a little more co-operative?"

"I'm with you, guv."

Green flicked off his radio and turned towards Bannen. "How persuasive do you think I'll need to be?" He drew back his right foot as the bells above began to chime five o'clock.

*****

Franklin was still groaning two minutes after the five o'clock chimes had died away.

"Next time, dear boy, assuming there is a next time, maybe you'll take my advice."

"You really believe that holding your breath makes a difference?"

"Positive. Now, what were we discussing before we were so loudly interrupted? Oh, yes. All that shouting down below. I was saying how I thought it indicated imminent rescue."

"I wouldn't bet on it. Not if they know about that video link and the fact that this place is sitting on several tons of high explosive."

"If they don't, we could always warn them. The video thingy can't possibly be picking up sound," Bill said, "It wouldn't stand the noise from the bells. All rather pompous, this bells thingy – they've been silent for more than a year already so to re-activate them for this little game is somewhat 'over the top', I feel. But to our advantage in an odd way."

"That's true," Franklin nodded, "And since we've been talking about the rescuers down there and nothing's happened so far, it's a pretty safe bet."

Their discussion was terminated when they heard footsteps on the stairs.

319

"Friend or foe?" Bill called as the footsteps grew louder.

"That depends on your view of the police," DS Green's voice came back at him.

"Very definitely a friend at the moment," Bill said, "But whatever you do, don't come charging into the bell chamber. Marcus Allen has us under surveillance, and on top of tons of explosive with more in the scaffolding, no doubt. We're even only talking with our heads turned away from the camera as far as possible in case he's using a lip reader."

Green reached the top of the stairs and stood in the tiny doorway, "I know about the camera feed," he was panting hard, "You mean that some of the explosives are up here with you?"

"Stop looking at the door, man," Franklin warned, "If Allen sees you doing that, he might get suspicious."

"Good reminder, dear boy." He turned to face Franklin, "Sergeant Green, I'm afraid the explosives are situated in the foundations and maybe the scaffolding also, and if what Allen said holds water, you will find access to them a near impossibility. He also suggested that if he sees any sign of Franklin and I trying to leave our little nest, he will detonate the charges regardless of his demands. I believe he used the term 'a public spectacle that will guarantee co-operation from the authorities'."

"Perhaps I could disable the video link?"

"I rather think that he might press the button should that happen. At the very least he would bound to send Benjamin Bannen to find out what's wrong."

"Bannen's been taken into custody. Where exactly is Allen, and who else is down there with him?"

"He *was* in some sort of self-built complex, deeper than the tube station. Given its defences, I very much doubt whether you could gain access to it, though. The only other person that was to stay with him was a gentleman by the name of Dennis, who he described as his communications expert or some such. I imagine he's staying on to assist with this ransom demand broadcast."

"Sounds likely," Green said, "Did you see any other sign of life down there?"

"There were maybe thirty or forty people down there a little while ago. Our mutual friend Alexandra Featherington was told to take them to a safe area. Goodge Street was mentioned I believe."

"That's right," Franklin added, "Must have been about an hour back. Maybe less."

"That ties in with something Special Branch told us," Green said.

There was a crackle from his radio, "Okay, Tony, I got all that." McCoy's voice filled the chamber, "I think the best bet up there is to sit tight for a while. As long as we don't give him a reason, Allen's not likely to do anything until he's got his broadcast out of the way. The bomb squad have just arrived, and I'll get that little weasel of a surveyor to show them where the access points to the foundations of the tower are along with the scaffolds. Taylor is sure that the explosives are down low there though, isn't he?"

"I'm positive, Inspector," Bill called.

Green spoke up, "Surely we'll have time to get this pair out during Allen's broadcast? He's bound to be distracted."

"We can't even be sure that it's a live broadcast," McCoy said, "He could be monitoring the video link all the time. Plus there's this Dennis guy to consider. Let's consider the options again once he's had his say."

"Fair enough, guv. You want me to stay up here with Taylor and Richardson?"

"There's no point in endangering anyone else, Tony. I trust Mr. Taylor can appreciate that?"

"Of course, Inspector—"

There was a sudden commotion in the background which evidently enraged McCoy to judge by the stream of oaths that followed it."

"What's up, guv?"

"That blessed little Kominski girl, that's what's up. Or rather, she's on her bloody way up!"

"I'll bring her back down with me, guv."

"You bleedin' well won't," Dot's voice echoed up the stairwell.

"Dot!" Franklin called, "Do as the nice policeman says."

She arrived at the top of the stairs, breathing hard, "No way. We're a team."

"Guv?"

McCoy gave an exasperated grunt, "That bloody little woman is impossible! We can't risk any more fuss and bother – we've not got the time. If the silly mare wants to hang around on top of a bloody great bomb, knowing her there's probably nothing we can do about it anyway. Just make sure she stays out of sight."

Dot gave DS Green a triumphant smirk, "See you later, Sergeant."

"You'd better start praying that you do," he said, "Good luck, guys."

When Green had gone, Bill gave vent to his annoyance, "This really is most unwise, my dear. I think that maybe Inspector McCoy was right when he described you as a silly mare."

"I would have called you a silly cow, at the very least," Franklin added.

Dot giggled, "Yeah, well… that's only 'cos you don't like mentioning horses at the minute."

*****

By the time Allen's broadcast was due, there were only a dozen people left within the exclusion zone around the clock tower. Four members of the bomb squad had been joined by three engineers who were attempting to gain access to the foundation chambers under the nervous watch of the surveyor, who had assured everyone that there were no entrances within the tower itself. A thorough but rapid examination had seemed to confirm this.

McCoy, Green, Robson and Cooper were pacing around, radios to ears as they attempted to organise the operation. Green looked up at the oddly re-activated giant clock tower and tapped McCoy on the shoulder, "One minute to go, guv."

They crossed the rolling lawns and climbed quickly into a plain white van which had arrived a few minutes earlier. Inside, portable television sets were displaying the main channels and a large digital clock informed them that there was ten seconds until five-thirty. Two engineers were tending to the screens.

"Allen'll never get this to work, guv."

322

McCoy was staring intently at the screen marked 'BBC 1', "I'll tell you what I think in a few seconds."

He'd no sooner finished speaking when the screen went first blank, then was filled with black. Twenty seconds passed.

"This isn't some sort of a problem with the screen, is it?" McCoy demanded of one of the engineers.

"It doesn't look–"

Marcus Allen's face suddenly filled the screen.

"Good evening, ladies and gentlemen. I apologise for the interruption of your programme, but I have a most urgent appeal to make. Time is pressing, so I will keep this brief." The image switched to the interior of the clock tower where Bill and Franklin were seated, trussed, in front of the giant clock face. Even from the rear, it was clear to see that the broadcast must be live.

"Thank Christ we didn't try to move them," Green muttered.

The image switched back to Marcus Allen, "As you have seen, there are two men being held captive in the clock tower of Big Ben. The middle-aged white man is William Taylor. Should my appeal fall on deaf ears, I will be making another broadcast at seven-thirty during which Mr. Taylor will be executed. If, on the other hand, the appeal has been successful, then my broadcast will be for the purposes of making a further demand. The choice in this matter rests with a mere handful of people.

"They are a group led by Peter Charno, and either the man himself, or one of his group will be watching this broadcast as I speak. My appeal is quite simple. Peter Charno is to present himself at the Queen Victoria Street police offices by seven o'clock at the very latest. Should he fail to do so by then, I repeat, Mr. William Taylor will be executed.

"For anyone doubting the veracity of my words, you may tune in later for an update, as the television people seem so fond of saying. And talking of television people, a message to all those engineers and technicians who at this very moment are striving to detect where this signal is coming from: Don't bother. My next broadcast will be made from a different location and should I find, in any case, that it is being blocked, I will execute both Mr. Taylor and his colleague anyway.

"Thank you all for your time, and just a final word. Should you be listening in person, Peter, be sure of my words. The battle is over, and you have been beaten. You have nothing left to lose and all that remains is find out if you really have a conscience. For now, at least, good evening."

There was another few seconds of blank screen before a ruffled-looking presenter appeared, apologising for the interruption and assuring viewers that this had not been some sort of publicity stunt.

McCoy and Green stared at each other.

"Guv? If he can manage that, surely he's as serious as he sounds?"

McCoy nodded, "I'm beginning to think you're right, Tony."

"In which case, we've got another little problem to consider."

"Such as?"

"What if Allen tries to contact Bannen for any reason? As soon as he realises his man is no longer standing guard, he could just go ahead and detonate the explosives."

"Shit, you're right. I don't suppose there's any chance of Bannen co-operating with us, is there?"

"Guv, he was willing to stand guard over tons of explosives for Allen. What do you think?"

"Point taken. We've still got his radio, though. It's a long shot, but maybe we could have someone imitate him. It might buy us a few extra minutes, anyway."

"You're right, guv. It's a bloody long shot."

"We haven't exactly got much choice, have we? We can't get men down there because of Allen's monitoring devices, which means our only way in is through those foundation doors which seem to be impassable. Even if we can get the captives out, there's no way we'll be able to do anything about the tower."

McCoy's radio crackled into life, and DCS Cox began to speak rapidly, "There's to be a special news bulletin in ten minutes, Graham. Are you convinced that I should go on air with a crazed appeal backing up what that madman just asked for?"

"We need every minute we can get, sir. I'm pretty much positive this guy's not bluffing."

"Wonderful," Cox grunted, "Any progress at your end?"

"Nothing so far, but I've called up Special Operations. Let's see if they can come up with anything."

"What's the shout if this Charno character does come forward?"

"I'll be back there if he does and we'll wait for as long as we dare before contacting Allen. I'm just hoping and praying that if he does come forward, Charno even knows *how* to get through to him."

"Well, good luck, Graham. Let me know as soon as anything develops."

"Will do, sir."

"The SO boys are here, guv," Green said.

"You handle them, Tony – I'm heading back to the office. Any problems with them, call me straight away."

*****

"What the bleedin' 'ell was that?"

The two captives tried hard not to look upwards to where a metallic clattering noise had just come.

"The cavalry?" Bill suggested.

"I can't see it makes much difference what way they come for us," Franklin sighed, "As soon as Allen sees us move he's gonna press his big red button anyway. It'll take at least five minutes for us to get down the stairs and even then we've gotta get well away from this place before we'll be safe."

Bill nodded, "It does seem that we're in a right old pickle, doesn't it? Dot, my dear, I really think it's time for you to take yourself off to a place of safety."

"And I keep telling you I ain't doing it. Just like the three musketeers, right?"

"It'll be more like the three kebabs if this place goes up," Franklin said. There was more clattering overhead, "What are they doing up there, Dot?"

Before she could answer, there were a series of clicks and a cool breeze filled the chamber. A head appeared, upside down, through a trapdoor. "Ah! There you are!"

"Don't drop down!" Dot yelled.

"No worries, miss, I know what the score is. I'm Liam Daniels, by the way, Special Operations. We're just rigging up an alternative escape route for you."

"Through the roof?!"

Daniels nodded, "Hope you've all got a head for heights since we're about ninety metres up, only the line will have to stretch almost all the way to St. James's Park to get you down fast enough and, more importantly, far enough."

"Line?" Franklin asked.

"One of those rope slide boys. Everyone reckons you won't have enough time to get out safely if you try going down the stairs. Abseiling will be the same. Besides, this way, we don't even need to untie your legs. Every second counts, and all that."

"You're being serious about this?"

Daniels withdrew his head for a moment and then returned holding three harnesses attached to ropes. After making sure that they would not be picked up by the video link, he lobbed them gently at Dot. "We'll use these to get you up to the roof, and my men will be waiting to attach you to the slide. You might as well put yours on already, miss. Now, I'd better go and see how everything's going. See you soon."

The cool breeze disappeared shortly after Daniel's head.

"The man's mad!" Bill said.

"Too right," Franklin nodded, "If he honestly thinks that I'm gonna jump off the roof of–"

"But we just agreed we'd never make it down the stairs," Dot pointed out, "And I'm sure they must know what they're doing."

"I can't stand heights!"

"You mean *depths*, dear boy."

"What?"

"You can't stand depths. After all, you're up high right now but you're not scared, are you? It's just when you get outside and see the depth–"

"Not scared! Man, I'm shit–"

"Language!"

*****

Once DS Green was satisfied that there was nothing left for him to organise at the tower, he left DC Robson with Bannen's radio and made his way back to the offices. He found McCoy pacing the reception area.

"No sign yet, guv?"

McCoy shook his head, "Four of the usual nutters, but not the man himself. It's six-thirty, Tony. We're running out of time."

"Special Ops have nearly finished the slide. We can have a go at getting them out any time now."

"We'll wait for Charno. If he doesn't show then we'll just have to try to distract Allen for long enough—"

There was a commotion at the doorway and DS Singh appeared leading a tall, elderly man by the elbow, "Inspector? Another one."

McCoy looked up, "He's nothing like the description we've got—"

"Inspector," the elderly man said softly, "I am aware that my appearance is not what you had expected. However, I assure you that I am Peter Charno. I am able to prove it."

There had been a quiet authority in his words and McCoy found himself nodding, "You have twenty seconds."

In succinct and concise fashion, Charno described details of his subterranean apartment and that of his murdered personal assistant, Monica Leigh. He offered to provide details of the deserted stations that McCoy and Green had visited, but the Inspector waved him into silence.

"This all sounds very convincing, but it doesn't explain your appearance. I was told that you didn't look a day over forty."

"Just one week ago, that was true," Charno agreed, "You will no doubt disbelieve me, but I have a number of special powers and during the past few days, I have been sacrificing one of those to build on another. You see, Inspector, as soon as I realised that Allen was making his final push, I knew that he would want one last showdown with his nemesis – myself, that is – and, I found myself unprepared. I needed the time to make myself ready for our final confrontation."

"And while you've been preparing yourself, innocent civilians have been murdered and others are at this very moment sitting on top of the

327

world's biggest firework. And all because of some petty squabble over property that no-one–"

"Inspector! Please! I'm aware of the situation, but I promise you that without my intervention, London will become a plaything for Allen. This is far, far, far, from being a petty squabble."

McCoy eyed Charno carefully, "We've no time for this right now. But, believe me, Mr. Charno, we shall be having some very long conversations when this is all over. Now, assuming you really are Peter Charno, I suppose you know how to contact Marcus Allen?"

Charno uttered a mirthless laugh, "Of course, Inspector. There is a specific broadcast channel set aside for just such a situation. I have the necessary equipment within my jacket."

"Okay. One more thing before we start. Those people in the tower claim that you employed their agency to search for missing persons. Did you?"

"Not persons, Inspector. Person. Alexandra Featherington is my daughter. She has the same powers that I have, which means that I cannot use the power of my mind to find her. Knowing that Allen was making his final push, I wanted to make one last effort to bring her back to my side. Believe it or not, a couple of unknown investigators would stand more chance than all of my people put together. They also had the additional advantage of being able to innocently create a little chaos wherever they went, maybe distract Allen just enough for me to be able to make my own last stand. It seems to me that they've succeeded admirably."

"They are minutes away from death, Mr. Charno."

"Then we must begin." Charno drew a strange looking radio telephone from his pocket, "Shall I make my call right now?"

"You'll need to be told what to do, Mr. Charno. You have to distract Allen long enough so that we can free the captives."

"I can do better than that for you once I am face-to-face with Allen. He'll be far more watchful until I'm within his sights."

"We can't take that chance–"

"Inspector, I can *guarantee* you a few valuable minutes once I am with Allen. I can't guarantee anything at all from this range."

"You can't know that! You can't even know where he is!"

"Oh, but I can, Inspector. And I also know that you've made life very much harder for yourselves by arresting his right-hand man, Benjamin Bannen. Let us hope that your man with the radio fools Marcus if that proves necessary. Given the excitement that will be coursing through my enemy's veins, I think it highly probable."

"But that's exactly why we must act now!"

"Nonsense, Inspector. I am offering you a chance to safely recover the captives – a chance which I, myself, owe them – and also prevent widespread destruction. If you act too early, they will die, and the Palace of Westminster will be destroyed. Allen will want this showdown to be as public as possible. My guess is that he will broadcast it live. You will see a clear indication of when to act."

"But–"

"Guv!" DS Green pointed at the wall clock, "We're almost out of time."

"I can't just allow…" McCoy trailed off as a strange tingling sensation ran along his spine, "What… what are you doing?"

"Trust me, Inspector." Charno punched one button on the telephone and lifted it to his ear.

*****

The chimes when the giant-sized hands passed seven seemed even louder than the earlier ones, but it was not their volume that brought tears to Dot's cheeks.

"What's taking them so long?"

"They'll be waiting for precisely the right moment, my dear," Bill said, imbuing his voice with as much confidence as he could manage.

"Yeah, Bill's right," Franklin nodded.

In the darkness above them, bodies were moving about.

*****

Afterwards, neither McCoy nor Green could remember a single word that Charno had said while he'd been in contact with Marcus Allen. When the mysterious elderly man told them that he was to be taken to Westminster Station immediately if there was to be any chance for the captives, they simply hustled him out of the building and into the waiting car.

It was only when he had disappeared into the station's dark interior that the strange trance lifted, and the two police officers stared at one another in astonishment.

"I don't believe we just let that happen!"

"Guv? I ain't sure we had a choice in the matter."

McCoy checked his watch, "Shit! It's seven twenty-five. Let's get to the communication van. He's due to make his next broadcast."

"What about Taylor and the rest of them?"

McCoy shook his head, "We'd better pray this Charno character knows what he's talking about. If anything goes wrong now, I'll be cleaning out the stables alongside Bradford – and I'll bloody well deserve to be. No-one outside of my office back there will ever believe what happened."

The co-ordinator of the Special Operations team had spotted them and arrowed across the lawns towards them. They arrived panting at the van at the same time and dived inside, startling the two technicians.

"Anything yet?" McCoy demanded.

"Just a message from DCS Cox is all," the shorter of the two grimaced, "He wants to know – and I quote – 'what the fucking hell McCoy is playing at?'."

The Inspector grabbed for his radio, finding it switched off, "How the…"

"Same here, guv."

McCoy switched his on and his superior's voice filled the van, "McCoy?"

"Sir. Situation's under control. Charno came to the–"

"I know he did! What I'd like to know is what you've been playing at for the last three quarters of an hour. There's only… less than two minutes to go before his deadline."

"We're aware of that, sir, but Charno assures us–"

"Charno *assures* you!?"

"Look, sir. I'll explain it all later. There's no time right now." He switched off the radio.

"Inspector McCoy? What the hell's going on?"

McCoy span round and looked at the SO's man, "Just make sure your boys are ready to go."

"They've been ready for the last hour, but I'm not leaving them up there sitting on a ton of explosives–"

"You won't have to. The signal should come in a few minutes."

"What bloody signal?"

"*The* signal," McCoy improvised desperately.

He was saved by one of the technicians, "Here we go again, Inspector."

As earlier, the screen labelled 'BBC1' blacked out for a few seconds before Marcus Allen's smiling face filled it. He appeared to be standing at one end of a long, brightly lit chamber and at the far end of it Peter Charno was standing motionless.

"Once again, ladies and gentlemen," Allen began, "Let me apologise for the interruption to your entertainment, but as you will shortly discover, events have developed apace since I last had the pleasure of addressing you." An image of Bill and Franklin looking frantically at the clock face, now displaying seven thirty-two, filled the screen for a few seconds before returning to Marcus Allen who had begun to walk backwards towards Charno.

"My captives are, as you have just seen, fit and well – for the time being, at least. William Taylor must be wondering whether he has just received a stay of execution, and once I have completed this next piece of business I will have my man inform him. What he informs him of depends on the co-operation of the person you see standing behind me.

"Ladies and gentlemen, allow me to present you with Peter Charno. This is the man who, during my earlier broadcast, I demanded made contact with me. It is a sign of his fading powers that he so readily acquiesced, and one look at his clearly failing health confirms that his time is drawing to a close."

331

Allen moved to one side and motioned Charno forward until they were facing each other.

Green nudged McCoy, "They seem to be trying to outstare each other. Surely if we act now–"

"No, Tony. I pray to God I'm not wrong, but I really think that Charno will let us know when the time's exactly right."

There was a full half minute's silence from the screen before Allen spoke again, still facing Charno, but directing his comments towards his wider audience, "Many years ago, Charno and I shared both power and property, but as is so often the case, opinions began to differ. For more than five decades now, we have waged a great war against each other, one that ended with my victory this very week. Time has come for me to take total control of the domain of the Dark Side. This may distress some of you watching, but I shall also have to take the last of Charno's fading powers.

"In the beginning," Allen went on, "Our powers were weak. Over the decades we have developed them in our different ways. For myself and my loyal followers, we choose to concentrate on the abilities that allow us to influence people's decisions. As a warning to anyone that might consider crossing me after my rise to power, these skills were utilised to... *persuade* seventeen people that suicide was a better alternative to standing against me, just a few days ago.

"Charno decided that he would resist me in a passive way – his own skills simply developed enough to allow him to keep track of people's locations, thereby enabling him to prepare to defend his own properties in advance. Useful in its own way, I suppose, but as you can see from my victory, ultimately rather pointless.

"Now, it has come to this. As a warning to you all, I will demonstrate just how powerful I've become." A smile flickered across Allen's face and he flicked back his mane of grey hair. Then froze as if he'd been slapped.

The old man facing him drew back his shoulders, "Always so arrogant, Marcus. I fear you've been spending too much time gloating in the past couple of years to notice what has really been going on around you. Nothing to say, all of a sudden?"

The muscles in Allen's jaw were working hard but he was clearly incapable of making more than a low keening noise.

"What Marcus failed to mention, ladies and gentlemen, is that our powers developed from the same source. Within one set of capabilities lies the other. For the past five and a half days I have been honing my own abilities with the help of the last of my followers. They are close by, just as we speak."

Sweat was beginning to form on Charno's brow, "Inspector McCoy, now that I'm sure of the level of control needed for this man, I can tell you that you have a minimum of approximately six minutes to release the captives. Hopefully, you have all the time in the world."

The Special Operations co-ordinator leapt from the van as soon as McCoy nodded at him.

Charno began to speak once more, "The cost to me has been great – I now look my true age and am sure that no amount of help is going to repair the damage. It grieves me deeply, but at least I can repay the people of London for some of my own foolishness.

"In your arrogance and pride, Marcus, you believed yourself victorious. In your conceit and contempt you never thought for one moment that the passive, pacifistic Peter Charno would be willing to discard his own principles for the greater good. This is the end for us both, Marcus. We shall leave London to the people it truly belongs to – those both above and below the streets."

Two figures appeared behind Charno.

*****

"Go, go, go!"

A figure dressed from head to toe in black, dropped down beside Bill and hauled him unceremoniously to his feet.

"Miss! Brace yourself!"

The harness Dot had donned earlier tightened around her shoulders and dragged her into the bell chamber. With a squeal of surprise she was lifted from the ground by unseen hands, the man that had dropped into the room steadying her ascent with one hand whilst struggling with Bill's bound hands with the other.

"Put your hands over your head!"

Dot disappeared into the darkness.

"Okay, old chap, slip this on."

Bill took the harness from the man and struggled into while Franklin's hands were freed. In seconds, Bill was dangling below the trapdoor as a series of grunts and groans filtered down into the chamber.

"Okay, young fellow, you're next."

"Thanks, man," Franklin managed as he struggled into the harness.

"You can thank me by doing exactly as you're told for the next two minutes."

Before he could reply, Franklin was hauled off his feet and yanked smoothly upwards. Eager hands dragged him through the trapdoor and into a smaller chamber. The only illumination came from the lights of London, shining brightly through an open doorway. A wiry looking man, also dressed in black, had already removed Dot's harness and was fitting some contraption around her wrists. He glanced up as Franklin stumbled onto the floor.

"All here? Good. No time for questions. This rope is attached to the main slide and will act as a safety device. You'll not fall off. This," he indicated a leather cuff which was attached to one of Dot's wrists, "goes over the slide and you simply hang from it until you reach the bottom. Don't worry about this bit, which is normally used as a brake, my men will control the rate of your descent. Got that? Good."

While he'd been speaking, other men had been stripping Bill and Franklin out of their harnesses and they now found themselves being attached to the slide which was anchored to the back of the small chamber.

"Oh, man!"

"Sounds like fun, dear boy." Bill swallowed hard.

The wiry man who had given them their instructions unceremoniously picked up Dot and held her high enough for another man to clip her onto the slide. Still holding her clip, he swung his own up and over the thick rope and then shoved her towards the doorway. All Franklin heard from her was a tremulous "Bleedin' 'ell" before the pair of them dropped out of sight.

Bill was next, followed down by the man that had freed his hands in the bell chamber, and then came Franklin's turn, just him and the wiry instructor remaining.

"I ain't sure about this, man!"

"It'll be fine. Just hang on a sec and I'll be with you."

"Take your time, man."

"With that lot down in the basement?"

"Good point."

A hand pushed him firmly out into the night.

"Oh, shit!" Franklin grimaced as he took in the scene. He could see across half of the Capital. Teetering on the small ledge outside, he could just make out Bill and his guide about half way down. It looked as if they were travelling at a hundred miles an hour. "Oh, man—"

"Enjoy the ride!"

His feet were kicked out from under him and for a terrifying second it felt as if he was dropping straight down. The strap snapped tight on his wrist and his feet kicked up in the air. "Just hang limp!" A voice yelled above the rushing wind.

Eyes tightly closed, Franklin did as he was instructed.

The first he realised of the approaching end of the descent was a ragged cheering and he risked opening one eye. Astonishment opened the other one as he descended the last few feet into the waiting arms of a pair of burly men. All around them, police were struggling to hold back a cheering crowd, and flashes strobed all over the scene.

Dot rushed up to hug him as his hands were freed, and he felt the familiar shoulder slap that indicated that Bill was present.

"Okay, you three!" DS Green appeared at their sides, "Come with me."

He led them through a police cordon and into a white van, refusing to answer any of their questions other than to say, "You'll see for yourself soon enough".

McCoy greeted them with a grunt and pointed to the monitor in front of him.

The two figures took up position on either side of Charno without a word.

"My friends," Charno said, his voice which had become strained, easing once more, "I have brought you here for two purposes. To help me end this all and, perhaps more importantly, to witness this event first hand. When this is over, you are to lend as much assistance to the police as is within your powers. It will take time, but your task ahead is to cleanse and heal. If at any time violence *must* be used, then use it. To those viewing, I would advise against it unless you are in a position of authority. To those, I say guard this well."

"Must you do this, Peter?" The man on his left asked. "Could we not preserve your life with our own powers?"

"This is the *right* way, I have no choice. Now, ward yourselves!"

He leaned forward until his face was mere millimetres from Marcus Allen's. Charno's eyes closed as Allen's opened wider. A silence settled over the two men until the faintest of cries escaped Allen's mouth.

There was another silence in the van, as the stunned spectators watched the two men lock wills.

Dot the first to break it, gasping, "That can't be happening!"

Franklin pulled her even closer to his side as they watched faint traces of lines begin to form on Marcus Allen's leonine features. There was more muttering from the others as they watched the process begin to speed up.

Allen's shoulders began to droop, his hair greying and then thinning. The faint lines became wrinkles, etching themselves ever deeper into his flesh, his mouth slowly drooping, the lips turning thin and blue. With a suddenness that startled everyone in the van, Allen threw back his head and let out a muffled scream. Blood sprayed out of his mouth in a fine, pink haze, and then began to trickle from his nose, eyes and even ears. His body convulsed seemed to hang in the air for a few seconds before crashing to the floor of the chamber.

Peter Charno was swaying, physically supported now by his followers, and he turned to the camera. His voice was barely more than a whisper. "Inspector, he is dead. My people will lead you here." He paused, trying to muster his strength, "Mr. Richardson, you exceeded my every expectation. I salute you. You will receive the rewards you so richly deserve..." Before he could say another word, his eyes widened for a moment before slowly closing.

With clear reverence, his two followers lowered him to the cold stone floor.

*****

In the van, the screen blanked before returning to a BBC studio where a stunned-looking presenter was speaking rapidly to his producer.

Green turned to McCoy, "Did we really just see that, guv?"

McCoy shook his head, "On the grounds that there hasn't been a massive explosion, I guess the answer must be 'yes'. Okay, let's get some men down by the station and wait for those two goons that were down there with Charno. We'll need to get the bomb crew ready and I guess we'll need some engineers to gain access. Meanwhile I want..."

Dot, Franklin and Bill sidled out of the van, DS Green following them, "We'll need to speak to you three."

"Oh, come on, Sarge," Franklin protested, "Surely Monday will do?"

"We'll see," he grinned, "I'll have a couple of cars brought over and we'll get you home. Although with all the fuss there's bound to be in the press, what I'd really recommend is a hotel somewhere. You'll be watched by us wherever you go in case there's any more trouble from Allen's lot."

McCoy joined them, "And if any of you three are thinking of disappearing for a few days, think again."

"I'm thinkin' of not even movin' for three days."

"Good idea," Franklin nodded.

Chapter 13

Sunday 25th November 2018

In the end, they were ensconced in a hotel for eight days until the worst of the furore had died down. The media finally realised that press statements were the only things that would be forthcoming while the news was still hot, and McCoy finally realised that the three of them really hadn't known more than they'd let on. When Alexandra Featherington was arrested after a tip-off from one of her own people, scores more came forward to confess their part in Allen's corrupt empire.

Dot and Franklin arrived home with a basket containing a mewling cat that had been in the temporary care of Mrs. Jenkins.

"What a relief!" Franklin sighed, stepping into the living room.

"You're telling me. Are you really sure, though, about me–"

"If you *don't* move in, I'll take you back down in the tunnels!"

"You wouldn't dare!"

"Try me." He unlatched the lid of the cat basket and the mewling abruptly ceased, "Out you get, cat."

"You can't just keep calling him 'cat'!"

"How about 'Weirdo' after the last couple of weeks?"

"No!"

"Dotty?"

"Don't even bleedin' think about it!"

"It's not–" Franklin was interrupted by the doorbell and groaned aloud, "Not more bloody reporters." He crossed the room with Dot in tow, a determined look on her face. "I've already told you," he began, starting to open the door, "That we've got... Oh, it's you!"

"Er, hello?"

Franklin turned to Dot and gave a sheepish smile, "Er, Dot, this is Melanie Forbes. Melanie, Dot."

Melanie gave Dot a nervous smile, "Hello. I'm not going to bother you, I just wanted a quick word with Franklin."

Dot shrugged, "Whatever."

The pretty young woman, about Dot's stature, delved into her pocket and handed Franklin three keys, "These are yours."

He took them, "I was wondering how someone got in…" He broke off when he saw the blush rise on her cheeks.

"I'm really sorry about the horse. I hope he didn't do too much damage?"

Franklin's jaw dropped open while Dot suppressed a giggle, "But…" he managed at last, "You were supposed to be on holiday with your father!"

Melanie shrugged, "He had to come home early, and I thought you'd never guess it was me if I did it as soon as we got back. And then… well, I got to feeling really guilty over it…"

"The cat?"

She nodded, "You did say you were going to get one. You do like him, don't you?"

"He's bleedin' adorable," Dot answered for Franklin, "It's a lovely way of saying sorry."

"Er, yeah, great," Franklin sighed.

"That's okay then," Melanie said, "I'd better pop down to the police stables and collect him. He's been hired from a riding club near us, and they're expecting him back this week."

"Good idea," Franklin said, rolling his eyes, "You know where he is, then?"

Melanie nodded, "There's a policeman lives down our street with his mum and he's just been posted to the stables. He was moaning about it in the pub the other night and mentioned a horse that'd been found in some guy's house. Funny little man, he is, Derek Bradford."

After she'd gone, Franklin double-locked the front door and made his way into the living room where Dot was playing with the furry peace offering. "Well, at least we know what happened now."

"True," Dot nodded, "At least about the horse and the cat. But what about that?" She pointed to a large holdall that had been wedged behind the sofa, "I didn't notice it until I started crawling round with Mister No-Name, here."

Franklin pulled the bag out, put it on the table and unzipped it. He peered inside and then turned to Dot, "He's going to be called Lucky."

"Oh?"

He hoisted the bag and turned it upside down. Hundreds upon hundreds of banknotes cascaded onto the table and spilled over to the floor where the newly-named cat began to chase them.

The End

Printed in Great Britain
by Amazon